Presently
PERFECT

ALISON G. BAILEY

A LOOK
BACK

Then I saw Him,
MY KNIGHT IN
PLASTIC
ARMOR...

"Noah you
don't have to
give me
ALL your
candy"

"I'm NOT
giving You
ALL of it.
I'm giving you
Half."

"I'll ALWAYS
take care of You
and make sure you have candy
Tweet

It was
the
FIRST TIME
He called
Me by
the nickname
that would
stick with me
FOREVER

PRESENT
PERFECT
Alison G. Bailey

"I've been unsure
about many things in my life
except that I have
always loved him.
Every **SINGLE MINUTE**
of every **SINGLE DAY**
that I have been on this earth,
my heart has belonged to him."

PRESENT
PERFECT
Alison G. Bailey

PRESENT PERFECT

Alison G. Bailey

NOTHING has ever been a waste when it comes to *You*
NOT my **TIME,**
my **THOUGHTS,** or
my **HEART.**

I don't regret anything about my life
with you,
even the times we were apart.
Those times showed me how much

I belong to You

I can't love you
you're my
everything

—Noah Stewart

Presently
perfect

PROLOGUE

Perfection is an illusion fueled by the perception of others.

"Noah, you're just a perfect little angel."

"Straight A's again. Noah, your mom and I are so proud. You never disappoint us."

"Damn dude, all you have to do is walk by and every pair of panties drops to the floor."

"Stewart, you impressed me out on the field today."

"I can't lose you, Noah. You're perfect and deserve better than me."

Being an only child I was never starved for attention. In fact, just the opposite. My parents beamed with pride, my teachers praised me, and my teammates looked up to me. I worked hard to fulfill everyone's expectations. At times my efforts left me feeling suffocated and fragmented—Noah the good son, Noah the honor roll student, Stewart the team captain. Everyone had a separate piece of me, except her. She had

1

all of me. And no matter what she said or did, deep in my soul, I knew I always had all of her.

The way others viewed me was all based on performance and achievement. Expectations were high. If I fell short their look would change, but never hers. She loved and accepted me for who I was, not what I did. Even when she looked through tears, I felt and saw the love she had for me. No matter how much she denied it or how often she pushed me away, her not being in my life was unimaginable and not a possibility.

Tweet was my heart, my soul, and my purpose. She was my *everything*.

Neither of us were perfect. We both made mistakes. Looking back, that was okay, because every choice brought us to where we needed to be at the time we needed to be there. The one constant... our love and friendship.

There are two sides to every story and I wouldn't trade our sides for anything in the world.

CHAPTER 1

My skin sizzled under the blazing sun. It was only noon but the temperature had already skyrocketed to heights unbearable to most living things. Stripping off my T-shirt, I tossed it onto one of the chairs as I walked to our pool. Without stopping, I took a deep breath and dove headfirst into the cool water, putting out the fire radiating off my body while drowning out the rest of the world. Completely submerged, I stayed under as long as my breath held before breaking through the surface above and swimming to one end of the pool. My hands raked up my face, wiping the water as well as the dark brown hair away from my forehead. I extended my arms out along the edge of the pool, closed my eyes, and tilted my head back.

After several seconds a tremor ran through my body. I lifted my head, squinted my eyes open, and attempted to focus. I blinked several times in disbelief at what I saw. My best friend, the girl I had known my entire life, was standing across from me looking hot. The tiny red string bikini she wore barely covered her firm round boobs that were the perfect size for my hands. The thin strings connected to a scrap of red material, ran along

3

the crease at the top of her thighs, and ended in loosely tied bows at each hip. Streaks of golden brown mixed through her usually dark hair, fell over her smooth shoulders, and disappeared behind her back. This was a far cry from the girl who stood at the bottom of the Dean's driveway, Halloween 1996, shedding feathers from her homemade Tweety Bird costume when we were six years old. Amanda Marie Kelly, my Tweet, had grown up, out, and all around.

A basketball sized lump slid down my throat with such force that the thud caused my head to snap back. Seeing Tweet's naked thighs, hips, and stomach, not to mention front as well as side boobage, caused all the oxygen and blood to congregate in one specific part of my body. Thankfully, this part was hidden under the water.

She slowly walked down the steps into the pool. With her chin tucked halfway to her chest, the hint of a sexy smile playing across her lips, and one cocked up eyebrow, her gaze locked on me. A heavy weight pushed down on my chest. The longer I stared at her the harder things got— like breathing, forming a coherent thought, speaking, and of course my dick.

Tweet's shapely legs disappeared little by little into the water. With each movement the top of her boobs jiggled slightly. In an instant, my dick grew ten sizes bigger and shot up, ready to crash through the dark depths of the family pool like the friggin' Loch Ness Monster.

She stopped at the last step, the water surrounded her mid-thigh and gently lapped against her skin.

I'd like to be lapping against her skin at mid-thigh.

Bending over, she brought her cupped hands together and scooped up some water. She lifted her face to the sun, raised her hands, and allowed the coolness to pour down, wetting her hair and skin. I followed one large droplet as it slid down her neck, over her collarbone, and between her boobs before vanishing into her bikini. My gaze flung up to meet hers. Raising one hand, she crooked her finger in my direction, inviting me to come closer. At first I didn't think I'd be able to move. I had had boners before but this was the granddaddy of all boners.

Adrenaline pumped through me, causing my entire body to vibrate from the inside out. As inconspicuously as possible, I lowered my hand into the water to adjust my rock hard business. Slowly I swam toward her, dunking my face in the water in hopes that it would calm me down before I lost complete control and attacked her. I emerged from the water hotter and more turned on because of her closeness. Our chests were only an inch apart, almost touching due to our heavy breathing. My eyes connected with hers and I got disoriented for a minute, with no awareness of anything except the beautiful girl in front of me. I stood there, getting lost in her, a fluttering sensation taking over my stomach and heart.

I caught the sight of Tweet's fingers making their way toward the skinny string draped over her shoulder, the only obstacle between me and paradise. One slight tug and my fantasy would be complete. She cocked her head to the side away from me, pushing her hair off her neck to reveal the bow that held up the scrawny triangles. The edges of her pale pink lips curled up as her fingers came together, the string resting between them. My gaze darted back and forth between her eyes and her hand a few times before the hand won out.

She pulled down on the string, letting it slowly untwist. I had to touch her now. The tingling sensation in my fingers was becoming more painful. My breath was coming out in quick short spurts. Every part of my body throbbed. I leaned in toward her neck. My mouth slightly opened, the tip of my tongue sneaking out between my lips ready to taste her. Finally the string broke and fell away.

A gust of oxygen rushed out of me, as waves of tremors invaded my body at the sight of her wet tits. I couldn't wait any longer to feel her nipples rub against my chest. I stepped in closer. The heat from her body radiated across my lips. She ran her fingernails down my chest and stomach, applying just the right amount of pressure to scratch the surface of my skin. Tweet's hand slipped under the waistband of my swim trunks and continued to travel down. My heart was pounding so loudly I could hear the echo all around me. The breath got stuck in my lungs as her fingers curled around my...

"Noah!" *Pound. Pound. Pound.* "Noah!"

My eyes shot open. I was disoriented. The sound of the doorknob clicking back and forth clued me in to where I was.

"Noah, it's time to get up. I have breakfast ready." Mom's muffled voice came from behind the door.

My chest caved in disappointment. The first attempt at an answer was an epic fail. My mouth went through the motions, but no sound came out. It felt like my throat was closing up. Swallowing several times, I slapped my hands over my face and rubbed, trying to come out of my daze.

Clearing my throat, I made an effort to sound unaffected. "I'll be there in a few minutes."

"Are you okay? You sound funny," she said while shaking the knob again, this time pushing against the door.

Bolting upright in bed, I snapped, "I'm fine! I just woke up!"

"Well, don't be much longer. Your dad wants you to cut the grass this morning."

As Mom's footsteps faded down the hall my gaze moved around the room, ending up on my bed. Half of the comforter was hanging off the edge of the bed, my sheets and pillowcase were soaked in sweat, and my dick was reaching for the sky.

It was just a fucking dream.

I'd been having these dreams a lot lately. All of them starring my best friend who had been in my life since day one. The girl who had been like a sister to me until recently. We shared everything—our first steps, our first words, even our birthdays. Hell, we used to take baths together as little kids. Thinking about taking a bath with Tweet now, her wet body covered in suds, was causing Mr. Johnson to do the dance of the horny bastard. How fucked up was I? I shouldn't be thinking of Tweet that way.

I dragged myself out of bed, heading straight to the bathroom and a very cold shower.

You would think the sound of my mom's voice would be enough to knock the image of a naked Tweet out of my head but that wasn't the case. And because of this I'd be missing Mom's great Saturday morning breakfast of eggs, bacon, and grits. Since she worked during the week

Mom always made it a point to fix a big breakfast on the weekends. It's just as well. I couldn't look at either of my parents right now, not with images of tiny string bikinis swirling around in my head.

Once I showered and relieved my situation I headed outside to the backyard. I rolled the lawnmower out and was filling the tank with gas when a high-pitched squeak flew over the fence from behind me. I wasn't in the best mood this morning. Keeping my head down, I tried to ignore it, hoping it would go away. No such luck.

"Heeeeeey Noaaaaah," Beth said. She was leaning against the gate of the chain-link fence that separated the backyards.

Her family had moved here a few months ago. Tweet introduced me to her after my final baseball game with the Tigers, when we won the league championship. Beth was fourteen like Tweet and me. She had black hair and big green eyes, was tall and skinny. Her bones stuck out all over the place and looked as if they'd cut you up pretty bad if you hugged her. I thought it was strange that she was so skinny because she ate like a horse.

Tweet, on the other hand, had curves. Lots of them, strategically placed, and they were awesome. She got them a month or so ago. That was the day I discovered curves and how much I loved them. Tweet was also soft. Not squishy gross soft. But warm and smooth soft. I really liked hugging her. I'd been noticing girls for a while— at least I noticed certain parts of them that were changing and growing. I never paid much attention to their complete package. Tweet's package was the only one that held my interest. The clearing of a throat got my attention. Jerking my head, I looked over my shoulder to find Beth standing a couple of feet away from me, smiling.

I twisted the top to the gas can back on, stood, and walked over to the patio, placing it down. "Hey Beth."

She was wearing a strapless blue and white checkered bikini, silver flip-flops, in full makeup, with big earrings dangling from her ears.

Why would she have earrings and makeup on with a bathing suit?

Tilting her head to the side and smiling, she asked, "What are you doing today?"

I glanced between her and the lawnmower. "I'm getting ready to cut the grass." I tried to keep the sarcasm to a minimum.

As I walked toward the mower Beth took a step in my path, causing me to bump into her. Stumbling back, she slipped out of one of her shoes. My hands shot out, grabbing her upper arms before she fell flat on her ass.

"Whoa!" she yelped.

"Are you okay?" I asked, helping her straighten up.

Looking up at me, she answered breathlessly, "Yeah. I almost fell right into your arms."

"Sorry about bumping into you."

My hands fell away from her.

"That's okay. Would you mind handing my shoe to me?"

I hesitated. It was a flip-flop. I didn't understand why she couldn't just slide right into it. When she didn't make a move, I squatted down, grabbed the shoe, and held it up to her. Before I was able to stand, one of Beth's hands landed on my shoulder while the other reached for the shoe. She leaned into me as she raised her leg, bringing it to my eye level. My gaze moved along her bare inner thigh until it met a small piece of blue and white material. I breathed in deeply and stood, causing her to sway a little off balance.

"Are you sure you're okay?"

"Yeah. Maybe it's just the heat. It's really hot today," she said.

I knew exactly where this was going. I didn't necessarily dislike Beth. She just annoyed me. She talked really fast and a lot, she asked me stupid questions like, 'what was I doing' when it was obvious what I was about to do, and she tried to touch me a lot. She wanted me to ask her to hang out at my pool. I focused on the mower.

"I plan on laying out and getting some sun today," she said. I started adjusting the mower settings. "I wish my parents would get us a pool. It'd be awesome to have a pool to lay out by." Silence. "Do you like having a pool? I think it would be awesome to have a pool." She paused before a nervous laugh escaped her. "I said that already."

I looked up at her with raised eyebrows and smirked. "Yeah, I gotta get going on this before my dad gets mad."

I turned my attention to priming the engine by pressing the pump on the side of the mower a few times, then opened the throttle to full speed as I pressed the handle bar switch.

The hopeful expression fell from her face, replaced with a pout. "Oh okay. Well, if you wanna hang out later just give me a call."

Grabbing the string handle, I yanked it toward me with a steady fast pull two times before the motor came to life, filling the air with a loud rumble. I threw a quick smile at Beth and then pushed the mower in the opposite direction.

After I finished cutting the grass I ran into the house, wiping the sweat from my face with the bottom of my T-shirt. I grabbed a Gatorade from the fridge and stood at the kitchen window as I downed it. Craning my head toward the window, I made sure the coast was clear of Beth. She must have gotten tired of waiting for me. I tossed the bottle in the trash before heading out the back door to Tweet's house.

I ran toward her yard, placed my hands side-by-side on top of the fence, and vaulted over.

Taking a few steps, I heard the voice of one of the top three females in my life, Tweet's mom, who was over by the clothesline hanging laundry.

"Mornin', Noah. You're up and out early for a Saturday," she said, clasping a clothespin to the top of a pair of light green panties that would cover Tweet's cute little ass perfectly.

Looking past her, my eyes froze on the panty rainbow hanging from the clothesline. Images of Tweet wearing each pair with a matching bra flashed through my head. Mrs. Kelly's chuckle jerked me back to the present.

Red heat crawled up my neck and over my face. Swallowing hard I answered, "I had to cut grass this morning."

"You feeling okay? You look a little flushed."

"Yes ma'am," I said, slowly coming out of my panty haze.

"She's inside doing what she does every Saturday," Mrs. Kelly offered and then turned her attention back to the laundry.

"Thanks." Taking one last eyeful of laundry, I backed away before spinning around and headed inside.

I found Tweet exactly where I always found her on Saturday morning—sitting on the sofa, with a bowl in her lap, a box of Cap'n Crunch cereal on the coffee table, watching *The Smurfs*.

Wow, that's a huge bowl of cereal she's scarfing down.

She had on her favorite thing to sleep in—a huge oversized long gray T-shirt with a big panda face on the front of it and striped multicolored fuzzy knee-high socks pushed down around her ankles. Her hair was piled high, shooting up from the top of her head like a spout. She was so focused on the stupid blue people that she didn't hear me come in. I decided to have some fun. Besides, after the panty parade outside and with her looking so damn cute I had to touch her.

I quietly approached. Standing directly behind Tweet, I collapsed over the back of the sofa, wrapped my arms around her, and rested my chin on her shoulder.

"Mornin', Tweet," I mumbled.

"Noah!" She gasped. "You're all sweaty! Let go of me!" Laughter flew out of her as she tried to wiggle free from me.

Holding on tight, I teased, "I've missed you soooo much, Tweet."

"You just saw me last night." She giggled.

The sound made me smile. Vibrations started in my chest and quickly spread to the rest of my body. I wanted to turn my head toward her neck and touch her skin with my lips. She smelled so good, like raspberries and Cap'n Crunch. The twitching in my shorts let me know I needed to back off. I wasn't sure what was going on with me and Tweet right now. All I knew was that she invaded my thoughts and dreams all the time. She was usually either naked or about to get naked in them. It made me feel like a creepy pervert thinking of her that way. She was my best friend. My Tweet.

Then when I was actually around her all I wanted to do was touch her—hold her hand, sit close to her, or put my arm around her shoulders. It was as if I had no control over what my body did. It just automatically moved toward her as close as possible.

Dropping my arms, I stood and walked to the chair next to the sofa. I sat on the edge, elbows propped up on my knees, and leaned forward.

"I'll never get why you still watch this stupid cartoon," I said, snatching up the box of cereal and tossing a handful in my mouth.

Placing the empty bowl down on the coffee table, a look of confusion crossed Tweet's face. "The question is why *wouldn't* I still watch *The Smurfs?* They live in a utopia with a 'one for all and all for one mentality.' Everyone is equal, but different, and they respect that. Plus, they're really cute and have a lot of fun screwing around with Gargamel."

"Yeah well, they're still little blue fuckers who give me the creeps."

The next thing I knew there was a pillow being pitched directly at my head. Holding my arm up, I caught it just before impact.

"Oh, it's like that, is it?" I jumped up and quickly stepped forward, placing me directly in front of her. I tried to keep my expression serious, but the smirk kept creeping across my mouth.

"Give me the remote," I commanded. "There's got to be something better on than these little Smurffuckers."

Tweet grabbed the remote and slipped it behind her back. "Don't call them that," she said, tilting her chin up defiantly, in an attempt to maintain her own serious expression.

I positioned my hands on the back of the sofa just above her shoulders. Leaning in, I looked into her eyes. "Give. Me. The. Remote."

"I seemed to have misplaced it," she announced, narrowing her eyes.

"Then you leave me no choice."

"Noah, don't you dare."

We held each other's gaze. The same feeling I had in my dream took over my body. Everything around me stopped and I got lost in those beautiful eyes. I felt a shiver come off of her. Tweet softly cleared her throat, which snapped me back to attention. A slow smile spread across my face. Moving with lightning speed, I placed my hands just below her rib cage and started to relentlessly tickle her. My heart almost stopped when the top of my hand brushed the bottom of her boob.

Whoa, she wasn't wearing a bra.

Tweet doubled over laughing and fell to one side, all the while swatting my hands away.

The remote was within reach the second she fell to the side, but I wasn't ready to take my hands off of her yet. Between fighting me off and laughing, she was having a hard time breathing, so I figured I'd give up my quest for another touch of her boob.

Grabbing the remote, I stepped back, leaving her a heaving mess on the sofa. I flipped through the channels.

"You don't play fair." She gasped.

I ignored her whining and continued to channel surf. "Let's go for a swim." "I can't." She sounded weird."

"Don't be mad at me, Tweet," I said.

"I'm not mad. Oh, go back one channel. I just saw Justin Timberlake." I scrunched up my face. "So what."

"So what? I like him. He's cute and sexy. Besides, my TV, my rules."

A burning sensation spread across my chest at the same time my grip tightened on the remote. I sneered at the TV and felt a slight growl rumble in the back of my throat.

What the hell was wrong with me? I liked Justin Timberlake.

I hated the way Tweet was drooling over him. She had this strange look on her face, like she was hypnotized. The more she stared at *him*, the more pissed off I got. I aimed the remote at the TV and clicked it off.

"Hey! I was watching that. Thank you."

I turned toward her. "Go get your suit on." I didn't mean for it to come out like an order, but it did.

"I told you, I can't go swimming today." She lowered her chin to her chest.

"Why?"

"I just can't."

I didn't know what her problem was. We spent every day hanging out together. She didn't act mad at me, but she wouldn't look at me either.

"Tell me."

"No. It's personal," she said, quickly glancing up at me.

I could tell my questions were making her uncomfortable. I didn't want her to feel bad. I wanted to make her smile.

"You know you can always talk to me about anything." Our eyes connected. I saw relief in hers once she realized I wasn't going to push her. "Besides, I think we are pretty personal. I mean, I've seen your drawers flapping in the wind."

All the blood drained from her face. "What do you mean you've seen my drawers?" She sat up from the sofa, looking past me out the window. "Oh. My. God! Is it that woman's goal in life to humiliate me whenever possible?"

Tweet bolted off the sofa and ran out the back door. I felt bad that I had a hand in embarrassing her. Although, I couldn't help but laugh as I watched her snatch each pair of panties off the clothesline one by one while ignoring her mom.

God, she was cute.

Turning with an armful of underwear, she headed back toward the house.

The second she hit the door, she said, "Noah Jeffrey Stewart, we are never to speak of this again."

Trying to hide the smile that was stuck to my face, I agreed, "Absolutely. In fact, I really didn't pay any attention to what was out there."

She let out one big sigh and nodded her head, looking relieved. She took one step toward her bedroom when my words stopped her.

"Oh Tweet."

"Yes?"

"The yellow pair are my favorite."

A loud groan escaped her as she sneered at me before heading down the hall.

CHAPTER 2

I placed my hand flat on the picnic table behind her and scooted closer until our bare thighs rubbed against each other. I was so happy Tweet wore her short shorts. I'd spent most of the summer thinking about touching her and then trying my best to touch her in subtle ways as often as possible. She seemed to be okay with it for the most part. Spending time with Tweet had always been effortless. I never started a day wondering if she would be in it. It was like breathing. I automatically knew I'd be doing it. And just like I wouldn't survive without oxygen, I knew I couldn't survive without Tweet. But things were changing, lines were blurring, and becoming confusing.

I didn't know if she was having the same feelings as I was. There were times when I thought maybe she did. Like when I held her hand, a shy smile appeared across her face, or the way she leaned into my side when I put my arm around her shoulders. And then there were the goose bumps that had popped up all over her thigh when our skin made contact. I wasn't sure how to tell her how I felt or if I even wanted to. My head kept telling me it was wrong to have the thoughts I had been having about her.

Somehow, my body started reacting to Tweet, the hot girl, but my mind was still seeing her as my best friend.

There was a slight breeze coming off the lake as we sat on top of the picnic table at *our spot*. This park had been a major part of our lives. Tweet and I played on the playground and in the sandbox as little kids. We had our birthday parties here, and family picnics, and Dad had pitched my first baseball to me here. We had one more week left of summer vacation before freshman year in high school started. Between classes and baseball practice Tweet and I knew time at our spot was going to be limited, so we made it a point to be here every night this week.

A tiny piece of dark brown hair brushed across her cheek. Tweet didn't pay any attention to it. She was too caught up in listening to the music that was pouring out of my ear buds that we were sharing. With her eyes closed, she swayed back and forth, getting lost in the music of our favorite band, Lifehouse.

"What do you think?" I asked.

"They're awesome," she said, still swaying with eyes shut. Her head was tilted back slightly and there was a peaceful look on her face. "The entire CD is brilliant. The song "Everything" is my favorite."

"Mine too. It reminds me of you." I was so close to her face that my breath caused that same piece of hair to glide back over her cheek.

Man, her skin looked even softer up close.

Her eyes shot open to meet mine. There was a look of surprise across her face. For a split second I had the urge to look away but I stayed focused. I wanted her to know I wasn't teasing. Maybe if she saw how serious I was she'd tell me if she was having these same feelings. Her gaze dropped back toward the ground, her eyes closing again. I continued to stare. She was so pretty. I didn't get a chance very often to take long looks at her. Whenever she caught me stealing a glance I turned away embarrassed. A smile crossed my face as I watched and thought about the surprise I had for her. I was so focused I hadn't even noticed the song was over.

"What are you smiling at?" she asked.

"You. I like watching you listen to music. You get so lost in it."

Our eyes locked and the air in my lungs rushed out. My mouth went dry watching her teeth glide across her lower lip as she sucked on it. The breeze that was helping cool us off suddenly wasn't doing its job. I was burning up. Tweet must have been warm too because her cheeks were turning pink. She smiled at me as she handed my ear buds back, then looked away, breaking our contact.

"Do you think they'll go on tour soon?" she asked, staring out over the lake.

Trying to act casual, I shrugged and answered, "Maybe."

"If they come to town we have got to see them. I bet they're unbelievable in concert."

I leaned away, put my iPod down, and jumped off the table. Her eyes narrowed as her brows squished together. The expression was priceless. Maintaining eye contact, I reached around to my back pocket. Slowly I brought my hand around and held up the two concert tickets.

"Performing Arts Center, three weeks, you and me, Tweet," I said, grinning.

Her eyebrows shot up as her head tipped to the side and her jaw dropped open. She blinked several times, not quite registering my words. I waved the tickets in front of her face hoping to snap her out of her shock and awe. I worked and saved all summer for these tickets, cutting grass in the neighborhood and doing extra chores for my parents. My dad must have asked me at least five times if I was sure I wanted to spend all the money I had worked so hard for on one thing. When the one thing was Tweet, the answer was a definite yes.

After several seconds I saw a flicker of recognition cross her eyes. "You're kidding?!"

Shaking my head, I answered, "Nope."

As she launched herself off the table I instinctively opened my arms to catch her. Stumbling back, I lost my balance, landing us both on the ground with Tweet straddling me. We were both laughing so much it was hard to catch our breath. The combination of her body, her laughter, and the excitement in her eyes had me "excited" in record time.

"Noah Stewart, you are the bestest best friend a girl could have."

"I *am* pretty awesome, aren't I?" I cocked an eyebrow and shot a flirtatious smirk up at her.

"Yes you are," she said in a low breathy voice.

Tweet squirmed slightly on top of me. This, of course, made me even harder than I was already. Our faces were so close that if either one of us puckered our lips they would have been touching. My gaze moved up and down her face before it froze on her eyes. Tweet had the most amazing eyes I'd ever seen. They were big, greenish blue, and my favorite things to look into. Her dark brown lashes made the unique color pop even brighter. The curves of her face were soft and smooth—from her high cheekbones, to the slope of her nose that turned up at the end, down to the little dimple in her chin.

She had to have felt how hard I was but she wasn't freaking out about it. After a few seconds when she didn't move I allowed my attention to focus more on how her body felt against mine. Her hands were between us, holding her up slightly, but I felt her boobs against my chest. Several months ago Tweet's body started to change or maybe I just started to notice. That's when my world flipped upside down and confusion took up permanent residence where Tweet was concerned.

The first thing that caught my eye was her ass. It was round, firm, and the way it curved out from her body drove me crazy. Then one day out of nowhere she got her awesome boobs. They were perky, full, and next to her eyes, my favorite thing to stare at. I especially enjoyed it when the top of her boobs peeked out from underneath her shirt. Tank tops and low cut T-shirts were the best. All the parts of her body fit together perfectly and felt fantastic on top of me. Glancing down at her pink lips caused a tremor to run through me. My tongue darted out, wetting my bottom lip. Her hair had fallen from behind her ear and brushed the side of my face. It was soft and as usual smelled like vanilla and raspberries. The tips of my fingers tingled as they trailed the length of her hair, tucking it back behind her ear.

"You were extremely sure of yourself, getting those tickets without asking me first. What if I didn't want to go with you?" she said, teasing.

"Impossible. I know my girl too well." We exchanged smiles. I wanted to kiss her so much right then, but I was too scared. I didn't know how to really kiss a girl.

She's not a girl. She's Tweet. Your best friend.

I couldn't take her being this close to me any longer. Clearing my throat, I said, "I guess we better get up."

"Oh. Yeah. Sorry about that." Her cheeks turned deep red.

As she rolled off of me her thigh slid over my dick, causing my eyes to shut tight. I sucked in a deep breath. The friction felt amazing. Pulling my knees up, I rested my elbows on them, and lowered my head. I needed a minute. Tweet must have gotten the message because she sat quietly next to me.

Once certain parts of my body relaxed I was able to stand up. Tweet slipped her hands into my outstretched ones, and in one fluid movement, I helped her off the ground, pulling her into my chest.

"That was fun. What would you do for tickets to see Green Day in concert?" I asked, smirking down at her.

Her body pressed up against mine had my head spinning and the rest of me vibrating. As we stood there the look in her eyes shifted from warmth to what looked like sadness. I felt a heaviness in my chest.

Should I have kissed her? Was she sad because I didn't? Couldn't she tell I wanted to? Maybe she was scared I was going to. She was probably grossed out by how hard I was and just didn't want to hurt my feelings by jumping away.

I opened my mouth to say something but my mind was cloudy. I wasn't ready and by the look on Tweet's face neither was she. I took in a deep breath and stepped back.

"I guess we should be getting home." I paused. I'd always been able to read Tweet so easily, knowing her thoughts like they were my own. It was getting harder and harder for me to figure out what was going on in her head. "Unless you have something you want to tell me."

Chewing on her bottom lip, she glanced down, twisting the edge of her shirt around her finger. "I was just going to say the same thing about getting home."

I waited a second for her to let go of her shirt so that I could take her hand. Her head tilted up, but her eyes were focused over my shoulder. A shy smile flashed across her face before she turned and walked away. As the distance between us grew so did the tightness in my chest. Something had happened. I didn't know what it was, but I saw it in her eyes. Things between us were no longer changing, they had already changed.

Travis collapsed against the set of lockers, clutching one hand over his chest. "Be still my beating heart."

I looked around my locker door at him. Chuckling, I said, "What's your deal, man?"

Travis and I met over the summer at baseball camp and had hit it off from the start. Even though he was a sophomore and I was a freshman he always acted cool about hanging out together. I followed his gaze. The hallway was crowded with students slamming lockers, talking, and rushing to their next class. He didn't need to tell me what had grabbed his attention. She was tall, blond, and very curvy. She walked down the hall with confidence, acting like she owned the place—head up, shoulders back, hips swiveling from side-to-side, causing the slightest bounce of her ass. The snug shirt she wore outlined the curves of her back, stopping at the top of her painted on low rise jeans. As she swayed, a little of her skin was revealed at the small of her back. I felt a twitch in my pants. My gaze stayed glued to that ass until it disappeared around the corner.

"Hey Amanda." The sound of Travis's voice knocked me out of my daze.

Glancing back I caught Tweet's beautiful teal eyes looking directly at me. I quickly lowered my gaze, turning back toward my locker, and pretended to be searching for another book.

"Hey Travis," she said. I jerked slightly when I felt her hand on my shoulder. "Are you okay, Noah?"

My throat closed up. I didn't know why I felt weird. I hadn't done anything wrong. I looked at a girl's ass. There was no crime in that. Tweet wasn't my girlfriend. Since the day at our spot when I showed her the tickets, I had tried to hold her hand again, but she avoided my reach. I wanted to touch her all the time, that hadn't changed, but things between us had. At times she acted nervous and shy around me. This was a good thing. I had no business touching her or thinking about touching her.

Clearing my throat, I snapped, "I'm fine!"

"Damn, you don't have to bite my head off," she huffed.

Stepping back, I closed my locker. "I'm sorry, Tweet. I'm just stressed about the Science test I have after lunch."

"You answered all the review questions perfectly last night when I quizzed you." She gave me a sweet smile.

My heart dropped into my stomach. Not only had I looked at another girl, I was lying about it. I was a lying ass-looker. I needed to get ahold of myself. It was becoming clearer that Tweet didn't want anything more than a friendship with me. She wasn't a freak like me. My head and heart kept arguing. My head tried to convince my heart that it was wrong to think of her as my girl but my heart knew better.

My eyes spent the first half of lunch period nervously darting around the cafeteria looking for "her". It wasn't that I wanted to see "her" really. It was more like I wanted to see certain parts of "her". When I spotted "her" walking down the hall I didn't get a look at the face. I wondered if the front was as curvy and large like the back. I shifted in my chair, adjusting myself. Even though I had every right to look at any girl I wanted to, I still felt uncomfortable doing it in front of Tweet.

We had only been in school for a week but it had become the norm for Beth, Tweet, and I to eat lunch together. Tweet and I sat beside each other as Beth's rapid-fire babble flew across the table. Every few minutes Beth would take a breather, look at me, smile, wink, and then go back to talking. I needed to focus on something other than the girl next to me, the girl across from me, or the girl whose ass had me disoriented. Taking out my notebook, I buried my face and concentrated on studying.

A chill ran over me. I shifted my gaze to Tweet. Tension rolled off of her as she stared straight ahead. I glanced up for a split second to see what had her so anxious. It was *her* and she was bouncing right toward us. I kept my head down trying to ignore my surroundings.

"Yay! I found y'all." Her southern drawl was squeaky and high.

"Hey, Brittani, I saved you a seat," Beth said.

My knee bobbed up and down under the table at a steady pace. The sound of the chair across from me scraping the floor caused my mouth to go dry while sending a stinging sensation down my arms to my hands. I could feel the stares aimed at me from my side as well as directly in front of me. I needed to get out of here.

Just play dumb, man. Like you're clueless that she's sitting across from you.

I lifted my head at the clearing of a throat.

"I'm Brittani Monroe." Her hand was extended toward me and it was right in line with her massive chest.

Focus on the hand. Focus on the hand. Wow, her shirt was really tight and low cut.

I took her fingers in my hand and shook. "Um... hey. I'm Noah Stewart."

I heard a sharp intake of breath from beside me when my hand touched Brittani's.

I turned toward Tweet with pursed lips, a slight smirk, and eyebrows raised, attempting to look as innocent as possible. Her expression mimicked mine except she didn't look innocent. She looked pissed. The fingers of her right hand started drumming on the table as she chewed her left thumbnail and shifted her gaze back to Brittani.

"It's very nice to meet you, Noah. I'm so glad Beth asked me to join you for lunch," Brittani interrupted.

My eyes moved back and forth between the two girls. Tweet's eyes shot daggers at Brittani while Brittani's eyes stayed glued to me. I was getting more uncomfortable as the seconds ticked by. I heard muffled voices as I turned facing forward. I guess it was the girls talking. I was too focused on getting the hell out of there. Then it happened. Brittani leaned in closer and propped her boobs up on the table. She squirmed a little in her seat squishing them together even more. I was going to look away, but I couldn't help myself. This was the closest I'd ever been to real ones that were almost unwrapped. These were halfway out of the package.

Suddenly a stabbing pain shot into my ribs. "Ouch! What was that for?" I asked, rubbing my side.

"You mentioned that you needed to get to class early," Tweet said, smiling innocently at me.

"Yeah, I guess I better go." I closed my notebook and shoved it into my backpack.

"I don't want you to go yet. I'll miss you too much," Brittani whined, pouting her lips.

I heard Tweet huff and mumble something under her breath that I couldn't make out.

My gaze darted toward Brittani, making sure not to look directly at *them*. "Yeah, well... um... maybe later." I stood. "I'll see you in Algebra, Tweet." Her eyes narrowed as she gave me a slight smile, but I could tell her jaw was clenched. "See you later, Beth and um..."

"Brittani!" she squeaked, biting her lower lip.

As I backed away from the table, my eyes locked with Tweet's. I thought I saw tears beginning to build before she turned her head away from me. "Um... yeah... Brittani," I said and then got the hell out of there.

Once I made it out into the hallway a deep sigh escaped me. I was so mixed up. I thought about Tweet all the time. Then Brittani showed up with her boobs pushed up, out, and directly placed in my sight line. The look in Tweet's eyes before I left the cafeteria had my stomach tied in knots. She didn't look mad like she did when Brittani first sat across from me. Tweet had a hurt look in her eyes and I felt as if I'd been the one that put it there.

CHAPTER 3

"We're finally alone." Although I'd heard the voice only once, there was no mistaking who it belonged to.

I was leaning against the brick wall at the entrance of the school, flipping through my iPod, waiting for Tweet to come out after her last class. I breathed in deeply before lifting my head to see Brittani standing in front of me. During the time between lunch and my last class I had already heard stories about her. Apparently, this should have been her sophomore year, but she was held back. During her freshman year she had supposedly spent more time with the baseball team than she had spent studying. Her parents decided a new school would be a good fresh start for her, so she transferred in. The way she kept eyeing me, though, it didn't appear like a fresh start interested her. I think she was still a *team player*.

"You were in such a hurry to leave at lunch I didn't get a chance to ask you something." Her finger twisted in the tip of her blond curls, that rested right above the deep V in her shirt.

"Hey... um...," I stammered. She made me nervous for some reason.

"Brittani," she pouted. Stepping closer, she untangled her finger and pushed her hair back over her shoulder, giving me an open view of her chest. "You wanna hang out?"

"I can't. I have homework."

I couldn't help notice her eye roll. "You do your homework right after school on a Friday?" she said sarcastically.

"Yeah. Tweet and I have always done it that way."

"Tweet? Was that the other girl sitting at the table today?" I nodded. "I thought her name was Ana."

"It's Amanda," I said, sounding slightly irritated. "Tweet's my nickname for her." I gave her a quick smile before glancing away.

"That's sweet." She stepped in closer, putting her only about a foot away from me. Taking in a deep breath, her chest lifted, causing her shirt to open up a little more. "And kind of hot."

Sweat started dripping down the back of my neck and my palms were wet. I fumbled with my iPod before shoving it into the front pocket of my pants.

Pushing off the wall, I straightened. "Yeah, well that's what I call her."

"So are the two of you, *together?*"

"No, we're not like that." I felt my stomach sink as my shoulder muscles tensed.

"Go out with me tomorrow night."

"I'm supposed to wait until I'm sixteen to date."

"It's not a date silly. A bunch of us are going bowling. My dad is taking me. We can swing by and pick you up. Come on. It'll be fun."

She tilted her head to one side, smiling up at me while touching my upper arm. My skin heated up where her hand landed. If I leaned forward just a little I would be able to see right down her shirt. Feeling the front of my pants press against me, I shifted into position to get a glance when an overwhelming feeling of guilt ran through me.

I needed to get it through my thick head that Tweet and I were just friends. The fact that she won't even let me hold her hand now makes it pretty clear she doesn't have the same feelings as I do. Feelings I shouldn't be having about my best friend. My parents had been telling me to make more friends. They loved Tweet but thought I needed to expand my circle beyond her and a few guys I played baseball with. High school was a chance to do that. Brittani wasn't asking me on a date. There'd be other people there. I'm sure my parents would be fine with it.

"Yeah, it sounds cool. I'll have to ask my parents first but I'm sure they'll be okay with it."

"Oh yay!" she yelped, tipping up on her toes as she slapped her palms together. "Write your phone number down for me."

"You gotta pen and paper?"

She shoved her hand inside the big purse that was slung over her shoulder and pulled out a bright pink pen covered in glitter. I hesitated, staring at it for a few seconds. I wasn't sure what had me frozen. Was it that I didn't want anyone to see me holding such a girly pen or the fact that this felt like I was leaving Tweet behind? The pen wiggled in front of my face.

"Do you have a piece of paper?" I asked.

"You can write it here," she said, smiling and holding out her hand.

She let out a deep sigh when my fingers slipped around her wrist to steady her hand while I jotted my number across her palm. I shot a slight grin in her direction as I handed her back the pen.

Finally she stepped back, putting distance between us. She kissed her palm. "Awesome! I'll call you later with details." I nodded. She turned and walked away. After a few steps she spun around and said, "I'm really excited that you're going."

I smiled again, not saying a word before she spun back around and headed across the parking lot.

Outwardly, the first week of high school was great—my classes went well, I'd been asked to try out for the junior varsity baseball team, I had a new friend in Travis, and a hot girl wanted to hang out with me. I should've been happy, but at that moment all I felt was sadness and frustration.

I was sitting at my desk while Tweet lay across my bed, her feet propped up on the headboard, crossed at the ankles with closed eyes. When I swiveled my chair around to look at her I had to smile. She was tapping her toes to the beat of the music while she played air guitar.

God, I loved watching her listen to music.

She had caught me a couple of times staring, but I don't think she felt it had reached creep level yet. I wanted to go ahead and ask her about Brittani now before Mom came to get me for my dentist appointment. I needed her to be okay with it even though it wasn't a date and Tweet wasn't my girlfriend.

I rolled my chair over to turn the music down and then closer to the bed. Clearing my throat I said, "Tweet?"

"Yep."

"You know that girl who sat at lunch with us today, Brittani Monroe?"

"Yep." Her answers were quick and clipped. She had no interest in discussing Brittani.

"What do you think about her?" I asked, bracing myself for her answer.

"She's a slut with a stripper name."

I couldn't help my chuckle. "Tell me how you really feel. Don't hold back."

She lowered her legs and swung them over the side of the bed. Leaning back on her arms, she propped herself up, causing her chest to stick out. Tweet's boobs were awesome. They didn't have to be pushed up and half naked to get noticed. They were just as hot in a T-shirt as they were in a bathing suit.

I was so caught up in my thoughts of Tweet's chest that I almost missed hearing her when she asked, "Why are you asking me about her?" She tried to sound casual, disinterested, but I could tell she was curious. It must have been the writer in her. She was always looking for more behind the story.

"She asked me out," I said, leaving out the part about other people being there.

"On a date?!" She shot straight up in shock. I loved her reaction.

"Yeah, I guess."

"That's crazy talk!" Her nose crinkled as her eyebrows knitted together in disbelief.

She was actually jealous and so damn adorable. Adrenaline pumped through me causing my heart to slam against my chest. If Tweet was jealous that meant her feelings matched mine. Maybe "us" being more wasn't that weird. Glancing up she caught me smiling at her.

"What's so crazy about it?" I asked.

"Um… well, number one, we're only fourteen and not allowed to date until we're sixteen. Number two…"

"I can date now," I said, locking eyes with her. Technically it wasn't a date. It was hanging out with a group of kids from school. She didn't need to know that, at least not yet.

Folding her arms across her perfect chest, she narrowed her eyes at me and said, "You're kidding?"

"My parents said it was okay."

"How are you going to get to the date? You don't even have your driver's permit yet. I'm pretty sure your handlebars aren't wide enough for her to sit on. I mean, have you seen the ass on that girl?"

"I've noticed her ass." I gave her a big smirk. By the look on her face I could tell she did not like my answer, but that was okay. Tweet was jealous and that made me happy. "She asked if I wanted to go bowling. Her dad's going to drop us off."

"So you're going to go through with this?"

"I guess. Why not? She seems nice enough and she's kind of pretty."

Looking down, she picked at her jeans, and huffed, "Well, do what you want. It's your life to ruin."

"It's just bowling, Tweet," I told her, trying not to let her see how much I was enjoying her being pissed off.

Her head tilted back and toward one shoulder as her eyes focused on the ceiling. "Yeah. Well, first it's bowling, then it's a movie, and then you'll get married, buy a house, and have little slutty stripper kids. But if that's what makes you happy. Who am I to stand in your way?"

I almost busted out laughing at her prediction. Drawing in a deep breath, I held it as long as I could. Several seconds passed before I was able to talk. "Can I ask you something else?"

"Shoot."

I hesitated for a second. I don't know why. I knew the answer, at least I hoped I did. "Have you ever kissed a guy?"

"I've kissed my dad and my granddad."

Shaking my head, I said, "I don't mean relatives. I mean a guy. Have you ever had a real kiss from a guy?"

"You know the answer to that is no." Her gaze fell to the floor as she nervously shuffled her feet back and forth.

"Well, I've heard from a reliable source that Brittani has kissed a guy, a few of them, in fact."

"That doesn't surprise me." We sat in silence for another moment. Suddenly Tweet bolted up. "Oh my god! Are you going out with her so you can get some?"

Jerking forward I answered, "What?! Get some what?!"

"Brittani lovin'," she accused, eyes narrowed and lips flattened as she shot a death ray glare at me.

"No! I'm going because... I don't know... she asked me. Besides, you know how much I love the fries at the bowling alley. If you don't want me to go, I won't go. Just say so."

Please tell me not to go. Tell me you want to be my girl.

All those times in the past I knew Tweet liked me touching her. I couldn't have imagined her reaction when we held hands or hugged. Then she started pushing me away for some reason. I could see it in her eyes and hear it in her voice that she didn't want me to have anything to do with other girls. Or was it just Brittani? I was so confused. She kept running hot one minute then cold the next. I needed her to say the words.

Her head turned away from me. "Go." She paused and my hope disappeared. "It's just... I don't think she's the right girl for you."

"Oh, I'm positive she's not the right girl for me."

Her eyes immediately shot up to meet mine. Maybe if I kissed her, got it out of my system, my head would clear, and things could go back to normal. Knowing Tweet, she'd need a lot of convincing, especially with the way she'd been acting lately.

Rubbing the back of my neck, I thought for a few seconds, and then I pushed. "The thing is... um... you know I haven't kissed a girl yet. I'm not saying it's going to happen but what if she kisses me and I don't do it right? Word would get out and I might as well go be a priest because no girl would want to go out with me."

I watched as the lump she swallowed slowly slid down her throat and I waited for her to say something. It seemed as if she was staring at my mouth as her eyes glazed over. If my Tweet-dar was working like it used to, my guess would be that she was thinking about what it would be like to kiss me. "Earth to Tweet," I said, snapping my fingers.

"Sorry. Um... don't worry about it. You'll do fine."

I leaned forward closer to her, rested my elbows on my knees, and pushed harder. "You know what would help me?"

"What?" she asked.

"If I could practice." I held her gaze for several seconds giving my words time to register with her.

"With me?"

"Yeah."

Shaking her head, she said, "No, I don't think that's a good idea."

"It's a great idea. We'll practice on each other, so we won't embarrass ourselves in front of anybody."

"I don't have anyone who wants to kiss me in the near future." A flush crept over her cheeks right before her chin dipped down to her chest.

"I wouldn't be so sure about that."

Her gaze rose and my grin widened.

One more little push.

Slipping out of the chair, I got down on one knee and begged, "Think of it as preparing for your future."

I could tell she wasn't buying it.

God, she was stubborn.

"Please Tweet. *I need* you." My head tilted to the side, eyes wide, eyebrows up, and bottom lip poking out slightly.

We stayed in this position for what seemed like a lifetime. Her gaze swung back and forth from mine to the floor. I could see her struggling with her thoughts as they flashed in her eyes.

Finally, she looked up and said, "Okay."

"Seriously?" I asked, shock evident in my voice.

"Yes."

I lunged forward tackling her on the bed. My fingers flew to her sides, tickling the sensitive spot just below her ribs. As the sound of her laughter filled my room so did the warmth through my body.

"Tweet, you're the bestest best friend a guy could have. You're awesome, incredible, fantastic…"

The more she laughed, the more I tickled until she was gasping for air. "Stop tickling me! I told you I'd help. I won't let you look like a fool."

I didn't stop. "Promise?"

Laughing with tears seeping out of her closed eyes, she choked out, "Yes."

"Say it!"

I eased up on the tickling. Placing my hands on either side of her head, I hovered over, looking at her. Tears rolled down the side of her face, her lips curled up into a huge smile, and her dark hair fanned out around her head. A jolt of electricity shot through me. My chest started pumping so fast I thought I was going to hyperventilate. Our legs were tangled together. Tweet opened her eyes and they locked with mine. The air in the room shifted in intensity. Something happened in that moment while looking into her beautiful teal eyes. A sensation I hadn't felt before. It was more than my body reacting to being pressed against hers. It was more than physical. It was more than wanting to kiss her or hold her. I wanted to make her happy and keep her safe.

"Promise," she whispered.

"This is becoming a habit."

Her eyebrows scrunched together, confused. "What is?"

"You and me on top of each other." I smirked.

Her lips parted slightly as a soft sigh passed over them. It would have been so easy to kiss her right then. Tweet deserved her first kiss to be special. My lips moved down toward her neck. I tilted my head to the side, the tip of my nose grazing just below her ear. Shivers ran through my body.

"Wow. You smell really good," I whispered. She shuddered beneath me.

"I had a sour apple Blow Pop before I came over."

I grinned.

Moving away from her neck, I said in a low voice, "Thanks for helping me, Tweet."

"You're welcome." Her voice was so quiet, I almost didn't hear her.

"You know what they say, don't you?" She shook her head. "Practice makes perfect. We may need to practice a lot. I'm kind of a slow learner." I waggled my eyebrows and chuckled, causing my chest to vibrate.

She took in a huge gulp of air. "Do you want to start now?"

Yes but you deserve something special.

I dipped down closer to her before pushing away and vaulting off the bed. "Can't right now. I got a dentist appointment. Mom's getting off work early to pick me up."

Propping herself up on her elbows, she said in a daze, "Oh... okay."

I held my hands out, pulled her off the bed, and into my chest, gently pinning her arms behind her back.

Looking down, I smiled, and said in a commanding tone, "Tonight. Seven o'clock. Our spot."

"Okay, I'll see you then," she said, breathlessly.

Taking a couple of steps back, I took off my Red Sox cap and ran my fingers through my hair a couple of times before putting it back on. We never took our eyes off of each other.

I swallowed hard and said, "Thanks again, Tweet, for helping me out. I'll see you tonight, okay?"

"Okay… yeah… tonight… see you then."

My gaze roamed up and down her body one more time before I turned and walked out of my room. I needed to leave before my instincts took over, or I would've grabbed her, and started practicing right there on the spot. As I walked into the family room I looked out the window and saw Mom pulling into the driveway.

"Tweet, my mom's here. Lock up when you leave. Okay?" I yelled.

"Okay." The sound of her shaky voice drifting down the hall made me smile as I made my way out the door and to the car.

"You look awfully happy. Did you have a good day?" Mom asked, backing up into the street.

My smile stretched wider. "Yes ma'am and it keeps getting better."

CHAPTER 4

My eyes scanned the picnic table at our spot as I mentally checked off all the items I needed for the night. Red and white plastic tablecloth—check. Paper plates and napkins—check. Diet Pepsi for Tweet and Mountain Dew for me—check. Candle—check. Flowers—check. IPod—check. The only thing missing was the guest of honor. I had to admit, I felt pretty proud of myself. Convincing Tweet to meet me tonight in order to help me practice kissing was pretty quick thinking and ingenious. Seeing the way she reacted to the news that Brittani wanted to hang out with me showed that Tweet was jealous at the thought of me with another girl. Where there's jealousy, there's hope that she wanted more than friendship with me. If she wanted more, then that meant I wasn't a total pervert for thinking of my best friend in a very friendly way.

During the dental appointment earlier today, I was pretty oblivious to all the scraping and jabbing going on inside my mouth. Instead my thoughts drifted to what my mouth would be doing later. I had hit the jackpot because I was going to be kissing my girl in a few hours. I didn't know if Tweet had ever dreamed about having her first real kiss, but I was determined it would be a kiss she'd dream about for the rest of her life. I was clueless about romance, having no idea how I was going to make things extra special tonight. Then it dawned on me.

Last Saturday, we were hanging out as usual. It was pouring down rain so we decided to have a movie marathon, each picking our favorite. While I waited around to watch my pick, *Field of Dreams*, Tweet forced me to watch the 80's chick flick, *Sixteen Candles*.

We were at her house in the family room, both stretched out at opposite ends of the sofa, our legs side-by-side with our heads propped against the armrests. I was lying on my back, totally disinterested in the movie. We'd seen it at least ten times in the past. Tweet was lying on her side turned toward the TV. We both wore our usual summer uniform, T-shirt and shorts.

"Would you toss that blanket to me?" she asked.

"It's ninety degrees outside. Why do you need a blanket?"

I knew why she needed it. I had already noticed the goose bumps covering her bare legs. I was about to grab the blanket earlier to cover her up, but then realized, the angle I was at, gave me a bird's eye view up her shorts that just covered her round little ass.

"Please, Noah," she whined, tapping my hip with her toe. "My legs are freezing."

I reluctantly got off the sofa and grabbed the blanket that was slung over the back of the recliner. As I turned toward Tweet, I wadded up the blanket and shot it over to her as if I were making a slam-dunk with a basketball.

"You do this every time we watch TV. Why don't you just turn the ceiling fan off and wear a pair of sweatpants?" I asked, plopping back down on the sofa.

She tucked the blanket around her legs. "Because I like being cozy under a blanket. If the fan was off and I had sweatpants on, I wouldn't get cold. If I didn't get cold there'd be no need for a blanket to get cozy under. Why is that so hard to understand?"

She was so cute when she rambled and made no sense.

Shaking my head, I huffed out, "Girls."

When the movie finally ended, Tweet rolled onto her back, hiking the blanket under her chin. "I love the end of that movie."

"Me too," I said sarcastically.

"Jake Ryan is so romantic." Her voice was all breathy.

"Why, because he brought the girl a birthday cake on her birthday? Duh."

"It's not about the cake and the candles. It's because he thought about what she would like and did it. He's sweet and thoughtful."

So there I was, standing in front of the picnic table waiting for Tweet. My heart pumping harder and faster in my chest as my stomach rode waves of nausea. My mind flipped back and forth constantly. Was this a good idea? Maybe not. What if I kissed her wrong? I did a quick search on the internet on how to kiss. I was pretty sure I got the gist of it, although some of the stuff that came up freaked me out. I was excited about her coming, then scared to death, then excited, then doubted she would even show up. Tweet had been so unpredictable lately.

"You and Me" by Lifehouse drifted from my iPod that was set up on the table. A huge smile crossed my face when I heard the gravel surrounding the picnic table crunch behind me. After a couple of deep breaths trying to calm my excitement and nerves, I turned around. The breaths were pointless because the second I saw her they rushed out of me. The hum that started in the center of my chest quickly spread over my entire body. My eyes doubled in size and stayed glued to her. I felt my jaw go slack. *Wow*, played on a continuous loop in my head. I may have said it out loud, I wasn't sure. Everything else was a blur except the girl in front of me.

I had changed into my black Nike basketball shorts, white T-shirt, and Nike Air Max sneakers with my favorite Red Sox baseball cap twisted backward on my head. Tweet had dressed up. She wore a light green dress that covered her legs, but left her arms completely bare. The front of the dress was just low enough that I could see the top of her boobs, especially with the deep breaths she was taking. Her hair was up with a few stray pieces falling down her cheeks.

I stepped to the side revealing the picnic table. The stunned expression on her face caused the air to return to my lungs, making my chest puff out with pride.

Nailed it!

I hated shopping, so when I asked my mom earlier if we could stop by Target after my dentist appointment she was more than a little confused. I told her Tweet was helping me with a school project and having a picnic was my way of thanking her. Mom simply tilted her head to one side, said, "Ah," and pulled me into a tight hug right there in the parking lot. Thankfully, she never asked for more details. Mom was awesome.

Tweet was so focused on the table that she didn't notice when I picked up the wildflowers and hid them behind my back. The flowers were Mom's idea.

Walking toward Tweet, I cleared my throat, grabbing her attention. I brought my arm around and held the flowers in front of her. "These are for you."

She blinked several times as her gaze went back and forth from my eyes to the flowers. She gently took them from me as if they were made of glass, raised them up to her nose, and inhaled. I heard and felt the pulsing of my heartbeat as it crawled up my neck and into my ears. The hair on my arms popped up one by one sending a prickling sensation down to the tips of my fingers. I wanted to grab her right then and start practicing, but she deserved better than my horny ass attacking her. Shoving my hands deep inside my side pockets, I rocked back and forth on my heels, trying to get a grip on my hormones.

"You look really pretty, Tweet."

The pale pink on her cheeks darkened. "Thanks. What is all this?" she asked, raising her chin toward the table.

Following her gaze, I answered, "I wanted to thank you for helping me out. I know it's a lot to ask." I threw a slight smile her way.

The look in her eyes went from shock to sadness. No one else would have caught it, but I did. I noticed everything about Tweet, even the tiniest things. There was a slight quiver in her bottom lip. I had no idea what just happened to cause this sudden shift. All I knew was that I had this overwhelming urge to take her in my arms and hold her.

Lightening the mood, I walked closer and nudged her arm with my elbow. "Stop standing there being such a girl," I teased. "It's just our regular old table. Sit down."

"Thank you, Noah. This is… it's…" She was speechless.

She had gotten her *Sixteen Candles* moment and I was her Jake.

We sat at the table in silence, listening to music and staring at each other. Any nerves I had were gone. This wasn't awkward. It was comfortable and natural.

"Can I ask you something?" she said, breaking the silence.

"You can ask me anything, Tweet."

"Do you think it's weird for us to be best friends?"

Of all the things I thought she would ask that wasn't even in the ballpark of possibilities. I felt the lump in my throat grow. "What do you mean 'weird'?"

Shrugging her shoulders, she stated, "Beth thinks it's weird."

I wondered if Beth had been filling Tweet's head with stupid petty girl shit. After years of being compared to her older sister, Emily, it took only a few words from someone to cause her self-esteem to bottom out completely. I hated that she thought so little of herself, that she doubted herself, and was doubting us.

Something inside of me clicked. In that moment all my confusion disappeared. It didn't feel strange sitting across from Tweet on a date or giving her flowers. I didn't feel like a pervert for liking the way she looked in her dress. I didn't know if it was the way the light from the sunset lit up her face or the sweet shy smile she gave me, but something was different. I couldn't keep my eyes off of her. My gaze intensified. I wanted her not only to see but feel how serious and confident I felt in what I was about to say.

Reaching across the table, I placed her hand in mine, and laced our fingers together. "It doesn't feel weird to me. When I'm with you everything feels perfect. I can't picture anyone else being my best friend and I don't want to."

Our eyes stayed focused on each other for a few seconds before hers dropped down to our joined hands. Her fingers began slipping away from mine. I tightened my grip, causing her head to pop up.

"I feel the same way." Her voice was soft and shaky.

I looked into her beautiful teal eyes filling with water. My throat felt as if it were closing up, causing my chest to pump harder for air. I hated when Tweet cried. Maybe she believed we were weird. Couldn't she feel whatever this was between us or was I just being a big pussy?

A deep sigh escaped her lips as a tear spilled over and down her cheek. Raising her hand that I had been holding for the past five minutes, I brought it to my lips and placed a soft kiss on the inside of her palm. My actions were pure instinct. I had no idea what I was doing.

"Don't cry, Tweet," I whispered.

The sound of a car horn cut through the thick air that surrounded us, breaking the moment. I needed to get this night back on track and lighten the mood.

Raising my free hand, I pointed my index finger in the air, smirked, and said, "I believe our dinner has arrived." Then I got up and walked to the waiting car parked at the entrance of the park.

By the time I got back to the table with the pizza, Tweet's smile had returned. We quickly fell back into *us,* laughing and talking about anything and everything. We ate pizza and then downed a handful of breath mints. Practice time had arrived.

Adrenaline shot through my body as I pounded the table with the palm of my hands, like a drum. I was nervous, but not because I was about to kiss Tweet, my best friend. I was nervous because I was about to kiss my girl for the first time. I'd been calling her my *girl* for a few months, mostly teasing her with the name. I wasn't teasing anymore. Tweet was my girl. I stopped drumming and looked at her. Her eyebrows rose up high, she smiled, waiting for me to get the show on the road.

"I guess standing would be the best way to do this," I said.

She nodded in agreement.

We both swung our legs over the benches and stood. As I rounded the table heading toward Tweet, I noticed her kicking at a few of the small rocks while her eyes shifted between looking at the ground and me. There was so much energy pulsing through me I could feel every muscle twitching as if they wanted to break free from my skin. My mouth was drying up while my hands were sweating so badly, they felt as if I had dunked them in water. I tried to clear my head and remember what coach told us to do when we felt nerves right before a big game.

My shoulders rolled backward and forward while I tilted my head from side to side, stretching my neck. I shook out my arms and then each leg separately, trying to get rid of the tingling sensation that rode up and down each limb. My breaths were coming out in short quick spurts, causing me to feel a little lightheaded. Bending down, I rubbed my wet hands over my shorts a couple of times so I wouldn't sweat all over Tweet, and inhaled several deep breaths.

With my hands resting flat on my thighs, I looked up at her and announced. "Okay, here it comes." I straightened.

"I don't think it's a good idea to slap a warning label on it."

"I'm not going to say that tomorrow."

"Sorry. I thought that might have been one of your moves." She smirked at me.

I moved in closer to her, leaving very little space between us. Looking down into her eyes caused vibrations to explode throughout me and consume every part of my body. My heart was thumping so loudly that I knew she could hear it and probably even saw it slamming against my chest. Holding her gaze, I brought my hands up and cupped the sides of her face. As one thumb moved over her soft cheek I felt a shiver run through her body. Her reaction made me smile. Being this close to her, touching her, knowing what we were about to do was making my head spin and my legs weak. I needed to go in for the kiss before I passed out. But knowing this could be my only chance made me keep things slow.

I studied every part of her gorgeous face. Her teal eyes looked up at me between each long dark lash, as if I were the only thing that existed on Earth. Her lips were parted slightly with light spurts of breath flowing over them. Her soft skin flushed a deeper pink with each second that passed. Raising my hand, the tips of my fingers lightly touched her jaw. My thumb gently moved toward her mouth, skimming across her lips a couple of times before gliding back to her cheek.

Our chests were pumping faster. The sound of blood surging through my veins got louder. My world felt like it was underwater. Nothing existed except me and Tweet. I barely heard our song, "Everything", fill the air as I lowered my lips to hers.

During baseball camp this past summer I had heard some of the older guys talking about making out with their girlfriends. I so wanted to make out with Tweet. It took every ounce of strength I had not to go full throttle. I wanted to shove my tongue down her throat, grab her ass, and pull her against me.

Jake Ryan. I had to channel my inner Jake Ryan.

As I placed my lips on Tweet's, her eyes closed and her head tilted back. I applied slow and steady pressure, nibbling along her bottom lip before sucking on it slightly. Her body swayed to one side, both her hands gripping my upper arms in an attempt to brace herself. I read this as a good sign, so I let the tip of my tongue slip out and touch her lips. Her mouth opened. Tongues met. My head and dick were on the verge of detonating. Our tongues spiraled faster and faster around each other's, deepening the kiss. My fingers twitched. I wanted to touch her everywhere. The reaction my body was having was getting out of control. I had never felt anything this amazing in my life. I needed to step back before I threw her down onto the table and pounced on top of her.

A slight moan from Tweet vibrated across my lips as I slowed down the kiss. Pulling away slightly, I rested my forehead against hers, eyes closed, our lips still connected, and whispered, "You're perfect."

We quietly stood in this position for several minutes trying to catch our breath. Simultaneously, her hands loosened their grip on my biceps as mine slid over her shoulders and down her arms, our hands clasping together.

I didn't want this to end. Finally, once our breathing returned to normal, I slowly opened my eyes but kept my forehead firmly glued to Tweet's.

"Wow," I whispered. My voice sounded as if I had just woke up.

"Man," Tweet said, breathlessly. "Are you sure you haven't done this before because you have some pretty awesome moves. Where'd you get moves like that?"

The excitement and pride I felt hearing and feeling how much she enjoyed our first kiss was like winning the Super Bowl, the NBA Championship, the Stanley Cup, and the World Series all at the same time.

"Wal-Mart," I answered. A cocky grin crept across my face.

Tweet's pink lips slowly curled up to form a smile. "How long did it take you to think that one up?"

"It just came to me actually. I thought it was pretty good."

I wanted to practice some more, lots more in fact, but before I could say anything Tweet stepped away and s cleaned up the trash from dinner. Neither of us said another word while we walked home. An awkward air surrounded us as we stood on the front porch of her house. It didn't come from me not knowing how to say goodnight. It came from me not wanting to say goodbye. I didn't have a name for the feelings I was having for Tweet. All I knew for sure was that they were getting stronger and not going away. I didn't know how to talk to her about what was happening. It was weird because we'd always been able to talk about anything.

Tweet let out a deep sigh, breaking the silence. "Well, goodnight. It sure was fun practicing with you. Brittani is a lucky girl."

Total shock and disbelief appeared across her face as if some force beyond her control spoke those words.

It pissed me off that she mentioned Brittani. Tonight wasn't about her. Tonight was just us.

"Don't bring her up, not now." My gaze ran from her lips to her eyes. "Thanks for tonight."

I glanced away for a second, trying to decide whether or not to tell her how I've been feeling. I looked back and connected with her beautiful teal eyes. They looked sad or scared, I couldn't figure out which. I also couldn't figure out the right words to explain what was happening between us.

"Goodnight, Tweet."

"Goodnight, Noah."

I walked backward down the steps, keeping my eyes locked on her until I had to turn away. With each step an empty feeling hit my stomach. The dim light from the porch brightened her eyes. They were full of tears. I didn't know what the deal was. We'd be seeing each other tomorrow. I mean we saw each other every day. But for some reason leaving her tonight was hard.

Stopping at the bottom of the steps, I said in a low voice, "Tweet."

"Yeah?" She tried hard to keep her voice steady but I could hear the shakiness.

"Tonight was amaz…" I paused. It wasn't tonight that was amazing, it was her. "You're amazing."

"Noah…" Her voice trailed off.

"I wish you believed it."

Before she could say anything, I turned and walked away.

Monday morning I was headed down the hall toward my locker. I hadn't seen or talked to Tweet the entire weekend since we kissed. I left voicemails and sent texts, but she never returned any of them. She was avoiding me for some reason. Could I have misread our kiss? I thought it was awesome, but what the hell did I know? Maybe it sucked and she didn't want to hurt my feelings. Maybe the sadness and tears in her eyes Friday night were because she knew I was destined for the priesthood.

I couldn't be a priest. Communion wafers made me gag.

I turned the corner and saw her standing at her locker.

"Mornin', Tweet."

She jumped a little when I whispered in her ear.

"Good morning." She wouldn't look at me.

I just had to play it cool. All she needed to do was look at me. If she could look me in the eye then chances were the kiss didn't suck.

Leaning one shoulder against the locker, I stared at her profile, willing her to turn in my direction. "I've missed you. I called you all weekend. I saw your mom yesterday. She said you were busy working on a paper?"

"English," she said into her locker.

I reached out to grab Tweet's arm, trying to get her attention when one of my teammates, Brad Johnson, slapped me on the back and said, "Hey Stewart, heard you had a great time this weekend. I just got out of class with Brit. She couldn't stop singing your praises, dude. Way to go."

As Brad walked off, I turned to Tweet and shrugged my shoulders. I had no idea what he was talking about. I barely spent any time with Brittani the other night at the bowling alley. A group of kids from school were there. The guys pretty much hung out and bowled while the girls talked. Brittani and Beth tried to flirt with me a few times, but I was too preoccupied with thoughts of Tweet and the night before. Brittani's dad dropped me at home around 11:30 p.m. That was all that happened.

Two other teammates, Jeremy and Spencer, were coming down the hall and stopped when they saw me.

Spencer tugged on the back of my neck and announced, "Heard you had a hot date this weekend. How about that, just a freshman and already a player."

I grinned as the guys walked off down the hall. When I turned and met the look on Tweet's face, my grin busted out into a full blown smile.

Innocently, she asked, "Your big date was this past weekend?"

"Don't do that."

"Do what?"

"Play dumb. You're no good at it, Tweet."

"Well, it sounds like your first date was a success."

She was pissed and jealous.

"I would say my first date was perfect."

I watched as her poor books took a beating while she shoved them around her locker. The more she banged things around the harder it was for me to hide my laughter.

"Uh… you about done beating up that innocent locker, Rocky?" I asked.

"Congratulations! I'm glad your first date was…"

"Perfect."

This is so much fun.

"Perfect," she snapped. "Oh, did I tell you that I joined the school newspaper? You know, maybe I could write an article about having the *perfect* date and interview you and your *perfect* date since your date was so perfect."

"Do you have any idea how adorable you are right now?"

Teal eyes narrowed in my direction.

"Those guys are talking about my second date," I admitted.

"You've already had a second date?"

"Saturday night."

"Saturday night?" Her eyebrows scrunched tightly together as her face turned three shades of red. "I thought Saturday night was your first date."

"Friday night was my first date."

"But you were with me all Friday night."

She still wasn't cluing in.

I leaned in so close our noses were almost touching. My voice was low. "You didn't think I wanted Brittani to be my first date and kiss, did you? I've shared all my firsts with you."

Her lips parted and a faraway look glazed over her eyes. I'd overheard girls talking before about other guys and how the guy made them swoon. I wasn't exactly positive what that meant, but from what I did know, I was pretty sure I just made Tweet do it.

I stared at her lips for a few seconds, remembering what they tasted like. Maintaining eye contact, I pushed off of the lockers, turned, and sauntered down the hall. Yeah, I wasn't the only one who thought our kiss was awesome. There'd be no Father Stewart title in my future.

CHAPTER 5

As our freshman year continued, I thought things between Tweet and I would get easier and less confusing. I didn't know much about girls but I wasn't a complete idiot, except lately when it came to Tweet. She still managed to constantly confuse me. Every time a girl talked, giggled, or innocently touched me, Tweet would shake her head, roll her eyes, and a huff of air would pass over her gaping mouth. This came to be known as the shake, roll, 'n' huff. She did it so often that I could tell from a mile away when the SRH had been launched. I also felt her body stiffen each time we made any physical contact. Even something as simple as a brush of our shoulders caused her to jerk away from me.

The idea of us drifting apart scared the shit out of me. We still saw each other every day but our time together was becoming less and less. She made up stupid excuses not to be around me, like she had to study for a specific class that I wasn't in, or her Aunt Flo was visiting. We always studied together no matter what and I didn't know who the fuck Aunt Flo was, but she seemed to visit a lot.

There was a one week break before summer school started. In order to get ahead academically, Tweet and I signed up for classes. This would look great on our college applications. We hadn't talked about it, but I always assumed we would go to the same university. We both had really good grades and the fact that we were willing to give up part of our summer would show our dedication and hard work. There'd be no question we'd have our pick of schools.

I leaned back against the counter in Tweet's kitchen while she popped open a Diet Pepsi and a bag of Sweet Sixteen donuts. I was getting annoyed. The last twenty minutes had been spent with me trying to convince her to come hang out for the day. Travis had just gotten his license and was coming to pick me up. We were headed to Folly Beach to go surfing.

She gulped down a couple of swallows of soda, causing a seismic burp to catapult from her body. If there was an Olympic belching event, Tweet would win a gold medal. I swear some of the sounds that came out of this girl were truly impressive. She was tired of the subject and this was her way of changing it. We stared, challenging the other to laugh first.

I shook my head. "You're so damn dainty."

"Thanks. It's my southern bellechness bustin' out." She tossed a bite-size donut coated with powdered sugar into her mouth trying to keep the smile from appearing. Her serious expression was beginning to crack.

We faced-off for a few more seconds until another burp bubbled up from deep down in her gut. I heard it rumble up into her throat. Tweet tried to stop it from escaping by clamping her lips shut. This caused her cheeks to expand like a blowfish and a couple of small puffs of powdered sugar to fly from her lips. Tweet slapped her hand over her mouth and both of us doubled over as laughter blasted out of us simultaneously.

She straightened, caught her breath, and said, "Did you see the puffs of sugar?"

I wiped tears from my eyes. "That was classic."

"That burp was like a freight train. Couldn't be stopped."

"You're crazy. Now, go get your stuff. I told Travis to meet us here."

"Noah, don't start on that again. I told you I don't feel like doing the beach today," she whined.

She sat her drink and donuts on the kitchen island before pulling herself up onto the countertop and sitting across from me. My annoyance came back in a flash.

"Lately you don't seem to feel like doing anything, at least not with me." Sarcasm dripped from each word as I held her gaze.

"That is so not true. We see each other every single day," she said, crossing her arms over her chest, which caused her boobs to push together and my gaze to drop down to them.

After a couple of seconds I brought my eyes back up to hers. "Sorry it's such a fucking burden to be around me."

"What is wrong with you?"

"What is wrong with you?"

Tweet and I had never really argued before, not even as little kids. We joked around, teased each other, but this was the closest thing to a fight we'd ever had. I hated it.

"Look, if you don't want to go to the beach we can do something else, like a movie," I said.

"No. You planned on going to Folly, so go. You don't need to change things because of me. It's not like we're joined at the hip." Her gaze fell to the floor.

At that moment, all the air was sucked from the room and time stood still. My heart shot up into my throat. I clamped my mouth shut in order to keep it from spewing out all over the kitchen. It was pretty clear that she didn't want me around.

I blew out a breath and pushed off from the counter. "Fine! Have a great fucking day."

I stomped across the room and swung the door open. As I stepped through, I heard Tweet yell, "Noah!" before the door slammed shut.

I waited for several seconds, hoping she would come after me, but the door never opened.

With one leg stretched out in front of me and the other bent with my arm resting on top of it, I stared at the waves rolling up to the shoreline. I was still pissed off and staring at the water wasn't doing a damn thing to help. Since walking out on Tweet, I'd been trying to forget her. Travis talked the entire way to the beach. Occasionally, I threw in a grunt or a nod, but had no idea what I was grunting and nodding about. Once we got to Folly I focused on surfing, but she kept creeping back into my head. I couldn't believe she let me leave that way. I didn't know if I was more pissed because she didn't want to hang out or didn't come after me, or because I couldn't seem to get her off my mind.

Suddenly, cold water came raining down on me. Looking up, I saw the silhouette of Travis hovering above.

"What the fuck, dude? You're dripping water all over me," I yelled.

Dropping down next to me, he wiped his wet brown hair back and said, "You've been a big drip since I picked you up."

"Fuck you."

"Jesus, what is wrong with you today?" Stretching out, he leaned back on his elbows and looked straight ahead.

"I wish everyone would stop asking me that."

We stared ahead, listening to the waves for a few minutes.

"Did something bad go down between you and Amanda? Is that why your panties are all twisted and shoved up your ass?" I narrowed my eyes in his direction, not answering. "Can I ask you something?" I didn't respond. "Okaaaay. I'll take that as a yes, Travis, happy to answer any and all questions." More silence. "Exactly what are y'all?"

For the first time in my life I didn't automatically answer we're best friends, because I didn't know anymore. All I knew was that Tweet, who had been in my life since day one, had become a girl. A girl I thought and dreamed about all the time. A girl who made me feel things, not just physically, but deep inside. Feelings that I didn't even have a name for.

"I like her," I finally answered, my voice low.

I couldn't believe I admitted it to someone. The words were out of my mouth before my brain registered what they meant.

"No shit. I didn't have to be fucking Einstein to figure that part out."

Looking over at him, I asked, "What do you mean?"

"Are you kidding me? The look you gave me the first and only time I tried to sit next to her was like the fucking superlasers on the Death Star. My balls actually shrank up and hid behind my massive dick."

"Thanks for that visual."

"Stewart, you kill me. There are half-naked girls crawling all over this beach and you sit here like a pussy, wasting time daydreaming about a girl who blew you off today. And I don't mean that in the good way."

"It's not that I don't notice other girls," I said.

"Then what is it?"

I thought for a long moment. "I don't know. They're just not Tweet."

"Don't get me wrong. I think Amanda is great and she is definitely hot, but..."

My muscles immediately tensed up as I glared at him.

"Oh shit! There's that look again." Rolling away from me, he got up on all fours and frantically patted the sand with his hands. "My balls! Where are my balls?"

"You're an asshole." I chuckled.

Standing, he rubbed his palms together brushing off the sand. "I just don't get wasting time on a girl who doesn't seem to want to be around you when there are so many on the prowl for manly specimens such as ourselves. Maybe it's not necessarily Amanda that you're interested in."

"What?"

"We're strong testosterone-pumping males. Born to hunt and gather. We live for the chase. Maybe you like the challenge more than the girl." Like a dog hypnotized by a piece of meat, his gaze caught a tall redhead wearing a bright green bikini walking by. "Excuse me while I go be a man." Jogging toward the girl, he stopped halfway, turned with raised arms, curled biceps, and shouted, "Hunt and gather!"

As I watched Travis sidle up next to the redhead, I thought about what he said. Was it the challenge that drew me to Tweet? It did seem like my feelings were getting stronger the more she pushed me away. I got turned on when I looked at other girls but I figured that was natural. I was jacked up on hormones. Tweet was the only girl who stayed in my head and in my dreams. Even when I looked at other girls' bodies, once I moved up to their faces they all looked like Tweet.

I'm so fucked up. Maybe Travis is right.

All of a sudden, a pair of hands pushed down on my shoulders.

"Boo!" There was no mistaking that drawl.

"Hey, Brittani."

"Hey, Noah." She cocked her head to one side.

"What's up?" I asked, trying hard not to stare at her body popping out of her bikini.

"My body temperature."

She plopped down beside me so close that we were touching from our shoulders all the way down to our legs. The white multi-colored polka-dot bikini top pretty much just covered her nipples while the striped short shorts she had on sat low on her hips.

I cleared my throat. "Yeah, it's pretty hot out here."

"It is now that I spotted you." Leaning back, she propped herself up with her hands, pushing her tits up, out, and really close to my bare upper arm. She looked from side-to-side and asked, "You alone?"

"Um… Travis and I c-ame out to s-urf," I stammered.

Brittani had always made me nervous when we were alone, which wasn't often. She'd corner me at my locker or outside school sometimes, but we never really hung out. She was a lot more forward than any other girls at school and from all accounts, a lot more experienced. I struggled to stay focused on the ocean but my gaze kept drifting back to multi-colored polka dots.

"What about Ana?"

My eyebrows scrunched together before I realized who she was asking about. "You mean Amanda."

"Whatever. She just always seems to be around you."

"She didn't want to come today."

"She passed up the chance to see your hot body all wet and glistenin'?" Brittani sucked her lower lip into her mouth.

"I guess." I flashed a shy smile.

"I'd never turn you down, Noah," she said, running her fingernails down my arm. Standing, she held her hand out. "Walk with me."

My gaze traveled up her long tanned legs to her thighs, over her curvy hips, and up to her huge tits. I felt the familiar twitch in my swim trunks. When I finally turned to her face, I saw plain regular blue eyes, not gorgeous teal ones. Maybe it was time for a new challenge.

I placed my hand in Brittani's. It felt gritty with sand, not soft and warm like Tweet's. As she helped me stand up a deafening squeaky laugh escaped her. Tweet had a great laugh. It started out deep in her throat and rose to the perfect pitch with a snort thrown in here and there.

I need to stop this shit. I need to get Tweet out of my head.

Brittani and I headed toward the pier. She walked slightly ahead giving me a good view of her body. I concentrated on the sway and bounce of her ass. We didn't talk, which was fine with me. She led me to a secluded area under the pier. Stepping forward, she pushed me back until I was against one of the posts. My gaze darted around, checking if we could be seen. I felt a gritty hand touch my rapidly pumping chest.

"You know I've always liked you," she said in a husky voice.

I choked out, "Yeah?"

"You're the hottest guy at school. You're even hotter than a lot of the seniors."

For some reason I looked everywhere except down at Brittani while I felt my breathing getting shallow, my skin burning up, and my dick getting harder.

"Noah, have you ever kissed a girl?" she whispered.

I swallowed hard. "Yeah."

"I mean *really* kissed a girl?"

"I'm fifteen. Of course I've really kissed a girl."

My girl.

Closing my eyes tight, I desperately tried to erase any thoughts of Tweet. I may not have been sure what she was to me anymore, but I knew for sure she didn't want to be mine.

I could feel how hard Brittani's nipples were through her bathing suit as she pressed her body against me.

Rubbing her tits up and down my chest, she asked, "Have you ever touched a girl's tits?"

"No." I breathed out.

"You wanna touch mine?"

Looking down, I completely bypassed her eyes and landed on her chest. "Yes," I said, my voice gravelly and barely audible.

The blood pulsing through my body drowned out all other noise. I couldn't believe what was happening. It was like my dreams were coming true except this was the wrong chest and girl.

Fuck! Get your head in the game, Stewart.

Brittani's fingers wrapped around my wrists. She lifted my hands and placed them on her tits. I gave them a little squeeze. In that second, all the blood and heat in my body concentrated in my dick, causing it to push against my swim trunks. The pressure was building fast and becoming painful. Removing her hand from mine, she reached for the strap of her bikini and slid it over her shoulder. I attempted to take a deep breath without success. I was becoming lightheaded. I tried to step back, but my back was plastered against the post. I felt trapped, suffocated, and ready to explode.

"Stop!" I said through gritted teeth.

"Why?"

"I feel sick. It must be the tacos Travis and I grabbed on the way here. I gotta go."

Dropping my hands, I wedged myself free and took off running, never looking back.

I found Travis, pried him away from the redhead, and told him I needed to go home. The second the car pulled into my driveway I jumped out and ran into the house. My chest hadn't stopped hurting and the knot in my stomach grew bigger every time I thought about what had happened with Brittani. I couldn't even look her in the eye. I was worried I'd see Tweet's face but scared I wouldn't at the same time. I wanted to be alone and forget this day ever happened.

I headed down the hallway. I almost made it to my room until I heard my dad's voice calling me as I passed his home office.

"Noah."

I stopped, tilting my head up to the ceiling. After a couple of deep breaths, I reluctantly backtracked until I was standing in the doorway.

"Yeah?"

"Where've you been?" he asked while clicking through something on his computer.

"Travis and I went to Folly to surf."

"Were the waves… gnarly?"

Chuckling, I answered, "Yeah, the waves were super gnarly."

My dad was great even though he could be a dork sometimes. He knew it and never made any apologies for it.

"Good. You need to pack as much fun into this week as possible. Summer school starts next week, right?"

"Yes sir."

"Were you able to get into the AP Science class?"

"Yes sir."

He swiveled his chair in my direction. "Noah, I know college seems like a long way off and studying isn't exactly the most fun way to spend your summer. Your sophomore year is important. It's one of the first steps in building a strong and solid foundation for your academic career. Not only do your grades count but also your extracurricular activities like baseball. It all plays a hand in showing universities how well rounded, dedicated, and hardworking you are. You've got to stay focused."

"I know and I will."

"Trust me, you'll have plenty of time later for all the other stuff like girls. I was young once, about a million years ago." He smiled and gave me a wink.

It wasn't unlike my dad to have these impromptu father-son chats, but the fact that he mentioned girls was weird. Could he tell I had just touched my first set of tits? I needed to get to my room.

"You don't have to worry about me, Dad. I'm focused." I turned to leave.

"Oh, by the way, I got our tickets to Fenway and the flight booked today. So, the summer won't be all work."

"Awesome." I made my second attempt to leave.

"Noah."

"Yeah, Dad?"

"I'm very proud of you."

"Thanks."

Walking to my room, I wondered if he'd be so proud of me if he knew what a total asshole I'd been today. Not only did I argue with Tweet but I touched a girl that I didn't even like just because I was hurt and pissed off. Definitely nothing to be proud of.

After supper I was at the sink rinsing off dishes before loading the dishwasher, staring out the window. Tweet's house was basically the reversed layout as ours, the kitchens faced each other with matching over-the-sink windows. Ever since we were tall enough, we'd look out the window to see if the other one was doing the same thing. We'd jump up and down, dance, and wave like crazy people trying to make each other laugh. I tried like hell not to look over there tonight, but when Tweet was involved it seemed as if my body did what it wanted to do.

The florescent light above the window shined down on her. No makeup, hair pulled back with several pieces falling into her eyes, and she was still the most beautiful girl I'd ever seen. I could see her only from the shoulders up but I knew she was washing dishes. Her parents never did get a dishwasher. Raising her forearm, she brushed the hair back. Her hand grazed the tip of her nose, leaving behind a blob of suds. A smile appeared across my face as I stared, willing her to look up at me, but her eyes stayed down, focused on the dishes. I finally tore myself away from the window and forced myself not to look out of it every time I passed by.

After finishing kitchen cleanup duty, I grabbed the trash bag, flipped on the outside light and headed out the back door. I froze when I got to the bottom of the steps. For the first time since this morning I could breathe. Tweet was sitting on the patio swing in my backyard. Not saying a word, I tossed the bag into the trash and then walked over to her. She stopped swinging long enough for me to sit down. We glided back and forth for several seconds in awkward silence.

Tweet twisted her body away from me and picked up something beside her. When she turned around, she was holding a packet of Little Debbie chocolate Swiss rolls. A huge grin stretched across my face. She tore open the plastic wrap and handed me one of the cakes.

"I'm really sorry about today," she said. Her voice was low.

"Me too."

"We've never argued before."

"I know."

"You walked out on me." From the corner of my eye, I saw bright teal eyes look over at me.

"I did and you didn't come after me." I turned my head in her direction.

"I didn't, did I?" Silence. "Let's not do that again. Okay?"

"Okay."

We tapped the Swiss rolls together as if making a toast, and just like that, we were back to *us*. At least this version of us, whatever that was.

The rest of the night was spent on that swing, talking and laughing. At one point, Tweet shifted closer to me and laid her head on my shoulder. Our hands rested side-by-side on top of our thighs. I flipped mine over, palm side up, hoping Tweet's hand would slide on top. I'd heard that if a person focused all his attention on an object, he could get it to move just by the sheer power of his mind. That's all bullshit. I put every ounce of energy from my body, mind, and soul into that one slight movement. Her hand stayed still, just like the door had stayed closed earlier that day.

Travis's words from earlier crossed my mind, that I liked the big challenge of trying to get the girl more than the girl herself. At first, I thought that he might have a point. But when I walked outside and saw her waiting for me on the swing, I knew that the only challenge I'd face would be if Tweet wasn't in my life.

CHAPTER 6

"Okay. I only have one more question then I'll set you free." She glanced up at me with that sweet shy smile I couldn't get enough of.

The varsity baseball coach had been impressed with my playing during freshman year and had asked me to try out for the team. I didn't think I had a real chance of making it, I was only in my sophomore year. You usually didn't play varsity until junior year. My dad taught me never to turn down an opportunity. Even though I was pretty nervous, I showed up for tryouts, and wound up making the team. The school paper had asked Tweet to write an article. I knew they asked her because we were friends. Tweet had been to every game I'd ever played in, but still knew zero about baseball.

Not much had changed between us. My feelings for her were just as strong, if not stronger than ever before. Her feelings for me had apparently not changed either. She continued to limit our time together and as far as touching her, that was almost nonexistent. The only thing that had changed over the summer was that I had become an even hornier bastard with a little more confidence and less patience.

Toward the end of the summer I started spending more time with Travis. Hanging out with him always involved girls at some point. We went to the movies with some, the beach with others, or hung out with a few at his house. All the girls were cute and seemed nice. They flirted with me. I held a few hands, touched a shoulder here and there, and even hugged one or two. Several of them had made it clear that they really liked me and wanted to make out. I got close to going with a couple, but when I looked into their eyes I froze.

These girls wanted boyfriends who took them on dates, gave them flowers, and looked at them as if they were the only girl on the planet. I couldn't do any of that, at least not with them. Travis gave me hell about it all the time. He kept telling me that I needed to release the beast within, forget about Tweet, and give other girls a chance. I tried.

After that day under the pier, Brittani and I met up a couple more times during the summer, once at the beach and again at a party. It happened when being around Tweet and not touching her got to be unbearable. I was lonely and the hormones were making me nuts. I needed a release and Brittani was more than willing to lend a hand. She was different from most of the girls at school. She didn't want hearts and flowers. She wanted to do whatever and whomever when the mood struck her. She had one goal in life and that was to have as many guys standing in line waiting to release their beast with her.

We basically rubbed up against each other, she let me touch her, and then we would go our separate ways. I attempted to kiss her a few times but always chickened out. She'd whine about it and I'd give her some excuse like my throat was sore. I didn't know what was more lame, my excuses or the fact that she bought it every time. I felt guilty enough doing what I was doing. I tried hard to convince myself that I had no reason to feel guilty, but deep down I knew it was a lie. I had a reason and it was right beside me gnawing on her pen.

We were sitting halfway up the bleachers at the school baseball field. Tweet was going to be a great journalist. She was able to set the mood so that the interviewee was comfortable. She knew I loved being out here and had decided this was the perfect place for the interview. She seemed really nervous today. Other than an occasional glance, she hadn't looked at me directly. I wondered if she had heard the rumors about Brittani and me.

She stopped snacking on her pen and continued with her questions. "What made you first fall in love with the game?"

"My dad. He loves the game. He introduced me to it when I was four years old. That's when I watched my first game on TV, sitting next to him on the sofa with a liter of orange soda and two huge bags of chips laid out on the coffee table."

I smiled thinking about how excited my dad got about all things baseball. He was like a little kid.

"I don't remember who was playing. It didn't matter. What mattered was I got to spend time with my dad sharing something that he loved."

I looked out over the field.

"The first couple of years I played T-ball and little league—I liked playing the game, but the best part was always the time he and I spent together. No matter how busy he got at work he would make it to every practice and game."

I remembered getting up in the middle of the night as a kid, and seeing the light on in Dad's home office. He was making up the work he missed in order to be at my practice or game. My dad was great and I loved him for all the sacrifices he made. I felt a lump forming in my throat. I swallowed hard a couple times before I continued.

I'm such a pussy.

"When I was six, he took me to my first pro game at Fenway Park. The Red Sox played the Minnesota Twins, 9-1, Sox. I was in awe of everything—the players, the stadium, the field, the stands, the dugout, the food, even the parking lot," I chuckled. "My dad gave me one of the best days of my life.

"As far as the game itself, I love everything about it—the teamwork, the way the bat feels in my hand, the sound of the ball hitting the leather glove, the smell of the grass, and the concession stand food. I love looking up into the stands, seeing the fans and the most important people in my life."

I turned back toward Tweet and caught her staring at me. Our eyes locked. The last time she let me look into them felt like a lifetime ago. I couldn't read her look. It didn't matter, though. The only thing that mattered was that she didn't look away. Her hair was down. One side was tucked behind her ear with the other falling down the side of her face and curling under her jaw. The wind had blown it into a tangled mess that was incredibly hot. I wanted to touch her so badly it made my chest ache. Digging my fingers into my thighs, I fought the urge to reach up and brush her messy hair off the side of her cheek.

I cleared my throat and said, "Sorry Tweet. I didn't mean to ramble on."

"You didn't ramble. You were perfect." She sounded as if she were in a trance.

"So, any more questions?"

"No. I'm good. Thanks for doing this."

"No problem. I wouldn't miss spending time alone with my girl." I hadn't called her that in a long time but it still felt natural.

Whatever the spell was that had surrounded us for the past several minutes broke. She looked down and fidgeted with her notebook for a second before her pen took off tapping at lightning speed.

"What's wrong, Tweet?"

When her eyes met mine again they were starting to fill with tears. This was becoming the norm and I couldn't figure out why. She took in a deep breath and looked back down at her notebook. The vise around my stomach kept getting tighter with each second of silence.

Blowing out a heavy breath, she finally asked, "Why didn't you tell me you were going to the dance with Beth?"

Fuck me!

I had completely forgotten about Beth and the dance. She'd asked me a month or so ago when we were at lunch. Tweet had to drop off one of her articles in the journalism classroom, so she left early. Beth was babbling away as usual while my gaze followed Tweet across the cafeteria. Just before walking out the door she was stopped by a large hand touching her upper arm. A tall, no-neck, dark-haired, muscle-headed Smurffucker was talking to her. The burning sensation in my chest spread like wildfire. He shifted back and forth on his feet, smiling and talking. I couldn't hear what he was saying but I knew what he was doing. He was asking her out. My teeth were clenched so tight that my jaw hurt. I saw Tweet's head shake just before the smile dropped from his face. After one more touch of her arm, the muscle-headed Smurffucker walked away.

Nodding my head slightly in satisfaction, my jaw loosened with a smile. Beth asked me to the dance at about the same time. Apparently, she had taken my reaction to Tweet turning down the Smurffucker as a yes to her question. She bounced in her chair a couple of times, squealing and clapping her hands. After Tweet disappeared behind the doors, I realized what I had gotten myself into. I was going to tell Beth she misunderstood me, but she had already gotten up and hopped away. I caught up with her later that day. She was still extremely excited. I felt bad, so I didn't say anything. Besides, Tweet sure as hell wasn't going to ask me to the stupid dance.

Letting out a deep sigh, I rested my elbows on my knees. I lowered my head, removed my baseball cap, and ran my fingers through my hair a couple of times. I needed to stall as long as possible while I figured out how to explain this without sounding like a complete asshole.

"You know what, forget I asked," Tweet blurted out.

She quickly packed up her stuff, shoving everything into her backpack, and stood. As she took a step in front of me, trying to get away, my hand shot out, grabbing hold of her wrist.

"Don't run away from me. Sit back down." I kept my voice steady and low.

After hesitating for a few seconds, she took a deep breath and then slowly lowered herself down onto the bleachers beside me. I turned my head and noticed she was staring at my hand that was still wrapped around her wrist. This was the first time in months that I'd touched her.

Reluctantly, I uncurled my fingers, sat up, and focused on the baseball field.

"I felt guilty. I know I'm getting ready to sound like a pussy but I was disappointed that you didn't ask me."

"I didn't know you wanted to go," she said.

"I don't give a shit about going to a dance. I wanted to go with you and I was hoping you would want to go with me, but you never said anything. When Beth asked I said yes for some reason. I wished I hadn't after it came out of my mouth. She seemed so excited and happy. I couldn't tell her I changed my mind."

"Why'd you feel guilty?"

"I don't know. It felt—like I was… cheating on you," I stammered.

I couldn't believe those words slipped out of my mouth. I was surprised but not sorry. I'd had enough of the mixed signals, raging hormones, pushing away, seeing Tweet in every other girl, rubbing up against Brittani, and watching some no-neck Smurffucker touch my girl.

Turning toward her, I said, "Tweet, I've been having certain thoughts and feelings about you."

She was completely frozen. Nothing moved except her blinking eyes that showed a different reaction each time they opened.

Blink.

Shock.

Blink.

Hurt.

Blink.

Sadness.

Reaching out, I placed my hand on top of hers, causing her to snap back to the present and look at me.

"I think about you all the time, Tweet." I said, lacing our fingers together.

"It's nice to be thought about."

It was a stupid response, but she hadn't expected me to tell her this stuff today. Hell, I hadn't expected me to tell her this stuff today. I had taken her completely off guard and it made her uneasy.

"When you're around I want to touch you, hold your hand, or put my arms around you. I want to kiss you again."

I continued to hold her gaze, searching for more than the scared shitless expression she had.

"Um... Noah, I have to go."

What the fuck?

My grip tightened around her hand and I huffed in disbelief. "You're leaving?!"

"I need to go check and make sure Tony got enough pictures and... um... look, I'm sorry. I'll see you later. Thanks again for the interview."

In one swift continuous move, she abruptly got up and walked off, breaking away from me. After I got over the initial shock of her completely blowing me off, again, I thought about going after her. I stopped myself, though. This wasn't over but I needed to corner Tweet where she'd have no option to escape me.

CHAPTER

7

Standing outside of Tweet's closed bedroom door, I attempted to take several deep breaths before knocking. My lungs filled halfway with oxygen and then stopped functioning. I was nervous but determined.

I wanted and needed to finish the conversation we had started at the baseball field. Correction. The conversation I started and Tweet ran from. When I got home, Mom had left a message telling me we'd be having dinner over at the Kelly's tonight. This was the perfect chance for me to get answers. Even if I had to barricade the door, there was no way Tweet was getting away from me this time.

I could hear rapid tapping coming from the other side of the door. She was working on her computer. Raising my hand, I knocked lightly. The tapping stopped and only dead silence was left. I started to knock again when she finally answered.

"Yeah?"

I cracked the door open slightly and stuck my head inside the room. She was sitting at her desk wearing a short gray and white striped sleeveless dress and no shoes. Her hair was damp, wavy, and draped over one shoulder. The strap of her white bra had slipped a little from under her dress and was creeping down over her shoulder. I felt a prickling sensation cover my skin and my stomach was flip-flopping all over the place.

"Your mom wanted me to tell you dinner is in twenty," I said. My voice was stuck in my throat and came out husky.

"Thanks." She glanced up, a slight smirk flashed across her lips.

Sensing it was safe to enter, I stepped inside the room, closing the door behind me. A little awkwardness stood between us, but no tension. I walked over to her. One eyebrow cocked up and an involuntary smile spread over my lips at the sight of her bare arms popping with goose bumps as I got closer.

Placing my hands on the back of her chair, I looked over her shoulder and asked, "What are you working on?"

"Your article," she answered, tilting her head straight back.

"Make me look good," I said, peering down into teal beauties.

"There's no other way for you to look."

From the shocked expression that flashed across her face it was obvious she didn't mean to say those words. My eyes shifted and I discovered, from this vantage point, that I had an excellent view down the front of her dress, revealing a white lace bra. A shiver ran through me causing my own goose bumps to surface. I gripped the back of the chair. My eyes followed the light pink blush that speckled her chest, went up her neck, and over her cheeks. Tweet's gaze quickly darted back down to the computer screen.

Needing some distance between us, I walked over to her bed and sat.

Trying to focus and not think about her boobs covered in white lace, I leaned back on my hands and asked, "Tweet, what was the deal today?"

She swung the chair around so that we were facing each other. "What deal are you referring to?"

I couldn't believe she was going to play the clueless card.

"Don't do that. Now's not the time to play dumb," I said, keeping eye contact.

"You seem to be under the impression that I play dumb."

"Why'd you run away from me today?"

"I really had to leave."

I stared at her, not responding to her smartass attempt to avoid my question. Her left leg subtly started to bounce, and sped up the longer I sat there waiting for her to give me a *real* answer. She swiveled back and forth in the chair a few times before hopping up and heading toward her dresser. I watched her fumbling reflection in the mirror as she searched for something. I was getting more and more annoyed with her stalling. Supper was going to be ready soon and I wanted an answer before we left this room.

She grabbed her brush and raked it through her hair several times. Then taking her sweet-ass time, she piled her hair on top of her head and pinned it.

Time's up.

"Why?" I asked, trying hard to keep my tone even.

"Because we were having guests for dinner," she answered with a smirk.

I sat up straight, shook my head, and huffed in frustration, "Dammit Tweet! Would you stop being such a smartass for one minute?"

She whipped around in my direction.

"You do this every time there's something serious to talk about," I accused.

"Do what?"

"Make jokes and then run away."

"I'm sorry," she whispered.

Running both hands over my face, I pleaded, "Please talk to me."

"I'm not sure what you want me to say."

It was time to go big or go home. After she ran from me today I knew she had feelings for me that went beyond friendship. I could tell in the way she looked at me, the jealousy, and how her body automatically reacted whenever we were near each other.

"Then I'll start." I kept my voice steady and strong. I got up off the bed and slowly walked toward her. "You're the first girl I've ever noticed and the last girl I'll ever notice. My first kiss was the greatest first kiss in the history of first kisses because it was with you. I can't stop thinking about you."

As I got closer she took a step back, bumping into the dresser. My eyes zeroed in on gorgeous teal ones. Standing directly in front of her, I placed my hands on either side of her hips, securely planting them on the edge of the dresser.

She wasn't getting away from me this time.

Heat radiated off both our bodies, causing the temperature in the room to rise to the point of suffocation. I leaned in closer until my lips barely touched her temple. She smelled awesome as usual. My fingers dug into the dresser as intense vibrations shot through me. A rush of air coming from my partially opened mouth caused tiny wisps of her hair to graze my lips as they moved down to her ear.

Running the tip of my nose lightly across the shell of her ear, I whispered, "I want you to be more than my best friend. I want you to be my girlfriend. What do you want, Tweet?"

Her warm breath floated over the side of my face. It took all the strength I had not to look down. If I did, I'd have another unobstructed view of her boobs, only this time they'd be moving up and down with heavy breaths. My dick was already so hard standing was becoming painful.

Tweet whispered, "I want you."

When her words hit my ears I thought I was going to explode. My heart slammed against my chest as every part of my body pulsated. There'd been so many days and nights spent thinking about her, wanting to touch her, and kiss her. I've wanted to kiss her again for so long. Now I was a second away from finally living the dream.

My gaze didn't go any lower than her pink lips before rising up to meet her eyes. "God, you're beautiful." I sighed.

As she tilted her head slightly, Tweet's eyes fluttered closed. The room felt like it was spinning the closer I moved to her. Our lips touched for a millisecond before I applied pressure. Out of nowhere, a loud noise that sounded like a gunshot reverberated around the room.

"Dinner!" The booming deep voice of Mr. Kelly barreled through the closed door.

You have got to be fucking kidding me.

I immediately jumped back, causing Tweet and the dresser to rock forward. Turning, I faced the wall, my back to the door. If Tweet's dad caught me in this condition I'd lose my dick before I ever had a chance to use it. My breaths were coming so fast I was a second away from hyperventilating. I glanced over my shoulder at Tweet.

"Don't worry. He won't come in," she said, as her hands smoothed over her hair, tucking stray pieces back into place.

Turning to the wall, I hung my head, rested my hands on my hips, and breathed deeply in an attempt to put the beast within back in his cage.

The room was quiet for several minutes. My heartbeat and dick were finally calming down. Then with the clearing of her throat that sounded a little like a moan and a few innocent words, things changed.

"Noah, are you coming?" Tweet sounded all breathy and sexy.

My chin sank deeper into my chest as I raised my index finger, hoping she understood I needed a few more minutes. She did because the next thing I heard was the clicking of the door as it closed.

Supper was awesome. We had spaghetti with a side order of squirming Tweet. It gave me an enormous amount of pleasure watching her get all flustered whenever I whispered in her ear or touched her skin. She was so thrown off balance that she skipped her favorite dessert, chocolate cake, opting instead to go to her room and work on a paper. At least, that's what she told the parental units. I gave her a little time to simmer down. Seeing as how I was the cause of her missing dessert, I figured the decent thing to do was to take her what I knew she was craving and the cake. Ever since we were little kids, Tweet and I solved most of life's problems over a piece of chocolate cake with extra frosting. Whether it was getting hurt after falling off our bikes or not doing as well as we expected on a class project, chocolate cake seemed to make everything better. I was hoping it would work its magic and help me get my girl.

Looking at her closed door I thought how quickly things change. Two hours ago I was standing in this exact spot breathing heavy because of nerves and now I'm breathing heavy because I'm about to kiss my girl, finally. I knocked on the door lightly.

"Yeah?" Her voice sounded weird, raspy.

I opened the door just enough to allow my hand holding the cake through. I let it float there for a few seconds so that Tweet could take in all the deliciousness headed her way.

Poking my head in, I smiled and said, "I brought you some dessert."

I stepped in, tapping the door closed with my foot. She was sitting on her bed, legs crossed, cheeks still flushed a deep pink.

Her intense gaze followed me while I walked toward her and placed the cake down on the nightstand. Neither of us said a word as I sat across from her on the bed. The corners of my mouth curled up slightly when I held up the fork already loaded with chocolate frosting. Our eyes never left each other's.

Taking the fork, she raised it up to her lips and slowly slid it between them.

Holy shit, that's hot.

The tip of my tongue swept along my bottom lip as I watched Tweet suck the fork clean. Beads of sweat popped up all over my skin and my mouth watered. I swallowed hard a couple of times as the fork slowly slipped from her lips. Not being able to take the show any longer, I reached over and took the fork from her. As I went to place it back on the plate, my lips brushed her cheek. She smelled like chocolate and raspberries.

Leaning back slightly, only half an inch away from her mouth, I whispered, "You have a little frosting in the corner of your mouth."

We sat there completely still and silent. I couldn't concentrate on anything except Tweet's mouth, the little blob of frosting in the corner, and how much I wanted to lick it away. I didn't care that both our parents were just a few yards away at the other end of the house. I was finally going to be with Tweet and she was officially going to be mine.

My vision became blurry and my breathing shallow as the temperature of my body burst off the charts. With each slight movement toward her I noticed she was leaning away until there was a huge gap between us.

Pulling back, I stared at her. I didn't understand what was going on. Earlier she said she wanted me. I hadn't imagined that and just now, she let me get almost on top of her and lick her face.

"We can't do this. I can't be your girlfriend," she choked out. Tears were filling her eyes as she bit down on her bottom lip in an attempt to stop it from quivering.

All the oxygen and blood rushed out of my body. It felt as if I had been punched in the gut. I couldn't believe she was doing this. I knew Tweet. Things had been weird and unpredictable between us lately, but deep down I knew she wanted me to be her boyfriend. She wouldn't fuck with my feelings like this.

I turned away from her and rested my elbows on my knees. "Why?" I was barely able to say the one word.

"I'm afraid if something happened to cause it to end, then it might fuck things up so badly you wouldn't want to have anything to do with me after that."

"That's bullshit."

"No it's not. You remember Tyler Evans? He and Emily were close friends. Not as close as we are, but very close. They decided to cross that line and date. It lasted six months and ended badly. They couldn't even stay friends. Emily and I saw him at the mall over the summer and he was so ugly toward her. I can't have that happen with us."

"We're not them."

How could she compare what we have to anyone else? We weren't like anyone else. She knew that.

"I know, but Emily does everything perfectly. If she couldn't make it work, I sure as hell can't. I have to have you in my life. I won't cross that line with you. It's too risky and I won't chance it, not with us. I'm sorry about tonight. I never should have let things go that far."

"I'm not sorry about what happened between us in here. Except that you won't be with me."

"It's not that I don't want to. It's just that I don't want to mess up our friendship. Besides, you deserve better than me, Noah."

"There isn't anyone better than you for me," I said, looking over my shoulder at her.

"These feelings will fade away and things will get back to normal. Our bodies are going through a lot of changes. Hormones are flying all over the place. We just need to control ourselves and ride it out. I can't lose you, Noah."

Her eyes filled with tears. I was so in shock at how things changed in just a few minutes. I went from having the girl of my dreams to being in a nightmare. I needed to try one more time. Tweet gets in her head too much and overthinks everything. I knew she wanted me. She wanted me to kiss her and she wanted to be my girlfriend. She was just scared.

"You'd never lose me, Tweet. I'll always be here if you need me." I raised my hand to her face and let my fingertips trace the outline of her jaw down to her chin.

Shaking her head, she leaned away. "Please, Noah. I can't."

The look in her eyes was sad, hurt, and determined. Anger ripped through me. I had to get away from her before I said something I would regret. In one movement my hand dropped, I stood, and headed to the door. I grabbed the doorknob before her words stopped me.

"I'll see you in the morning when Mom and I pick you up for school, right?" she asked in a gravelly voice.

I couldn't turn around and look at her. "I don't need a ride tomorrow. Coach called a meeting for the team before classes. Travis is going to give me a ride."

"I'll see you at school then."

I couldn't comprehend how she could turn her feelings off and talk about school as if nothing happened between us tonight.

"Maybe. See ya around, Tweet."

I clicked the door shut and leaned against it. After a few seconds I heard the sound of muffled sobs before walking away.

It felt as if I were living behind a glass wall. Everyone was going about their business, living their lives while I just stopped. I was completely numb. I didn't think, feel, or say anything for the next couple of days. I also didn't see Tweet very much. This was the first time in our lives that we didn't have contact with each other. It sounded pathetic, but I literally didn't know how to get through my day without her. I decided that maybe part of the reason I couldn't get her out of my system was because I was around her all the time and that the best course of action was the *out of sight, out of mind theory*.

She called and texted several times a day but I never responded. My plan was to completely ignore her until these feelings I had for her were gone. I tried like hell to stay away and not speak to her. I did okay for the most part, although there had been a couple of times at school when my legs had a mind of their own and carried me over next to her. I said *hi*, but that was it. I didn't want to look at her either but failed at that too. She looked as lost and hurt as I felt.

Tweet lived in her head too much, analyzing every angle of a situation and its outcome. If I had only followed her back to her bedroom right after supper instead of waiting the other night, I had no doubt she'd be by my side now. I gave her too much time to think. Every time I thought how she compared us to Emily and that douche-bag Tyler Evans I got more and more pissed off. I didn't understand why she doubted us so much. I thought not being constantly around Tweet would help me get control of my feelings, but the longer I stayed away from her the more I wanted to be with her.

I was sitting in the family room staring blankly at the TV while Beth jabbered at my mom. I vaguely heard her tell my mom that she stopped by because of something to do with her dress for the stupid dance.

"Noah, do you like the color?" Beth asked.

I ignored her, pretending to be too caught up in the *Everybody Loves Raymond* rerun on TV.

"Noah!" Only the stern voice of my mom could penetrate the glass wall I currently lived behind.

"Huh?" I grunted.

"Beth asked you a question. Turn the TV off. You have a guest."

I huffed out a loud sigh and aimed the remote at the TV.

"I have to run to the grocery store. Beth, from the way you describe it, your dress sounds beautiful and the color is so pretty," Mom said.

"Thank you, Mrs. Stewart. I just love it to pieces." She clutched a tiny piece of cloth to her chest.

"It will look great next to Noah's black suit," Mom said.

"Hold up. What do I have to wear a suit for?" I snapped.

"To the dance silly," Beth answered.

Fucking dance. Fucking suit. Fucking Raymond.

"Mom?"

Standing, my mom smiled, and crossed over to me. "You'll look so handsome." She bent down kissing the top of my head and then placed her palm on my forehead checking to see if I had a fever.

Walking around like a zombie over the past couple of days had both my parents thinking I was coming down with a virus. Since I came right home after school and Tweet hadn't been around, they must have put two and two together. They never asked what was wrong. They were waiting for me to come to them and talk when I was ready. Mom still checked my temperature whenever she was near me just in case I was coming down with something more than a broken heart and shattered ego.

"Don't worry, you'll survive." Mom turned and headed out the door, leaving Beth and me alone.

"Sooo...?" Beth came and plopped down at the end of the sofa.

"So what?" I reached for the remote.

"Do you like the color?"

"The color of what?" I narrowed my eyes at her in annoyance.

"The color of my dress." She held out the scrap of material.

Glancing down, sounding completely disinterested, I said, "It's pink."

A small chuckle escaped her. "Actually, its razzle dazzle pink begonia. It comes with a wide black satin belt with a big bow attached at the end and the skirt is bustled up. My corsage doesn't have to match exactly. I mean, I don't think razzle dazzle pink begonia is your typical color, which is why I love it because it's so unique. Maybe a pale pink with some white baby breath sprinkled in… just no purple. God, purple would be horrible."

Her mouth was like a machine-gun firing words at warped speed.

I looked at her expressionless. "I have no idea what language you're speaking."

"I'm talking about my corsage." Awkward silence. "Are you excited?"

"About?"

"The dance, silly. God, Noah, you're so out of it."

"Beth, maybe you should go to the dance with someone else. I'm not in a very partying mood lately."

Her eyes doubled in size as her jaw dropped open. "The dance is one day away. I can't ask anyone new to go. I've already shown your mom the color of my dress so she knows what color my corsage should be. Besides, there's no one else I want to go with."

Reaching over, Beth placed her hand on my forearm, causing me to jerk it away.

I'm such a prick.

I liked Beth for the most part. She just wasn't the girl I wanted sitting on my sofa or touching my arm or the one I wanted to go to the dance with. This wasn't her fault. She deserved to be treated better than I had been doing.

"I'm sorry, Beth. I've just got a lot on my mind with school and being on the varsity team, there's a lot more pressure."

"Oh, that's okay. I understand. I was starting to think it was something about me that put people in a horrible mood. I was just over at Amanda's and she just about bit my head off. I know she's been really moody lately, but I've never seen her like this."

I perked up. "What was she upset about?"

"I don't know. She wouldn't say. She's been kind of like this ever since I told her we were going to the dance together."

With everything that had happened over the last two days it never crossed my mind how Tweet found out I was going to the dance with Beth.

"What did she say when you told her?"

"She said it was crazy. I thought she was mad because you know… I asked *you*."

Beth had my full attention. "What'd she say?"

"She said she didn't like you that way. Then she rambled on about her being the glue and that you and I couldn't hang out unless she was around. It was so stupid."

I tried to hide the smile that crept across my face.

Tweet's been as miserable as I've been.

The past couple of days had gotten worse instead of better. Even at my age I knew without a doubt that my feelings for Tweet would never change. I tried to distance myself, but it was like I didn't have a choice, always finding my way back to her. She was right about being the glue. The glue that I couldn't seem to pry myself free from. Tweet would always be my heart and soul no matter what she said or how many times she pushed me away.

CHAPTER 8

The heat from our bodies and heavy breathing swirled around my truck, coating the windows in fog and me in sweat. An intense cramp crawled up my leg and even though the seat was as far back as possible, the gearshift kept digging into my side. Her jean-covered thighs were clamped around my hips like a vise while she bounced up and down, trying to achieve as much friction as possible between her legs. Her long dark hair repeatedly slapped me in the face with every bump and grind. Slipping my hands under her shirt, they traveled up in search of the clasp to her bra. I grabbed and fumbled with it several times, but it kept slipping from my sweaty fingers.

"Oh god Noah. Touch me," she moaned.

"I would if you'd stay still long enough so I could unhook your bra," I said, spitting out the ends of her hair that had flown into my mouth.

After that night in Tweet's room, I was only able to stay away from her for three days. Not long after Beth and I arrived at the dance I saw Tweet run across the gym floor with tears running down her face. I found her tucked away in a dark corner, sitting on the steps outside of the school. I didn't know why she was hiding or what made her cry. The only thing that mattered was that she needed to be held and I needed to be the one to hold her. We shared another first that night. Swaying back and forth in each other's arms, I sang "Everything" in her ear while we had our first dance.

For the rest of our sophomore year things gradually got better between us. We started to hang out more. She continued to want our old friendship back while I still wanted to move into new territory. We hovered in this weird holding pattern up until our junior year.

I made the decision to move on with a *fake it till you make it* game plan, so I started going on dates with random girls. None of them turned into anything serious. I tried to act interested, but there always came a point when the girl was talking, that all I heard was *blah, blah, blah*. It was impossible getting to know someone when your heart wasn't in it. Being that there was only one girl who truly held my interest and heart, I abandoned the idea of new and shiny, trading it in for familiar and convenient.

Beth had never made it a secret that she wanted more than a friendship with me. A couple of months into our junior year, we were invited to the same party that John Murphy, one of the senior baseball players, was having at his house. I had spent a week trying to convince Tweet to go but she kept refusing as usual. This party was the first one I had been to where the alcohol flowed freely and openly.

I arrived at John's in less than a partying mood, having just come from Tweet's, making one last-ditch attempt to get her to come. I wasn't a big drinker. Travis and I had tried some of his parents' stash one weekend when they were out of town and his grandmother was staying at their house. She was out like a light by 8 p.m. and we broke out the beer ten minutes later. We both got buzzed, but I had never been completely drunk until that night at the party. I spent the entire time drinking beer, watching couples make out, and not listening to whoever sat next to me on the sofa. Beth wasn't drinking so she offered to drive me home.

She walked me onto my front porch and leaned me against the door while searching my pockets for my keys. I was drunk, lonely, and horny. I needed to feel soft hands slide up my chest and snake behind my neck. I needed to feel warm lips pressed against mine. I needed to feel wanted by someone, even if it was the wrong one. With the dim light of the front porch and her dark hair, the girl in front of me could pass for *my* girl. Placing my index finger under her chin, I tilted Beth's head back. Lowering my lips to hers, my eyes closed, and I imagined touching soft curves, the smell of raspberries, and teal eyes.

It's been a month since that night when I started using Beth in an attempt to move on with my life. A year had passed since that day in Tweet's room when she first pushed me away. For an entire year, I've been kidding myself that she'd come to her senses and finally give us a chance. I knew what I was doing was wrong. I didn't want to hurt Beth. She genuinely liked me and wanted to make me happy. But even after a month of countless hookup sessions the only part of me that reacted to her was my body.

Beth reached around to unclasp her bra while at the same time leaned forward trying to kiss me. She teetered back and forth a few times before her lips and teeth crashed into mine. A deep groan flew from the back of my throat. Clutching her hips, I quickly lifted her off of my lap and placed her in the passenger's seat.

"I got it unhooked now," she said eagerly.

"I think you bit my lip. Is my lip bleeding?" Hooking up with Beth was clunky at best and a little hazardous.

She craned her neck toward me. "No it's not bleeding." Shifting in her seat, she crawled back on top of me.

I grabbed her shoulders, gave her a weak smile, and said, "I gotta get home and study."

"Are you kidding me? You didn't have to study a few minutes ago."

"Well, my mouth is hurting pretty bad since you rammed into it," I snapped back.

We didn't say anything while I wiped the windshield clear. I was about to start the car when out the corner of my eye I saw Beth on the verge of crying.

Sitting back, my chest deflated, pushing out a deep sigh. "I'm sorry."

"Noah, we need to talk."

I didn't respond. I knew what was coming.

"When are we going to tell Amanda?"

"Tell her what?" I wasn't trying to be mean to Beth, I just didn't want to tell Tweet what was going on between the two of us.

"That we're dating," she said, sounding annoyed.

"We don't really go out on dates."

I never considered what Beth and I were doing as dating. I really didn't know what to call it. What I did know was that I wasn't ready for Tweet to find out. I never acted any differently around Beth at school. Our time together consisted of parking behind a closed store after hours making out.

"That's because of you." She scooted closer to me and ran her fingers through my hair. "She needs to know. I'm tired of sneaking around. Besides, I don't even know why Amanda finding out is even an issue. I mean, you can date whoever you want and so can she."

My head jerked in her direction. "Is she seeing someone?"

"I don't know. Maybe. Who cares?"

Staring straight out the windshield, my fingers automatically tightened around the steering wheel, causing my knuckles to turn white. My pulse was racing at just the thought of someone touching Tweet.

"Look Beth, we've only been at this for a month. There's no need for her to find out just yet. I'll be the one to tell her when the time is right. I mean, we're just messing around."

"I'm ready to do more than just mess around."

With scrunched eyebrows, my gaze darted to hers.

"Don't look so shocked." She chuckled. "Noah, I want you to be my first."

My response should have been, *no, you deserve your first time to be with someone who loves you or at least likes you a lot.* But being the pathetic selfish asshole that I was I said, "Okay."

A week later, I was regretting more than anything all that had happened over the past month. I had the strangest feeling come over me right before my last class. Walking to my truck after school I noticed that Tweet's car was already gone. We didn't always ride together because of my baseball practice and her working for the school paper, but we always parked beside each other. She had a free period at the end of the day but rarely went home early. I called and texted her several times with no response.

As I pulled up to Tweet's house, I saw that her car was the only one in the driveway. Our parents had already headed out to Myrtle Beach for their annual trip. Getting out of my truck, I headed to the back door. Ever since we were kids our back doors were always left unlocked when someone was home because we were in and out so much, going from my house to Tweet's.

Grabbing the doorknob, I twisted and pushed, but it was locked. I moved the large potted plant sitting right next to the door that hid the extra house key. When I lifted the pot the key was missing. I thought at first that it might have gotten kicked under the doormat by mistake. I looked all around but never found it. For the next fifteen minutes I went back and forth, knocking on the back door and then the front, still with no answer. I even drove to our spot to see if Tweet was there, but the table was empty. For the rest of the afternoon, I alternated between checking my phone and looking out the kitchen window hoping to see her waving at me.

After a couple of hours I decided to head back over to Tweet's. If I had to, I'd stay there all night pounding on the door until she let me in. I was about to walk out of my house when my cellphone rang.

Shit!

Beth's number popped up on the screen. My thoughts had been so preoccupied with this weird feeling I couldn't shake, that I had forgotten she was coming over. Since my parents were gone for the weekend, Beth and I had decided that tonight would be the night we would have sex. I was seriously messed up. What guy in his right mind forgets he's going to have sex for the first time?

"Hey," I said, trying to sound excited.

"She knows."

With those two words my heart plummeted deep into my gut.

"What do you mean, *she knows*? I told you I would be the one to tell her if there was anything to tell," I growled.

"She didn't find out from me," Beth snapped.

"Then how the fuck did she find out?!"

"Don't yell at me." Her voice was shaky as if she were trying to hold back tears. "She said Stacy and Kim told her."

I breathed in several times and kept my tone steady, trying not to sound as pissed off as I was. "I thought we agreed not to say anything to anyone for a while. How the fuck did those two find out?"

"I haven't told anyone. Apparently, they saw me trying to hold your hand at the movie the other day."

Christ, the one time we go out on an actual date and I get caught.

I paced back and forth in the family room several times, running my hand through my hair. Stopping in front of the window, I noticed that a light was on over at Tweet's. I was in a trance as I stared across the yard, hoping to get a glance at her.

"Noah? Are you still there?" I heard Beth's voice faintly through the phone.

"Yeah."

"I guess *you* should to talk to her. She didn't want to listen to me."

"Alright. I will," I answered robotically.

"You should have told her a long time ago."

"I know."

I was getting more irritated with Beth for pointing out the obvious and at myself for letting this happen. A shiver of electricity ran through my body. I turned my head and saw Tweet standing in the middle of the room.

I was so focused on that damn window I hadn't even seen or heard her come in. We exchanged quick smiles. Beth was telling me something but all I heard coming through the phone was *blah, blah, blah.*

"I need to go." Beth's voice trailed off as I lowered the phone, pressed the end button, and slipped it into my pocket.

"Hey Tweet." I tried to sound cheerful.

"Hey, hey, hey," she countered, attempting to sound carefree and happy. She was a terrible actress.

"Everything okay?"

"Yep," she answered nonchalantly.

She walked behind the sofa and leaned back on it. I couldn't take my eyes off of her. It was like watching one of those nature shows where the female panther slinks around all stealth-like, looking beautiful, and sexy. Then *bam!* Out of nowhere, she gouges your eyes out, rips your chest open, and eats your heart.

"Whatcha wanna do tonight? Since both our parents are gone for the weekend, the world is our oyster. We can hang out the whole time." She threw a slight smirk in my direction.

The tightening in my chest made it hard to breathe. This was it. I had to tell her. The only thing worse than hearing Tweet was hurt was being an eyewitness to it.

"Pepperoni with extra cheese good for you?" She was looking directly at me.

The sound of her voice broke through my haze and I noticed the cellphone in her palm. "What?"

"On our pizza. Pepperoni and extra cheese?"

"Yeah. That's fine."

She tapped out the number then raised the phone to her ear. A tingling sensation crept down my arms and legs. I closed my eyes and inhaled a calming breath. It didn't help. My heart felt as if it were going to burst from my chest at any second. Rubbing the back of my neck, I knew this *happy-go-lucky best friends hanging out* charade was over.

"Um... Tweet... I kind of have plans tonight," I choked out. The inside of my mouth felt like it was stuffed with cotton.

"What kind of plans?" she asked innocently, putting her phone in her pocket.

Time stopped, all the air was sucked from the room, and we stared at each other. We held this position for what felt like an eternity. At some point, I unknowingly moved toward her because we were only a couple of feet apart. With my arms crossed over my chest, I tore my gaze away from hers and nailed it to a spot on the floor.

I couldn't look at her when I said, "I sort of have a date." The words barely made it out, wanting to stay lodged in my throat.

"A date? With who?" I could hear the quiver in her voice.

A slight smirk crossed my face as my eyebrows shot up. She was going to make me sweat this out.

Glancing up, I said, "Don't do that."

"Do what?"

"Play dumb. I've told you before, you're no good at it. Besides, I just got off the phone with Beth."

"Did ya now? Are you referring to your *girlfriend* Beth?" Thick sarcasm dripped from each word.

"I'm sorry. I've been meaning to talk to you about it," I said, sheepishly.

"So talk."

I tilted my chin toward the sofa. I thought we needed to be sitting for this conversation but Tweet had other ideas. She shook her head and stayed planted firmly in her spot.

"I don't know where to start," I admitted.

"How about where you lied to me."

"I've never lied to you," I shot back.

"Lie of omission! That's just as bad."

I shook my head, keeping my tone even, and said, "Look, I know you're upset."

"Genius!" she yelled, throwing her arms up in the air.

"Would you please shut your mouth and listen for five seconds. It's not a big deal," I told her through clenched teeth.

Her entire face scrunched up in confusion. "What's not a big deal?"

"This thing with Beth. It's...," my hands ran up and down my face as a frustrated growl rumbled in the back of my throat. "No matter what I say, I'm going to sound like the biggest dick in the world. I already know that, so keep your smartass comments to yourself." I paused, taking in a deep breath. "This thing with Beth is just convenient."

Her head tilted to the side, brows shot up, mouth dropped open, and eyes doubled in size. "Convenient?"

"Yeah. We've known each other for a long time. I knew she wanted something to happen between us."

"Why was I kept in the dark about this?"

"I didn't want you to know." I made an attempt to pry my eyes away from hers, but the magnet force held them firm in place.

"Why?"

A chuckle escaped me as I shook my head. I was completely dumbfounded. I couldn't believe she was asking me this. She was acting as if last year never happened, like I never told her how I felt.

"The same reason why I never want you to know when I go out with a girl. I feel like I'm cheating on you, which is fucking ridiculous because we're not even together in the first place,"

"Why her?" Tears were building in her eyes.

"Because I didn't have to work for it." My chest caved in with shame when I heard the words come out of my mouth. Beth deserved better than what I was able to give her. She deserved the truth.

"She thinks she's in love with you, you know."

Closing my eyes, I tilted my head back toward the ceiling.

Why did things have to be so fucking complicated?

"I'll handle things with Beth." I lowered my head and peered into watery teal eyes. "I don't love her. You know that, right?"

Please believe me.

"What are you going to say to her?" Blinking away tears, she sucked her bottom lip into her mouth trying to stop the quiver that had become more prominent.

"I guess I'll let her know I don't feel the same way about her. That I never meant to lead her on. I'm not looking for anything permanent. If she's okay with that we can continue on."

"What do you mean *continue on?*"

I braced one hand on the wall, the other hand resting on my hip, and said, "I have needs."

"Needs? What kind of needs?"

"The kind a guy has." I looked over at her, confusion plastered all over her face. "I need to get laid.

"You *need* to get laid?" Her tone was high-pitched and condescending.

"I do," I bit out.

"You're saying if she's okay with your terms then you'll fuck her?"

"Yes." It came out as a soft whisper. I wasn't sure she even heard me, but when I looked over at her, there was no mistaking the pain in her eyes.

"Don't."

"Don't what?" I asked.

"Don't have sex with Beth. Don't date Beth."

We were standing face-to-face, frozen. Both terrified of what was on the other side of this moment. Standing in front of me was the one thing I wanted most in my life, but she might as well have been a world away, because I couldn't reach her. I saw it in her eyes. Even with the threat of Beth and I being together, she had made up her mind. We weren't worth fighting for. Heat flooded my body and my muscles tensed as this realization sunk in.

"I don't even know why we're having this conversation. What difference does it make to you? You made your choice. You and I are just friends." My words were coated with venom.

Her expression was a mixture of shock and pain as if I had just slapped her in the face. "Just friends? Don't say it like that," she whispered.

"We don't have to ask each other's permission for who we can date," I said coldly.

Tears pooled in her eyes, on the verge of spilling over while a large lump slid down her throat. The slightest tremor ran through her body as she tried not to fall apart completely in front of me.

"You're planning on doing more than having a date night with her," she said in a raspy voice.

I couldn't take this anymore. I was done with trying to understand Tweet and her fucked-up way of thinking. She wanted me to go back to a time when I didn't have these feelings. A time when I didn't love her, but I couldn't. I couldn't go back to a time that never existed.

I turned away from her, raking my hands up my face and through my hair. All the confusion, frustration, and hurt burst out of me as I rammed my fist into the wall, shouting, "Goddammit!"

Whipping around, I was met with a tear-soaked face and a body convulsing with sobs.

My eyes pierced hers. A low deep voice broke through my gritted teeth. "Yes, I plan to fuck her, screw her, bang her, and be balls deep in…"

"Shut up!!" Sobs were gushing at a rapid pace. Her words and breaths barely able to come out. "Please don't do it, Noah! Please!"

"Why not?!"

"Because you're mine!" she screamed.

I ran up to her as her body caved in. Grabbing her upper arms, I pushed her back against the wall.

Placing my mouth right at her ear, I said, "Then why don't you fucking take me and stop this bullshit you keep putting us through? You're going to tell me that you're okay with my hands running up and down *her* body, touching *her* ass and tits? You're okay with my tongue licking every inch of *her*? You're okay knowing that while you're over in your bed, I'll be over here sliding into her when we both know it should be you?"

The convulsions continued to jerk her body violently. I stepped back. As I watched her body give up and slide down the wall, her face beet red and coated with tears, I couldn't figure out which one of us was responsible for this. Did Tweet bring it on herself or was this my way of getting back at her? The only thing I knew for sure was that we kept hurting each other and it had to stop.

CHAPTER

9

I left Tweet a crumpled heap of sobs on the floor of my family room. It took every ounce of strength I had to keep me from running back in there, wrapping her in my arms, and reassuring her that we could work through this. At least I had to figure out a way to work through this. Tweet didn't have a problem with controlling her feelings like I did. My options were limited. I had to have her in my life. I just needed to figure out a way to do that without it driving me completely insane.

An hour had passed before I was calm enough to head over to Tweet's house. Standing at the back door, I held the paper plate with a big piece of chocolate cake in one hand, and twisted the doorknob, testing to see if it was locked. When the door opened a heavy sigh of relief flowed from my lungs. She didn't hate me for the way I treated her earlier.

The house was dark except for one lamp that was on in the corner of the family room. A quiet stillness filled the air. Even though our friendship was becoming more complicated, our natural connection was still strong. I knew instinctively where to find her.

From the doorway of her bedroom, I stared at her body stretched out across the bed. Starting at her crossed ankles, my gaze slowly traveled up her toned legs, and over her flat stomach where her bright pink iPod rested. Her chest moved up and down at a steady pace with each soft breath that flowed over her slightly parted lips. Dark brown hair fanned out over her pillow. One of the earbuds had fallen from her ear and dangled just above her shoulder. No doubt she'd been listening to The D-Bags. Tweet always said Kellan Kyle's voice was soothing. I swallowed hard, the knot in my stomach twisting tighter with each step, as I moved cautiously toward the bed.

I placed the cake on the nightstand and sat on the bed beside her. My hand reached out, wanting to sweep a few stray pieces of hair off her forehead. I stopped myself. I couldn't act on instinct anymore and keep doing what felt natural when it came to Tweet. As I drew my hand back, I saw her eyes squint open.

"I know you're not sleeping."

The edges of her mouth curled up slightly as dark lashes rose. The stream of moonlight coming in the window lit up her eyes. They were red and puffy from crying, but still the most beautiful eyes I'd ever looked into.

Clearing her throat, she asked, "How long have you been here?"

"I don't know, not long." My voice sounded weak, deflated, and unrecognizable.

"What are you doing here?"

Tweet sat up, bringing us face-to-face. Being this close, seeing the pain in her eyes that I caused made it hard to breathe. I wanted to run my thumbs over her cheeks and wipe away the tear stains. Instead, my fingers flexed, dug into the tops of my thighs, and kept their distance.

"What about Beth?" There was a tremble in her voice.

"She's not coming over. We're done."

"Why?"

"I told her there was someone else." I gave her a slight smile while our gaze stayed connected.

A prickling sensation radiated from my head, chest, arms, and legs until my entire body was one huge electrical current. Tweet squirmed. I could tell she felt it too. This wasn't the first time it had happened between us. The air shifted and crackled as our gaze locked on each other. It was in these intense moments that we weren't Tweet and Noah. We were a boy and a girl who had an inherent need for each other.

In front of me was the girl of my dreams, the only love my heart would ever know, and the one person I was meant to make a life with. During these times I believed we would be together. Then the trigger would get pulled, her demeanor would change, and the moment vanished. All the crap involved with being Tweet and Noah would come crashing down around us. It was a pattern and until I broke away from it, I'd never be able to move on.

"Come on, it's cake time," I said, tilting my chin toward the nightstand. "Let's go to the park."

I stood and reached out my hand to Tweet. The second her skin touched mine, I couldn't help but pull her off the bed, wrap my arms around her waist, and hold her against my chest. Her hands immediately gripped my biceps. Slowly, I leaned forward until our foreheads touched.

Tears that I'd been holding back burned my throat. I closed my eyes, pushing them down once again, and said in a low husky voice, "I'm so sorry. I never should have said any of that stuff to you. Please, don't be mad at me, Tweet."

The feel of her hands making their way up my arms, over my shoulders, and curling behind my neck caused my arms to tighten around her. Turning my head, I nuzzled deep into her neck.

Her lips brushed the bottom of my earlobe when she whispered, "I'm so sorry, Noah, for everything. I don't know how to change and make things better."

I wanted to scream at her and tell her I would figure out how to change things, but I knew she wouldn't listen. Her mind was made up and it had been for a long time. I don't know how long we stood in her room in this position. I could have held Tweet until the end of time and it still wouldn't have been long enough. I needed this night to be over and for the hurting to stop.

Pulling my head away, I stepped back, took in a deep breath, and said, "I think it's time for cake."

Without another word, I picked up the cake, grabbed Tweet's hand, and headed out the door.

My footsteps dragged along the sidewalk as the air became thick and suffocating the closer we got to the park. My sweaty hand gripped Tweet's tighter, but I couldn't let go. My head knew I'd have to soon, but my heart wouldn't let me, not yet.

Instead of heading to our spot I led Tweet to the playground area where we sat side-by-side in the swings. I unwrapped the cake, holding it and the fork out to her. The tips of her fingers grazed the top of my hand as she tentatively took the fork. She aimed for the biggest glob of frosting, scooped it up, and lifted it to her mouth. I watched mesmerized as Tweet's lips wrapped around the fork, the frosting completely disappearing. A slight moan rolled up from the back of her throat as she slowly slid the fork out her mouth.

She tilted her head back, passing the fork off to me. Moving her lips, she said something, but I was too fixated on the movement to hear anything that came out of them.

I gulped a large amount of air and said, "You really know how to eat cake."

The fork passed between us until the cake was gone. I kept the pace slow, not wanting time to move forward, focusing on the present, because the future was about to become irreversible.

After tossing our trash in the can, I headed back to Tweet. As I approached she stood and took a few steps in my direction. Her face scrunched up in confusion when she realized I wasn't making a move to leave. An overall numbness invaded my body.

Huffing out a strained breath, I whispered, "We need to talk, Tweet."

Her shoulders sank as her chest caved in, and fear took over her expression. I could tell she wanted to run, but she stayed firmly planted in front of me. We moved back to the swings and sat. I made several attempts to form the words, but they kept taking a detour, getting lost somewhere in between my head and my heart.

Tweet finally broke the silence. "Why are we sitting over here?"

"I didn't want to talk at your house or our spot," I admitted.

"Why?"

"Since you left my house, all I can see when I walk into the family room is you sitting on the floor, screaming and crying."

I felt the beginning of a sob tremor run through my body. I bit my lip and held my breath, riding the wave in silence, and not letting it pour out of me.

"I don't understand."

"I don't want you to have the same pain as I do whenever you're in your room or at our spot." Pausing, I tried to focus on anything other than Tweet's eyes. They were on the verge of spilling over with tears. "I don't think it's a good idea for us to be around each other for a while." My voice cracked on each word.

All the oxygen rushed out of my lungs and my head throbbed. Tweet's face was getting redder and more contorted. I gripped the metal chain of the swing as hard as I possibly could, trying to hold myself together and not reach out to touch her. Her eyes were the size of saucers as she concentrated on my face. The silence between us strangled my throat, but I was frozen, not knowing what else to say. I stayed put, waiting for Tweet to make the next move.

"Why?" The word barely made it across her lips.

"I think you know why," I whispered.

"I think I do too but I'd like to hear it from you, just in case I'm wrong."

I hesitated. I was scared to continue the conversation, worried that my pain and frustration would explode in anger like it had earlier. I didn't want to fight with her anymore. "Tweet, I don't know," I paused again. "This thing is confusing."

"What thing?"

Pointing back and forth between us, I said, "This thing between us. It's so different."

"Different good or different bad?"

"Different confusing. I know you've always been down on yourself. I know you think you're doing what's best for me. I hate that you think so little of yourself and I hate that you don't think we belong together. I've tried to be around you and stay in the friend zone. I've tried so fucking hard." Tears flowed freely down her face, causing my own to spill over. "I can't be around you right now. It hurts too much, because I am so completely and desperately in love with you, Tweet."

Silence.

Tweet, say something. Tell me you'll at least try. Don't let me give up on us, please.
Silence.

"There hasn't been a day in my life that I haven't loved you. I wish you would just let me love you," I choked.

A look of devastation flooded her eyes when my words registered. I knew she loved me. I could see it and feel it, but she was incapable of saying it. She didn't know how to free herself from whatever it was that had a hold on her and the struggle was ripping me apart. I didn't know how to help her. If I couldn't take care of Tweet then what the fuck was my purpose?

I reached my hand up and gently stroked one of her tear-drenched cheeks. Resting our foreheads together, I whispered. "You'll always be the most important thing in my life. I'll always be there for you no matter what or who else comes into my life. I have no past without you and I can't imagine a future that doesn't include you. I just need some time to figure out how I can have you in my life without having you *be* my life."

Tears continued to gush in a steady stream from her eyes as she clamped them shut. After several seconds they opened and peered directly into mine. Starting at my cheek, the tips of her fingers touched my skin and timidly traveled down to my jaw. "I'm so sorry."

The entire night still felt surreal as we walked back to Tweet's house. We stood on her front porch, our arms wrapped around each other like a pair of lifelines. First, I concentrated on the feel of her body, the softness of her skin, and the smell of her hair. Then my focus moved to how right it felt belonging to her. No matter what happened in our past or what will take place in our future, I will always belong to Tweet.

I shifted my weight from side-to-side, each time thinking the movement would break our connection. It only caused my fear and pain to intensify. Last year during one of the playoff games, we were so far behind, the entire team knew there was no way for us to rally and win. Coach told us there are no magic answers in life. You could want something so deeply and desperately, do everything in your power to achieve it, and still fall short. That there are just times in life that you have to suck it up, be strong, and get through it.

I allowed my lips to brush the shell of Tweet's ear and whispered, "I need to go or I won't, and I have to do this."

"I know," she choked out.

I took a step back. Our faces were drenched in tears and our chests were pumping heavy from our sobs. The look in her eyes reflected what I was feeling. The heartache and fear of facing a life without my soul mate.

My gaze lingered on every inch of her beautiful face before I forced the words out. "Goodbye, Tweet."

"Goodbye, Noah."

Walking backward down the steps, I was still unable to take my eyes off of her. Once at the bottom, I hesitated, praying that she'd listen to her heart. For a brief second I swore I saw her lips form the words, *I love you.* But she never moved and the only sound I heard were the crickets chirping around us. I turned and left behind the only life I knew and wanted. No more hearing her laughter or seeing her smile. No more watching her devour spoonfuls of frosting or getting lost in our favorite music. No warm hugs, soft hands in mine, or shy sweet looks. No one to share and live my dreams with. All I could do was wait for this new life to feel like my life, but deep down I knew that would never happen.

CHAPTER 10

The rest of junior year inched along as I continued to distance myself from Tweet. At school, I stopped using the locker next to hers, opting for one in the locker room, I stopped eating lunch with her, and I found a new parking spot as far away from hers as possible. Out of school, I forced myself to stop riding by *our spot* and severely limited my time staring out of the kitchen window over at her house. It wasn't easy but I managed. I had to. The hardest times were when our families did things together, like a cookout or spending a day on the Kelly's boat. I was amazed how exhausting it was not to do what came naturally. It took herculean strength not to hug her, hold her hand, or sit next to her. Not making eye contact and not talking to her was unbearable.

I made plans to be gone most of the summer visiting the campuses of potential colleges to attend after graduation. I doubled my workouts, was taking part in The Citadel baseball camp, playing in the summer league, and volunteering at a sports program for underprivileged kids. I forced myself to stay in perpetual motion until the urge for Tweet to *be* my life went away. I was an idiot because the urge never faded and deep down I knew it never would.

One night, a month before senior year started, I was sitting alone on another sofa, drinking another beer, at another party Travis dragged me to. They all blurred together at this point—same crowd, same conversation, same music, same everything. I wasn't exactly the most fun person to be around, but Travis continued to hang out with me. I felt bad for him. He was a good friend and put up with my moody ass. I faked having a good time for the most part, except for tonight.

Earlier in the day Travis and I met at the mall to pick up some baseball equipment the Sportsman's Shop donated for the kid's program where we were assistant coaches. After loading up my truck we decided to grab some lunch at the food court. As I stood in line waiting to place my order an intense vibration shot through me. When I turned, my gaze crashed into teal eyes. Everything stopped. I hadn't been this close to Tweet in months. She stared at me with a blank expression. My heart dictated my movements and I took a step toward her. Whirling around, she sprinted in the opposite direction before my foot even hit the ground. My body headed in her direction until Travis stood between us, blocking my view and progress.

A large hand came down and landed on my shoulder, causing my umpteenth beer to slosh over the sides of the red cup. "What the fuck?"

I bounced slightly when Travis plopped down on the sofa next to me. "Hey buddeeey. How's my buddeeey?" he slurred, sliding his upper body along the back of the sofa closer to me.

I glanced over and threw him a lazy smirk.

With a cocked eyebrow and lopsided grin, he informed me, "I gotta surprise that's gonna make that smile and other parts of you grow bigger."

"You're making me really uncomfortable," I said, leaning away.

"There are two lovelies that want to spend time with our pulsating masculinity. Their names are Heather and Melanie."

Travis's head flopped to the side, his gaze and wave aimed at a cute blonde and brunette standing across the room.

"They're all yours, buddy. I'm not in the mood." I downed more of my beer.

His head rolled back toward me. "Heather won't leave Melanie. They travel in pairs. I want to get my hands on Heather's pair, so you *get* in the mood."

"I'm sure your immense charm will pry her away."

"Come on. Be a friend."

"Sorry, not tonight."

Glaring at me, he bit out, "Not tonight... then what fucking night? I'd like to put that date on my calendar so I can stop wasting my time."

"What's your problem?"

"You're my problem. You and this pussy-whipped, no balls, coochie slave attitude you've been sporting around for months instead of a rock-hard dick."

"Fuck you! You don't understand."

I pushed off the sofa, stumbling a few steps toward the back door. I needed some air and to get away from Travis's bullshit. The room spun, and then I spun as Travis grabbed my upper arm, turning me to face him.

"I understand. You've been hung up on this fucking girl ever since I've known you."

My fingers curled into fists as I got in his face and snarled, "Don't you ever refer to her as *this fucking girl.*"

Travis took a step back, ran his hands over his face, and huffed in frustration. "What's the deal? I thought I was finally getting my friend back. You see her for like two seconds today and it sends you into a fucking tailspin. You gotta get past this."

I could see the sincerity in his eyes. He wasn't telling me these things in anger or because he didn't like Tweet. He knew I was in a constant struggle and he was being a friend.

"I'm trying," I whispered.

"Try harder, dude."

"I don't know how." It was pathetic how weak and defeated my voice sounded.

After seeing Tweet earlier, the rest of the day had been spent replaying the few seconds encounter over and over in my head. She looked incredible except for the sadness in her eyes. A pang of guilt pinched my stomach because I was glad to see that sadness. It meant she was as miserable as I was. She disappeared in a flash but I didn't need a lot of time in order to take her all in. Her hair was that summer mixture of dark brown and gold. The light sprinkle of red across her nose and cheeks was either a result of being at the beach or seeing me. I hoped it was the latter. She had on a plain white tank top and a pair of black shorts that were molded to her adorable round ass. Tweet was the only girl I knew who could wear the plainest clothes, little makeup, and still look like a supermodel. The memory of her hips swaying back and forth as she darted away had my dick twitching. I turned from Travis and headed out the back door, needing that air more now than before.

Once outside, I propped myself up against the house, closed my eyes, and sucked in all the oxygen my lungs could handle.

I need to get her out of my head.

There were a few people hanging out around the pool so I concentrated on them. That was a dumbass move because most of them were hooking up. Sounds of kissing, moaning, giggling, and more moaning filled my ears. I shifted my attention to the sounds coming from inside the house. Another dumbass move. The only thing I could hear was the pounding music, which made me think of Tweet's swaying hips, which made me think of grabbing those hips and pounding into… I had to get out of there.

As I shoved off of the wall, the back door swung open, Travis stepped out, and headed over toward me.

"It kills me to see you like this." He paused, his eyes shifting from me to something over my shoulder. "I didn't want to say anything because I don't play into the rumor bullshit."

"What are you talking about?"

His expression showed how much he was struggling with whether or not to continue. "I heard Amanda is hooking up with some guy."

My brows scrunched together as my jaw went slack. A small chuckle of disbelief escaped me. "Why are you telling me this?"

"Because I care about you. You're like a brother to me. Noah, stop pissing your life away waiting for something that's not gonna happen."

Glancing away, I shook my head, and said, "It's a fucking lie."

"How do you know?"

My eyes pierced his. "She wouldn't do that."

"Why not?"

"Because she's *my* Tweet!" I screamed.

Out the corner of my eye, I could see the people around the pool unhooking from one another.

"She's not your anything! When are you going to get that through your fucking head?!"

I lunged forward, landed both hands on Travis's chest, and shoved. He stumbled back, but made no move to come after me.

"I'm not going to fight you, man."

"Who's the no-balls pussy now?!"

I shoved.

He stumbled back.

Party people scattered into the house.

"I'm sorry," he said, his voice full of pity.

I shoved.

He stumbled back.

And then I tackled him to the ground.

I landed one hard punch to his jaw before he flipped me onto my back, wrapped his massive arm around my neck, and held me down. I jerked and twisted for several seconds trying to break free of his hold. Finally, the alcohol and pain took over and I gave up.

Pressing the heel of my hands into my eyes, I choked back tears, and mumbled, "We've shared all our firsts together."

Travis stood. "Let's go inside and have another beer."

I sat up, staring at his outstretched hand for a second before grabbing hold and lifting myself off the ground.

"I'm gonna stay out here for a while and get some air," I told him.

We exchanged one more look of understanding before he turned and headed toward the house.

"Travis."

He spun around. "Yeah?"

"Thanks for looking out for me."

"That's what brothers are for. Besides, someone's gotta keep an eye on your sorry ass." He gave me a weak smile and went inside.

I walked to one of the lounge chairs by the pool, sat, and dropped my head in my hands.

Christ, was it true? Was that the reason Tweet barely looked at me and ran away today? Had she been with someone? Had she given that part of herself away?

I thought the sadness in her eyes was because she missed me. I concentrated on the quick glimpse I got of her. Travis's words, the beer, and the overwhelming feeling of emptiness were clouding my memory. Maybe it was guilt and embarrassment for having moved on, leaving me behind. I hadn't even thought about being with anyone since that night I told her I needed time.

Soft footsteps approached and then the cushion on the chair shifted as someone sat down. A small hand began rubbing circles between my shoulder blades. My elbows stayed grounded on my knees as I looked up at Brittani. She had on a tight strapless bright orange dress that pushed her tits almost up to her neck. Her hair was curly and ran down her back.

"Hey," she said. Her eyes were full of concern. "Are you okay?"

"Yeah."

"You don't look okay. You look sad."

Pursing my lips together, I forced a slight smile in her direction.

"I've missed you." The tip of her tongue poked out and swept across her bottom lip.

The hand that had been rubbing my back made its way to my shoulder as her other hand rested on my upper thigh.

"Noah, stop pissing your life away waiting for something that's not gonna happen."

"She's not your anything! When are you going to get that through your fucking head?!"

The hand on my leg began to inch its way up and over heading for my crotch.

Leaning away, I said, "Brittani..."

"I can make you feel better."

I inhaled a sharp breath and stared into her glassy eyes. It was obvious she had been drinking. My emotions and willpower were drained. I was tired of feeling with my heart because all that got me was pain. I wanted to disappear for just a little while and get lost in sensation.

It was like I had stepped outside of my body, watching my hand find its way around the back of Brittani's neck. I clamped my eyes shut, leaned in, and slowly brought her lips closer to mine until they connected. Her hand slid to my crotch, applying slight pressure as it rubbed up and down my dick. I pushed on the back of her neck with more force, taking her farther into my mouth. My tongue corkscrewed around hers. She tasted like stale beer and smelled like Fritos. I thought I had seen snacks in the kitchen on one of my beer runs.

She pulled back and said, "Let's go to my room."

"This is your house?"

"You didn't know that?" she asked, giggling.

Without waiting for an answer, Brittani grabbed my hand and tugged me toward the house, through the crowd, up the stairs, and into her room, locking the door behind her.

I stood frozen, not sure what my next move should be. I thought we were just going to make out at the pool and now I'm standing in her bedroom with the door locked.

Kicking off her shoes, she moved toward me, a slow smile crept across her face. I stepped back until my legs hit the side of the bed, causing me to plop down.

Brittani stepped in closer, straddling one of my thighs. Her fingers twisted and tugged in my hair.

Tilting my head back to look up, she said, "I've always liked you, you know."

"Yeah?" I breathed out.

Her lips crashed into mine. It was a sloppy kiss, loaded with spit. Grabbing the back of her thighs, I shifted her to one side. I needed to wipe my mouth. She was sucking and yanking on my bottom lip so hard that when she finally released it, it snapped back with a loud pop. I jerked slightly, grasping the edge of the bed to brace myself. She pulled my hair one more time before her hands made their way down my chest to the bottom of my T-shirt. Brittani dug her fingers into my shirt, ripping it over my head and tossed it behind her. Once the shirt cleared my field of vision, I looked up, and saw bright pink lips barreling toward me.

I was confused. Brittani and I had fooled around before and I had heavy make-out sessions with Beth, but I never had gone all the way. I assumed all of this was leading up to having sex, although neither of us had mentioned it.

I placed my hands on her shoulders, holding her back, and said, "Brittani, we should slow down."

"Why?" she asked, shoving her body forward.

I held her back. "I don't have protection."

"I have condoms in my nightstand." She leaned forward.

"What about your parents?"

"They're never home."

I stared at her, drew in a deep breath, and debated whether to continue. My body wanted to and my head knew that this was the drastic step I needed to take in order to escape the pain my heart was constantly in.

"I've never had…"

"Listen, I like sex and I like baseball players. Just close your eyes. I can be whoever you want me to be."

Taking a step back, her fingers hooked in the top of her dress, and slid it down to the floor. She stood in front of me naked, no bra and no panties. I had seen naked girls before in magazines and on the computer. I had even seen Beth's tits. But I had never seen a completely naked girl in the flesh until now. Heat, vibrations, prickling skin, pounding chest, pumping lungs, trickling sweat, and throbbing dick all assaulted me at the same time.

When she got close enough, I grabbed her waist and buried my face between her tits. My lips sucked their way across her chest until they found a hard nipple. I slid my hands down to her ass, squeezed and pushed her roughly against me. Her chest vibrated against my cheek. I assumed it was from a moan. Everything around me was blocked out. The only thing I was aware of was *my* body's reaction. I was getting lost, which was exactly what I wanted to do.

Brittani pulled away and walked quickly to the nightstand. "Take your jeans off," she ordered, as she searched through the drawer.

I slipped off my retro Jordans while my fingers fumbled to unbutton my jeans. Jeans and boxers hit the floor and were kicked to the side, leaving me standing naked in front of a girl for the first time. Well technically, this wasn't the very first time I had been naked in front of a girl. When we were little kids Tweet and I used to take baths together.

Naked in front of my girl.

The final stage of my dick's launch sequence was getting close.

Adorable round ass.

Swaying hips.

Gorgeous teal eyes looking up at me.

Pink pouty bottom lip being sucked on.

Tweet naked.

My dick felt like it was about to explode.

Is it physically possible for a dick to explode?

Brittani pushed me back onto the bed. Instead of handing over the condom, she ripped the foil, and rolled it down over me. We then traded places, with her flat on her back and me hovering over. Wrapping her fingers around my dick, she guided it into position. She ran the tip of it up and down her entrance a couple of times before pushing it inside of her. It felt hot, slippery, and tight. I buried my head in her neck and began to move. With each thrust, I fell into a trance-like, robotic state. I was there physically, but my mind was blank. I didn't think of anything, not even the girl underneath me.

My thrusts got quicker and my breathing was erratic, as muscles stiffened. An intense burst of energy shot through my body. In less than four seconds it was all over. I rolled off of Brittani, laid on my back, and tried to calm my breathing. My gaze dropped to the deflated condom. The hollowness that had become a permanent resident in my chest seeped back in at a rapid speed. I felt movement next to me. When I turned my head I saw Brittani sitting on the edge of the bed, her back to me.

"Hey, are you okay?" I asked in a husky tone.

Looking over her shoulder, she answered, "Yeah. It was fun. Glad my little chat with Travis did the trick."

"I don't understand."

"Noah, I've wanted to fuck you for a long time now, but *she* was always in the way."

"You started the rumor about Tweet?"

"When I saw you sitting all by yourself, looking so sad and incredibly hot, I wanted to make you happy. I asked Travis what was wrong with you, and as always, it had something to do with *her*. I mentioned to Travis that maybe, possibly, I wouldn't be surprised if she was screwing around. You're so hung up on her for some reason and from what I've seen, she doesn't give a shit about you."

Without saying another word, Brittani got up, grabbed her clothes off the floor, and headed into the bathroom.

I sat up and swung my legs over the side of the bed. I removed the condom, tossing it into the trashcan, and then got dressed. The disconnect that came with each thrust was a welcome relief that I thought I'd be able to sustain for at least the rest of the night. Instead, I was flooded with the same pain and emptiness that I'd been living through except it had intensified. I didn't think it was possible to ache for Tweet more than I already did, but my stomach bottomed out and my lungs were barely working.

Don't think of her.

I focused on the door, willing my legs to move forward, but I couldn't stop the rush of thoughts. With Tweet, it would have been mind-blowing instead of mind-numbing. We would have taken our time discovering each other's body. I would have kissed her slowly and gradually undressed her. Then afterward, I would have held her, making sure she knew without a doubt how much I loved her.

The sound of the bathroom door opening snapped my mind back to the bedroom. I was out the door, down the stairs, and in my car in record time. I didn't even bother looking for Travis. I'm sure he had his hands full of someone. I dropped my head on the back of the car seat and sat in the driveway. I figured unless someone offered to drive me home I was spending the night in my car waiting to sober up.

I tried not seeing her, not talking to her, and not thinking about her, and it all failed. Not even being inside another girl got Tweet out of my system. That night I realized more than any other time that I was fucked in more ways than one.

CHAPTER 11

Four months, two weeks, five days, thirteen hours, twenty-seven minutes, and eight seconds—that's how long I had been Tweet-less. It was hard avoiding her during the summer, but avoiding her at school was almost impossible. By the end of the first day into my senior year, I had already tracked down her classes and where her locker was located. I was tired of being miserable and lonely. Senior year was a big deal and I wanted to share it with my best friend. This was one of those times in life that I would just have to suck it up. I needed her back in any way, shape, or form she would allow.

Two weeks had passed and I still hadn't talked to Tweet about renewing our friendship. I was scared that she wouldn't want to have anything to do with me at this point and not quite sure how to approach her.

I had been assigned my first chemistry project of the year. I was sitting at a table in the back of the school library, my head and concentration buried in research, when a large two-headed shadow with big hair crept across the page of the book. I lifted my gaze to see Stacy and Kim, the two canyon mouths who told Tweet about me and Beth last year. They stood, staring down at me with a strange look.

I didn't know either one of them very well even though we had always attended school together. In the classes we shared, they spent the entire time talking and smacking gum. They simultaneously slid the two chairs out that were across from me and sat, uninvited.

Stacy propped her elbows on the table, resting her chin in her hands. Thick dark eyebrows squished together while her bottom lip poked out, turned down in a frown. Kim's cocked head shook slowly, causing her blond ponytail to swish back and forth, as an audible *tsk* echoed in the quiet library. My gaze shifted, trading stares across the table between the two until Stacy finally broke the weirdness.

"We are so shocked," she said in a loud whisper.

"Totally," Kim chimed in.

Leaning in closer, Stacey continued, "It's just so unbelievable."

"Like the Easter bunny," Kim agreed, nodding her now straightened head.

My leg bounced under the table as my fingers clenched the edges of my book. Letting out a deep sigh, I narrowed my eyes and said, "I have no idea what you're talking about."

They looked at each other and then back at me with pity in their eyes.

Stacy sat back in her chair. "The fact that Amanda and Brad Johnson are *allegedly*," she raised her hands, crooking her fingers into air quotes, "an item now."

"Mmmhmm," Kim added.

Stacey shot a quick glance at Kim. "Brad is so hot."

"Scorching." Kim panted, her head tilted back with eyes closed.

I had no idea if what these two were saying was true or just stupid high school girl gossip. Brad was a teammate of mine and a total Smurffucker. I didn't doubt that he had been on the prowl for Tweet. Since freshmen year, other than baseball, collecting girls had been his main extracurricular activity. It was only a matter of time until he worked his way through the entire female population at school and made his move on Tweet. The part that seemed unbelievable was that Tweet would give him the time of day. She was frustrating and infuriating at times, but Tweet wasn't stupid. She would see right through his Smurffuckery ways.

"What makes the two of you think they're together?" I asked.

They exchanged knowing glances before turning back toward me.

"Well, we *allegedly* may have been on our way to cheerleading tryouts and saw Amanda and Brad standing at her locker," Kim stated.

"And we *allegedly* might have overheard Brad ask Amanda to Jeremy Pratt's party," Stacy continued.

No question half a brain was being shared between these two.

"Just because he asked doesn't mean she said yes." I pointed out.

"No. No it doesn't, but *allegedly* we followed them out to her car and they were standing really, *really* close to each other." Kim leaned forward with each *really*.

My blood went from a simmer to a full boil with the mention of Tweet being close to the Smurffucker. I didn't know what Stacy and Kim's game was, but I wasn't going to let them spread rumors about Tweet.

"Why did you follow them?" I asked.

"Um… cause Brad's hot," Stacy said sarcastically.

Giggles poured out of them.

Kim stopped in mid laugh and gasped. "Oh my god! I wonder if they'll be going to the prom."

"Isn't that a year away?" My tone was condescending.

Two sets of eyes bugged out at me.

"You have to start planning early," Stacy informed.

Kim turned to Stacy. "My color this year is going to be periwinkle."

"With your skin tone that color will be gorgeous. You're gonna be a big bucket of awesomesauce." Stacy squealed.

I slammed my book shut, tossing it onto the pile I had collected, and then shoved my notes into my backpack. Both girls jolted at the noise, but never stopped talking. My stride was purposeful as I headed out of the library, leaving Tweedledee and Tweedledum in their own little world.

My need to protect Tweet replaced any nerves I had about

approaching her. She may not have been my girl, technically, but I'd be damned if that Smurffucker was going to be a part of her life.

It took me the rest of the afternoon to figure out exactly what to say to Tweet. I had to talk to her tonight. I still wasn't a hundred percent sure that Stacy and Kim were telling me the truth. They were both known troublemakers. But to be on the safe side, I needed to set Tweet straight on the Smurffucker.

I rounded the side of the house where Tweet's room was located. I waited until it was dark, so I could see the light on in her window, making sure she was there. I didn't want her parents to see me. It was obvious to both sets of parents that something had drastically changed between me and Tweet. I had overheard Mrs. Kelly asking my mom on a few occasions if I had confided in her or my dad about what was wrong. Of course, my mom was as puzzled as Tweet's mom.

I loved Mrs. Kelly like a mother, but she scared me sometimes. When Tweet and I were eight years old, we nicknamed her mom *The Interrogator.* Tweet was great at dodging questions, having perfected the art of the non-answer at an early age. I sucked at it. The Interrogator knew my weakness. The first time I fell victim to her ruthless strategies was when I let Tweet talk me into riding our bikes from her house to mine. I've never been able to say no to her. The training wheels had just been removed from Tweet's bike and Mrs. Kelly told her several times she could ride only a couple of houses away.

Tweet and her bike took a huge spill that day as she came around the corner onto my street. She was terrified her mom would find out and take her bike away. After cleaning her bummed-up knee and having dinner at my house, I helped her home. No one seemed to notice her limping. Since nothing was said, Tweet and I thought we were in the clear.

Two days later when I walked into the Kelly's kitchen, the smell of potatoes frying hit me. It was late afternoon, Mrs. Kelly was making homemade French fries, and it wasn't even the weekend. I was invited to sit down at the table. A plate of fries, a bottle of Heinz ketchup, and a large Mountain Dew were placed in front of me. I knew I was a goner.

Somewhere between the first golden fry and licking the last grains of salt off my lips, I had given The Interrogator all the information she was looking for.

I drew in a shaky breath and stretched my neck from side-to-side. Lifting my hand to her window, I hesitated for a few seconds while the butterflies in my stomach landed. I tapped once and waited. It felt as if I stood there for a lifetime. I tapped again, harder. I was just about to turn around and leave when I saw her silhouette fill the window. As the window slid up so did the corners of my mouth until both were as high as they could go. The most exquisite shade of teal peered down at me, accompanied by a dazzling smile. I hadn't been allowed to get lost in those eyes in such a long time and it was intoxicating.

"Hey, Tweet," I said in a raspy voice.

I missed the feel and sound of her nickname passing over my lips.

"Hey," she whispered.

We were locked in place, eyes frozen on the other.

"Can we talk?"

Can I just stare at you forever?

"Sure. What do you want to talk about?"

"Not here, at our spot," I said.

A sparkle flashed across her eyes as her head quickly bobbed up and down in agreement. She disappeared inside her room for a few seconds. I was so excited I almost flew into her window and wrapped my arms around her. I waited, shifting from one foot to the other as adrenaline pumped through me. Once back, she swung one leg at a time over the windowsill. The sight of her cute round ass easing out the window had me temporarily spellbound. I shook my head, clearing my thoughts before stepping forward to help her.

As she slid down, her shirt moved up her body exposing her stomach. I placed my hands on either side of her, right above the curve of her waist. My breath stopped and my dick twitched the second my hands felt skin. When she was firmly on the ground, I stepped back, needing to put some distance between us. We walked in silence the entire way to our spot.

Tweet seemed to be more on edge. I figured it was because we hadn't been alone in a long time. My nerves reappeared the closer we got to the park.

When we arrived, I extended my hand and helped Tweet climb up on the end of the table. I stood, leaning back on the edge next to her with my legs crossed at the ankles and my arms covering my chest. Tweet didn't face me, but I caught several flashes of teal as she glanced at me before I aimed my focus at a spot on the ground. I had all the points I wanted to cover mapped out in my head earlier today, but now I was struggling to remember even one of them. Finally, I decided simple and obvious would be the best opener.

Clearing my throat, I asked, "How have things been going?"

"Pretty good. How are things going with you?"

"Okay. Coach thinks we have a pretty good chance at the championship this year."

"Really? That's fantastic." She sounded annoyed.

"Yeah. We'll probably make the playoffs at least." She caught me smiling as I stole a quick glance. "How are your classes so far?"

"Good. How about yours?" She huffed.

Why is she getting pissed off?

"Good," I answered.

"Noah, why did you ask me here tonight?" Her voice was low and hesitant.

My eyes stayed glued to the ground as I whispered, "I miss you."

"I've missed you, too."

For the first time in four months, two weeks, five days, seventeen hours, thirty-two minutes, and eleven seconds—my throat opened, my lungs expanded, oxygen swirled through my body, and I could breathe.

"It hurts being away from you. I think about you all the time," I said.

I wasn't going to pretend that I didn't love her. I was just going to make an attempt to manage it.

"What do you think about?" Tweet asked, her tone sounded flirtatious.

Don't get your hopes up, dumbass.

I pushed off from the table and stood in front of her. The glow from the streetlight washed over us. At first, my eyes were frantic, wanting to take in every little dip, curve, and slant of her face all at once. I forced my gaze to slow to a steady pace as it glided across each feature. Her dark brown eyebrows were raised, causing tiny crinkles to run across her forehead. Bright teal eyes peered up at me from behind long dark lashes. Smooth pale pink cheeks turned a deeper shade with each second that ticked by. The color of her barely pressed-together lips matched the shade of her cheeks. And then there was that dimple smack dab in the middle of her chin. I had dreams about that dimple and my tongue.

Fuck! I needed to get control of myself.

I'd only had quick glimpses of Tweet over the past few months. They weren't enough to satisfy me, so I had resorted to digging through old pictures of us just to see her smile, those eyes, and that dimple. I realized it was pathetic or *pussy-thetic* as Travis liked to call it. He caught me one day after practice shuffling through a stack of photos I kept in my locker. Being this close and looking for this long, I realized that my memory and those pictures didn't do her justice. Nothing compared to the real thing. The real thing was breathtaking and perfect.

The sound of a horn blasting as a car drove by caused my head to jerk up, breaking the spell. I hesitated for a second, trying to get my thoughts together.

My gaze fell from her face and I told her the truth. "I think about how lonely I am without you. How boring my day is without you. How much I miss hearing your voice and your laugh. How much I miss listening to music and eating cake with you."

I glanced up at her, we traded brief smiles, and just like that, I was lost in those eyes again.

"I miss taking care of you." I paused for a moment, scared of her reaction to my next sentence. "I miss my best friend and I want her back in my life."

In a split second I saw thoughts spinning out of control flash across Tweet's face.

Relief.

Excitement.

Happiness.

Fear.

Doubt.

She was considering all the possible *what if* scenarios. I wasn't going to give her time to overanalyze us. I had no doubt she wanted me back her in life. I could see it in her eyes when she opened her window.

Placing my hand on either side of her hips, I grabbed the edge of the table, lowering my forehead to hers. "So Tweet, will you be my best friend again? I *promise* I will stay in the F-zone."

Deep pink cheeks lifted and teal eyes squinted, as Tweet's face lit up with a heart stopping smile. "I never stopped being your best friend."

I tilted my head slightly to one side and brushed my lips gently across her cheek. Pulling back, I smirked and said, "Hi bestie. Glad you're back where you belong."

She beamed with joy.

I am so fucked.

When I sat down on the table next to Tweet, I could feel the jolt of electricity as our shoulders and arms brushed against each other's. I picked up her hand, lacing her fingers with mine, and placed a soft *friendly* kiss on the back of it. She giggled and her grin grew even bigger. Mindlessly, my thumb gently moved back and forth over her wrist as I weighed out how to bring up the subject of the Smurffucker.

Releasing a long deep sigh, I said, "Tweet, there's something else I need to talk to you about."

"Shoot."

Turning toward her, I asked in a serious tone, "Is it true that Brad Johnson asked you to Jeremy's party?"

Her eyes widened as her mouth opened and closed twice before answering, "How did you find out so fast? It's only been a few hours since he asked me."

"It doesn't matter *how* I found out. What matters is that I found out just in time. You're not going on a date with him, Tweet."

She glared at me in disbelief and jerked her hand from mine. "Hold on now. Is this why you suddenly wanted me back in your life, so you could dictate who I could and could not go on a date with?"

"No!"

She leaned in, a sassy head wobble emphasizing her point. "Because, for your information, I haven't been on one single date. Unless you count Vincent Chamberlain in tenth grade, which I do *not* since he dumped me in the middle of the damn date for Sarah Grice."

"He's a Smurffucker and you're not going out with him Saturday or any other time," I shot back.

Tweet's back stiffened as she glared at me. Heat rose through my body, hands clenched firmly around the edge of the table.

God, she's stubborn and infuriating.

She jumped off the table. I moved to do the same, but she quickly turned on her heels, facing me. With hands firmly planted on her hips, she narrowed her eyes in my direction. For a split second my anger eased up. I bit my bottom lip to keep the smile from forming across my lips.

God, she's adorable.

"Who the hell do you think you are? For four months, I was close to being completely ignored by you. You know what I had to watch while I kept my mouth shut? Bitchanni sniffing around you first thing in the morning at your locker. Then there's Amy, Paige, and Tiffany. Anyone else? Oh yes, let's not forget what started the four month sabbatical, the day you planned on fucking Beth." The words flew out of her mouth in rapid fire succession. Her chest was pumping so fast and heavy I thought she was about to hyperventilate.

"That's different." I was standing directly in front of her now. The veins in my neck strained against my skin as the two words broke through clenched teeth.

"How so?"

Because you made it clear you weren't an option for me.

"It just is. Look, it's my job to take care of you and look out for you."

"Noah, it's just one date. The party is only a few days away. I've already accepted his invitation. I'd feel bad if I canceled on him now. It would be rude."

My eyebrows shot up. "Accepted his invitation? What the hell do you think you're going to, some debutante cotillion bullshit?" Sarcasm was dripping from my voice.

"I know exactly where I'm going. Jeremy's party! Saturday night! With Brad!" she shouted, as she brushed passed me.

"I can't figure out why he even asked you," I said more to myself.

"Thanks a lot."

I whipped around and immediately zeroed in on the hurt in Tweet's eyes. I opened my mouth to explain what I meant, but was stopped by a hard shove against my chest.

"That was a shitty thing for you to say to me." She turned and walked away.

I ran to her, grabbed her elbow, and spun her around to face me. "Tweet. I'm sorry. That didn't come out right. You know what I meant."

She shrugged out of my grasp and stepped back. Tears were already threatening to spill from her eyes. "It came out just fine. I know exactly what you meant. No one like Brad could ever want to go out with anyone like me, unless he had an ulterior motive."

My muscles quivered from the tension radiating through my body. I wasn't going to tolerate her putting herself down.

"Dammit! That asshole is nowhere near good enough to even be talking to you."

I took a step toward her, but she held up her hand, letting me know that was as close as she would allow me to get. The hurt in her eyes cut into my chest and made it ache. She should know I would never say anything to hurt her on purpose. I was going to do everything within my power to keep her safe and away from Brad, though. There was no way that Smurffucker was going to get his hands on what was mine. Tweet belonged to me and I belonged to her. No amount of pushing away or denial would ever change the fact that we were put on this earth to be together.

"It's fine. I've had the exact same question playing repeatedly in my head since he asked me out. It just hurts like hell when your best friend wonders the same thing."

"I told you I didn't mean it that way." My jaw was clenched so tight it was hurting.

"I need to go," she said. I stepped toward her. "Noah, don't."

One more hurtful glare from those gorgeous teal eyes was sent in my direction before she turned and stomped away from me.

"Where are you going?" I shouted.

"Home!" she yelled back over her shoulder.

"You're not walking home by yourself at night!"

"Yes I am!"

I knew she'd be fine on the walk home—our neighborhood was extremely safe, but I couldn't let her walk away from me, not like this. I just got her back in my life and I was going to hold on to her tight this time.

I followed a few steps behind her, in silence, the entire way home. I was hoping by the time we reached her house she would have cooled off. Even though she was pissed at me, I couldn't help watching her ass as it quickly swayed from side-to-side while she walked faster and faster toward her house. Just watching her walk got me hard and had me thinking of all sorts of things I would like to do to that sweet round little ass.

Fuck! I needed to get my head in the game and out of my crotch.

Once at her house, I stayed at the bottom of the steps as Tweet fished her key out of her pocket and slipped it into the lock.

Clearing my throat, I said, "Aren't you going to say goodnight?"

"Goodnight, Noah," she said. I could hear the tremble in her voice.

"Goodnight, Tweet."

I couldn't leave like this. I needed to feel that connection. I needed to be physically close to her. I needed to know things between us were all right.

Walking up behind her, I placed my palms on the doorframe, caging her in. I leaned in close. I felt a shiver run through her body as my warm breath hit behind her ear and over her neck. She smelled awesome. Apparently, my dick liked the scent of raspberry and vanilla because it started twitching like it had been tasered with one thousand volts of electricity.

My mouth was so close to her ear, my lips lightly brushed against the shell of it when I whispered, "Please don't be mad at me. I just want to protect you."

"I'm not mad. I'm scared," she said, breathless.

"Of what?"

"That we're not going to be able to go back to the way we were. You've been back in my life for an hour and it already feels like we're crossing that line. I just got you back. I don't want to lose you."

"I promised you I'd stay in the friend zone and I will. But the line has already been crossed, Tweet. I wish you'd step over it with me."

When she leaned back against my chest I knew I had to get out of there. I was already so hard it was becoming painful. All I could think about doing was turning her around, pressing her back against the door, and shoving my tongue down her throat.

I pushed off from the doorframe and wrapped my arms around her waist.

Placing a soft kiss behind her ear, I said, "I'll see you tomorrow."

I kissed the top of her head, dropped my arms, and headed home for an ice cold shower.

CHAPTER
12

I leaned up against the wall in one of the darker corners of the room. I got to Jeremy's party early and picked this spot specifically so I'd have a clear and direct view of the front door. I didn't want to leave anything to chance and possibly miss seeing Tweet and the Smurffucker when they arrived.

I purposely hadn't talked to her for a couple of days. Things got pretty intense between us the other night. I figured a little breathing space was a good idea. I had to control myself. If I did what I wanted to do, my arms and lips would be permanently attached to her body. I had to prove to her that I could keep my promise and stay in the friend zone.

From the first day I met Brad, I didn't like him. There was just something about the guy that made my skin crawl. He was up to something and it was my job to make sure that *something* wasn't Tweet. Since she refused to break the date, I decided keeping a close eye on him was the next best thing.

For the past two days, whenever I knew Brad had access to Tweet, I followed him. When they came out of the class they shared, I was outside the door. When they ate lunch together, I was a couple of tables away.

When they met at her locker, I was across the hall watching. All the time making sure he was aware of my presence. A piece of my heart splintered each time I saw them together. I wanted to slam my fist into the wall or, better yet, Brad's face, every time he touched her as they walked down the hall or he leaned in to whisper in her ear. I held it together fairly well. The one thing that I couldn't bring myself to watch was when Tweet looked up at him with that shy smile, the one that had always been reserved for me. It was *mine* and she was giving it away to him.

Earlier today I had reached my limit. Usually, our baseball practice didn't start until a couple of hours after classes were over, but today Coach called an early practice starting right after school. The team drifted toward the locker room when I overheard Brad talking with Spencer about this sweet virgin piece of ass he had his eye on. A burning sensation invaded my body as my hands clamped down like a vise on his shoulders and I throttled him against the brick wall of the building. Through clenched teeth and a few harsh shoves, I attempted to convince him to break the date. Tweet rounded the corner of the building and saw us seconds before I threw my first punch. The fear and hurt in her eyes made me back off and go inside the locker room. I didn't want her to think I had gone back on my promise and was acting like a jealous boyfriend.

Each time the front door to Jeremy's beach house opened, my body stiffened. I thought it was Tweet. The party had been going on for a while and they still weren't here. The knot in my stomach twisted tighter as I considered the fact that the Smurffucker may have taken her somewhere else.

Shit! I should have followed them.

While I was mentally kicking myself for being so careless, a pair of wet lips crash into my upper arm. I looked down to find Beth propped against me. She looked up with a drunken smile plastered across her face.

"Hey, baby," she giggled. "You want to go upstairs?"

"Beth, you're drunk."

"Sooo what."

"You know it's not going to happen between us."

Since the night I had told Beth we were done, she tried to hook up with me at every party. She got drunk, made a pass, and then got pissed when I turned her down. Beth deserved better than someone who loved and dreamed about another girl. But she never got the message, no matter how blunt I delivered it.

"Why not?!" she said angrily as she straightened and stood directly in front of me.

My eyes focused back on the front door. Beth's hands slowly slid underneath my shirt and over my stomach at the exact time I spotted Tweet and Brad walk in. I grabbed Beth's wrists, tugging her hands out from under my shirt.

"Beth, knock it off."

I took a step to the side, trying to get away from her, but she mimicked my movement, blocking me in.

"You're such an idiot, Noah. You could have me any time you want, but because your precious fucking Tweet says no, you won't even give us a chance." She looked over her shoulder, following my gaze. "She obviously doesn't want you. When we were still talking I asked her a million times if she liked you more than a friend and she always said no. When are you going to wise up? I know Brad. He's a fast worker. I bet before the night is over, he'll have his dick in her."

I pushed Beth back slightly, got right up in her face, and growled, "Don't you ever fucking talk about her like that again. I don't give a shit if you're drunk or that your feelings are hurt. You and I are never going to happen."

Tears streamed down her face as her bottom lip quivered. "You won't even try because of her," she whined.

Tweet and Brad walked toward the double French doors leading out to the back deck. My already fisted hand pounded into to the wall behind me as Brad's fingers, which had been touching the small of Tweet's back, slipped underneath her shirt. I walked away from Beth without uttering another word and headed to the kitchen.

On the back wall of the kitchen was a sliding glass door. This allowed me to keep an eye on the Smurffucker, but stay out of Tweet's sight. She was staring out at the ocean, the breeze pushing her chocolate brown hair away from her gorgeous face. She wasn't looking at Brad, but he was staring intensely at her. I could tell it made her uncomfortable. She was lightly drumming her fingers on the railing. The movement was so small no one else would even notice.

Tweet had no clue that she was hot. She always made a joke of it, never believing that a guy would think of her in that way. By the look in his beady eyes, I could tell Brad thought of her that way. I hated that cocky asshole. He thought all he had to do was snap his fingers and girls would do whatever he wanted. The stupid girls did, but Tweet wasn't stupid. She was just naïve.

After a few minutes, she turned to face him. Whatever she said made him laugh. The look on his face got serious as he slowly moved in closer to her. Brad's head tilted to the side, Tweet's head tilted up slightly, and their lips touched.

She let the Smurffucker kiss her.

A constant rush of breath caused my throat to dry up. My muscles and veins strained against my skin as if trying to break free. I had tunnel vision as I elbowed my way through the crowd.

I grabbed the handle of the glass door and slid it open so hard it bounced off of the frame. I ignored the muffled voices yelling at me. My actions were pure instinct. The only thought in my head was I had to get that Smurffucker off of my girl.

It took only three strides to reach them. In one fluid movement, I grabbed the back of Brad's shirt, jerked him away from Tweet's lips, and dragged him down the steps onto the beach. The second my feet hit the sand my fist hit his pretty face.

"I fucking warned you about touching her!" I screamed, slamming my fist into his face again.

He shoved me, followed by his fist connecting to my jaw. I stumbled back, shook off his punch, and barreled straight into his chest, tackling him to the ground. Sweat poured from my face and bounced off Brad with every punch to his head.

I was so in the zone I didn't realize anyone else was around until I heard Tweet's voice scream, "Noah stop it! You're going to kill him!"

Two sets of hands latched on to my arms and pulled me off of Brad. Tweet immediately went to his side, knelt down, and draped her arm around his shoulder. She looked up at me with tears in her eyes, pleading for me to calm down.

What the fuck was she doing?

I thought she would come with me and we would leave together. When she didn't make a move, but instead stayed by Brad's side, comforting him, I got lightheaded and my stomach hardened.

She's actually choosing him?

As I shook my head in disbelief I saw Spencer and Travis standing on either side of me, their hands still attached to my upper arms.

Shrugging out of their grasp, blue eyes pierced teal ones, and I snarled, "Is this what you want? Some mother fucking son-of-a-bitch who just wants to get into your pants?"

I waited like I always did for her answer, for her to make the next move. Tweet did what she always did and turned away. I should have been used to it by now, it wasn't the first time she had chipped away at my heart. But when you love a person so completely, there was that part of you that constantly held out hope that this time they'd be more careful with your heart.

I spun around and bulldozed my way up the steps and into the house.

Why wouldn't she listen to me?

She knew I would never lie to her. I warned her and she still chose him over me. I couldn't get the image out of my head of his lips and hands on her. She was mine and those were my lips the Smurffucker was kissing. I had never felt this much rage in my life. I had to calm down and get numb. Passing through the house, I grabbed the two things that I knew would do the trick.

Forty minutes and two and a half beers later, I was upstairs in a bedroom, relatively buzzed and about to ram into Brittani. We had been hooking up on a regular basis over the past few weeks. I realized during the second time we had sex I was able to block everything out and get lost in the unconscious physicality. All I wanted was to get to that moment I craved the most. When I closed my eyes and pretended that the girl I was inside of looked at me with love in her teal-colored eyes as I ran my fingers through soft dark brown hair. That moment when the hands touching me and the legs wrapped around me belonged to Tweet.

After pushing Brittani's skirt up, I grabbed her hips, buried my face in her neck, and shoved her against the bedroom door with a loud thud. A deep groan rumbled from my chest as I lowered her onto me.

"Oh baby. Yes. Fuck me hard," she moaned.

Shit! The picture of Tweet I had in my head, lying naked across my bed was just erased by that fucking high-pitched drawl.

I pressed against her with more force, thrusting faster. Brittani's legs clamped around my hips, pushing me deeper. Her fingers twisted and tangled in my hair.

With one hard tug, she yanked my head up, and demanded, "Kiss me." I kept thrusting. "Why won't you kiss me on the lips?"

She was ruining everything. I couldn't pretend if she kept talking.

"Shut the fuck up," I grunted.

"I can't talk now either? Fine, then finish fucking me."

I tore my face away from hers and thrust two more times. My body stiffened, her body shook, and I was done.

I eased out of Brittani as she uncoiled her legs from around me and placed them on the floor. I stepped back, removed the condom, tossed it in the trashcan, and zipped up my jeans. Brittani readjusted her clothes and fluffed her hair. Our movements were a silent routine. Void of emotion or connection. And when I didn't get the moment I was chasing, the one in which I could pretend I was with my girl, the emptiness overwhelmed me.

I walked to the door, placed my hand on the doorknob, and inhaled a couple of deep breaths before cracking it open. I peered out, making sure the hallway was clear. Rumors were already flying about me and Brittani hooking up. I didn't want to add any more fuel to the fire.

With my head down, I stepped out of the room and left Brittani applying another coat of gloss to her lips. An immediate prickling sensation covered my body. The hallway wasn't empty like I thought. I had this reaction around only one person. Out of everyone at this party, why did she have to be the one standing outside the door? I looked up and felt the blood drain from my face as my heart and stomach took a nosedive. I stood motionless, having lost the ability to speak or think clearly. Panic flashed through my mind as Tweet's shocked expression stared back at me.

I hurt her.

I disappointed her.

I disrespected her.

I loved her.

I'd do anything to make this up to her.

I couldn't lose her.

She's my everything.

I hadn't noticed that Brittani was behind me until her squeaky voice pierced my ears.

"Well, hello Amanda. What are you doing here?"

I remained silent and in the same position until I felt arms creeping around my waist. I quickly stepped to the side away from Brittani's grasp while my gaze stayed glued to Tweet.

Brittani moved toward me. Hot breath mixed with the smell of beer and bubblegum lip gloss hit the side of my face. "Baby that was amazing as usual. No one fucks me like you. The way you suck my..."

"Shut up, Brittani," I bit out.

From the corner of my eye I saw the shadow of Brittani's hand approaching. Angling my head away from her, I cut off her attempt at weaving her fingers through my hair.

"What's wrong?" she whined.

"Get out of here," I spit out through clenched teeth.

Tweet's gaze shifted to Brittani. Little by little her expression transformed from stunned blankness to devastation. There was a slight tremor taking over her body as her eyes glazed over with tears.

"Blah, blah, blah," Brittani said and then headed downstairs.

I wanted to start everything over—this night, this year, last year. I wanted to go back to the first time Tweet had a negative thought about herself and beat the shit out of that thought. That one thought led to the next, and the next, and the next, until she was buried under an avalanche.

Suddenly, Tweet's hand slapped over her mouth and she ran toward the bathroom, slamming the door behind her. Slowly and mindlessly, I headed in her direction. I was scared to death that our friendship was irrevocably shattered. I had no clue what to do or say. I just knew I had to go to her, explain, and pray that she'd forgive me.

As I got closer to the bathroom the sounds coming from behind the door ripped into me. Sobs broke in between bouts of gagging. Tweet was sick to her stomach because of me. The sobs got louder and faster. I couldn't stand it any longer. I had to get to her.

I knocked softly on the door.

Silence.

I knocked again and asked in a low voice, "Tweet, are you alright? Can I come in, please?"

She gasped for air, trying to get control of her crying.

"No and no!" she screamed.

I quietly jiggled the doorknob and found it unlocked. I inched the door open, stuck my head in, looking for her, and then swung it wide enough to step in. Tweet scrambled to her feet, moving toward the sink as I closed the door.

Staring at me through blood red eyes, she choked out, "Stay the fuck away from me Noah!"

"I know you don't want to hear this right now." My throat felt thick, the words struggled to get out. "I am so, *so* sorry."

"For what? I'm not anything to you," she said in a cold flat tone.

Her words slapped me in the face. I knew it was the hurt and disappointment talking. She didn't mean it. When she said shit like that, part of me wanted to shake some sense into her and the other part of me wanted to kiss her senselessly.

"It doesn't mean anything. She's just a fuck."

"Wow! What a romantic you are."

I'm not perfect like you think, Tweet.

I raked my hands up and down my face, considering whether or not I should admit to her that I'd failed at staying in the friend zone.

"I was angry with you for choosing him."

"You're not going to blame me for what you just did with her. How could you with *her?*"

Tweet stomped toward the door. As she brushed passt me, I reached out and grabbed her upper arm. She looked straight ahead, not wanting to make eye contact.

My gaze traveled up her blotchy tear-stained faced up to her lifeless eyes. "I don't know. When I saw you kneeling by that Smurffucker, helping him… it tore me apart."

"So you fucked Brittani to get back at me?"

"No! I wasn't trying to get back at you. I just wanted to feel numb."

I wanted to be with you.

She turned her head in my direction. Tears trickled down her face as we looked at each other for a brief moment.

Jerking out of my grip, she stepped back, and said, "Why with *her?*" She paused, choking back a sob. "You didn't see the look on her face when she came out of that room and saw me standing there." She drew in a shaky breath. "She looked so goddamn smug. She knew she had something that I never would."

Tweet bit down on her bottom lip, her body jolted before the sob finally broke free. I couldn't stand it any long. I wanted to touch her and wipe away the tears. I raised my hand slowly to her face. Her gaze fell and she shrugged away from me.

I dropped my hand and said, "You *do* have me. Every part of me. You always have. You just don't want me."

Tweet's head snapped in my direction. Her body became rigid, her jaw locked, and her lips flattened into a straight line. When I saw the intensity of her glare I knew I had hit a nerve with my last words. She took a slight step forward, placed her hands on my chest, and shoved me back, away from the door. The next thing I knew, the door flew open and she took off, running like always.

Going after Tweet wouldn't have accomplished anything at that point. She was terrified. I could see it in her expression. She overanalyzed things, playing out every possible scenario in an attempt to control her feelings and reactions. Tonight when she saw me step out of that room, that control was stripped from her. Instead of letting go of her heart and head on her own terms, all the emotions came crashing down, and the sheer force was devastating.

I walked downstairs. The party had quieted down with most people either passed out or making out. Even though it wasn't the time or place to talk, I sure as hell wasn't going to leave Tweet here with the Smurffucker. I looked around the room but there was no sign of them. I didn't know if that was good or bad. I was glad to see she wasn't part of one of the couples hooking up, not that I thought she would do that on a first date. I checked out the back deck. Still no Tweet. I walked out to the front porch. Scanning the cars, I breathed a sigh of relief when I saw Brad's car still here.

Coming back inside, I looked up and witnessed the Smurffucker dragging Tweet by the hand, up the stairs. By the time they made it to the second step, my hand was wrapped around Tweet's wrist stopping them. She stumbled back against the banister. The strong smell of tequila hit me in the face. Her glassy eyes looked at me in confusion for a few seconds, and then finally registered that it was me.

"Noah!" she slurred, a huge smile plastered across her face.

I was standing one step below Tweet when she broke free from Brad, twisting her body in my direction. I let go of her other wrist and caught her as she fell toward me. Her arms wrapped around my neck as I grabbed hold of her hips, trying to keep her steady.

Tweet's head tilted back as she clung to me. "Look, Brad! It's Noah! My Noah!" Her voice was ear-splittingly high. "He's so sweet and sexy. He's swexy. He licked my thigh under my parents' dinner table." She straightened her head, bringing her forehead to rest on mine. The look in her eyes had turned smoldering, her voice husky when she asked, "You remember licking me, Noah?"

We had a huge fight just a little over an hour ago and now she was completely wasted; her clothes were rumpled, she had pieces of sand stuck to her face, her hair was a tangled windblown mess, and she reeked of tequila and the ocean. But she was still the most beautiful thing I had ever laid my eyes on. My expression teetered from snarling at the Smurffucker to wanting to smile at Tweet.

God, even drunk she's adorable.

I was either the biggest idiot known to mankind or so beyond in love with this girl that all my common sense and self-preservation got obliterated when I was around her. My heart was pounding against my chest while the temperature in the room soared. The tension in my muscles was beginning to disappear and I was getting lost in teal eyes. I needed some distance.

My hands moved to Tweet's shoulders and I helped her stand upright. "I'm taking you home."

"But Brad was going to do some *things* to me on purpose. I don't know what, but I'm having fun. Hey! You want to come with us?" she asked, hooking her arm around mine.

My gaze zeroed in on Brad glaring down at me, his jaw clenched tight. My priority was to get Tweet home safe. I'd deal with this asshole later.

I snaked my arm around Tweet's waist and led her down the steps. She was abruptly yanked away from me. I whipped around and saw Brad clutching Tweet's arm.

"Haven't you done enough to her tonight? She's having a great time with me, so get your fucking hands off of her," he growled.

Tweet smiled up at him, then turned to me, and said, "I really am having fun. He's not a Smurffucker at all."

Glaring at Brad, I grabbed Tweet's hand, and led her toward the front door. We had taken two steps when I felt her being tugged away from me again. I let go of her hand, walked over to Brad, and punched him in the stomach. His hand fell from Tweet as he doubled over and dropped to the floor. I picked up Tweet, tossed her over my shoulder, and finally headed out uninterrupted.

Just before reaching the front door Tweet grabbed the waistband of my pants, lifting herself up slightly, and yelled, "Bye-bye, Brad! Thanks! Maybe you can lick my thigh next time! Bye-bye!"

Once we were at my truck, I lowered Tweet off my shoulder until her feet touched the ground. Her eyes struggled to stay opened, losing the battle, right before she passed out. I wrapped my arm around her waist, holding her body against mine while I unlocked my truck. I placed her in the seat and leaned over to fasten her in. The click of the seatbelt caused her to stir. Reaching my hand up to her face, my thumb brushed away the dusting of sand that clung to her cheek.

Her eyes stayed closed as a lazy grin slowly appeared across her pink lips. "Mmmm...," she moaned. "Noah." She sounded breathy.

"Yeah, Tweet?"

"You're my knight in plastic armor."

A slight chuckle escaped me as I remembered our Halloween costumes from when we were six years old.

"You always take care of me and make sure I have candy," she said, her voice trailing off.

I stared at her for several seconds, simply enjoying the view. As I inched away from her, she shifted in the seat.

Another slight moan flowed over her lips, and she whispered, "I love you Noah."

I knew she wouldn't remember saying those words to me tomorrow, but that didn't matter. The only thing that counted was that for the first time she let go of her heart, her head, and allowed herself to love me. There was nothing better than when the girl of your dreams made all of yours come true.

CHAPTER

13

"Noah, your room is like a ride at Disney World," she said, half moaning and half whining her words.

Tweet was fast asleep when I pulled into my driveway. Once I had the door to the passenger side opened and the seatbelt unfastened, her eyes fluttered in an attempt to wake up. She giggled when I scooped her up, lifting her from the truck. Her arms tightened around my neck as she nuzzled up against me, her lips touching the spot right below my ear. Our parents were spending the weekend at Myrtle Beach on their annual getaway. Tweet was in no condition to be by herself and I knew in the morning she'd really be feeling the effects of tonight, so I brought her back to my house to take care of her.

I carried her to my room, sat her on the bed, and then went to my dresser to grab a pair of boxers and a T-shirt for her to change in to. I turned around to find Tweet sprawled out on her back across my bed.

When I walked over to the bed, she lifted her head slightly. One eye squinted open, spotting the clothes in my hand.

Her nose and lips squished up in confusion. "You wear plaid underwear?"

Before I had a chance to answer, her head fell back onto the bed with closed eyes and a relaxed face.

"Sometimes. Why?"

"I never dreamed of you wearing plaid boxers."

The idea of her dreaming of me in my underwear made me grin.

I sat the boxers and shirt beside her and said, "Change into this. I'm going to get you some water and aspirin."

"What am I going to do about my parents? I can't go home like this." Panic flowed through each word.

"Both our parents went to Myrtle Beach this weekend. Remember?"

I took two steps toward the door before her plea stopped me.

"Noah! I can't sit up. Help me!"

Tweet was in the same position, lying on her back, except now with both arms pointing straight up toward the ceiling. My grin grew wider, I shook my head, and walked back to her. When our hands connected, I pulled her into a sitting position. Her body swayed and her head wobbled from the movement.

Tweet's fingers fumbled, trying to unbutton her jeans, never quite making contact with the actual button.

After several failed attempts, she looked up at me, batted her lashes a couple of times, and said, "I seem to be having difficulty locating the actual boot-ton and zip-pah."

She flashed me a lopsided smirk and giggled.

I hesitated for several seconds, staring at the button. My pulse rate and temperature were rising at warped speed with just the thought of helping Tweet undress.

This was not a good idea.

I knelt down in front of her, tore my gaze from the button, and whispered, "I'll help you."

First, I removed her flip-flops and carefully placed them to the side. I then decided they were too close and a tripping hazard.

What if Tweet had to get up in the middle of the night to go to the bathroom? She could trip, fall, and hit her head. If she hurt herself I'd have to rush her to the hospital and call her parents. If I called her parents, I'd have to explain to Mr. Kelly why his youngest daughter was in my bedroom, wearing next to nothing...

I slid the shoes farther away.

My chest expanded and contracted as I took in a deep breath before bringing my hands up to the top of her jeans. As I freed the button and pulled down the zipper, the tips of my fingers grazed the skin just below her navel. A shiver ran through both of us. I couldn't tell where it originated from, me or Tweet. All I knew was a whole lot of shivering was happening. Our eyes locked and we both downed a supersized gulp of air.

"I'll go get your water and aspirin while you change."

I got up and made a second attempt at leaving for water and aspirin. The bed squeaking caused me to spin around just in time to see Tweet flop back down on it.

"Noah, I can't stand up. I need you," she hollered.

I rushed over. "Tweet, are you okay?"

She looked at me with an adorable pouty expression. "Yes, but I *need* you. Don't leave me."

I knelt back down in front of her and said, "I won't ever leave you. Hold on to me."

I slid my hands on top of hers, lifting them to my shoulders. As Tweet pushed off the bed to stand, her chest brushed past my face. The breath caught in my throat. Through her thin shirt, Tweet's nipples strained against the material. I turned my head to the side in order to end the staring contest between me and the perky *just my size* awesome rack in front of me. I huffed out a breath and tried to focus on the task at hand.

Placing my hands on either side of her hips, I carefully hooked my fingers around the top of her jeans, making sure not to touch skin or the purple lace panties that were peeking out from behind the zipper. As the jeans slid down her thighs my gaze darted away. I struggled to keep it focused on something... anything—the floor, the lamp, my baseball trophies. Nothing held my interest quite as much as those purple lace panties above those smooth naked thighs. It was like they had this indestructible superpower and my eighteen-year-old male eyes were no match. I helped her sit back down and pulled the jeans off the rest of the way.

Tweet stood as I held the boxers out at arm's length for her to step into, while I angled my head back as far away as possible from her body. She slipped one leg in followed by the other. My gaze drifted up, catching a side view of her. I followed the purple lace wrapped around her hip and over her curves. A hint of her ass where it met the back of her upper thigh peeked out. I got lightheaded and blew out spurts of air like I had just run a hundred- yard dash. And of course my dick was moving around like a cat trapped in a paper bag.

I waited for her to pull the shorts up, wondering why it was taking her so long. Then I realized she could barely stand, much less bend down. Tweet's fingers dug into my shoulders as I slid the boxers up her leg. My thoughts ping-ponged between placing my hands on her hips or her hands.

I really wanted to touch those hips.

I held Tweet's hands while she slowly sank back down on the bed.

"I'm sure you'll be able to handle the rest on your own. I'll go get the water and aspirin," I said, my voice husky.

Out of nowhere Tweet ripped her shirt off and tossed it to the side.

Holy shit! The bra matched the panties.

A magnetic force slowly pulled my eyeballs out of their sockets. I had seen Beth's tits and Brittani completely naked, but neither of them held a candle to Tweet with messy hair, wearing my plaid boxers, and a purple lacy bra.

My foggy thoughts cleared when I heard her ask, "What are you looking at? I never struck you as a lacy bra kind of girl?"

She sucked in her lower lip and then released it slowly.

"I have a black one, a red one, a white one, a pink one, a yellow one, and of course, you see the purple one." Her gaze bounced from one boob to the next. "They *all* have matching lace panties too."

The corners of her lips slowly crept up to form the hottest smile that had ever been aimed at me.

Fuck me on a slow boat to China.

I was unable to tear my eyes away from her while my hand searched for the T-shirt. I inhaled a shaky breath, handed the shirt to Tweet, and demanded, "Put this on. Now!"

Fortunately, she listened and pulled the shirt down over her head, breaking my lacy hypnotic trance. Unfortunately, her inner calf slowly rubbed up and down my hip, occasionally making contact with the side of my ass. Sweat popped up on my forehead, trickling down my neck, and collecting in my palms. I didn't know how much more of flirty Tweet I could take before I caved. Even Superman had his kryptonite. Plus, my dick was growing by leaps and bounds and becoming quite intimate with my zipper.

"You want to see how talented I am?" she asked.

Yes.

No.

Yes.

No.

Yes.

No. No. No. I needed to put an end to this.

"What are you talking about?"

"Watch and learn, buddy boy." A wink was aimed in my direction.

She's killing me.

I sat back on my heels, nervous and excited about what was coming next.

Tweet placed one arm behind her, squirmed for a second, and then brought it back to the front. Reaching up into one of the shirt sleeves, she pulled the strap of her bra down, twisting her arm until it was free. She then repeated the same move on the other side, only this time, she tugged the entire bra out.

Tweet's nipples rubbed against my T-shirt.

My nipples had rubbed against that T-shirt.

Mine and Tweet's nipples rubbing against each other's.

Swinging the bra over her head, she hollered, "Ta-dah!"

God, she was hot and fun.

"You're nuts." I chuckled.

"And talented." She puckered her lips, blew me a kiss, and threw another wink my way.

"Yes, very talented." I smiled.

The air in the room stilled as our eyes stayed on each other. Tweet leaned back onto the bed. Using her elbows to prop herself up, she tilted her head slightly to the side, her chocolate brown hair falling over one shoulder. The look in her eyes changed from flirty into a hot raging inferno.

"Do you want to know what Brad did to me?" I opened my mouth to answer but she cut me off. "He ran his hands up and down my bare back, over my hips, and grabbed my ass."

The second she said his name I tensed up. My fingers dug into my thighs, automatically curling to form fists. My chest pumped deep and heavy. The constant thud of my heartbeat echoed in my ears. Tweet watched me like a hawk, gauging my reaction. Raising her leg, she slowly rubbed my hip again.

All the emotions of the night, the week, the months, and years mixed together and flooded my senses. My heart and my head were no longer separate. They were one being and that being wanted his girl.

My hands grabbed the back of Tweet's legs, pulling her to the edge of the bed and into my chest. Her hard nipples pressed against me throttled my body into overdrive. My hands squeezed and massaged her upper thighs. We were half an inch apart and on the verge of getting lost in each other.

"Do you want to touch me?" Tweet sighed.

My eyes clenched as my head fell back. I needed a minute to clear my mind. My brain was shutting down. All coherent thought and common sense were being forced out by what my body needed. I should have gotten up and walked out of the room, that would have been the right thing to do, but my body wasn't in the mood for *right*.

"Fuck yes," I whispered.

"Then do it." She challenged.

I lifted my head, bringing me face-to-face with Tweet. My hands traveled up her thigh and over her hip, slipping just underneath her shirt. The feel of her bare skin sent me to the edge of sanity. My dick was hard, hot, and about to slash my jeans open.

Get in there, dumbass. You've been waiting for this to happen.

"Touch me, Noah."

There was a slight catch in her voice. The tone wasn't hot, flirty, or playful any longer. It was pleading. She was begging me to push her out of the friend zone. She struggled, wanting to cross that line, but couldn't bring herself to do it, drunk or sober.

I wanted Tweet more than anything in the world, but not like this. She had to come to me on her own, ready to put aside any fears because we were worth it. I'd hold her hand as she stepped over the line, but I wasn't going to force her.

My common sense finally returned along with all the other reasons the line wouldn't be crossed tonight.

I removed my hands from under her shirt, pulled away, and sat back on my heels.

"Fuck. Fuck. Fuck," I muttered.

Tweet lowered her gaze, dropping her chin to her chest. We were silent for what felt like a lifetime. Her hunched shoulders rose and fell with each unsteady breath she inhaled. When she looked back up at me there were tears in her eyes.

"What's wrong with me?" she asked, her voice cracking.

"There's absolutely nothing wrong with you. It's just that... you've been drinking and I don't want anything to happen between us while you're drunk."

She looked down and whispered, "I want to go home now."

I leaned forward, placing my index finger under her chin, and raised her gaze to meet mine. A gentle stream of tears spilled from her eyes. I moved my hand to her jaw, cupping the side of her face as my thumb slid over her cheek, wiping the tears aside.

"Don't cry, Tweet. Talk to me."

Shrugging away, she said, "It's just that I could tell Brittani was drunk and you still... Please let me go home now."

My arms wrapped around Tweet, pulling her in, and I said, "I'm so sorry about tonight. I hate myself for hurting you." Leaning back slightly, I rested my forehead on hers. "It didn't matter if *she* was drunk. We both use each other. You're not just a warm body that a guy screws when he's trying to numb himself. You mean everything to me."

I gently kissed her forehead then whispered, "Don't go. Stay with me."

She gave me a slight nod.

When I pulled back our eyes connected. I hoped mine conveyed just how sorry I was for tonight, how hard it was to stop things, and how much I loved her. Not saying another word, I grabbed a pair of pajama pants and a T-shirt and walked out of the room.

I changed my clothes and headed to the kitchen. As the glass filled with water, I stood at the sink staring at my reflection in the window. I had no idea how this night went from losing Tweet forever to having her in my bed.

She said it, I love you, Noah.

I smirked, thinking how incredible it felt hearing her say the words. Sure, she was drunk but the alcohol didn't make her love me. The love was already inside of her heart. All the tequila did was create a small crack in the wall she'd built up. I needed to be patient until the day came when she willingly crossed over the line and into my arms.

After I cleared my head, I went back to my room with water and aspirin in hand. I smiled when I saw that Tweet had made herself at home in my bed, lying on her side under the covers. I walked over to her and held out the water and aspirin. After downing the pills, she lay her head back, nuzzling into the pillow. I went to my dresser, turned the lamp off, and crawled into bed. I was taking a big chance, but I couldn't help slipping in behind Tweet and draping my arm around her waist. She placed her hand on top of mine and squeezed it slightly. I buried my nose in her dark hair, breathing in the scent of raspberry and vanilla.

This was where we belonged.

"Noah, can I ask you something?" she whispered.

"You can ask me anything, Tweet."

"Even if it's about Brittani?"

"Yes," I sighed.

"Why didn't you want to kiss her or hear her talk?"

The room fell quiet. I tightened my arm around Tweet and whispered, "Because she wasn't you."

Gripping my hand, she pulled my arm around her even tighter before we both drifted off to sleep.

The mattress jostled slightly as Tweet slid from underneath my arm and scooted off the bed. This morning, we were still in the same position we had fallen asleep in, the only difference was... at some point during the night, our legs had tangled together. I rolled onto my back, peeking at her from out the corner of my eye as she slinked across the room toward the door, her hand covering her mouth. She slipped out and quietly closed the door. Her pounding footsteps echoed down the hallway as she made a beeline for the bathroom. Tweet was about to have retro-tequila for breakfast. Once the memory of last night started to seep back into her mind, I knew embarrassment would follow. I decided it was best to give her a few minutes to get herself together, so I didn't get up. Besides, I had a history of being a reflex puker. There was no need for both of us to be spewing all over the place.

Lying in wait, I let my mind wander to how incredible it felt having Tweet with me for the entire night and all we did was sleep.

I flung the comforter up, partially hiding my face, when I heard the bathroom door close. Soft groans drifted toward my room. A few seconds later my bedroom door opened, and in stepped a rumpled and slightly green-tinged Tweet. She walked to the foot of the bed to pick up her shirt and jeans. Her head turned. She spotted her shoes that were on my side of the bed, but made no attempt to get them. Her puffy-eyed gaze scanned the room. I bit my bottom lip to keep from laughing when I saw the look of pure terror cross her face. Her eyes squeezed shut. I knew exactly what caused her reaction. Slowly she lifted her eyelids, cringing at the sight of her purple lace bra slung over the lamp on my dresser.

She tiptoed over to it and studied how the bra was twisted and tangled around the lamp. She had positioned herself at the perfect angle for me to have a great seat for the show. She unhooked the strap from the switch and carefully slid the bra off the lampshade. When she almost had the bra completely freed, she got cocky, thinking she was in the clear, and yanked. The bra snagged, sending the lamp tumbling. Fortunately, she caught it before it hit the floor. She placed the lamp back on the dresser and glanced over her shoulder, checking to see if I was awake. When I didn't show any signs of life, she turned back to her project. Her face squished up as she bit down on her bottom lip, trying to decipher the lace maze. It was becoming harder to keep quiet and not laugh.

"Leave it. I like having your pretty little lacy things scattered around my room," I said in a deep throaty voice.

Tweet froze.

"And how is my Tweet feeling this morning?" The smile was evident in my tone.

She was mortified and gorgeous.

Trying to sound chipper, she squeaked, "Great. I'm going home to shower and wash my hair."

I got out of bed and walked up behind her, placing my hands on her hips. We looked at each other in the mirror.

I pushed her hair to one side, lowered my mouth to her ear, and said, "Don't go. You can shower here."

I backed up, pulled my T-shirt over my head, and flung it onto the bed. I noticed Tweet's expression in the mirror. Her eyes traveled up and down my torso several times as her breathing picked up speed.

Moving in behind her, I said, "I'm going to go jump in the shower and then I'll make you some toast. It will help your stomach."

I kissed the top of her head and then glanced down at my shirt she was wearing, splattered with the effects of her first tequilathon drunk. "You can keep the shirt."

Our gaze simultaneously shifted down and then back up as a blush crept over her face. Smiling, I gave her a slight smack on her cute little ass before leaving the room.

I jumped in the shower and quickly washed. I wanted to get back and help Tweet recover from her hangover. Plus, I'd learned from experience if I gave her too much time alone she'd start overanalyzing and build up the wall again. I needed her to know that I'd be patient and that she could set the pace for us moving out of the friend zone.

Once I was done, I grabbed a towel and dried off. My thoughts were a little cloudy after my palm felt Tweet's ass, causing me to forget about grabbing clothes to change into, so I threw on the pajama pants from last night. I hurried to the kitchen to make breakfast. I had the toast, a Diet Pepsi, a glass of water, and bottle of aspirin set up on the coffee table in the family room with the TV tuned in to the Smurfs. I kept the volume low in case last night's aspirin had worn off completely. I then headed down the hallway to get my girl.

Stepping into my room, I said, "Breakfast awaits you in the family…"

The room was empty and all of Tweet's stuff was gone. A knot formed in the pit of my stomach.

She was probably in the bathroom.

I knocked softly on the bathroom door. "Tweet, is everything okay? I have breakfast ready."

Silence.

Placing my hand on the doorknob, I turned it, and opened the door slowly.

Empty.

The knot in my stomach twisted tighter. Tweet just up and left without saying a word. No goodbye, see ya later, or kiss my ass. Not one fucking word. She ran like always. My heart rate went from sixty to one hundred eighty in two seconds flat. One by one, the veins in my neck popped out as blood traveled through them with such velocity I thought they were going to explode. I stood in the middle of the hallway, hands on hips, with my head down, inhaling long deep breaths while I counted, in an attempt to calm down.

One.

Two.

Three.

Fuck this.

I ran to my room, threw on dark blue basketball shorts and orange sleeveless T-shirt, before bolting out the door to get answers.

CHAPTER
14

"Tweet!" I yelled, stepping through the back door.

First stop was her bedroom.

Empty.

The water was running in the shower, so I headed in that direction. Without slowing down, I flung the door open and found a startled Tweet. A big red towel hugged her body while her hair was hidden under a white one. I didn't allow my focus to linger long on the fact that the only thing she was wearing was a towel.

A towel that was soaking up the drops of water that clung to her soft skin.

Shaking my head, I cleared out thoughts of a naked Tweet, and refocused on being pissed. I stood in the doorway, one hand gripping the doorknob while the other braced against the doorframe, as I glared at her.

Leaning in I growled, "You and me are talking. Now!"

"Can I at least put some clothes on?" she huffed.

Attitude? Really Tweet? Unbe-fucking-lievable.

"No! You have about ten seconds to get your sweet little ass out here." I abruptly turned and stomped away, leaving the door wide open.

I stomped to the family room, sat down on the sofa, but immediately jumped up. Too much adrenaline was pumping through me to stay still. I paced back and forth, thinking it would burn some energy. As the seconds ticked by and she hadn't shown, my agitation grew. Widening my distance, I circled the room several times before ending up in the kitchen. Hoping that by grounding myself I'd calm down, I leaned back against the counter by the sink, crossing my arms in front of me, and took steady deeps breaths while I waited.

The Kelly's home was an open floor plan. From where I stood in the kitchen I had an awesome view straight into the family room and the front door, so I'd be able to catch Tweet if she made a break for it. Moments later, she rounded the corner into the family room. Her gaze bounced around the space. When she didn't see me, her chest caved with a sigh and a look of relief washed over her face. I cleared my throat letting her know our talk was still on and happening right now.

She timidly shuffled into the kitchen, landing on the other side of the island across from me. Neither one of us said anything at first. She still had the towel wrapped around her body, but the one on her head had been removed, replaced with damp wavy hair falling down her back. The anger that I had built up lessened while my gaze slowly glided down the length of Tweet's body. My tongue inadvertently darted out slightly, licking my lower lip.

Remember, you're pissed off.

Tweet shifted and began to nervously bite on her thumbnail while I waited for her explanation. My anger returned the longer I waited for her to speak.

She shifted a few more times and continued to feast on her nail. At this rate she was going to hit bone at any moment. I'd had enough of her stalling.

My tone was strong and determined when I demanded, "Talk."

"About what?" She looked up at me with innocent eyes, as she continued the Feast of the Nail.

A low, deep growl escaped me as I shook my head, not believing we were going to play this game. "How many times do I have to tell you not to play dumb? You're no good at it."

Releasing her thumb from its torture, she said, "I'm not playing this time. I really don't know what you want me to say."

"Okay. How about we start with, why did you leave this morning?"

"I felt icky and needed a shower," she said.

"You could've showered at my house."

"I didn't want to."

"Why?" I shot back.

"Because... my shampoo is over here and... I like my shampoo."

My breathing deepened and picked up speed. The muscles in my arms tensed and relaxed with each flex of my hands. My patience had reached its expiration date.

"You're a piece of work," I snapped.

A tremor of anger mixed with frustration ran through me. I needed to get hold of my emotions. If I went nuts and started yelling we wouldn't get anywhere. Unwrapping my arms, I took one step forward, placed my palms flat on the kitchen island, and leaned in her direction.

In a steady low-pitched voice, I said, "Why did you run out this morning, and don't give me any bullshit about shampoo."

"I was having a hard time remembering what went on last night. I knew we needed to talk, but I needed to clear my head first." She paused. "I don't remember anything that happened after the tequila," she admitted.

"You don't remember a thing after you got drunk?"

She shook her head. "No. Not a thing."

"You don't remember me carrying you out of the party and taking you to my house?"

Her head was shaking before I finished the sentence.

"You don't remember me undressing you? You don't remember my hands sliding up under your shirt, touching your back? And you don't remember asking me if I wanted to touch you and then *telling* me *to* touch you?"

A large lump slid down her throat.

"None of that rings a bell?" I questioned, my voice low and gruff.

I held her gaze waiting for an answer.

She was on the verge of passing out last night when I put her in my truck, so I knew the chances of her remembering that she said *I love you, Noah* was slim. But she remembered every minute once we were in my bedroom, even though she still shook her head in denial. She tried to keep her reaction hidden, but I could tell my words affected her. Her lips were slightly parted, her cheeks had turned three shades of pink in the past minute, and her fingers clutched the towel tighter as she shifted from side-to-side. My words and her memory of last night were turning her on. The hair on my arms and legs bristled. Warm vibrations originating from my chest quickly spread over my entire body.

We stayed in standoff mode for a long time, neither of us backing down. I figured Tweet was concentrating on just the right words for her answer. She wanted to be clear, concise, and explain why she left me.

"No," she said in a low voice.

All this time waiting and *no* was the only word she uttered.

"That is such bullshit and you know it!"

Looking down, I concentrated on the countertop. I blew out a long breath and grunted in annoyance before looking back up at her.

This was exhausting.

My tone reflected how deflated I felt. "Last night, when I saw you standing in the hallway... the way you looked... broke me. You were so hurt and disappointed. I thought I'd lost you for good. I couldn't think straight after I saw that Smurffucker kiss you. Then you ran to his side. I've never felt that out of control before. I wanted to be numb and forget, so I grabbed the easiest piece of ass around."

"Noah...," she whispered. Sorrow filled her eyes.

The muscles of my arms tensed, bracing myself for what I was about to admit to her. "I always tell her not to talk so I can pretend it's you. It's pathetic, I know. I don't want to pretend anymore, Tweet. I'm trying my damnedest to stay in the friend zone. It's just hard and I thought after last night in my room... The way you were acting... I knew you had been drinking. I just thought things would be different for us now."

"Always?" Her voice choked on the word.

It felt as if a huge boulder had been hurled directly into my stomach. I wanted to erase all those times with Brittani but especially the first time. I gave that part of myself away because I thought Tweet had done the same.

"A few times," I whispered, lowering my gaze.

"Was she your first?"

Tears seeped from her hurt eyes. I was ashamed of what I had been doing. I was with Brittani out of loneliness and spite.

I looked up at her, but couldn't bring myself to say the words. Besides, Tweet already knew the answer.

Turning her head from me, a strangled sob tried to escape. "I'm sorry I can't be with you like that."

Her gaze made its way back to me and I held it with all the strength I had. Anger, frustration, desire, need, and want all crashed over me. I pushed off from the counter and rounded the kitchen island, headed directly for Tweet. Once in front of her I cupped the sides of her face, tilting her head back, and forced her to look straight into my eyes. We were so close our warm breath mixed together and swept across each other's lips. Tweet shivered in my hands.

Skimming my nose across her soft cheek up to her temple, I ordered in a whisper, "Stop pushing me away."

I ran my left hand down her neck and over her exposed shoulder. My lips hovered a hairsbreadth above her skin, sliding toward her jaw, and stopping on her neck. I felt her body give and lean into me. I was on the verge of getting lost in her.

Let go of your head, Tweet, and follow your heart.

"Noah, you promised you'd stay in the zone." She sounded out of breath.

"That was before last night," I said against her skin.

My lips glided down the rest of her neck and across her shoulder.

Tell me to kiss you.

Suddenly, her body stiffened as she pulled away from me. I let my chin drop to my chest, and my hands fall away from her body, landing on my hips.

"I can't do this with you. Don't you understand that? *Please*, Noah, stop pushing me," she pleaded.

"You're my knight in plastic armor."

"I love you, Noah."

I straightened, and without another word, walked out the door.

I was desperately trying to be patient and understand Tweet's thought process but it was almost too much to handle when I was that close to her, especially when the only thing between us was a towel. My body reacted on its own, clouding my judgment.

I decided to go for a run to clear my head and stop my body from craving Tweet, knowing full well it was only a temporary fix.

I went back to my house, threw on my Nikes, grabbed my iPhone, and headed out the door. I shoved the earbuds in my ears and scrolled through my music, finally stopping on Snow Patrol's "Open Your Eyes". I chuckled, thinking how fitting the song was to my situation. If Tweet would only stop wasting time and open her eyes to *us*. I picked another song. After all, the point of the run was to clear my head of her for a little while. As I flipped through my playlist I realized it was pointless. Every song I had reminded me of Tweet.

I let the opening electric riff of the guitar invade my head. The repetitive rhythm setting the pace of my warmup while I ran backward. As the drum beat joined in, picking up the tempo, I turned and allowed it to propel me forward. Gary Lightbody's clear lone voice echoed in my ears. I concentrated on my steps, syncing them with the beat of the music. After several seconds my left foot pounded the pavement on the downbeat.

Right foot—up beat.

Left foot—down beat.

Right foot—up beat.

Left foot—down beat.

Repeat.

Sweat burst from every pore, soaking my hair and clothes. My chest pumped to the pulsating rhythm, oxygen and carbon dioxide exchanging places at a rapid speed. Muscles were aching and on the verge of fatigue. A tingling sensation sparked in my chest, intensifying as the music made the steady climb toward its destination. My mind screamed for my body to slow down, but it was too late. The music and my movements had become one, pushing my body faster and faster to its limits. The sensation in my chest erupted into an all-consuming seismic vibration, devouring my body as the song exploded.

Faster.

Faster.

Faster.

Faster.

Faster.

I rounded the corner onto my street. As I approached my house, a break in the music caused me to trip and stumble, landing me in my front yard. I collapsed and rolled onto my back. I was completely exhausted. My mind relaxed and numb from the run as I lay in the grass staring up at the clouds. Then the familiar notes of the song started playing. I jolted back into awareness of all things Tweet as "Everything" drifted from the earbuds. Sitting up, I yanked out the earbuds and walked into the house.

Once inside, I downed a bottle of water and jumped in the shower. The entire time my thoughts were of Tweet—last night, our conversation earlier, what she was doing now, when would I see her again.

I was in the kitchen fixing myself something to eat when there was a soft knock at the back door. I opened the door to find a plate with a piece of chocolate cake floating in midair. I couldn't help but smile at the *white flag*, her attempt at calling a truce.

I grabbed the cake and teased. "Thanks. I wanted something sweet." Then I shut the door.

I got a fork from the drawer, leaned back against the counter, and dove into the cake. A few seconds later Tweet walked in and moved toward me. She was trying to hide it, but I could tell she was smirking.

With my mouth full, I asked, "Did you want some?"

149

Narrowing her beautiful teal eyes, she said, "Not if it's going to make you cry."

And just like that, we were Noah and Tweet again, best friends.

She grabbed the fork and plunged it into the side of the cake that had the most frosting. I always left that part for Tweet since it was her favorite. She handed the fork back and then lifted herself up onto the counter next to me. We continued to pass the fork between us until the cake disappeared. Twisting, I placed the empty plate behind me and then turned back around.

I dragged my hands up my face and through my hair, blew out a breath, and asked, "What are we going to do, Tweet?"

"I need you in my life."

"I need you in mine, too."

"Be my friend," she said.

"Always."

She cleared her throat, hesitating before speaking. "Noah, next to my dad, you are the finest man I know. I can't bear the thought of you not being in my life."

"Tweet…"

I started to turn to her, but she stopped me. I shifted back in place against the counter, looking down, and sighed.

"You deserve better than me. If we were together, eventually I would screw it up. Then I wouldn't have any part of you. I'm scared to death of losing you. Those four months that we were apart was the loneliest time of my life." Her voice cracked on the last few words.

The tension was coming back into my body listening to her. I wanted to shake her and make her understand all this crap was in her head and not real. My arms folded across my chest to keep them from reaching out and grabbing her.

"I'm surprised I haven't screwed up our friendship already. Although, I might be doing that now. I just want the best for you and I'm not the best. I wish I were. You have no idea how I wish I could let you pull me across that line, but there's something that's got such a hold on me and I don't know how to let it go. It's nobody's fault. It's just the way I am. I've tried to think better of myself, I really have. Please stay my friend. Things are safer if we keep our relationship as friends. You're the only one I have and the only one I need. We have to move past this."

My voice was shaky and deep in my throat. "I don't know how or where you ever got it in your head that you're not good enough. You're beautiful, smart, funny, and kind. You're perfect for me and always have been. I wish you believed it."

"Me too," she whispered.

I tried to make my voice steady and strong before I asked, "What does Brad mean to you?"

"Nothing." Her answer came quick. "He asked me to the party and we had fun, until you punched him in the stomach, of course."

Both of us chuckled, breaking the tension a little.

I couldn't stand there any longer and not look at her. I turned to Tweet. "He's not close to being good enough for you."

I raised one hand to her face and cupped her jaw, running my thumb across her cheek. "If he does anything to hurt you, I swear to god, I'll kill him."

"Thank you for caring about me," she said quietly.

I leaned slightly forward, resting my forehead against hers.

"I don't just care about you, Tweet."

A sob escaped her as the tears trickled down her face. She wrapped her arms around my neck as mine hugged her waist. I wanted so badly to push her into being with me, but I knew I couldn't. I had to be patient. She needed to come to the realization on her own that we were meant to be together. In the meantime, I needed to ease off. I had just gotten her back in my life. I wasn't willing to give her up again. If I couldn't have all of Tweet right now, a part of her would have to do.

CHAPTER 15

Several months had passed since Tweet and I talked in my kitchen. I struggled but managed as best I could to stay within the boundaries of the friend zone. I didn't really have much of a choice. I had already tried putting distance between us but all it did was turn me into a robotic shell. Our senior year was coming to an end. Tweet and I would have the summer together and then she'd be moving away to the University of South Carolina in Columbia to earn her journalism degree. I was staying in town, attending the College of Charleston and then the Medical University of South Carolina, working toward my degree in orthopedic surgery. Life was going to get busy and force us to be apart soon enough. I wanted to spend the summer with *my girl* and if that meant following her rules then that's what I was going to do.

The first rule of *friend zone* was to spend time with other people.

Tweet continued to hang out with Brad.

I fucking hated rule one.

I asked her a few times if they were dating, which was code for "Is he putting his slimy hands on you?" She always denied it, saying they were just friends and since they shared three of four classes, they studied together a lot. I had a gnawing feeling Brad had ulterior motives where Tweet was concerned, so I maintained surveillance on his Smurffucker ass as much as possible.

I didn't set out to really *follow* rule one, it was more like I woke one day and found I'd tripped into it.

Shortly after the zone boundaries were reestablished, Brooke appeared in my life. Mike McCarthy, one of my teammates, introduced us after practice one day. She attended a school across town and, apparently, had come to a few of our games, then started showing up at practice. I never thought much about it at the time. She was Mike's cousin, so for her to be at games made sense. As far as her showing up at practice, I figured she really liked baseball.

After some of the home games I'd go hang out and grab a bite to eat with a group that consisted of teammates, their girlfriends, and various unattached people. On rare occasions, I was able to talk Tweet into going with me, but because of the fucking zone, most of the time she felt it was better if I went alone. I noticed that Brooke had become a regular member of the group. The only reason this got my attention was because we were usually the last two left after the couples headed off and everyone else had paired up. We talked about people we knew in common, graduation, plans for the summer. She asked me to the movies, to dinner, and kept showing up at practice. By process of elimination and my general cluelessness about any other girl besides Tweet, I had found myself in a relationship with Brooke for the past two months.

Brooke was a cross between Beth and Brittani. She was sweet and wanted to make me happy, like Beth. Then there were times when she looked at me, ready to pounce, like Brittani. Outwardly, I was a lucky son of a bitch. I had an intelligent, tall blonde with big blue eyes and a supermodel shape who wanted to be my girl. The problem was, the position of *my girl* had already been filled a long time ago.

The way Brooke's eyes lit up when I mentioned medical school told me she was looking for a serious boyfriend/potential husband. Brooke deserved a guy who saw only her in his eyes and I was incapable of being that guy. I tried to back off but she was persistent, and determined for us to be together. I went along because I was eighteen, she was pretty, and I liked how it felt to be wanted.

Brooke's best quality was she seemed cool about mine and Tweet's relationship. The two girls had been around each other a few times. Although she never said it, I could tell Tweet wasn't a big Brooke fan. Part of me got a thrill at Tweet's reaction, hoping it had more to do with jealousy than simply not liking Brooke.

On her end, Brooke didn't act threatened or jealous. A few times she asked me to explain exactly what Tweet meant to me. It was always awkward because I didn't want to hurt her feelings, but I also didn't feel I owed her an explanation. So I'd change the subject and Brooke would get the message.

My gaze was like the ball in a pinball machine, bouncing from the clock, to the TV, to Brooke's hand. We were at her house watching some lame movie. Brooke was curled up next to me on the sofa, her head resting on my shoulder. For the past ten minutes her hand had been inching its way along my outstretched leg heading toward my crotch.

"Brooke, knock it off," I said, shoving her hand away.

"Why? I can tell you really like it," she whispered in my ear.

I smirked, glancing at her out of the corner of my eye. "I also really like my balls, which I won't have if your giant of a father catches us."

Make-out sessions with Brooke were fun and becoming hotter, but tonight I had other plans.

I hadn't seen or talked to Tweet in a few days. She was hiding herself away for some reason, not even answering her phone or texts. My natural instinct was to immediately go to her when I didn't hear back, but I was still playing by her rules, staying in the zone.

Brooke's glossy lips trailed down my neck, causing a shiver to run through my body.

"Come on No-No, let's have some fun."

Of all the possible nicknames that could have been bestowed upon me, she comes up with the stupidest one I'd ever heard.

"Brooke, I have to leave," I said, shifting away from her.

She flopped back against the back of the sofa in a huff, her arms crossed over her chest.

"Already? We haven't finished the movie." Her words came out as a high-pitched whine.

"Sorry, I have a big Biology exam I need to study for." I stood.

"We could have studied together."

I glanced at my phone, looking for any reply from Tweet, and noticed the time. I needed to check on her before it got too late.

Bending down, I kissed Brooke on the forehead. "I wouldn't be able to concentrate on my Biology with *your* biology distracting me."

She giggled and I was out the door.

Pulling into the neighborhood, I glanced over at the park and saw her sitting at our spot, staring out across the pond. My heart automatically pumped faster, my breathing became shallow, and a prickling sensation covered my skin.

I parked my truck on the street, got out, leaned against it, and took in the beautiful view. Her light blue T-shirt hugged the curves of her back, stopping just above her waistband. Her head was turned slightly to the left. Her dark hair was down and hung over one shoulder, exposing her profile.

I pushed off from my truck and headed toward Tweet.

When I was at the edge of the picnic area, I teased, "So you don't answer calls or texts anymore?"

Her back straightened and I could see her lips curl up in a half smile.

"Bitch, bitch, bitch," she said in a singsong voice.

I walked over and sat next to Tweet, where I belonged.

The crickets sang in the trees around us while we stared out at the pond. There was just enough of a glimmer shining on the pond from the lights around the park to be able to make out the occasional fish breaking through the surface, coming up for a bit to eat. We sat quietly for a while enjoying the sounds of the park and being with each other.

I couldn't put my finger on it, but something was off. Tweet seemed sad and distant.

"What are you doing out here this time of night?" I asked.

She cut her eyes over to me. "I could ask you the same thing."

"I was looking for you."

A hint of a smile crossed her lips before her gaze swung back to the pond.

"Where have you been keeping yourself lately?" I continued.

"Around."

"Have you *been* with *him*?"

Her head whipped around to face me. Her eyes had doubled to the size of saucers and her jaw had gone slack.

"What... are you talking about?" she stammered.

"Brad. Are you two hanging out a lot more? Are you getting serious about him?"

Her expression relaxed as she sighed. "No. I haven't seen him in several days."

"Good. Keep that up."

A small giggle escaped her.

The glow from the streetlight reflected in her eyes that were glassy with tears.

Facing away from her, I gripped the edge of the picnic table to keep me from reaching out and grabbing her.

"You can tell me anything, you know."

We simultaneously turned to each other.

With tears on the verge of spilling over, she whispered, "I know."

My arms shook from the strain of keeping them planted. I wanted to pull her into my lap and wrap them around her so badly.

"I need to get home," she said, scooting off the table.

I jumped up. "I'll drive you."

She shook her head. "No, I want to walk."

"Okay."

I couldn't help myself. Reaching up, I wiped a stray tear away from her cheek with my thumb. We locked eyes for a brief moment before Tweet lunged forward, wrapping her arms around my neck. My right arm eased its way around her waist, holding her tight, while my left hand stroked her hair.

"I am so, *so* sorry," she whispered through a sob.

I had no idea why she was apologizing. Whatever happened had kept her away from me for several days. If I found out Brad played a part in it, I would end him.

Angling my head toward her, I buried my nose in her hair. "Don't disappear from my life like that again."

When Tweet pulled away that sweet shy smile of hers beamed up at me. She then turned and headed out of the park. I jumped in my truck and started it. The stereo blasted, I flipped on my hazard lights, and slowly followed behind her. Rolling down the window, "I'm Yours" by Jason Mraz filled the night air. Tweet's hips swayed back and forth in time to the music. She never turned back to acknowledge my presence as the side-to-side swishing of her cute little ass wrapped in her jeans became more exaggerated. In typical Tweet fashion, she pushed aside whatever brought tears to her eyes earlier, opting instead to act silly and make me smile.

When we were almost to her house, Tweet jogged to the front steps, twirled once, and then ran up to the front door. Before stepping inside, she turned, winked, and tossed me a wave. I stared at her for a few moments.

God, I loved her.

I gently tapped my horn, flashed my lights, and drove off content and happy, having seen my girl and knowing she was safe.

CHAPTER 16

Graduation day had finally arrived. During the ceremony, I racked up a few scholarships and the I Dare You Award for leadership. Tweet earned a couple of scholarships as well as an award for journalism. I was so proud and excited for her. The shocked look on her face each time her name was called was priceless.

To celebrate the graduates in the neighborhood, all the parents got together and had a party at the park. Dads gathered around the grills, joking and drinking a few beers. Some of the moms were congratulating each other on their son's or daughter's achievements, while others chased down the younger brothers and sisters running around.

I'd been lugging coolers of ice from my truck to where the drinks were set up. Hauling the last one, I weaved my way through the crowd, dodging kids, Frisbees, balls, and various other flying objects and set the last cooler down.

My gaze roamed over the park, searching for Tweet. She was right where I knew she'd be, at our spot.

"Hey Dad, I got all the coolers out of my truck. Anything else?"

Draping his arm around my shoulders he said, "That's my boy!" He turned to Mr. Sutton. "Tony, isn't my boy something?"

Dad had a little buzz going on already. He never shied away from showing me affection, but when he started asking random people their opinion of me, I knew an adult beverage was involved.

"He's a great kid," Mr. Sutton replied.

"Kid shmid, he's a man now." Dad's one-arm hug tightened around me. "A great young man. Your mom and I are incredibly proud of you, son."

His eyes began to mist.

Slapping me on the back, he said, "Now, go have some fun."

Tweet didn't notice as I approached. She continued to stare across the pond, off in her own little world.

"Earth to Tweet." I waved my hand in front of her face, bringing her back to the present.

Clearing her throat, she said, "Sorry."

"What do you have rattling around in that beautiful head?"

She blew out a sigh. "Nothing much, I was just thinking about all the times we've spent here."

"You're not getting all sentimental and mushy on me, are you?"

"Maybe just a little." She threw a slight smile my way.

Swallowing hard, I admitted, "It's going be hard not having you around."

I hated the idea of Tweet not living in town. I knew we'd call and text, and USC wasn't that far away, but the idea of her being gone made my chest ache. Travis graduated high school last year and was attending USC. Being a sophomore in the fall, he had already made friends, knew the campus, and had gotten used to college life. I didn't tell Tweet I had asked Travis to keep an eye out on her. Making sure she was finding her way around campus, having fun, and letting me know if any Smurffuckers came sniffing around her.

"It's going to be hard not having you around. You'll come visit me, right? USC isn't far, only about an hour and a half." There was a hint of panic in her tone.

She'd asked me this same question every day since receiving her acceptance letter. It made me feel good to know she would miss me.

"Nothing could keep me away from my girl. I'll be up there so often you'll get sick of me."

"Impossible."

I picked up her hand and placed a gentle kiss on the back of it. Then we sat quietly enjoying our spot. The moment was interrupted when my name shot through the air.

"Noah!"

I let go of Tweet's hand and stood as Brooke walked up.

Damn, I thought I'd have more time with Tweet.

"Hey, baby. I've been looking for you," Brooke said, wrapping her arms around my neck and planting a kiss on my lips.

I shifted slightly, hoping to break the kiss, but Brooke had a vise grip on my neck as she shoved her tongue farther into my mouth. Heat ran through my body more from embarrassment than the intensity of the kiss. I didn't want Tweet to see this.

I was so fucked in the head.

Tweet clearing her throat interrupted Brooke staking her claim.

Setting my lips free, Brooke snaked her arm around my waist. "Sorry, Amanda. I love kissing my fella. I just never want to stop."

Tweet turned her head, but not enough to hide her eye roll from me.

"Congrats on graduation," Brooke said.

"Thanks. Back at ya."

I looked back and forth between the girls thinking more chit-chat was on the way.

Silence.

Silence.

Silence.

After a few seconds of extreme awkwardness and the annoyed expression on Tweet's face, I decided to take matters into my own hands.

"You hungry?" I asked Brooke.

She looked up at me, waggling her eyebrows. "I'm always hungry when you're around, No-No."

"Oh my god!! That's your nickname?" Words and laughter flew from Tweet's mouth, causing her body to lurch backward. "Oh man, that is rich." Snarkiness dripped off of each word.

I forced the corners of my lips down, in an attempt to hide my smile. I hated the nickname, but Brooke liked it, and I didn't want her feelings to be hurt.

Brooke's arm tightened around me, her eyes narrowed at Tweet, and she spit out, "I think it's cute and Noah loves it when I call him that, especially followed by a moan."

Shit! The claws were coming out.

A small gasp caught in my throat, causing a cough to fly out of me. Rubbing the back of my neck, I glanced over at Tweet and smirked. She didn't hide her DEFCON 1 glare or her sneer from Brooke. I could tell by the look in Tweet's eyes that the wheels were turning and she was about to unleash one of her smartass comments. I needed to separate these two before Brooke pushed her over the edge. Just when I was about to drag Brooke away, she giggled, further rubbing the moan comment in Tweet's face. It was too late for me to implement rescue efforts. I could see the snark bubble up in Tweet's eyes.

Her arms folded across her chest, her head did that little wobble thing, and Tweet blasted back, "Did I give you the impression that I didn't think it was cute? I'm sorry. It's as cute as a Smurffucking button."

Brooke's back stiffened as another awkward silence fell over us.

I glanced at Tweet put my arm around Brooke's shoulders, and stammered, "Well, let's get you fed. See ya later, Tweet."

As Brooke and I walked away, she tossed her last snippy comment over her shoulder, "See ya, Tweet."

Several yards away I stopped and whispered in Brooke's ear, "I'll be right back."

"Where are you going, No-No?"

"I need to tell Tweet something."

A huge smug grin appeared across Brooke's face as she looked back.

I jogged over to Tweet, keeping my expression neutral.

Leaning in close to her face, I promised. "You will be severely punished later tonight."

I let the concerned expression sit on her face for a few seconds before I allowed my devilish grin to slowly appear. I knew it was wrong, but I got a huge thrill out of Tweet being upset because of Brooke. Since she would never tell me her true feelings, I had to read her body language and reactions. They were the only indications I had that nothing had changed.

You still love me, Tweet.

Maintaining eye contact, I took a few steps back, then turned, and jogged back to Brooke's side.

Grabbing our plates of food, Brooke and I sat side by side, several tables away from Tweet. I positioned myself so that I would have a clear view of her table. I tried to keep the staring to a minimum, but found myself glancing over often. Tweet's sister, Emily, had joined her. I couldn't hear what they were talking about, but I could tell Tweet was uncomfortable and ready to bolt. Her gaze shot toward me with every laugh that erupted from Brooke. The longing in her beautiful teal eyes intensified each time they were aimed in my direction.

A ripple of excitement moved through me. Maybe between the thought of us living in different cities, seeing Brooke's antics, and listening to Emily, Tweet's walls were coming down and we could finally step out of the friend zone.

As the party went on, I had a nice little buzz going from a few beers, and I basically let Brooke be *Brooke*. We hugged and kissed off and on. As Brooke laughed, squealed, and giggled loudly, I watched for Tweet's reaction. I knew what I was doing bordered on douchedom, but I was a man on a mission. Somehow making Tweet jealous didn't feel like pushing her to be with me. I was positive she wanted me, but her thoughts were just all jumbled up. This was my attempt at helping her straighten out her head and it seemed to be doing the trick.

The sun had set, a couple more beers consumed, the party ended, and the park emptied. I closed my eyes and slid my hand behind her neck, lacing my fingers through her soft dark hair. Her right hand twisted in my T-shirt as she tugged me closer to her body, while the left rubbed up and down my dick. A breathy moan slipped from her lips as my tongue slid between them. The second we made contact the kiss became frantic as we pushed as far into the other's mouth as humanly possible. The deep husky tone of Jason Wade's vocals floated from the speakers as "Everything" surrounded us. Pulling back, I sucked on her bottom lip hard and then nibbled my way across her jaw and down her neck.

"Let's go back to my house," she panted.

I nipped at her earlobe.

"Noah, I want you."

"God, I want you too, Tweet." I moaned against her skin.

"What?!"

Two hands shoved hard on my chest, throwing me back against the seat of the car. My eyes shot open to a snarling Brooke.

I shook my head, trying to get my thoughts to fall into place. "What?"

"You called me Tweet!"

Fuuuck me like a jackhammer!

Jabbing at the button on her dashboard, she silenced the voice of Jason Wade. I had walked Brooke to her car after the party and got into the passenger's seat. The car ran idle while we said goodbye. The emotions of the day along with Tweet disappearing from the party without a word to me, mixed with four beers, had my head foggy.

Say something, dumbass.

I raked my hands up my face and into my hair. "I'm sorry. It's been a weird day with graduation and…"

Think. Think. Think. I'm drunk!

"I'm drunk."

"You didn't drink that much," she snapped.

"I'm a pussy when it comes to alcohol, ask Travis. I'm like a little girl. A little girl wearing a bright pink tutu. It was a slupid stip of the tongue… a stupid slip of tongue."

With raised eyebrows, I gave Brooke the most innocent look I could manufacture.

Her expression softened. "I'll give you a pass this time."

"Thanks."

My hand reached for the door handle.

"The offer still stands," she said.

Squinting my eyes, I looked at her, confused. "Offer?"

She huffed. "To come back to my house. My parents are away for a few days."

"Brooke, I don't think that's such a good idea."

"Why not?"

Pushy much?

"Um… because I've been drinking, and…" I stammered.

"Noah, I've been wanting to have sex with you since the second week we met."

"Brooke…"

Things with Brooke had gotten more intense over the past few weeks. There were several times during our make-out sessions when she wanted to go further, and they would have if I hadn't stopped.

"…we can talk about it later."

I reached for the door handle again when her words stopped me.

"Is it because of *her*?" There was venom in her voice.

My head fell back against the seat and I stared at the roof.

"I'm not an idiot, Noah. I see the way y'all look at each other. Are you cheating on me with *her*?"

"No. Tweet's been in my life from day one. She's my best friend," I explained, my voice low.

"Then what is it? I think it's pretty obvious how I feel about you. I love you, Noah." I felt her hand touch my bicep.

Turning my head in Brooke's direction, I said, "You don't even know me that well. How can you love me?"

"I don't need to know specifics to know how I feel."

She waited patiently for me to say the three words back. As I looked into her hopeful eyes I wondered what made one person fall in love with another person. On paper Brooke made sense. She was smart, had goals, was pretty, wanted to make me happy and have a future with me. Everything was present and accounted for except for the most important thing. That intangible connection. That sweet spot, where the mystery of falling in love lies in wait until the right person comes into your life. You can't force it, predict it, or manipulate it. It's what trips your heart for the fall to begin. My heart was tripped eighteen years ago and had been falling ever since.

"Can we talk about this later when my head is clear, please?"

She stared at me blankly for a few seconds before shifting in her seat and placing her hands on the steering wheel. Without another word, I got out of the car and she drove away.

I cared about Brooke and part of me wished I could love her. It certainly would make my life easier. But easy was just easy, it didn't make something worth it.

My head was telling me to go home and think about my relationship with Brooke. I could put her off for only so long. She was going to want to continue the conversation we started tonight at some point. Instead, I pulled out my phone and ended the day like I wanted, listening to my heart.

Me: *Our spot. Now. Come alone. I want you all to myself. ;)*

Tweet: *You're not the boss of me. I'll come when I'm good & ready.*

Several seconds went by before my phone chimed.

Tweet: *See you in a sec. ;)*

A sigh of relief mixed with excitement ran through me. I thought Tweet was mad at me from the way she disappeared tonight without saying goodbye. I couldn't wait to be alone with her and give her the graduation gift I'd been holding on to for the past months.

I grabbed the gift from my truck and headed to our spot. As I sat looking out across the pond waiting for Tweet, my mind drifted over the happy memories we shared of this place—her excitement when I gave her the tickets to our first concert, our first date, and our first kiss. We've spent so much time here talking about everything and nothing at all, sharing our dreams, our fears, and now a new chapter in our lives. Tweet's sentimentality was rubbing off on me.

The crunching of the gravel around the picnic area let me know my girl had finally arrived.

After several seconds when she didn't come any closer, I teased, "Are you going to come and sit down or look at my back the entire night?"

"Quit your bitchin," she said, rounding the table and sitting by my side.

We automatically took our positions—fingers laced together, bodies huddled close, Tweet's head on my shoulder.

"Where'd you run off to earlier?" My cheek rested on top of her head.

"I didn't run off. The party was winding down, I was tired, and so I went home," she said.

"You left without saying anything to me. I thought you were mad at me."

"Why would I be mad at you?"

"I don't know. I was just disappointed when I realized you'd left." I squeezed her hand slightly.

"Well, you seemed to have had your hands full."

The corners of my lips curled up slightly.

"By the way, you guys were a bit much, don't you think? I mean, jeez, get a room."

"We did."

I thought my tone was teasing, but apparently I missed the mark in a big way. Lifting her head off my shoulder, Tweet jerked her hand from mine and leaned away.

"Don't joke about something like that with me." Her lips flattened into a straight line, as teal eyes with a hint of green glared at me.

"Are you jealous?" It came out more sarcastically than intended.

The wheels were spinning in her beautiful head, trying to decide the appropriate response. Would she go the angry or smartass route?

"Brooke's nickname for you is stupid." There was a sneer on her face, but her tone was smartass.

That's my girl.

I smirked. "I know. And, you are so damn cute when you're jealous."

"It's lame. In fact, after I got through being embarrassed for you, I felt sorry for you, and then I threw up." She held eye contact.

Damn, she made me happy.

Placing my hand over my heart, I said, "Oh baby, you've just gone from damn cute to smokin' hot."

"Bastard." She forced the corners of her lips to stay down.

"I love when you talk dirty to me. Say something else."

"Asshole."

I let a long deep moan slowly float from my mouth. "Oooh yeah. That's the ticket."

"You're ridiculous," she said.

"And you are beautiful."

Tweet shook her head and gave me an exaggerated eye roll before turning away in an attempt to hide the smile that was beginning to break across her lips.

"Now that all that's out of the way, it's gift time." I clapped my hands, rubbing my palms together. "Me first."

Shifting to the side, I reached into my front pocket and pulled out the dark blue velvet heart-shaped box with a white ribbon. She looked stunned and confused.

"Um... I think you brought me Brooke's gift by mistake."

"I brought the right gift to the right girl. Take it." I held it closer to her.

She glanced down at it, then back up to me, then back down to the box before finally reaching out for it. She stared at it for several seconds as if she were in a trance.

"Open it Tweet. It won't bite you." I gave her a slight smile.

Slowly, she untied the ribbon and lifted the top of the hinged box. The tips of her fingers gently touched the gold feather charm necklace. She looked up at me with tears running down her face.

Nailed it!

"I can take it back if you don't like it." I winked.

Her voice was shaky when she said, "It's the most beautiful thing I've ever seen. You're not going to touch it except to put it on me."

Tweet handed over the necklace and twisted her body slightly away. I removed it from the box and brought it around her neck. My mouth was an inch away from her ear. I could feel the heat radiating off of her skin. Gathering her hair in one hand, she held it up and I clasped my gift around her.

"You'll always be my number-one girl. Congratulations, Tweet," I whispered.

Her chest rose and fell with heavy breaths. I heard the thud deep in the back of her throat as she took several hard swallows.

"Thank you, Noah. I'm never going to take it off," she choked out.

Tweet turned back around and our eyes locked for a few seconds before she handed me my gift.

As I tore through the wrapping paper, Tweet anxiously said, "I hope you like it."

I opened the box and couldn't believe what I saw. It was a chain attached to a ballpark dog tag. I'd been wanting one for a long time. It was made from a piece of the original stadium seats.

"Fenway, isn't it?"

The biggest smile appeared across her face as she nodded. "It has it written on the back."

I flipped it over to read the words. I was completely speechless. Tweet knew nothing about baseball even though she had come to every one of my games since we were kids. She always complained that it was too hard to remember all the rules. But she remembered Fenway. She didn't just go to a sports store and tell a salesperson to give her something a baseball fan would like.

She remembered how special Fenway was to me.

I pulled the chain over my head. Wrapping my arms around her waist, I scooted her closer to me, her head resting on my chest.

"I love it. Thank you, Tweet. I can't believe you remembered Fenway was my favorite. It's the best gift I've ever gotten." I placed a kiss on the top of her head.

We sat there for a long time in silence just holding each other. It was the perfect end to this chapter in our lives—just me, my girl, and our spot.

CHAPTER 17

There was nothing different or special about the day when it started, just the typical morning routine. I got up early, went for a run, showered, dressed, and sat at the kitchen table eating a bowl of cereal for breakfast. Mom put the last glass in the cabinet after unloading the dishwasher and then she'd be off to work. Dad walked in, already dressed in his suit, grabbed his travel mug, and filled it with coffee. As he passed by Mom, he placed his hand low on her back and gave her a kiss on the cheek.

"Noah, did you get a chance to ask your supervisor about getting off next month for the trip to Fenway?" Dad said.

"Yes sir. He said it would be fine and already put the dates on the schedule."

"Good deal. I'll check on flights when I get home tonight. I was afraid we wouldn't get to go this year with you working at the hospital and getting ready for college. I know life will get busy, but I'd like to keep this tradition going as long as possible."

"Me too, Dad."

I could see the pride in his face as he smiled down at me. My dad was a good man. If I developed into half the man he was, that'd be pretty awesome.

Patting my shoulder, he looked toward my mom and said, "Hey good lookin', your car's blocking me in."

"Sorry, I'm leaving now. I'll walk out with you," Mom said, grabbing her purse.

She walked over to me and kissed the top of my head.

"The dishwasher is empty, so when you're done, bowl goes in the dishwasher."

"Yes ma'am."

"And if you get home before me, there's a chicken casserole in the fridge. It'd be great if you'd put it in the oven."

"Yes ma'am."

"At three hundred fifty degrees."

"Yes ma'am."

"Now that the boy has all his instructions, can we go?" The corner of Dad's lip quirked up in a smirk.

"Right after I grab my sweater," Mom replied as she rushed down the hallway.

"It's ninety degrees outside, why do you need a sweater?" Dad chuckled.

"It gets cold in the office."

Turning back to me he said, "By the way, it wouldn't be the worst thing in the world if you forgot to put that casserole in the oven. There's always pizza." He winked.

"Ready to go," Mom hollered as she went out the door.

"Women, wouldn't want to live without them." He picked up his briefcase. "Have a good day at work, buddy. I love you."

"Love you too, Dad."

I'd gotten a summer job as a transporter at Medical University of South Carolina hospital. I took patients for tests, therapy, or to their cars after discharge. I'd be attending the university once I earned my undergrad degree. This job was an opportunity to meet staff and learn the hospital. It also gave me some insight into what my life would be like for the next several years with classes and residency.

I was pushing a new mom and her twin boys in a wheelchair through the lobby of the hospital. The new dad walked slightly ahead of us, arms draped with two car seats and bags of baby stuff, his hands full of flowers and balloons.

"Mr. Burgess, you can go ahead and get the car, just pull up right in front of the door," I told the already frazzled-looking guy.

"That'd be great. Thanks." He looked down at his new family. "Honey, I'll be right back." He picked up speed then finally disappeared out the front exit.

As I continued to head toward the door, I glanced down at the tiny heads peeking out from under the blankets. I couldn't help the smile that broke across my face as I thought how great it would be to have a son or daughter one day… way in the future.

I rolled Mrs. Burgess and the little dudes outside. Mr. Burgess made it to his car and waited for an ambulance to pass before he could drive up to us. After fifteen minutes of the dad checking and rechecking the security of the baby seats, the new family was on their way home.

Before heading back upstairs, I pulled my phone out of the front pocket of my scrubs to check for any messages. I always kept it on silent while at work, but checked it during the day. I scrolled through my texts. The first two were from Travis, one asking me to hang out tonight and the other his usual *sex position of the day* picture.

Delete.

I felt a slight tremble in my stomach when I saw the next name listed. There were at least five missed calls and texts. I'd stopped scrolling to open the first one that had been sent a little over fifteen minutes ago.

Mrs. Kelly: *Come to the ER.*

I had to read it twice before the words registered.
Why would Tweet's mom be texting me?

My legs moved on their own in the direction of the emergency room. My hands shook as I called Mrs. Kelly back.

Straight to voicemail.

I pulled up my mom's number and pressed Call.

Straight to voicemail.

My dad's number was next.

Straight to voicemail.

Mr. Kelly's number—called.

Straight to voicemail.

Why the fuck wasn't anyone answering their phones?!

I tried to stay calm, but the thought of Tweet being hurt was too overwhelming. It became harder and harder to take in a deep breath. I was lightheaded and overheated. I rushed across the hospital, cutting each corner sharp as I navigated the maze of hallways.

I finally made it to the ER. Judy, the admit clerk, saw me coming and directed me to Room 10. Without stopping, I sprinted the rest of the way down the hall and around the corner. Doctors and nurses hovered just outside the room. When they saw me coming they parted like the Red Sea. I got to the door and froze.

My dad was on a stretcher lying flat on his back, his arms straight by his side, with a white sheet covering him to mid-chest. My mom stood on the other side of the stretcher. Tears poured down her face as her chest heaved uncontrollably. She brought a trembling hand up and gently stroked the side of Dad's face. Leaning down, she placed a soft kiss on his forehead, then over each eyelid, then each cheek, finally placing a lingering one on his lips.

My gaze swung up, landing on Mrs. Kelly standing in the far corner of the room. Her face drenched in tears, her hand covering her mouth in an attempt to quiet her sobs. It was like watching a silent horror movie. When my mom straightened, the bright fluorescent light beamed down on my dad's face. It was relaxed and lifeless.

Memories of when my grandmother died flooded my mind. She was the only grandparent I ever knew. Both my mom's parents and my grandfather had passed away when I was still a baby. When Grandma died I was eight years old and scared beyond belief to go to her funeral.

"Dad, I don't wanna go today."

"Noah, there's nothing to be scared of. You're a strong boy and I'll be right by your side, buddy," Dad said as he straightened my tie.

It was the first time I wore a complete suit with a jacket and tie. The collar of my shirt made my neck itch and the tie felt like it was choking me, so I kept tugging on it.

I twisted my head back and forth, trying to loosen the chokehold the collar had on my throat. "What's she going to look like?"

Dad finished fixing my tie, brushed the hair off of my forehead, and looked at me with reassuring eyes. "She's going to look peaceful, like she's sleeping."

I stayed glued to Dad's side that entire day. Whenever I felt scared all I had to do was look up and he was there protecting me.

Mom's gaze connected with mine. No words were needed. She saw the question in my eyes and I read the answer on her face. Someone's hand touched my shoulder, moving me through the doorway and into the room. With each step I felt my body get weaker. Mom rounded the foot of the stretcher, walking toward me.

Dad would want me to stay strong for her.

Mom flung her arms around my neck and collapsed against me. I caught her and held on to her tight. I pressed my hip against the side of the stretcher in order to brace myself. I looked over at my father's face. Biting on my bottom lip, my body jerked as I tried to contain my sobs.

"Noah, there's nothing to be scared of. You're a strong boy and I'll be right by your side, buddy."

There was a light knock on my bedroom door. "Noah, it's me."

I don't know how long Mom and I spent at the hospital. Everything about this day was covered in a fog. The only thing that was clear was that I had to stay strong for her. Once we got home, I waited for as long as I could before coming back to my room. The second the bedroom door clicked shut I broke down. Never in my life had I experienced the deep gut-wrenching sobs that took over my body.

"Come in." The words scratched my throat, causing my voice to sound raw.

I lay in bed on my back with the heels of my palms covering my eyes. I heard the door open and close. Lowering my hands, I sat up and looked at her through red swollen eyes. For the first time since I read Mrs. Kelly's text I could breathe. My oxygen had just walked into the room.

We held each other's gaze. In that moment, nothing she could have said would have comforted me more than the way she looked at me. It was in the moments between the words that said the most. That's when your heart does the talking.

"He had a massive heart attack at work. He was gone before the paramedics had a chance to get there." I gasped, trying to hold myself together. "I just saw him this morning and he looked fine. We were going to Fenway next month, Tweet."

Suddenly, my body convulsed and the sobs tumbled out. The bed dipped behind me, then her arms and legs wrapped tightly around my body as I leaned back against her chest. She buried her head in the crook of my neck, her tears dripping down my skin.

I felt the brush of her lips when she whispered, "Your dad was a great man and he was so proud of you."

Our sobs came in waves. We clung to each other as we rode the peaks. When they subsided I took the opportunity to check on my mom. The doctor had given her a mild sedative and Mrs. Kelly stayed by her side while she rested. Most of our extended family lived out of town and were on their way here. Each time I returned to my room, Tweet and I would resume our position—my back resting on her chest, her arms and legs holding me close. With my eyes shut, I mindlessly ran my hand up and down her forearm that was draped over my shoulder and hung down across my chest.

After a while there was a knock on the door.

A female voice said, "Noah, it's Brooke. Can I come in?"

Before I could answer, I heard the door creak open and the sound of Brooke's shoes click on the floor as she stepped inside. My right hand continued to stroke Tweet's arm while my left arm pulled her leg closer to my side. I was surrounding myself with her because that's where I felt safe.

"What's going on?" There was a sharp edge to Brooke's tone.

Never looking toward her, I rubbed my forehead and replied, "Brooke, I really don't want to be around anyone right now. I'm sorry. I'll call you tomorrow."

The next sounds I heard were a huff of breath, footsteps, and the door closing.

"Maybe I should go and let her stay," Tweet said.

Turning over onto my stomach, I wrapped my arms around Tweet's waist and nuzzled her chest. Slowly, her fingers combed through my hair, the tips of her nails skimming lightly over my scalp.

I mumbled, "Don't leave me. I need you. I don't want to be around anyone but you, Tweet." I clung to her, my body trembling as another wave of sobs crashed over me.

She tightened her hold and whispered, "I'm here. I'm not going anywhere."

The clock on my nightstand read 2:18 am. I was stuck between the worst day of my life and the day I dreaded the most—planning my father's funeral.

I drifted in and out of sleep the entire night. Each time I opened my eyes Tweet was there letting me be whatever I needed to be at that moment—hurt, angry, confused.

Our position shifted, landing us in the middle of the bed. I was on my back, my right arm behind my head. Tweet lay on her side, facing me. With fingers laced together, our thumbs mindlessly circled each other's like a slow thumb-wrestling match. Moonlight from the window washed over our faces.

My gaze was glued to the ceiling. I didn't need to look at Tweet to know whether or not she was awake. I knew she would be.

"You wanna hear something ridiculous?" I said, my voice low.

"Always." She squeezed my hand.

"I was eight years old when Grandma passed away."

"I remember that. You kept tugging on your tie the entire day."

"Yeah." I paused, intensely aware of how prominent Tweet has been in my life.

I didn't have to connect the dots to who a particular family member was or explain any history about an event in my life to her. She was an extension of me.

"So I realized at an early age that people in your life die. But I've never thought about my parents not being here." I glanced toward her. "Isn't that weird?"

She snuggled closer to me, resting her head on my shoulder. "I don't think it's weird. I've never thought about my parents..." Her voice quivered.

My gaze turned back to the ceiling. "I saw the ambulance. I was helping a discharged patient to their car. There were no screeching tires or sirens blaring. I had no idea it was him inside."

Tweet let go of my hand and hugged my arm, molding herself closer to my side.

"People love to talk about the miracle of birth. No one ever mentions the miracle of death. They're both extraordinary events, considered acts of God. The difference is that one leaves you completely devastated."

"Your dad bought me an orange push-up at every single one of your games. When you first started playing T-ball, I'd get so antsy waiting for the game to be over."

"You used to twirl around until you got so dizzy and fell flat on your ass in the dirt."

We shared a chuckle.

"Then once I was older I'd walk up and down the bleachers and around the field, over and over, waiting for that game to end. He always knew just the right time to show up with that ice cream."

"You know why he did it, right?" I glanced at her. A smile crossed her lips a she thought of the sweet memory.

"Cause he was an awesome man who knew I liked orange push-ups."

"There was that, but that wasn't the only reason. It was also for the good of the game."

She narrowed her eyes. "What are you talking about?"

"When I played T-ball, Dad caught me sneaking off the field. I saw you twirling around and I wanted to go play with you. He figured you'd sit down and be still for an ice cream."

"I was had. I mistook his bribery for gentlemanly Southern charm."

"Pretty much." I smirked.

"He continued it even up until your last season."

"Well, your bleacher walking was extremely distracting, especially as you got older and curvier."

"Noah." She pretended to be offended. "He was an incredible dad." She hugged my arm.

"Yeah, he was." I paused for a few second. "When I was wheeling that new mom across the lobby yesterday, I looked down at those little guys in her arms... for a brief second it flashed through my mind how awesome it was going to be to go to Fenway with our son and my dad."

Raising her head, Tweet propped herself up on one elbow and said, "What?"

I turned my head toward her. "Hmm?"

"You said *our* son."

I sat up, raking my hands down my face. "Shit. I'm sorry. I'm not thinking straight and..."

"Noah, stop." Her fingers curled around my forearm, tugging my hand away from my face. Our gaze connected. "It's okay."

We stared at each other. Tweet raised her hand. Her fingertips timidly moved across my jawline to my chin, grazing the outline of my bottom lip.

"Noah." She sighed, looking at me like she'd take all my pain away if possible.

"Tweet."

I placed my hand on her wrist and guided it down to my chest, pressing it to my heart. Having Tweet close gave me peace and hope that I would make it through this pain. She was my strength. I needed a break from the pain.

Let me get lost in you, Tweet.

I leaned in, the tip of our noses touched. The hot thick air surrounded us. I tilted my head and moved closer. Our lips almost touched when I felt the pressure on my chest.

"Noah, we can't do this," she said, pulling away.

I was so caught up in the moment, the pain, and in her that the words sounded like a foreign language. "What?"

"You're hurting and I'd do anything to take the pain away from you, but not like this."

Sitting back, I blinked away the haze of the moment.

"I'll be right back." Tweet must have seen the panic in my eyes, because she quickly followed up with, "Promise. I'm just going to the bathroom."

She climbed off the bed and walked out of my room. I flopped back down, breathing out a deep sigh. As much as I wanted Tweet, she was right to stop us. I knew in my heart we'd be together some day, we had to be. But it wouldn't be today and it couldn't be like this.

CHAPTER 18

Mom and I went to the funeral home the next morning to make the final arrangements for my dad. So many details had to be ironed out—choosing the casket and the type of lining for the inside, the suit Dad would wear, what prayers would be said during the service, the eulogy, the music. The list was endless. I sat beside Mom trying to stay strong for her and take all the information in. It was heartbreaking to see her this way. She looked dazed and you could feel the loneliness radiate off of her. Thankfully, Tweet came with us. Without her I wouldn't have been able to handle all the decisions that Mom was incapable of making on her own.

I had this constant need to have physical contact with Tweet. Whenever she was near me I held her hand, let my arm brush against hers, or just plain hugged her. Each time my strength wavered, I reached for her. When I felt her touch and looked into her eyes it gave me the courage to move forward.

By the time we were done at the funeral home Mom and I were completely drained. We headed back to our house. Tomorrow after the funeral, people would be coming back here and all the Kellys were helping to get the house and yard ready. Mrs. Kelly was assigning and overseeing all the activity that was taking place—friends and neighbors constantly stopping by with food and wanting to give their condolences. Mr. Kelly was outside working in our yard—cutting grass, clipping hedges, planting more flowers. He needed to keep busy, so he wouldn't fall apart. Emily was taking care of dusting and vacuuming while Tweet was assigned laundry duty.

After making sure Mom was in the capable hands of her two sisters Marie and Carol, I headed down the hallway toward my room. I needed a few minutes to decompress from the morning. My footsteps slowed as I got closer to my dad's home office. I hesitated briefly before stepping inside. I half thought I'd find him sitting behind his desk like I had so many times in the past. I walked over, rolled the chair away from the desk, and sat down.

Everything remained exactly the way he'd left it before he went to work. His calendar was opened to yesterday's date, *check flights for Noah and me,* scribbled across the note section. I starred at his handwriting like it was encoded with a top secret message. His autographed Ted Williams baseball along with the 1978 Vintage Topps Sporting News Baseball Card was displayed proudly under its acrylic dome, sitting front and center on the desk, right next to the baseball card made of me when I started T-ball. His candy jar was halfway filled with Skittles. He always had candy. When Tweet and I were kids, he used it as a bribe in order to get us to play outside while he was working. The *World's Greatest Dad* mug that I had given him when I was seven had been converted into a holder for pens and pencils. I remember how excited he acted when he opened the cheesy gift. It was as if he'd won the lottery.

I ran my palms along the armrest of the worn brown leather chair. Dad's office chair was the most uncomfortable thing in the world, but he liked it that way. He told me one time that it kept him alert, and made him work more efficiently, so he would finish before his ass got numb. Laying my head back, I closed my eyes trying to feel his presence. I needed to experience what the world felt like with him in it one more time.

Every minute detail of yesterday morning played in my head—the playful way he looked at Mom, the way his hand felt when he patted me on the shoulder, any sign that he was sick, and the sound of his last words to me.

"Have a good day at work, buddy. I love you."

Tears were building behind my lids.

God, how many tears can one person cry?

Opening my watery eyes, I swiveled the chair to the right and gazed over at the bookcase. In the corner of the second shelf was his stack of baseball caps, all Red Sox plus one College of Charleston. On the day I got my acceptance letter and signed to play for C of C baseball, Dad wore that cap proudly. I choked back a sob. He was such an awesome dad.

Closing my eyes again, I allowed my mind to go blank. My quiet escape was cut short with the ringing of my phone. Looking down at the screen, I cringed. It was Brooke. She'd been calling or texting practically every hour on the hour since she left yesterday. I ended up turning off my phone last night. I knew I was being a complete asshole to her. She was trying hard to be understanding and wanted to be with me. But if Brooke were here I couldn't have Tweet, and I *needed* Tweet.

Taking in a deep breath, my finger slid across the screen, and I reluctantly raised the phone to my ear. "Hey."

"Hey." There was a hint of annoyance in her tone.

"I'm sorry I haven't gotten back with you. It's been crazy here," I apologized.

"I wanted to come over but I didn't know if you were back from the funeral home. You know I would have gone with you. Then I thought about just coming on over and waiting…"

"No! Don't come over. I wouldn't be able to spend time with you anyway." My words came out sharp like a command.

I could hear Brooke suck in a deep breath and then slowly let it out. "The point is for me to be there for *you*. You don't have to play host to me, Noah."

"I'm sorry. I didn't mean for it to sound…"

"Is *she* there?" Brooke snapped.

"I can't do this right now."

Ever since that night we were making out in her car and Tweet's name slipped out, Brooke has been overly suspicious of any time I spend away from her. She's been pushing more for me to explain my relationship with Tweet, not buying the *just best friends* line any longer.

"Well, when can you do it? She probably *is* there. In fact, I bet you were with *her* the entire night."

"Christ, Brooke, my dad just died and my mom is a basket case."

"Are you cheating on me with *her?*"

"I've told you a thousand times she's my best friend."

"Best friends don't usually wrap themselves around each other in bed."

"I know what it must have looked like, but she's not going anywhere. She's a huge part of my life, so you'll have to get used to it if we're together."

"I don't think it's possible to get used to another girl crawling all over my boyfriend."

I huffed in frustration. To say I wasn't in the mood for this conversation would be a huge understatement. "That's up to you. I need to go. I'll see you tomorrow at the funeral." I removed the phone from my ear and pressed End.

I couldn't blame Brooke for being pissed. But just the thought of trying to get through this without Tweet caused my stomach to twist in knots. Brooke would just have to understand. There was no other option.

I walked out of the office and almost ran smack into Tweet. She had an armful of folded towels and an apologetic look across her face.

"I guess you heard that." Tweet's gaze followed the path of my hand as I mindlessly placed it on her shoulder. "You think it's weird?"

"What?"

"That I can't seem to go more than two seconds without touching you."

"It's a good weird." She gave me a slight smile.

"I'll quit if you want." She shook her head and I breathed a sigh of relief. "It's just... I feel like if I let go of you for too long, I'll lose you."

"I'm here as long as you need me. You don't have to let go until you're ready. But I don't want to cause trouble for you with Brooke. She wasn't happy last night when she saw us in your room."

"She'll be fine... eventually." The corners of my mouth curled up slightly as I leaned my shoulder against the doorframe. "Brooke is pissed. Can you believe that? My dad just died and she's pissed because I need you."

"She wants to help, Noah."

"She has to understand that what I *need* right now is you. Nobody can take your place in my life, Tweet."

Hugging the laundry to her chest, she glanced down, a pale blush popping up across her cheeks. "I better go put this up before my boss catches me slacking off."

She turned, taking a couple of steps away.

"Tweet."

Looking over her shoulder, she responded, "Yeah?"

"Thank you for being in my life."

"There's no other life I'd rather be in." She threw me a wink before heading down the hallway.

Ditto.

The funeral was surreal. Judging by what everyone kept saying, it was a beautiful service. I tried to pay attention, but my focus was singular. I comprehended what was happening, I just couldn't get my head around the fact that my dad was inside that box, and I'd never see him again. Walking behind the coffin as the pallbearers carried it out of the church, my heart sank deeper and deeper. I wanted to scream and demand God to rewind the past few days. Instead, I held my tongue, linked arms with Mom, and tried to make Dad proud.

Our house overflowed with family and friends stopping by after the burial. There was a ton of food, people chatting, family members who hadn't seen one another in years hugging. It was like a party except that the guest of honor was a no-show. Mom and I were stationed in the family room greeting people as they arrived. I had mastered the post-funeral posture—a small smile, no teeth showing, slight head tilt to the side, firm handshake for the men, and a hug for the females accompanied by two soft pats on the back between the shoulder blades.

Brooke stayed glued to my side most of the day, being very touchy-feely even for her. I wondered if somehow she could see the guilt I felt over what I had done last night. In a moment of weakness, pain, and too many beers I had crawled through Tweet's window into her room for comfort.

Tweet followed behind as I stumbled my way over to her bed, plopped down, and immediately grabbed her hips, pulling her into a hug. Her bed sat high up, bringing her chest to my eye level as she stood in front of me, my cheek resting against her warm chest.

Wrapping her arms around my neck she pulled me close, and gently combed her fingers through my hair.

"I wish I could take your pain away," she whispered, giving me a light kiss on the top of my head, causing my arms to tighten around her waist.

We stayed like this for a long while, then my fingers slowly moved underneath the skimpy T-shirt she wore. Since leaving the hospital, my concept of time was nonexistent. All I knew was it was late. Tweet was dressed for bed, wearing long pajama pants and a T-shirt. I turned my face toward her. I could feel the hardness of her nipples as I nuzzled deeper into her chest.

She tried to take a step back, which caused me to tighten my hold. I looked up into beautiful teal eyes and saw everything I would ever need in my life.

Our breathing became heavier. I never broke eye contact as I placed open-mouth kisses over her tits. The flimsy material became wet and transparent the longer I worked the area with my mouth. It felt incredible to run my tongue along Tweet's body even on top of the shirt. My skin was on fire while waves of vibrations ran through me. Tweet's fingers gripped my hair, one second trying to tug my head away and the next pushing me harder against her chest. She wanted this to happen as much as I did.

My lips moved down until I found the small spot of exposed skin right above her hip bone. A slight gasp escaped her when my tongue circled her navel and then dipped deep into it. My hands slid down her back, landing on her adorable round ass that I had dreamed about. My lips traveled slowly up her torso, inching her shirt up as I gently sucked and licked her blazing skin. My dick was about to burst through the front of my pants.

"Noah…," she said, breathlessly.

"Your skin is so soft and sweet," I mumbled against her stomach.

"We can't do this."

In one fluid movement, Tweet's fingers disentangled from my hair and her hands slid down my arms, landing on top of my hands that were glued to her ass. She pulled, trying to remove them, but I couldn't let go. I needed to get lost in her. I brushed my lips along her collarbone, nibbling my way to the spot right beneath her ear.

I inhaled a deep breath of her and whispered, "I need you. You're the only one I want. Every time I'm with her, I think of you. I need to be inside of you so bad. Please don't make me leave."

"Noah, you're drunk and hurting. You're not able to think straight. You have a girlfriend. You're not that guy. You don't cheat."

Like a bucket full of ice, reality came crashing down around me. I was being selfish. No matter where my heart belonged, I had a girlfriend. Brooke deserved more respect than this and Tweet didn't deserve to be used.

Loosening my grip, I curled my arms around Tweet's waist as hers slid behind my neck. We hugged each other so tight it was hard to catch a deep breath. My body trembled slightly as my tears dripped down her neck.

"Please don't leave me," I begged against her skin.

I couldn't remember much after that. I woke up this morning alone in Tweet's bed wearing my boxers and T-shirt. This was the second time in two days that things got intense between the two of us.

I managed to shove the guilt aside until I saw Brooke. Each time I looked in her direction, the question she asked me on the phone yesterday played in my head.

"Are you cheating on me with her?"

Even though Tweet stopped things both times before they got to the point of no return, Brooke seemed to sense something had happened. She was being a caring girlfriend while staking her claim in front of Tweet. At first, it was subtle touches of my arm or holding my hand. Then she got bolder, reaching up to brush the hair off of my forehead, then letting her hand slowly slide down the side of my face.

I tried to find comfort in Brooke's efforts but it was no use. My gaze always ended up scanning the room for Tweet when I needed strength. At one point, Tweet caught my attention, tilting her chin toward the back door, letting me know she was stepping outside. I wanted to follow her. We'd been separated most of the day and I needed to be near her for at least a few minutes.

I was listening to another one of my long-lost relatives go on and on when I noticed Brooke had left my side, was walking through the kitchen, heading out the back door.

I turned to Mom and said, "Will you be okay if I take a little break?"

Cupping the side of my face, she looked at me with hazy eyes. "Yeah, I think so." I bent down and kissed her on the cheek. "Noah, your father and I are so proud of the man you've become. We love you so much," she whispered in my ear.

She was talking as if Dad were still alive. It was going to take a lot of time for her to go from an *us* to an *I*. My parents had been together for twenty-six years. They met at a freshmen dance when they were fourteen years old. The way Dad always told the story, mom fell for him the second she laid eyes on his impressive teenage physique. The way Mom always told the story, Dad's *scrawny self* stepped on the hem of her dress, ripping it and causing her to fall flat on her face.

"I love you, Mom."

I motioned to my Aunt Marie, who was across the room, and she hurried over to take my place.

I moved through the crowd as quickly as possible, but kept getting stopped by the *sorry's* and *if there's anything we can do's*. I'd made it halfway to the kitchen when an older man, who worked with Mom, blocked me. He began with the prerequisite *sorry for your loss* before launching into some story that started with *in my day*.

Concentrating on the back door, I willed it to open and for one of the girls to walk through. It didn't matter at this point which one appeared first.

"...and I don't understand the internet stuff. My grandson was telling me about the Twitler. How you twitle and retwitle people. Then there's the other one... oh, what's it called? My Face! It all seems like a big waste of time to me. When I was young... *bah, blah, blah,*" the old man rambled.

I smiled and nodded, while my gaze bounced from the old man to the doorknob. I knew realistically only minutes had passed since the girls had gone outside, but it felt like hours.

Finally, the doorknob twisted. My breath hitched. The door opened and in walked Travis.

Inching away from my mom's co-worker, I said, "Thank you for coming, sir. We really appreciate it."

I was able to reach Travis without any more interruptions.

"Did you see the girls?" I moved to the window over the sink and craned my neck, trying to spot Tweet or Brooke.

Travis followed behind me. "What girls?"

"Tweet and Brooke are in the backyard... together... alone."

"Shit."

"Exactly," I said, looking back at him.

Just then the door opened and Tweet walked in. We locked eyes. She was more upset than before she went outside. She headed toward the family room, but I made it to her before she got there. My hand immediately landed on her arm. It felt incredible touching her.

"Are you okay, Tweet?"

"I'm fine. Just tired. I'm going to see if my boss-mom has any orders for me." She gave me a weak smile and pulled away.

The door clicked shut behind me. I spun around and saw Brooke. I couldn't read her expression, but she didn't seem upset. I walked over to her, grabbed her upper arm, guiding her over to an empty corner of the room.

"What did you say to her?" I tried not to, but even to my ears the words sounded accusatory.

"To who?"

"Tweet."

"I followed her outside because she looked upset and I thought she needed a friend. It was a good thing I did too. She's taking your father's passing pretty hard."

"And that's all y'all talked about?"

Clearing her throat, Brooke continued, "That, and she wanted to let me know how happy she is that I'm in your life, especially during this horrible time. Since she'll be busy this summer getting ready for college and then moving there, it gives her peace of mind that you can turn to me. Amanda thinks we are an awesome couple."

I should've been happy that my best friend and girlfriend were seemingly trying to get along. Not that they didn't get along. You have to associate with each other to either get along or not, and neither of them had ever made much of an effort in that direction. The fact was, I didn't want them to be friends and I sure as hell didn't want Tweet to think Brooke and I were an awesome couple.

CHAPTER 19

The week following Dad's death passed in one continuous blur. Two days after the funeral Mom insisted on going back to work. My aunts, Mrs. Kelly, and even her co-workers tried to talk her out of it. Arguing that it was too soon, she needed time for herself, to mourn the loss until she got over the heartache. My mom was a strong woman. Each time I looked at her, I knew she'd get past my dad's death, but she'd never get over his loss. Mom was going to mourn no matter where she was, work or home. You can't hide from the constant sorrow that embeds itself deep inside your heart from the abruptness of death. She needed to keep moving or she'd suffocate from the pain. I understood that because I was in the same boat.

Our surroundings looked familiar—the house, the yard, the cars, the neighborhood, the grocery store, etc. But the world felt disjointed now. In my warped thinking, trying to grab on to anything that would lessen the pain, I had convinced myself that I'd miss Dad only during the hours he was normally around, like at night, on the weekends, or at one of my games. But I missed him everywhere and all the time.

I went back to work at the hospital on the same day Mom returned to her job. Stepping through the doors for the first time since *that* day my body went into sensory flashbacks. I spent the first half of the day trying to breathe and make my arms and legs work. I talked to or texted Tweet when I got overwhelmed with the memories. Just the sound of her voice calmed me enough so that I could hold my emotions in check and not break-down at every turn.

Other than when I was at work, the majority of my hours were spent with Tweet. It was ironic how the worst week of my life ran alongside the best week of my life. Brooke had backed off somewhat, giving me what I needed, space and time. I asked Tweet again about the chat she and Brooke had after the funeral. She didn't offer up a lot of information, saying only that they had a better understanding of each other. I didn't push further. As long as I got to spend time with Tweet without it causing an argument with Brooke, I was fine with not knowing all the details.

Tweet and I were headed to *our spot*. It had become a nightly ritual this past week that I hoped would continue the entire summer. I hated that our time together felt as if it were zooming by and then she'd be leaving for college. I wasn't sure how I was going to make it through a day without her. I knew we'd call and text, but I wouldn't be able to see the reassuring look in her eyes or feel the warmth of her hug over the phone.

Once at our spot, I lifted our joined hands in the air, stiffening my arm to help her up onto the table to sit. Tweet shook her head, unlacing her fingers from mine and dropping her hand in the process. She hadn't said very much this week. Most of her time had been spent listening to me, but tonight something felt different. On our walk over here it was as if she had something she needed to say, but purposely kept silent.

Leaning back against the end of the table, I looked at Tweet standing directly in front of me. Tears had already formed in her eyes, threatening to spill over.

Confusion and concern took over my mindset. "What's going on? You've been so quiet this past week."

Tweet stood like a statue. The only movement was from her eyes as they attempted to blink away the tears. She'd been strong for me this week and it was obvious that all the emotions she held on to were now rising to the surface. She loved my dad like a second father.

Reaching out, I grabbed her wrist and scooped her into a hug. The second our bodies connected, I felt the sobs rumble in Tweet's chest before they broke free. Her arms latched around my neck, tightening with each second that ticked by. My right arm snaked around her waist, while my left angled across her back, pressing her hard against my chest. I buried my face in the crook of her neck. The scent of raspberry and vanilla consumed me. It was my turn to be strong for her.

I don't know how long we stayed holding each other before I felt her shift in my arms. She lifted her head away from my shoulder while my arms remained around her. I moved to rest our foreheads together, but she avoided the contact.

"Noah, I need to say something." Her voice was unsteady and weak.

"Okay."

She hesitated for several seconds before stepping back. I always hated how it felt when we broke from a hug. It not only left my arms feeling empty, but my heart as well.

Tweet wouldn't make eye contact with me at first. Instead, her gaze focused down on her fingers twisted together, attempting to stop the tremble in her hands.

"Promise me you'll listen before you say anything."

"What's going on Tweet?"

"Promise me," she said, finally looking up.

"Okay, I promise."

She bit down on her bottom lip, raking her teeth across it slowly, as tears rolled down her cheeks. "You are the most important person in my life. Your happiness is my number one priority. Don't ever doubt that because it will never change."

"You're scaring me." My voice cracked with emotion.

I had no idea what she was going tell me, but I had this sinking feeling that my life was about to be irrevocably changed for the second time within a week.

Squaring her shoulders, she looked directly into my eyes and tried to sound confident. "I need to step away from us for a while. Seeing you with Brooke is harder than I thought it would be."

"I'll break up with her." The words quickly flew out of my mouth with such conviction, the force knocked Tweet off balance.

"Brooke is who you should turn to now, not me. She's your girlfriend." A loud gasp escaped her as she tried to keep her emotions under control. "She's good for you, Noah."

"You're a liar. You can't stand her."

"You need to stop being so attached to me."

"Stop being so *attached* to you?" I shoved off from the table and took a step toward her.

"We're not kids anymore. I'm getting ready to go off to school…"

"Don't do this. I won't touch you again. I swear, not even a hug. You can't do this. I can't lose you too," I pleaded, moving in closer to her.

The inside of my mouth turned into a desert. Swallowing several times, I tried to get an ounce of moisture to appear. My tongue kept sticking to the roof of my mouth and my throat began closed. With each pump of my chest my lungs felt like they were filling with cement. I was on the verge of hyperventilating. A prickling pain covered my skin, like a thousand pins jabbing me all at once. I was familiar with the sensation. Its level-one devastation, a pure physiological reaction, before your mind has had a chance to process what's about to happen. I felt it a week ago when I thought Tweet was in the ER and again when I saw my dad on the stretcher. A sob pushed against my chest, the pressure intensifying the longer I stared at the determination in her eyes.

"I love you," I finally blurted out.

I was a walking contradiction, touching her whenever possible, then telling her I wouldn't, before blurting out my feelings. I grasped at anything that had a chance at stopping her from what she was about to do.

"Well, you shouldn't. I've told you over and over that I can't be with you, but you keep pushing. The truth is, I *don't* want to be with you, Noah."

Every muscle in my body tensed as I glared at her. "So this is my fault? You always said the reason we couldn't be a couple was because *you'd* do something to mess it up and we'd lose our friendship. Now you're blaming me for being too *attached*, too *clingy*?"

"No one is to blame," she squeaked out.

"Oh yeah? I blame you," I snapped.

Heat shot through my body as memories bounced from one corner of my mind to the other. All the times I showed her how I felt, told her how I felt, was patient with her, and tried to understand her screwed-up way of thinking. None of that ever sunk into her thick bullheaded skull.

"You don't give a shit about me or my happiness. All you care about is *you*. You want to dictate and control *us* in order to protect yourself."

Tweet took a step back and turned her head away.

I grabbed her chin between my thumb and index finger, forcing her gaze up to meet mine. "Don't you dare look away from me. You're not going to run this time." She froze and remained silent. "I've tried to stay away from you, to not touch you, and I've tried so fucking hard not to fall in love with you."

I moved in closer until our chests rubbed together with each heavy breath we took.

Dropping my face, so that our lips were almost touching, I gritted my teeth and said, "I know you want me in every way. I could tell that night in your room how wet you were through your pajamas. You were so ready for me to slide into you. All I did was kiss your stomach and you almost came right in my arms… didn't you?"

Deafening silence.

"Didn't you?!" I yelled, causing her body to jerk.

She inhaled a ragged breath and simply nodded.

Stepping back, I shook my head and chuckled humorlessly. "You always said I deserved better than you. Maybe you really thought it was you who deserved better than me. You always have to have everything so fucking perfect. Nothing is ever good enough. I'm not good enough."

"That's not true! *You* are perfect. I'm the loser. You deserve perfect."

"And you think Brooke is perfect for me?"

"I don't know. I just know that I'm not."

"Shut the fuck up! I'm tired of hearing you say that. All these years I hated how you looked at yourself. I know you think everyone is constantly comparing you to *perfect* Emily." I looked at Tweet through blurry eyes as I choked back a sob. "I never have and I never wanted to. I put up with you pushing me away, convincing myself that all you needed was some time. If I kept telling you how incredible you were and how much I loved you, one day you'd believe it, and stop all this bullshit. You're not a loser, Tweet. You're a coward, because you're throwing away the chance to be with the person who wants to spend the rest of his life loving you and telling you how perfect you really are."

"Please don't hate me. Once you calm down and have a chance to think clearly you'll see this is for the best right now." Her voice quivered, the words barely making it out.

I stood looking down at the ground in silence. My body was rigid, my hands rested on my hips, fingers clawing into my skin. I blew out heavy breaths as I held on to the tension in my body. If I let it go, I'd collapse. I couldn't believe she was doing this.

You fucking promised you wouldn't leave me.

The first tear splashed to the ground. Tremor after tremor coursed through my body. A second tear fell from my eye. I was not going to crumble in front of this girl. A third tear dripped, followed by a fourth, a fifth, a sixth, a seventh... until a steady stream gushed out of me.

Lifting my head slightly, I saw her out of the corner of my eye. She was still standing in the same spot. For the first time in my life, I wanted and needed to put some distance between me and my *best friend*. She had lost the privilege of seeing her effect on me.

"Get the fuck away from me." My voice was low and controlled.

"Noah..."

My head shot up, light blue eyes pierced teal ones. Her face was coated in tears, her body shaking uncontrollably. I felt the life drain from my face. She gasped, cupping her hand over her mouth.

In a slow, clear, and determined cadence, I ordered, "Get. The fuck. Away. From me. Now."

She hesitated for a moment before stepping away. I stared straight ahead as she brushed past me. The crunch of the gravel diminished as the love of my life disappeared across the park and into the darkness. With each step she took, my heart slammed harder against my chest until it completely shattered.

My gaze moved toward the table, *our table.* The blood that had drained from my body was replaced by pure adrenaline. All my systems went into overdrive—my breathing, my pulse, my temperature—all shot up to an explosive level.

I kicked at the table a few times before ramming my fist into it. The more I brutalized the piece of wood, the more my anger was fueled. Growls and grunts flew out of me along with incoherent and incomplete sentences.

"Mother fucking… selfish… bit…!"

I stumbled back. Drawing in several deep breaths, I tried to get some control of myself. There had to be another reason why Tweet did this to me now. I attempted to piece together some logical thoughts, but nothing made sense. I was fed up with trying to figure out her actions. What kind of a person abandons her best friend at the lowest point in his life?

Looking back at the table another wave of rage flooded my body. I stepped forward and grabbed the edges. Inhaling a huge breath, I flipped the table over.

"Goddamn her!"

I pounded one of the wooden legs with my foot until it finally broke off. Grabbing it, I used the last of my energy to throw it full throttle in the direction of the pond. Exhaustion took over, my knees buckled and gave way, causing me to collapse to the ground. Tears and sweat soaked my clothes and hair.

Robotically, I walked back to my house. I rounded the corner of the family room, heading to my room when my mom's voice broke through my haze.

"My god, Noah. What have you been up to?"

"I went for a run," I answered flatly.

"*Blah, blah, blah,*" she said as I continued my nonstop trek toward the bathroom.

I can't be there for Mom right now. Please don't be disappointed in me too much, Dad.

I peeled off my clothes and stepped into the shower. Hot water poured down my back as the room filled with steam. Placing my palms flat against the tile wall, I dropped my head down, letting it hang between my arms. I was numb from the inside out. As I focused on nothing, wanting my mind to stay blank, the pain slowly sliced through the numbness. Once the first cut was made, it took only seconds for it to rip me apart. I felt lightheaded. My legs shook, barely able to hold my weight. My stomach, followed by my heart, plummeted, as my body seized out of control. The bottom dropped out and the pain overpowered me.

I squinted my eyes, staring at the door in confusion. I couldn't remember driving over here. I tossed and turned in my bed for an hour after I had gotten out of the shower. I was physically drained, but my brain wouldn't shut off. Thoughts of *her* flashed through my head—the shy smile, the teal eyes, the soft curves, the laughs and dreams shared. Just when I allowed myself to enjoy how the memories felt, the picture of her walking away from me shot through my consciousness, the pain invading every corner of my body. Finally, I bolted out of bed, threw on a black T-shirt and gray cargo shorts, slipped on my black Nikes, and then jumped in my truck.

Raising my hand, I knocked on the front door. A light shined from behind the etched glass inset of the dark wood. The door swung open. Her eyes lit up and a smile broke out across her pale pink lips. She was dressed for bed in a white tank top and red shorts covered with white polka dots. Her hair fell down over her shoulders. She looked like an angel, with the light bouncing off the soft blond curls.

"Are you alone?" My voice was scratchy and hoarse.

"Yeah. Dad is on a business trip and Mom went with him."

Brooke stepped back, opening the door wider for me to walk through.

I stood in the entryway as the door clicked shut behind me.

Brooke's hand landed on the back of my shoulder. As she circled around to stand in front of me, she let her hand slide down my arm and meet up with mine.

Looking up through long blond lashes, she asked, "Are you okay?" My gaze dropped to hers. A slight chuckle drifted from her as she rolled her eyes. "God that was a stupid question. Your dad just died." Another chuckle paired with a smile appeared.

"Let's go to your room," I mumbled.

"What?"

I jerked my hand away, cupped the sides of her face, shut my eyes, and crashed my lips into hers. Brooke clung to my biceps as I backed her up toward the bedroom. Stopping abruptly, her fingers curled around my wrists, pulling my hands away from her face.

"What's gotten into you, Noah?" She gasped for air.

"Isn't this what you've been wanting?"

"Yes, but why now? Did something happen to change your mind?"

"No. I just wanted to kick the summer off with a bang." I smirked at my lame joke.

Without another word, Brooke took my hand and led me into her bedroom.

I hadn't been in Brooke's room before. I'm not sure what I expected, but it definitely wasn't the pink nightmare I had just walked into. At first I thought she had made a mistake and taken me into her younger sister's room, but then I remembered Brooke didn't have a younger sister.

The walls were covered in Pepto-Bismol pink that made me queasy. The bookshelf was pale pink and lined with a few books, some framed pictures of Brooke throughout the years, and a collection of stuffed animals. Bears, cats, lambs, unicorns, horses, all stared at me. In one corner sat a white desk and chair with a bright pink lamp and more stuffed animals, only these were miniature. The blanket covering the bed looked like a pink Muppet had been killed and skinned for Brooke's warmth and comfort. To top off the pink nightmare, hanging over the bed was a chandelier decorated with white pearls and crystal beads. Four small lamps with pink shades surrounded the fixture. The bottom edges of the shades were wrapped in pink fluffy feathery material. No doubt another Muppet sacrificing its life for Brooke's decorative desires.

A sexy smile crossed her face as she walked back toward her bed. I concentrated on the movement of her body, working hard to ignore the Muppet carnage that surrounded me. Brooke's fingers hooked under the hem of her tank top. I mimicked her by grabbing the bottom of my own shirt. We stared for several seconds, challenging each other to be the first to strip. My hesitation was confusing. I needed to move on with Brooke. There was no reason not to. She cared about me. She loved me. She looked good on paper.

Finally, I hiked my shirt over my head and let it drop to the floor. Brooke lifted her shirt, torturing me with a slow striptease. Her tits bounced slightly as they were released from the shirt. Brooke's body *was* hot. She was tall and thin, not curvy like...

You're about to fuck your girlfriend. Do not think or compare her to "the other one."

"Well, what are you waiting for, No-No?"

What was I waiting for?

To feel something.

Once I touched her I was sure I'd start responding to the hot half-naked blonde looking at me with big blue eyes full of lust. I walked over to her, grabbed her hips, pulling her into me. Her hands shot to the back of my head. Tangling her fingers through my hair, she tugged, bringing my lips down to hers. My eyes closed as I slid my tongue between Brooke's soft lips. The deeper she allowed me inside her mouth, the more my fingers dug into her hips. My dick finally woke up as I pressed it against her. Several moans rumbled out of her, each one louder than the last.

I moved her toward the bed until the back of her knees hit the edge. We tumbled down on top of the pink fur almost knocking a large yellow stuffed duck to the floor.

Brooke reached for the duck. "Watch out for Mr. Puddles."

Hovering over her, I said, "You name your stuffed animals?"

"Not all of them silly, just the special ones. And Mr. Puddles is very special." Bringing the fake fowl up to her face, she puckered her lips, kissing its felt bill. "Aren't you?"

As she gently sat Mr. Puddles to the side, I shook my head trying to clear it of what I had just witnessed. I began a trail of wet kisses across her jaw, and down her neck until I reached her chest. The entire time that fucking duck watched me. I ran my tongue across one stiff nipple before closing my lips around it and sucking it hard. Brooke's nails buried deeper into my head. Her hips rocked against me accompanied by a high-pitched squeal.

"Oh god, No-No! I love you!" she yelled out.

Her body, her movements, her moans, her voice all should have urged me on. Instead, they had the opposite effect. I stilled, dropping my forehead against her chest. I couldn't do this to her. Passing the time with Brooke waiting on Tweet to come to her senses was already bordering on using Brooke. I couldn't be with Brooke like this until I knew for sure that she'd be the one I was having sex with and not just a stand-in.

Scrunching up my face, I inhaled a deep breath, and slid off of her. Sitting on the edge of the bed, I saw out the corner of my eye Brooke propping herself up on her elbows. I took a quick glance at her. Her eyes fluttered, growing bigger and more confused with each blink.

I hung my head and whispered, "I'm sorry."

"What's wrong?" There was a slight catch in her voice.

I turned toward her and our eyes locked. "I gotta go. I'm sorry."

I bolted off the bed, snatching my shirt from the floor as I rushed out of Brooke's bedroom.

CHAPTER

20

Twisting in the passenger side of my truck, she faced me. Her eyes lit up with excitement. "This trip is going to be awesome."

Brooke had been invited to her friend, Rachel's, bachelorette party this weekend. Rachel lived in Columbia, South Carolina—the state capital, where the famous Five Points shopping district was located, and home of the fighting Gamecocks of USC. Travis was in his sophomore year at the university and had been begging me for months to come hang out for the weekend. Since I didn't like the idea of Brooke traveling alone, this seemed like the perfect opportunity.

The guilt I felt after running out of Brooke's bedroom was relentless. Because of it, I made more of an effort to be an actual boyfriend. I explained to her that I hadn't been thinking straight that night. That the emotions of the week had me out of sorts. Our first time needed to be special and I wanted a clear head for when that time came. She said she understood and that it was okay. She never asked if Tweet had anything to do with my behavior. In fact, she hadn't mentioned Tweet since the funeral, nor had she commented about us heading straight into Tweet territory this weekend. Brooke wasn't an insecure girl. Confidence oozed out of each pore. She was, however, the suspicious type, but apparently, the increased attention I was giving her had helped relax her suspicions.

Placing her hand on my thigh, she said, "Are you excited?"

I glanced over with a smirk. "Yeah. It will be great to hang out with Travis."

It was the weekend before Thanksgiving, six months since Dad had died and I had any contact with Tweet. My life was split into two time dimensions. In the first one, days and months flew by at lightning speed. Mom and I missed Dad every day and it was hard to believe months had passed since we last saw him. But we were moving forward, focusing less on the painful memories and more on all the great times we shared with him. The second dimension was the Tweet time warp.

Tweet-time dragged on so slowly that it felt like it never budged. Each day we were apart the hole in my life expanded. I *tried* to stay angry at her. I *wanted* to stay angry at her. She *deserved* for me to stay angry at her. And I *was* angry at her… for about a week. As the days leading up to our break up replayed in my head, I understood why she did what she did.

Until Dad's death Tweet and I had managed to stay within the boundaries she had set for our friendship. It was a struggle, but we maintained the friend zone pretty well. When Dad died, our instincts kicked in. I turned to her and she was there for me. One hug became two, two became three, and three became four, etcetera. Our gaze lingered, our hands squeezed harder, and the innocent kisses on the cheek moved closer to the corners of the mouth. And then there were the two times we almost let nature take its course. It was obvious that neither one of us had a lot of self-control when the other was involved. Before we knew it the line blurred even more than before. She tried to get us back on track, even though it was a shitty way to go about it.

Brooke unbuckled her seatbelt and scooted closer to me. Her hand slid to my inner thigh while she placed light kisses up and down my neck.

Sucking in a quick breath, I shrugged. "We're gonna crash if you keep that up."

Her chin rested on my shoulder. "How about we get a hotel room for the night?"

"I thought all the girls were staying at Rachel's place."

Brooke may not have questioned me anymore about that night in her room, but she kept dropping not so subtle hints about us having sex. I really cared for Brooke, but every time I closed my eyes I still saw Tweet.

"They are, but I don't have to."

"You'll probably be out late, though," I countered.

She moved back to her side of the truck, buckled her seatbelt, and stared straight ahead. Something was going to have to give soon. My girlfriend wanted to have sex and I was running out of plausible excuses to hold off.

I reached over, placing my hand on top of hers. "We'll have our time. I just don't want to fit it in during a busy weekend."

I squeezed her hand slightly. When her head turned in my direction, I held her gaze for a brief second and gave her a smile. She flipped her hand over, pushing her fingers between mine... and held on tight.

"I know... it's just with us both living at home and being busy with classes... we don't have a lot of chances to be alone for any length of time. It's frustrating, Noah. I love you and I want to show you how much."

That was another thing I was going to have to deal with soon... those three words that Brooke liked to say... often. I found it weird that she never got upset when I didn't return them. She always went along with my subject change, never showing one sign of being hurt. The *I love yous* continued to flow out of her mouth regularly, like she had them scheduled in two-hour increments.

"Don't worry. You show me all the time how you feel. Those cookies you made me last week were tasty."

"I have something else that you might enjoy tasting." The fingertips of her free hand skimmed the length of my arm, causing a shiver to run through my body.

"Did you bring brownies?" I teased, needing to lighten the mood.

Brooke released my hand and shoved it away. When I glanced over, she had her arms folded in front of her chest, her bottom lip poking out in a pout, as her gaze froze out the windshield.

Unlike Tweet, Brooke wasn't much on teasing, unless she was the teaser. The way this usually played out was—I'd let her act like an eight-year-old for ten to fifteen minutes, then say something that I knew would make her smile. She'd pretend for another few seconds that she was mad before giving in. Our relationship was routine, predictable, and generic.

I let the silence hang in the air for another... *three, two, one.*

"So that'd be a *no-ah* on the brownies?"

Half a second later the corners of her mouth curled up.

After dropping Brooke off at her friend's, I drove around exploring the USC campus, hoping to get a glimpse of Tweet. At first, I wondered if she went home this weekend, but with the Thanksgiving break a few days away, I doubted she'd bother.

The rest of the afternoon was spent helping Travis and his frat brothers get ready for the party they were throwing that night.

Travis and I were hanging out in his dorm room drinking a couple of beers he smuggled in before heading back out for the party.

Sitting at the standard-issue dorm desk, I tilted the bottle up to my lips and took a swig.

"If there's gonna be free beer tonight, why did we go buy this stuff?"

"The shit they serve at the frat house tastes like piss," he said, cracking open another beer.

Travis sat across from me, his back leaning against the wall and long legs sprawled over his bed.

"You're quite the wordsmith."

"Of course I am. Why do you think my major is English?" I chuckled and took another swig of beer. "So, how have things been?"

"Fine. Classes are pretty good. You know I decided not to play baseball this year. I need to focus on the books. And…"

"I don't mean that bullshit."

Travis was the only one who knew what happened between me and Tweet. He also knew I had ulterior motives for coming up here this weekend. He planned on keeping me busy over the next two days so I couldn't follow through on those motives.

"I'm getting by," I answered.

In reality, I'd been miserable, although I slapped a smile on my face and pretended like everything was good. Two of the most important people in my life had disappeared. There was nothing I could do about my Dad other than adjust and accept the fact that he was gone. But with Tweet there was no acceptance.

I knew that to Travis, I looked like some pussy-whipped idiot wasting time. He didn't get why I wasn't satisfied with Brooke. The thing was, Travis had no frame of reference. He'd never been in love. How could I explain Tweet and I, when his soul hadn't connected with its mate yet? There was no way he'd be capable of understanding the completeness I felt when she was with me and the pull I experienced when I knew she was out there.

I fidgeted with the beer label, peeling off a corner, while I considered whether or not to ask him the one question I'd been dying to know the answer to since Tweet left for school.

I lifted my gaze to the ceiling, not wanting to see his expression when I said, "Have you seen her?"

"Seen who?"

I dropped my look to him. "Don't do that. You know *who*."

"Yeah, I've seen *who*."

"How'd she look?"

"Hot as usual. Looks like she lost some weight."

I leaned forward. "She didn't need to lose any weight. Had she been sick?" Even I could hear the panic in my voice.

"Dude, I said she looked hot."

I relaxed back in my chair. "Have you talked to her?"

"When are you going to stop this?"

"Stop what? She's a friend."

"Callin' bullshit!" he said, shaking his head.

"I'm concerned about all my friends."

"Call-ing bullshiot!"

We both concentrated on finishing our beers before I pushed him for more information.

"Have you talked to her?"

"Dude!" he snapped.

"What? I'm just trying to make conversation."

"Come on." He waved his hand toward himself. "This is your one and only shot. Get it all out now 'cause I'm not spending the entire night talking about your girl. They'll be a lot of lovelies vying for my attention. They gotta stock up on the Travis experience to get them through the holiday break."

I knew it was probably just a slip of the tongue, but a small smile crossed my lips when he referred to Tweet as *my girl*.

I seized the opportunity and repeated. "Have you talked to her?"

"Yes, a few times."

"And…" I was annoyed at his dribble of information.

"She said hey and see ya around."

"Did she ask about me?"

Travis slid off his bed and walked to his dresser. Raking his hand through his hair, he checked out his reflection in the mirror.

"She wanted to know how you were. I told her you were great. End of story."

"What was her reaction?"

Quirking one brow, he looked up in search for the words. "I don't know… blank."

Blank? That could also mean sad.

"Is she with anyone?" I needed to get as much out of him as I could while he was willing to talk.

He didn't answer right away. I hated that he didn't answer right away because it meant I wasn't going to like the answer.

He put his USC baseball cap on and blew out a deep breath. "I've seen her around with a couple different guys."

Clenching my jaw, I bared down, grinding my teeth together. Deep long intakes of oxygen, followed by quick exhales, pumped from my body. It sounded like a mad bull just before skewering a matador. I grabbed the edge of the chair, grounding myself, so I wouldn't bolt out of the room and blindly go track down these Smurffuckers.

"Let's go have fun and not... Fuck!" Travis huffed.

I turned my attention toward him. "What?"

"That look."

"Yeah... so."

"My balls and dick just got hoovered up into my body. Damn Stewart, I really needed those tonight."

Travis's dorm was within walking distance of the frat house. The booming base of the music, laughter, and squeals could be heard before the place was even in view. As we approached the steps leading up to the porch, a tall lanky dude placed his hand on Travis's shoulder, pulling him to the side for some type of frat boy business.

"Go on inside and grab us a couple of beers. I'll come find you when I'm done," Travis instructed as he and the lanky dude walked around to the back of the house.

I walked up the steps to the front door, squeezing between the overflow of bodies on the porch. Inside looked like the typical frat party. Every inch of the place was covered with bodies—some standing, most drinking, some dancing, a handful already passed out, and some hooking up.

The minute I walked through the door, I heard it and felt her. "Everything" by Lifehouse poured out from the speakers, drifting over the noise of the crowd. My pulse sped up and my breathing became shallow. I did a quick scan of the room and eyed a guy tugging a dark-haired girl toward the back of the house. I didn't know for sure that it was Tweet, too many people were blocking my view. I slowly maneuvered my way in their direction and then I heard her voice.

"Matt, I don't want to!"

I shoved and elbowed drunk bodies out of the way, giving me a clear path to Tweet and the motherfucker who had her hands pinned behind her back. Without slowing down, I grabbed a fistful of the guy's shirt and yanked him off of Tweet.

"Shit! What are you doing, dude?!" the asshole yelled.

"She doesn't want to go with you, dickhead."

My gaze concentrated on Tweet while I tightened my grip on the guy. Her eyes doubled in size when she realized who was standing in front of her. Travis was right. Tweet looked thinner but hotter than ever.

I was so caught up in Tweet that my grip loosened, allowing the asshole to shrug free. "I'm her boyfriend," he spit out.

Hearing those words come out of his mouth felt like a punch to the gut.

"I don't give a fuck who you are. She's not going anywhere with you," I snarled.

"Fuck you, dude. Come on, Stick."

Stick? Who the hell was that?

The asshole reached for Tweet's arm. She stepped out of the way as I grabbed his shirt and spun him around. One blow to his stomach and then his jaw had him stumbling back, falling into the crowd of people behind him. I took hold of Tweet's hand, weaved us through the room and out the door.

Once we reached the front yard, my body jerked back as Tweet stopped walking and pulled her hand from mine.

God I've missed the feel of her skin.

Her eyebrows furrowed as she blinked her beautiful teal eyes in disbelief. "Noah? What are you doing here?"

I turned, moving in closer to her. "Are you okay? Are you hurt anywhere?" Tweet shook her head. "It's cold, put this on."

I shrugged off my jacket and held it open for her. As her arms slipped through the sleeves, the familiar scent of raspberry and vanilla swirled around me.

Wrapping the jacket around her, I said, "I'll go back and get your coat later."

"How did you know where I was?" She still sounded like she was in a daze.

"I didn't know. I walked in and…"

Felt you.

"…saw you. Brooke came up here for a bachelorette party with some of her girlfriends."

The strangest look appeared on Tweet's face. Tears filled her eyes, spilling down over her cheeks. Before I knew what was happening, she brushed by me and left.

"Tweet!"

I hadn't said her nickname in months. It felt incredible passing over my lips again even though I was yelling as she hightailed it away from me.

She was moving fairly quickly, but I managed to keep her in sight. Each time I called out her name, she gained more speed until she broke out into a full run. My arms and lungs pumped faster as I matched her steps.

When the hell did she get so fast?

We had run three blocks when Tweet made a sharp right toward the campus. She got halfway across the courtyard when I saw her crash to the ground. I amped up my speed and tore off toward her.

By the time I reached her, she was sitting up, rubbing her left ankle. She was crying harder now. I fell to my knees next to her.

"Are you okay?" I gasped.

"Just leave me alone, Noah."

"I'm not leaving you alone out here. Why did you run from me?"

Without answering, Tweet struggled to stand and then tried to take a few steps. She barely touched her foot to the ground when her face squished up, wincing in pain. I got to my feet and reached for her arm, but she pulled it away. She tried to take another step, but then fell into a heap on the ground.

Damn, she was hardheaded.

I knelt back down next to her. "Would you let me help you?"

Turning her head in the opposite direction, she choked out, "Noah, just go back to your fiancé."

"Is that why you ran from me?" She stayed quiet while continuing to rub her ankle. "Tweet, she's here for a friend. It's not Brooke's bachelorette party. I haven't asked anyone to marry me."

My cheeks were on the verge of hurting due to the ginormous smile slapped across my face.

You still love me, Tweet.

"Then why are you here?" She wiped away a tear with the back of her hand.

"Travis goes here and has been asking me to come up. Brooke didn't want to drive all this way alone. I figured it would be safer for her if I came, and…"

"How boyfriendy of you."

There's the smartass mouth I love and missed.

"…*and* I was hoping to see you."

Finally, she gazed up. I took my time examining her gorgeous face.

"God, I've missed you. You have no idea how much," I whispered.

Moving in closer, I cupped the sides of her face and ran my thumbs along her tearstained cheeks. "I hate when you cry, Tweet." The shy smile that I thought about every day for the past six months tugged at her lips. "Let me take care of you."

I stood, extending my hand to Tweet. When our palms made contact, an electric jolt passed between us. I could tell she felt it too. Not one thing had changed in six months. She was still *my girl.*

Gently, I pulled her to a standing position.

"Can you walk?" I asked.

She timidly placed the foot down, but immediately drew it back. Biting down on her bottom lip, she shook her head. I scooped Tweet up, cradling her in my arms. My breathing accelerated and warmth traveled through every inch of me. The feel of her body in my arms soothed the ache that had taken up permanent residence in my chest for the past six months.

"Won't Brooke be mad if she finds out you carried me all the way back to my dorm?"

Swinging Tweet from side-to-side, my gaze scanned the area. Laughter bubbled up and burst out of her.

"I don't see her around. Besides, she wouldn't want me to leave you out here. She's not like that, Tweet."

I was seventy-five percent sure Brooke wasn't like that.

Tweet's lips pursed into a straight line. I could tell she was holding back one of her choice smartass remarks.

Following her directions, we headed toward Tweet's dorm. We didn't say much as we made the trek across the campus. I was too distracted by the feel of Tweet's arms around my neck and the friction between our bodies caused by the slight jostling as I walked.

Tightening her hold around my neck, Tweet shifted, causing her chest to press against mine. My body reacted and walking got... *harder.*

"Oh, by the way, I live on the fourth floor." Her lips were only a few inches away from mine.

"Okay," I answered, swallowing hard.

Christ, everything was getting harder—walking, swallowing, breathing. Stop thinking about getting hard.

"And there's no elevator." Her eyebrows pushed up to her forehead as she threw me a smirk.

I wasn't sure I'd be able to make the entire trip without taking a break. Tweet wasn't heavy at all. It had been a long time since we were this close and my body craved even the slightest contact with hers. I needed to calm things down.

Cy Young holds the record for most wins at 511.

She rested her head on my shoulder.

Top three record holders for consecutive games played. Cal Ripken, Jr., at 2,632. Lou Gehrig, at 2,130. And Everett Scott, 1,307.

Nuzzling into my chest, a breathy sigh escaped her.

Travis' naked ass.

CHAPTER
21

I was relieved to find out Tweet actually lived on the second floor, not because I was tired of carrying her. I wanted to hold her for the rest of my life. But with each step across campus my body's reaction took control. There weren't enough baseball stats in the world to keep my mind focused. When picturing Travis's naked ass didn't cool things down, I picked up the pace, practically jogging the last block.

I was still holding her as she unlocked the door to her room. Once inside, she reached back to the wall, flipping on the overhead light, and then pointed to the bed across the room. I put her on the bed, helped her take my jacket off, and sat down next to her. Tweet shifted, angling her body toward me. Sliding my hand behind her ankle, I carefully lifted, and then placed it in my lap. My gaze shot to hers when I felt her body tense in pain. When our eyes locked, she immediately relaxed. Heat radiated through my chest at the trust she still had in me.

Slowly, I removed her shoe and sock. The ankle was already starting to swell and a mild bruise had formed on the top of her foot. I gently ran my hand over the area, pressing slightly, to see if she had broken a bone. Nothing felt unusual.

I placed my palm on the sole of her foot and asked, "Can you push on my hand?"

Inhaling a deep breath, she tentatively flexed the foot. Tweet bit down on her lower lip as her eyes shut, crinkling at the edges.

Her foot was cold to the touch. Taking my other hand, I placed it on top, sandwiching her foot between my palms, in an attempt to warm it up a little.

"I think we should go to the hospital, Tweet."

"It's just a little sore," she said, holding her breath.

"Let me take you, just to be on the safe side."

"I'll be fine." Wiggling her toes to prove her point.

God, she was stubborn.

"I'm at least going to get some ice for the swelling."

Her chin dipped slightly as a sweet smile worked its way over her face.

Luckily, there was a twenty-four-hour convenience store directly across the street. I made a quick trip to pick up some ice. Before heading back I texted Travis to let him know where I disappeared to... kind of.

Me: *I met up with an old friend. Will check in later.*

Travis: *Hope you know what you're doing. By the way, a redheaded lovely found my dick and balls.*

Me: *So she's a Microbiology Major.*

Travis: *Fuck you. :)*

Running up the stairs to Tweet's room, I felt more energized and happier than I had in six months. I lightly tapped on her door as I let myself in. My lungs fully expanded at the sight of her sitting on the bed waiting for me. It never ceased to amaze me how *right* things felt whenever she was around.

"Dude, that's a lot of ice," she teased, squishing up her face.

I may have overdone it with the five-pound bag of ice.

"It won't go to waste. You have ginormous ankles." Her head tilted to the side as she looked up at me and laughed. "It's nice to hear that again."

"What?"

"Your laugh." I admitted.

Not only had I brought Tweet ice, but also a little surprise, but that would have to wait. I tossed the shopping bag onto her absent roommate's bed, then took the ice into the bathroom. I grabbed a small towel but then realized I needed something to put the ice in so it wouldn't melt all over her.

Poking my head out the door, I said, "Do you have like a plastic sandwich bag?"

"Yeah, I think Lisa keeps some on top of the mini-fridge."

I snagged the bag and went back to work. Scooping up a couple of handfuls of ice, I placed them in the Ziploc, and then wrapped it in a towel.

She scooted up to the head of the bed, leaning back on four huge pillows propped against the wall. I joined her, sitting far enough away, so that her foot rested comfortably in my lap. I rubbed my hand over the towel- covered ice, trying to warm it a little so the cold wouldn't be such a shock, and then lowered it onto her ankle.

"Does that feel alright?"

She nodded. "Thank you, Noah. Sorry you had to carry me all the way here."

"No problem. You aren't as heavy as you used to be."

She sat up slightly, grabbed one of the pillows from behind her, and bopped me on top of the head. For the first time in months genuine laughter flew out of my mouth.

"Are you saying I was fat before?"

"No!" Cocking an eyebrow, I smirked at her. "Your curves are awesome and nicely arranged."

The pink on her cheeks darkened, as my eyes involuntarily scanned her body. I swallowed hard and then swung my gaze around the room, hoping to ride out the flirt.

Tweet's half of the room suited her. On the wall I was leaning against, hung a large quilt with a multicolored pattern of a bookshelf stacked with books. On the other wall, at the head of the bed, was a poster of an antique typewriter with famous literary quotes hovering above it. Her bed was covered with a gray comforter and the four big pillows were a mix of garnet and gold, which were USC's colors.

The only plan I had coming up here this weekend was to track down Tweet. What I did when I found her was another question. I didn't know if I would even be talking with her, let alone sitting in her dorm room by ourselves. This was my shot to get her back in my life and I wasn't going to waste it.

I cleared my throat and glanced over at her. "Um… Tweet?"

"Yeah?"

My mouth suddenly went dry. I sucked on the inside of my cheeks, trying to get the spit flowing before taking a big gulp of air.

"I've missed you." Looking down, I shook my head. "No, I've more than missed you. It's like when my dad died…" I saw the sadness in her eyes as she thought back to that time. "I couldn't imagine a life without him. Nothing would bring him back, so I had to adjust. But there's still an emptiness that I can't fill. You and my parents have always been the three most important people in my life."

You're rambling. Get to the point, dumbass.

"I've been going through the motions each day, mainly for my mom's sake. Being here with you… laughing and joking… It's the first time I've done that since you left that wasn't fake." Pausing for a moment, I summoned up the courage and then said, "I need you."

I blinked away the moisture in my eyes. I had been disappearing in the sadness. I didn't realize how numb I'd become until I saw Tweet again. She made me feel.

"What about Brooke? How do you think she'd react to me being around again?"

Shit! Brooke.

"I think she'll be fine with it... eventually. Besides, Brooke doesn't dictate who my friends are."

"You don't hate me for what I did?" she asked, glancing down at her fidgeting hands.

Placing my finger under her chin, I lifted it up until her gaze met mine. "I could never hate you, Tweet." I stared for a moment, soaking her in. The familiar crackle of electricity surrounded us. I needed to tone it down or she'd be scared off. "I did, however, severely dislike you for a while."

I threw her a wink.

"I'm sorry I hurt you like that. I was just wanting..." Her voice cracked with emotion. "I think I understand why you did it. I promise I will stay completely in the friend zone. I will not tempt you at all with my body."

She giggled. "Okay."

"Really?" The shock and excitement in my tone was evident.

I couldn't believe she wasn't putting up a fight, giving me one excuse after another or spouting off lame-ass rules we needed to follow. She simply nodded her head in agreement.

"Don't take this the wrong way, but I'm so glad you fell."

"Yeah me too."

We stared for several seconds, exchanging smiles in the process. I wanted to lunge at her, wrap my arms around her body, and stay by her side for the rest of the night. Instead, I opted for a slightly subtle approach, the small surprise I had bought her.

"Hold this on your ankle for a second. I got you something," I told Tweet.

Gently lifting her leg, I took the pillow she swatted me with earlier and propped up her foot. I walked over to the roommate's bed where I had tossed the bag, dug through it, and got what I needed. I went back and sat on the bed, hiding the items behind my back.

"Well, what is it?" Tweet wasn't a very patient person.

"Close your eyes," I said. She did as she was told for once.

"Don't open them until I say so."

"I won't."

"Promise?"

"Mmmhmm."

"Say it." I tried to sound demanding but she could hear the humor in my voice.

She giggled. "I promise I won't open my eyes."

"Good." I brought the items around, holding them in front of her. "Okay, open your eyes."

Beautiful teal eyes looked back at me, not even noticing what I was holding. I glanced down. Tweet took the cue, letting her gaze drop. Her head lifted, with sparkling eyes and a huge smile plastered across her face. You would have thought I'd just given her a pot of gold instead of a box of chocolate snack cakes, the container of chocolate frosting, and the plastic spoon.

"Hey bestie. It's great to have you back." The corners of my mouth curled up, forming the first *real* smile I'd had in months.

"It's great to be back."

We ate cake and frosting. Well, Tweet actually ate the frosting, while we caught up each other up on our lives. She told me Emily had moved back to Charleston after law school and was working at a firm downtown, specializing in corporate law. She had just bought a condo in the historic Radcliffborough section of town. I already knew all of this. Our mothers talked daily. But I didn't stop her. I loved the sound of her voice too much. I could listen to her talk forever. She went on to tell me how much she loved her classes. Then filled me in on her roommate, who sounded great and more than a little crazy.

When it was my turn, I filled her in on how much I liked the College of Charleston and that I decided not to play baseball this year. I told her, like I told everyone, it was to focus on my classes. But by her expression, I could tell she saw right through me and understood the real reason. The game hadn't been the same for me since Dad's death. I was sure I'd learn to love it again someday. It was just going to take time.

We were both enjoying being back together so much that we avoided the subject of Brooke and the asshole from the party as long as possible.

I was leaning back against the wall, massaging Tweet's ankle when my phone chirped with a text. I looked at it and smirked. It was a picture from the bachelorette party. Brooke was wearing a tiara, and a bright pink feather boa, posing seductively with a male blowup doll with the message, *I'd like to come blow you. Where you at?*

"Brooke?" Tweet asked.

"Yeah. She sent me a picture. Looks like they're having a good time."

I typed out a quick reply.

Me: *Ha-ha. I'm beat. Headed to bed. See you tomorrow. Have fun.*

I switched my phone to silent before tossing it to the side.

"You can go if you want. I'm fine. Thanks for taking care of me..." The words shot out of Tweet's mouth like a machine gun firing.

"Stop it. I'm not going anywhere."

"I don't want to cause any problems for you, Noah."

"You're not."

"Are you in love with her?" Her body jolted once she realized what she just asked.

I slowly let out a deep sigh. I was torn about how to answer. The answer was a definite no. I didn't love Brooke. How could I when the girl in front of me had always owned my heart? I had to be careful of my words. I didn't want to step over the newly drawn line and scare Tweet off. But I wasn't about to lie to her either.

"Honestly? Between my dad passing away, taking care of my mom, and missing you, I haven't thought about my feelings for Brooke. I know I sound like a dick."

Her warm hand landed on top of mine. "You're just being honest. You've had a lot to deal with this year."

"She tells me she loves me all the time. I never say anything back. I just smile and change the subject." I paused for a moment. "I care about what happens to her."

"I shouldn't have asked you."

"You can ask me anything, Tweet. I just don't know how to answer you right now."

"Fair enough," she said.

"So who was that Smurffucker you were with at the party?" I asked, keeping my tone calm and controlled.

My jaw inadvertently clenched as the veins in my neck pushed against my skin. I was trying hard not to go all jealous boyfriend.

"His name is Matt. And you know, I don't refer to Brooke as Princess Bitchella." She gave me a sarcastic smirk.

There's that smart mouth I love.

"You've been thinking on that one for a while haven't you?"

"Nope. Actually, it just came to me."

"Matt..." The name left a bad taste in my mouth. "Is he your boy... friend?"

"Yes."

Knots of queasiness twisted in my stomach. This Matt was a grade-A asshole. I could tell the second I laid eyes on him. I kept my cool and continued to ask her about him in a calm manner.

"Why does he call you Stick?"

"It's just a stupid nickname he gave me."

"I heard what he said to you, Tweet."

"How long had you been at the party? I walked all over that place and never saw you."

"I had just walked in when I saw you and... Matt." I cringed saying his name. "Has he forced you to do anything you didn't want to do?"

She shook her head. "No." There was a hint of defensiveness in her voice.

Her gaze shifted down. I knew right then and there, I'd be getting Travis to enlist some of his big frat brothers to keep an eye on Matt the mother fucker.

"He's not usually like that. He was drunk. He's a theater major and is under a lot of pressure with this upcoming production... plus with classes..."

She was rambling and fidgeting with the hem of her shirt. I placed my hand on top of hers, stopping the fidgeting.

"Does he treat you right, Tweet?" Not looking up, she nodded. "If he does anything to hurt you, I'll make sure every fucking bone in his body gets broken."

Note to self: Tell Travis—Every. Fucking. Bone.

At 2 am, the door to Tweet's room slowly creaked open and a glassy-eyed redhead, who I assumed was Tweet's roommate, poked her head in cautiously.

"You can come in," Tweet told her.

The girl staggered over to her bed and plopped down. She never once glanced in our direction.

"Lisa?" Tweet said.

"Mmmhmm?"

"This is Noah."

Lisa's eyes shot open as she bolted upright.

Swinging her legs over the side of the bed, Lisa turned toward us, blinking. "*The* Noah?"

I glanced over at Tweet, curious to know how I got the title.

"Yes." Tweet chuckled, rolling her eyes.

I slid to the edge of the bed and extended my hand. "Hey, it's great to meet you, Lisa."

Her drunk gaze bounced from my face to my hands a few times before she finally slipped her palm into mine.

"Well, hellooo, *The* Noah. It's really great to see you... here... with Amanda."

She looked back and forth between me and Tweet. A huge grin slowly appearing on her face.

"I guess I should be going." I stood and collected the trash from our snack.

Lisa jumped up, swayed a little to the left, and then intercepted me. "I'll take that for you, so you can say toodles to each other."

She walked to the other side of the room, pretending to give me and Tweet some privacy, while blatantly glancing over her shoulder at us.

Turning to Tweet, I said in a low voice, "I'm not sure what time I'm heading back tomorrow. I want to see you before I go, but I don't know if I'll be able to. You know?"

"I know."

"I'll definitely talk to you tomorrow."

"And I'll be home for Thanksgiving in a few days." Her face lit up with excitement.

God, *I don't want to leave.*

We must have stared at each other for what Lisa felt was an abnormal amount of time because it sounded as if she were hacking up a lung trying to get our attention. Leaning down, I placed a kiss on Tweet's forehead. I couldn't help closing my eyes and savoring the feel of her skin.

"Goodnight, Tweet," I whispered against her.

"Goodnight, Noah."

I turned to Lisa who had gotten a little closer to the action, standing only about a foot away from me. "Goodnight, Lisa."

"Goodnight, *The* Noah."

I smiled, looking over at Tweet. Apparently, I lingered a little too long again for Lisa's taste, because it sounded like the other lung was getting ready to make an appearance. Before the girl lost any more organs, I grabbed my phone, my jacket, and headed out the door.

When I got back to his dorm, I was surprised to see a sleeping Travis and shocked to see him alone in bed. I stripped down to my boxers, leaving my T-shirt on, and crawled into the other bed. On my back, hands behind my head, I lay in the dark, grinning, and feeling alive again.

"About time you showed up," Travis mumbled.

"Sorry. I didn't mean to wake you. I lost track of time."

"Mmmhmm."

"How's your redhead?"

"Satisfied. How's your *old friend?*"

"Back where she belongs."

The next morning I woke up early and headed over to the frat house to get Tweet's coat. The place looked like a massacre. Passed out drunk bodies covered almost every inch of the main room—sprawled over sofas, chairs, tables, the stairs, and the floor. I walked down the hallway, opening doors until I found the designated pile of coats and jackets. I recognized Tweet's coat immediately. I was with her last year on the day she bought it. I started to leave when my phone chirped with a text.

Brooke: *Good morning No-No. I missed you last night. Rachel is going to drop me off at Travis's dorm in a half hour. We can go grab breakfast. See you in a bit.*

Me: *Okay.*

My mind was spinning trying to figure out how I could see Tweet before meeting up with Brooke. I wasn't ready to tell Brooke that Tweet was back in my life. Before walking out of the room, I raised Tweet's coat and inhaled her scent. It would have to hold me for the next few days until I saw her again.

I pulled into the parking lot of Travis's dorm with five minutes to spare before Brooke was to show. Picking up my phone, I had every intention of calling Tweet to let her know I wouldn't be able to see her today. But I knew if I heard her voice, I'd be too tempted to put the truck in reverse and haul myself over to her place, so I sent a quick text.

Me: *Mornin' Tweet. How's your ankle?*

Tweet: *A little better. Thx.*

Me: *Not able to stop by. Sorry.*

Tweet: *That's ok. Have a safe trip home.*

Me: *Last night was amazing. See you in a few days. Look outside your door.*

Tweet: *Ok. Just a sec.*

When several seconds had passed, I smiled, knowing full well she hadn't noticed what I had put at her door. Her coat was in a shopping bag that Brooke had left in my truck. In front of that was something I knew would make her smile, a wind-up yellow bird Koosh toy.

Me: *Look down.*

Three.
Two.
One.

Tweet: *Thx for getting my coat back and for my tweet. I love it!!!!!!! :)*

Me: *:)*

CHAPTER
22

Vibrations ricocheted through my body each time my foot slammed against the concrete. The only evidence of the cold and that I was still breathing, were the spurts of hot air morphing into puffs of white smoke the second they hit the atmosphere. My neighborhood whizzed by me, so I knew I was moving, but it felt like I was sinking in quicksand. The repetitive thumping of my heartbeat drowned out all other sounds. When the words tried to bulldoze their way into my mind, I shoved them away. I had to focus on getting to her and not on *those* words. If I allowed them to invade my thoughts, I'd collapse.

I found her exactly where I knew she'd be, at our spot. Why none of the others thought to check here first was beyond me. I stopped at the edge of the park, placing my hand against the bare-leaf large oak tree, catching my breath, and trying to gain the courage I needed to have for her.

The overcast sky covered everything in gray tones. There was an eerie stillness surrounding our spot. The park was quiet except for the sound of her phone blowing up with calls and texts. We were only two days into our

Christmas break. With the semester ending and exams, I hadn't seen Tweet since Thanksgiving. Brooke had gone out of town for the holiday, so Tweet and I spent the entire time together. Even though we talked and texted several times a day, there was nothing like having her by my side.

She was sitting on the new picnic table. The one I'd destroyed last summer had been replaced. Her back faced me, shoulders slumped, as she stared straight ahead. The sleeves of the USC hoodie she wore were pulled down over her hands. She was cold. As I approached, the crunch of dry grass, leaves, and gravel sounded ten times louder in the bubble Tweet and I were in.

"Tweet." That was the only word that came out before I felt the tremor in my throat.

I moved in closer, my arms ready to hold and protect her. She leaned away and held up her hand, signaling me to stop.

"Don't touch me," she said, in a weak voice.

Please let me take care you.

"Why?"

"Because, if you touch me, I'll fall apart. I've already pulled myself back together once today. I don't think I could do it again."

I sent a text to her parents and Emily to let them know I found her, she was safe, and I'd bring her home when she was ready. I sat next to her on the table, but kept a safe distance. I was going to give her whatever she needed. If she needed space, then she got space, even if it meant I had to wait the rest of the day and night before wrapping her in my arms. Tweet would talk when she was ready.

As the silence ticked by, my mind drifted back to earlier.

Mom and I were wading through our year of "firsts" without Dad. The first Fourth of July, my first college semester, the first autumn, and the first holiday season. The Kelly's had been incredibly supportive over the past months, having us over for dinner several times a week, but ramped it up big time as the holidays approached. I had been at Brooke's and told her that I needed to leave in order to help Mrs. Kelly put up some Christmas decorations as a thank you for all the dinners.

Walking through the back door of the Kellys' home, I felt the tension immediately. My gaze landed first on Mr. Kelly, who was pacing back and forth in the family room. His expression was blank. I was confused as to why he was home this early from work. Then I saw my mom sitting on the sofa with her arm draped over Mrs. Kelly's shoulders. Emily was on the other side of her mom, holding her hand. All three women were in varying stages of crying.

Mom's head shot in my direction as I took a few steps forward.

"Noah, thank god you're here," Mom said, standing and walking toward me.

"What's going on?"

She wrapped me in a hug. "I need to tell you something."

In that moment, I decided to do a mental head count. Everyone who was important to me was in this room except for the most important one.

Pulling away from Mom, I asked, "Where's Tweet?"

Mr. Kelly stopped pacing, Mrs. Kelly sobbed a little louder, and Emily looked up at me with tears running down her face.

My gaze shifted back to Mom. The look in her eyes was exactly the same as the day my dad passed away. I went numb.

"Sit down, son."

My head was shaking even before she finished the three short words.

"I don't want to sit down."

"Noah…"

"Mom, just tell me where she is." I begged, my voice was already hoarse from swallowing several huge lumps.

"We don't know." She paused for a moment, inhaled a deep breath, and then continued. "Amanda had a doctor's appointment today."

My brows pushed together as I narrowed my gaze at her, not understanding what she was getting at.

"Her leg has been hurting since you saw her that weekend at USC. Her mom insisted she go get it checked out." Another pause, this one accompanied by a slight quiver of her bottom lip. "Amanda has cancer, sweetheart."

A loud thud came from the other side of the room. Mr. Kelly was leaning against the wall, his hand fisted by his side, his shoulders shaking. Mrs. Kelly's sobs echoed around the room while Emily's whispers of comfort were like white noise.

"She doesn't have cancer, Mom."

"Noah, sit down and I'll..."

I took a step back. "I'm not sitting down because Tweet doesn't have cancer."

The pressure was building in my chest, up my throat, and behind my eyes.

"She has bone cancer in her leg."

"Tweet just sprained her ankle, Mom. She was running like a bat out of hell that night she fell."

"She's been in pain since then. You've seen her limping."

"She limped because she sprained it. I carried her all the way to her room that night. I checked her out. I ran my hand over her ankle. I didn't feel anything, not even a broken bone..."

A tear must have escaped because Mom's hand came up to my face and wiped across my cheek.

"I held ice on it..." I trailed off.

"She was lucky you were there to help her, sweetheart."

"The doctor must have made a mistake. You've seen how beautiful she is, Mom. She can't be sick. Just because her ankle still hurts a little doesn't mean she has cancer."

"She's been in a lot more pain than she let anyone know. She's lost weight and has been tired."

I chuckled. "It's her first semester at college. Of course she's tired and she might have lost a little weight, but she's crazy busy just like me."

"Noah, they saw the tumor on x-ray." The deep scratchy voice of Mr. Kelly pierced my ears.

I backed up as Mom came toward me. Turning on my heels, I bolted out the door and headed to our spot.

"You talked to my mom?"

Clearing my throat, I answered, "Yeah. She didn't know where you were and you wouldn't answer your phone."

I didn't tell Tweet her mom was too upset to speak. She didn't need that guilt right now.

I took a chance and scooted a little closer to her. "It's cold out here, Tweet. Let's go somewhere warm."

"I've been trying to figure out what I did," she said.

"What do you mean?"

"What am I being punished for?" A tear trickle down the side of her face.

Hold it together Stewart. You have to be her strength.

"You're not being punished." My voice was confident and reassuring, because that's what she needed from me. But in the first few hours or even days after you're given devastating news, your mind seeks every possible answer as to why this is happening.

My fingers twitched. I was getting antsy. I needed to hold her. Finally she looked at me. We stared at each other for a moment before I finally gave in and threw my arms around her, pulling her onto my lap. Her face buried in the crook of my neck, her body convulsed with sobs, and we both shattered into a million pieces.

"You're frozen baby. Let me take you home."

Her lips grazed my neck as she shook her head. "Not yet."

"Tell me what you need, Tweet."

"For you to hold me."

Pressing her securely against my chest, I whispered, "I'll never let you go."

I can't lose you.

No matter how advanced treatments are or the thousands of people who survive, the word "cancer" translates into death when you first hear it applied to yourself or a loved one. A future without Tweet was inconceivable. I couldn't let my mind go there. Instead, I focused on my girl, at our spot, letting me take care of her.

The two days following Tweet's diagnosis were one colossal blur for me. An MRI had been scheduled, followed by an initial visit with her oncologist. Mrs. Kelly had contacted USC, told them the situation, and that Tweet wouldn't be returning next semester. Since it was the holiday break, the campus was almost deserted, with the exception of a few administrative workers, so arrangements had to be made for us to go and pack up Tweet's things the day before all the tests and doctor visits started.

When I told Brooke the news about Tweet she seemed genuinely sorry. When I told her I'd be spending as much time as possible with Tweet, she got pissed.

"It's not like you can cure her, Noah," she bit out.

"I can't believe you just said that."

We were standing on her front porch. I had stopped by to tell her my plans for the next several weeks.

"What I mean is, she has family to help her through this." Her tone was a little less bitchy.

"I didn't come here to discuss whether or not I was going to be by her side. I *will* be there for her no matter what. I can't do it with you laying a guilt trip on me or bitching at me every second."

"Well, I'm not sure what you're asking of me."

"To understand that I won't be around very much."

"But it's our first Christmas." Her lip poked out in a pout.

"I know."

"And if I don't *understand?*"

"Then maybe we should take a break."

Jesus, Brooke why are you with me?

She froze. "That's drastic, don't you think?"

"Tweet has cancer. That's drastic." I paused. "I gotta get going. We're leaving early in the morning to go pack up her dorm room."

Brooke looked away for a few seconds. When she turned to face me there was an icy determination in her eyes.

"Okay, do whatever you have to do. Can I ask for one thing?"

"Sure."

"Spend Christmas day with me and my parents."

I didn't know why I was being such a douche. Maybe I was angry that the girl who loved me wasn't the one I loved. Maybe I hated that the girl I loved was the one I couldn't protect. Whatever it was, Brooke didn't deserve to be treated like this. She hadn't done anything wrong.

"Deal." I kissed her on the forehead and whispered, "Thank you."

"I love you, Noah," she said.

"I'll call you tomorrow once I'm back in town."

Brooke stayed on her front porch, watching me as I backed out of the driveway. I thought about going back and just ending things with her. But our relationship wasn't a priority to me, not even the breakup.

Noah

The next day, Tweet, her parents, and I headed up to USC. Tweet rode with me while her parents went up in their SUV. No one said a word as we boxed her things up. My stomach twisted each time I looked over at her. She was trying to hold it together for her parents' sake, but I caught glimpses of the sadness and fear in her eyes. We were packing up her future and shoving it in a closet until some stranger gave her permission to dream again.

Before heading back home to Charleston, Tweet insisted on stopping to see Matt the asshole. She wanted to tell him face-to-face about her diagnosis. I knew she said he was her boyfriend, but my gut told me it wasn't your typical relationship. Of course, who was I to talk? I had a hot girlfriend who said she loved me all the time, wanted to have sex, and I hadn't done either of those things with her.

Tweet didn't think it was a good idea for me to go upstairs to the apartment with her. I didn't think it was a good idea for me not to go. Instead of arguing about it, I simply followed her, staying far enough back so she wouldn't spot me. Slowly, she walked up the stairs, her body tense. She was nervous. I couldn't tell if it was because of the news she was about to tell him or that he always made her feel uneasy. Either way, I wasn't letting her out of my sight.

The door at the top of the stairs opened and a hand grabbed Tweet's arm, pulling her inside. I jogged up the rest of the stairs, parking my ass directly across from the door Tweet had just entered. I hated that she was with this dick. My blood boiled as I thought about how he talked to her and treated her at the frat party. The door was closed, but the walls were thin. I couldn't hear exactly what they were saying, but I heard muffled voices go from soft, to sharp and loud.

It felt as if I'd been waiting for hours. I moved closer to the door. They must have also because their voices were getting louder. My chest tightened at the sound of his.

"Stick! Wait! You caught me off guard! I didn't know what to say to you. I thought you were coming to break up with me because you were mad about Danielle."

The asshole cheated on Tweet?

"I don't care about you enough to be mad about Danielle. I have to go. Noah's waiting downstairs to drive me home."

That's my girl.

"Are you fucking him?"

"What? Matt, let me go. You're hurting me."

That was it. I burst into the room and saw the asshole tightening his grip around Tweet's upper arm. I rushed over, clamped my hand around the front of his neck, and pushed him against the far wall. When I looked back and saw Tweet's upper arm starting to bruise, I squeezed tighter, causing the asshole to gasp for air.

Getting right up in his face, I snarled, "A tight grip doesn't feel so good when you're the grippee, does it, Smurffucker?"

I put more pressure on his neck, completely cutting off his airflow. Douchebag's eyes popped from their sockets and he was turning a lovely shade of blue. "Tweet, go get in the truck."

"Noah, he can't breathe. Don't kill him."

"Go get in the goddamn truck. Now!" I yelled.

Tweet actually did what I asked her to do and left.

Loosening my grip slightly, I allowed Matt to take a breath, before slamming him back against the wall.

"If you ever touch her, talk to her, think about her, or say her name again, I will fuck you up. After that, my good friend, Travis, who's the star hitter on the baseball team, will fuck you up. The entire team is made up of our friends, so they will definitely fuck you up. When they're done, I'll call some football players I know. Those no-neck, hard-headed bastards are crazy and always looking for an excuse to get out their aggression. They'll fuck you up real good. Then Travis will give his frat brothers a call. Greek boys are competitive. Other frats will get in on this, and so on, and so on. Any way you slice it, you will be so fucked that prison will look like a vacation at Disney World." I let go of his neck, stepped back, and landed a hard punch to his ribs.

Matt doubled over in pain, taking a small end table and lamp with him as he fell to the floor. I walked out the door, suddenly stopping at the sight of Tweet in the hallway.

I should have known she wouldn't listen completely.

Grabbing her by the hand, we ran down the stairs, and back to my truck.

I flung open the passenger door, one hand gripping the frame while the other rested on my hip. My expression was tight as my eyes narrowed in her direction, clearly indicating how pissed off I was and for her just to get in the truck. The second her sweet little ass hit the seat, I slammed the door.

Adrenaline coursed through me as I paced back and forth in front of the truck, trying to cool down. Once I felt calm enough, I walked over to the driver's side. My hand grabbed for the door handle at the same time the image of Tweet's bruised arm flashed across my mind. With a will of its own, my hands balled into fists and repeatedly pounded the side of my truck. When the last drop of rage was drained from my body, I looked down at my clenched fingers, the knuckles bright red and raw from the blows. I jerked the driver's door open and slid into the seat.

"Noah, are you okay?" she asked timidly.

"Has he hurt you before?" I forced the words out through gritted teeth.

Her silence gave me the answer.

Clearing her throat, Tweet admitted, "He's never hit me."

"Has he *ever* hurt you?" My restraint was hanging on by a thin thread.

"Just grabbing my arm a few times too tight, but he was drunk and…"

Oxygen pumped in and out of me in quick spurts. "Has he ever forced himself on you? Don't lie to me."

She hesitated for several seconds before answering. "Yes."

I hammered relentlessly on the steering wheel but instead of giving me relief, it only pushed another wave of anger to the surface. Shoving my door open, I jumped out.

Once again, using the side of my truck as a punching bag, I pounded the metal and yelled, "Fuck! Fuck! Fuck!"

I got back in the truck, turned the ignition, and sped out of the parking lot. Beads of sweat dripped down my forehead as my fingers gripped the steering wheel.

"Noah…"

I raised my index finger, stopping her words, and said, "I can't talk right now."

We rode the entire hour and a half drive home in silence. I hated Matt but was pissed off at Tweet. How could she let herself be treated like that by that asshole? I knew her self-esteem was low, but to let a slime like that guy treat you as if you were worthless… I didn't understand. My anger was still simmering. I needed to hold it together before I said something hurtful that I'd regret.

When we arrived at Tweet's house, it was late and I was too tired to unload her stuff, so I just walked her to the front door.

She fumbled to find her keys. "Thank you for everything and I'm sorry about…"

"What time is your appointment tomorrow?"

"The MRI is at 10 o'clock and I see the doctor at 3 o'clock."

"I'll be over at eight to unload your stuff. We'll have plenty of time to get to your appointment."

"You don't have to go. Both my parents will be with me."

"I know I don't have to go. I want to go. Get some sleep. I'll see you in the morning."

I kissed her on the forehead, letting my lips linger for several seconds as a calm washed over me. Without another word, I tore myself away and headed down the steps.

CHAPTER 23

Mr. Kelly and I were mirror images as we sat across from each other in the waiting room. We nervously checked our watches, his right knee bouncing as rapidly as my left one, and we jumped whenever the door leading to the exam area opened. They allowed one person to accompany Tweet to the back during the MRI. It was a no brainer that Mrs. Kelly would be by her daughter's side.

After the longest hour of my life, Tweet and her mom appeared in the doorway of the waiting room. While Mrs. Kelly chatted with the nurse, Tweet shuffled forward. As always, I noticed her beautiful eyes first. With each blink they grew glassier and filled with fear. Her body tensed—fingers curled around the strap of her purse, the pink shade of her bottom lip turning a milky white as she bit down on it. She had just gotten a glimpse into a world she didn't want to be a part of and this was only the beginning. I wanted to trade places with her. It sounded like a cliché. Something people say to make themselves look good because they know it's not possible. But I would give anything for this to be happening to me instead of her. Tweet's gaze finally zeroed in on mine. It might have been wishful thinking, but I thought I saw relief flash briefly across her face.

We had a little time before the appointment with the oncologist, so we decided to go to lunch instead of heading all the way home. We ate in relative silence except for the occasional chitchat about unimportant things. After lunch we headed to the appointment, sitting in the waiting room for forty-five nerve-wracking minutes before being ushered back into the doctor's office.

Dr. Lang was a chubby, balding, middle-aged man. What hair he had managed to hang on to flew out from the sides of his head, giving him a mad scientist look. Tweet sat in front of his large desk, flanked on either side by her parents. I stood in the back of the room like some uninvolved bystander, watching a scene play out. Only it wasn't a scene from a medical show and I wasn't uninvolved. I was witnessing the love of my life go through something that I wouldn't wish on my worst enemy, and I wasn't able to protect her.

"Well, I have some good news," Dr. Lang said, looking down at Tweet's records. "There doesn't seem to be any evidence of cancer elsewhere. Your left leg appears to be the only area affected." Four audible deep sighs filled the office. "But there does appear to be infiltration into the surrounding soft tissue. Because of this, I recommend a below knee amputation."

Oxygen rushed from my lungs as my legs caved in slightly, causing me to stumble back. Reaching out for the table on my right, I steadied myself. The three bodies whose backs faced me stayed stock-still. The news wasn't shocking, it was expected, but hearing the words in such a definite manner was like a punch to the gut.

Dr. Lang's gaze stayed on Tweet for several seconds, gauging her reaction. I tried to put myself in his shoes. If I made it through medical school and my residency, the reality was that I'd be delivering devastating news to a patient someday. I knew doctors tried to remain unemotional, but Dr. Lang was struggling. I saw a picture of his family when we first walked in the office. He had a daughter who looked to be around Tweet's and my age. I could tell he was thinking about her while telling Tweet that her life was about to be flipped upside down.

"They've come a long way in prosthetic limbs. I've seen some that look so real, you wouldn't even know they weren't," he said.

Mr. Kelly cleared his throat and asked, "So if it's just in her left leg… Once the…" His voice cracked and he took a moment to compose himself. "Once the surgery is done, she'll be cancer free, right?"

Dr. Lang kept his eyes focused down when he answered. "Technically, yes. She'll still have to go through chemo, though."

"But if it's just in her leg, why does she need to go through chemo?" Mrs. Kelly said.

Dr. Lang looked up. "Mr. and Mrs. Kelly, Amanda, and young man."

Tweet glanced back at me. "That's my best friend, Noah."

The doctor and I exchanged nods.

"Amanda has osteosarcoma. It's a very aggressive form of bone cancer. From what I know about your case, I'd say aggressive is an understatement. Your symptoms came on very quickly. We need to make sure we kill any stray cells that could potentially metastasize to your lungs. The chemo will give us the best chance of stopping that from occurring. I know this is extremely overwhelming. Let's take it a little at a time. My nurse will talk to you about scheduling the surgery. She'll also give you information on amputation and names of prosthetists in the area."

"Prosthetists?" Tweet's voice was flat.

"They're the ones who will make your new leg," the doctor explained. "It will be a few weeks before you'll be able to get fitted for that and start chemo. We want you to heal from the surgery first. Do you have any questions?"

There was so much information being tossed out, none of us could think clearly enough to ask anything. I did my best to pay attention, running through major points in my head in order to fill in any blanks Tweet or the Kellys might have missed.

"I'm sure I'll have a million questions as soon as I walk out the door." A slight chuckle escaped Tweet.

Dr. Lang glanced over at me before directing his gaze back to Tweet, his brown eyes warm with sympathy.

"I have a daughter a couple of years younger than you, Amanda." He paused, swallowing a large lump in his throat. "I'm going to do everything I can in order to help you survive this."

"I know," Tweet said.

There are times in life when the right person is chosen by some random force to be placed in your path. Tweet connected with Dr. Lang. I trusted what he said and knew he would fight for her.

The doctor hesitated before continuing. "I don't usually talk to patients about this. But because of the type of cancer you have, the strength of the chemo treatments, and your young age, I feel compelled. Amanda, you may want to discuss the type of *arrangements* you want with your parents, just in case... To be prepared."

"I'm going to be staying with my sister, Emily," Tweet told Dr. Lang. "She has a ground floor condo in Radcliffborourgh close to the hospital. My parents' house has steps going into it. We figured Emily's would be a good place to stay."

The room spun and the bottom dropped out of my world. She didn't understand that he was basically telling her to plan her funeral.

"He's not talking about living arrangements, sweetheart," Mr. Kelly said.

I pushed Dr. Lang's last statement out of my head. I couldn't let my thoughts go in that direction, no matter how real the possibility was, and it just got very real hearing a doctor tell Tweet to think about her own funeral.

We filed out of the office with a stack of information on bone cancer, what to expect from surgery, the treatment plan, and a list of prosthetic companies for her to choose from.

Tweet didn't want to go home just yet. She hugged and kissed her parents goodbye in the parking lot of the medical office building. I reassured them that I'd take care of her and bring her home when she was ready. Mr. and Mrs. Kelly were visibly shaken as they walked to their car.

Tweet and I sat in my truck in silence, processing what just happened at the appointment. All I wanted to do was disappear with her, inside our own bubble where nothing could touch us. I fidgeted, tapping my fingers on the steering wheel, the words *I love you* ready to burst out of me. Taking in a deep breath, my mouth opened, but her words were faster.

"Noah, don't. I need a little time to think about what was said in there." She stared straight ahead out the windshield.

"What do you want to do?"

"Run away," she said softly.

Without another word, I started the truck and pulled out of the parking lot. I had something I wanted to show Tweet and there was no better time than the present.

We drove farther into downtown Charleston, passing Colonial Lake and the College of Charleston, before pulling into Emily's tree-lined neighborhood. I parked the truck in front of a three-story, pale green Charleston home with white trim, a huge wraparound porch on the first level, and screened-in porches on the two upper levels. A lot of the historical homes in town had been renovated and divided into condos, with each floor being a separate unit.

I cut the engine, turned to Tweet, and said, "I'm staying here for a few weeks."

"It's really nice. Why are you staying here?"

"It's Carter Perry's place. I hang out here all the time. It's within walking distance of school. He asked me to stay while he was out of town for Christmas. You know, keep an eye on the place. He won't be back until after New Year's. It's great having some privacy."

"Emily's place is only a couple of blocks away. After my surgery, you'll be so close by."

"I know, funny how it worked out that way." I smiled at her before getting out of the truck.

I wanted to be as close as possible to Tweet during her recovery. It wasn't a coincidence that I would be only a few minutes down the street from her. When she told me she'd be staying with Emily I asked Carter if I could hang out at his place during Christmas break. If I had my choice, I'd be in the same room with her, but I knew there wasn't a chance in hell of that happening, so Carter's place was the next best thing.

I rounded the front of the truck and opened the passenger door. Placing her hand in mine, I helped her down, and we walked inside my temporary home.

The two-bedroom condo had all the essentials—huge sofa, huge flat screen TV, fridge full of water and beer.

We both shrugged off our coats, tossing them onto the sofa.

"Do you want anything to drink or eat?" I said.

"No. I'm fine. Thanks."

"Make yourself comfortable. I'll be right back."

"Okay."

I walked down the hall to the bathroom. I closed the door behind me, leaned against it, and inhaled several deep breaths. Today was intense and I needed a minute to get my head together before I fell apart in front of Tweet. After several minutes I put on my game face and went back to Tweet.

She was standing by the floor-to-ceiling windows, staring out over the courtyard. She was so deep in thought she didn't hear me walk back in the room. I stood at the entrance to the hallway, leaning my shoulder against the wall, my arms folded over my chest. I stared, taking in every inch of her, and thought what a lucky bastard I was to have her in my life. As I got lost in Tweet, my guard weakened, and the negative seeped into my consciousness. If she didn't survive this, neither would I.

I swallowed the huge lump in my throat, then asked, "Tweet, are you sure you don't want anything?"

I walked to the kitchen, grabbed a bottle of water from the fridge, and stood by the counter.

Not turning around, she continued to gaze out the window. "I don't want to die."

I froze. The word had been hanging out there, it had crossed all of our minds, the doctor had alluded to it, but this was the first time it had been said out loud. My mind searched for the right thing to say, something profound that gave her peace, but nothing came. Instead, my pathetic attempt at support shined through.

"You're not going to die," I said with confidence.

She turned toward me. "How do you know?"

"I don't want to talk about this right now." I unscrewed the bottle cap and took a swig of water.

"But I do. I need to talk about it with my best friend. I know it's not easy. We haven't talked about it at all. Things are going to get bad, and I need you to understand that."

Lowering my head, I inhaled a deep breath. I was so pissed off at God for allowing this to happen to Tweet. I tried to shove down the anger mixed with fear, but it was too strong. The tremble started in my shoulders and quickly spread to the rest of my body. The feeling was overwhelming. I was helpless and weak. This wasn't fair. I couldn't lose her. She was my life.

The plastic water bottle flew across the room, smashing into the wall. My blurry eyes looked up into beautiful scared teal ones.

"You don't think I understand how bad things are? I'm going to be a fucking orthopedic surgeon one day. I've done a ton of research. I know that if the cancer doesn't eat you up, the meds they're going to pump into your body might. The stats show you have a sixty-five percent chance of surviving for five years. For most people, that would be pretty good odds, but not for you. You deserve one hundred percent guaranteed survival."

Tears and sobs were now gushing from both of us.

I moved toward her in three quick strides. Pinning her to the window, I placed my hands on either side of her face.

Our lips were almost touching when I whispered, "I can't lose you. You're everything to me. Those months you weren't in my life wrecked me, but not having you in my world would completely destroy me. My purpose is to take care of you and protect you, but I can't do either of them. I don't know how to make this better, to make you better. I don't know how to help you."

"Noah…" Her palms lay flat against my chest.

"Please, don't push me away, Tweet."

"I'm not pushing."

My eyes closed as her hands slid up my chest, over my shoulders, finally tangling in my hair. Grabbing the back of her thighs, I lifted her up, pushing her hard against the window. Tweet's legs wrapped securely around my waist, squeezing tighter, pulling me closer, as I grinded my hips into her. We both knew this would be the only time we'd experience the sensation of both her legs around my body. My gaze shifted from her mouth to her eyes. Tilting my head slightly to the side, my lips brushed hers.

"Noah, I lo…"

The front door swung open and the sound of my name being called echoed through the condo.

Tweet untangled herself from around me and slid down my body, until her feet hit the floor. I ran my hands through my hair a few times, as I stepped back. A second later Brooke rounded the corner, stopping dead in her tracks at the sight of me and Tweet.

How the fuck did she get a key?

"I didn't know we were having company." Brooke's words were clipped with a nice sheen of snide bitchiness.

Never taking my eyes off Tweet, I said, "Brooke can you give us a minute, please."

"No, I can't," she snapped.

"Please."

"Noah, we were supposed to have this place all to ourselves through New Year's Eve."

Turning on my heels, I walked toward Brooke, grabbed her arm, and dragged her down the hall into one of the bedrooms.

"Noah…"

I raised my index finger, indicating for her to stop talking long enough for me to close the door. The click of the door was like a starting gun, causing Brooke's mouth to take off running.

"I'm sorry she's dying, but she's not going to use that to come between us and ruin our time here. The world does not revolve around Amanda Kelly."

My world does.

"Don't talk about her that way."

"I'm not trying to be a bitch. It's just... this is our time. No worries about roommates or your mom walking in on us..."

"That's not the reason I'm staying here." I growled, my fingers linking behind my neck.

I hadn't planned on telling Brooke I was spending the next few weeks at Carter's. I failed to mention that to Carter, however, who had let it slip. Brooke assumed it was a surprise I had planned, so that we could have time alone. Carter must have been the one to give her the key to the place. I wasn't thinking Brooke would show up when I brought Tweet here. When Tweet was involved, my mind only focused on her and no one else.

"Then why are you staying here?"

"Brooke... I can't do this right now. I need to get back to..."

"*Her?*" She lurched forward.

"She needs me."

I turned and reached for the doorknob when Brooke's words stopped me.

"I need you." There was a slight quiver in her voice.

I leaned forward, resting my head on the door. "Brooke, why are you with me?"

"That's a stupid question."

"It's not stupid. It's pretty simple, actually."

"Because I love you."

"Why? I'm a horrible boyfriend."

"No you're not."

"We don't have a lot in common or even know each other very well." My voice was low.

"Opposites attract. And what do you mean we don't know each other?"

"Who's my favorite band?"

"What?"

"My favorite band, who is it?"

"Um… Nsync."

"You don't know me at all."

"I know you're smart, hot, and going to be a doctor one day. That's all that matters, not some stupid group."

"You like the idea of me more than you like me. That's not fair to either of us."

Twisting the knob, I flung the door open and headed down the hall. Once I reached the main room, it was empty. Tweet was gone.

Fuck!

I grabbed my phone and texted her.

Me: *I'm sorry. Where are you?*

The sound of Brooke's heels clicked across the hardwood floors as she walked up behind me.

"I don't know what you're thinking, but you will not break up with me right before Christmas. I've put too much time into this relationship. You promised you'd spend Christmas day with me and I refuse to be humiliated just because I don't know the name of your stupid favorite band."

She jerked open the front door and stomped out, never looking back.

Happy fucking holidays to one and all.

CHAPTER
24

The knot in my stomach twisted tighter as beads of sweat formed across my forehead. I weaved in and out of traffic, inching closer to the hospital at a snail's pace. Tweet's surgery was scheduled for 7 a.m. and I was sitting in downtown Charleston on Calhoun Street, only blocks away from the hospital at 6:27 a.m. If cars didn't start moving soon, I planned to abandon my truck and haul ass the four blocks to get to her before she went to the OR. I flipped on my flashers and laid on the horn a couple of times, hoping people would get a clue and let me pass. Finally, whatever had caused the congestion let up and cars started moving forward.

Street parking in downtown was almost nonexistent, so I didn't bother looking. Instead, I drove straight to the parking deck. There were two main hospitals within a few blocks of each other along with several doctor offices in this area. Crowds of people were already hustling to work and appointments. Rather than wait on the elevator I took the stairs, two at a time, and flew across the street into the main entrance of MUSC, I was glad that I had been working here since the summer. Because the place was huge and easy to get lost in, I already knew the layout, so I headed straight to the surgery floor. My heart thumped into my throat the closer I got. I checked my watch: 6:45.

Shit!

More than likely, Tweet was already back in the holding area getting prepped. We both agreed to shelve any discussion about what happened the other day at the condo. In the grand scheme of things, it wasn't a priority at the moment. Tweet getting better was our focus. Last night I tried to talk her into letting me ride with them to the hospital this morning, but she said no. Just because she had to be here at the ungodly hour of 5 am, there was no reason for both of us to suffer. Tweet wasn't a morning person and she wasn't allowed to have her Diet Pepsi before surgery, so I knew she was helping me dodge a bullet by having me hang back and come in later.

I skidded around the corner into the waiting area at 6:48 am. The place was practically deserted, no sign of the Kellys anywhere.

I landed in front of the admit desk where a blank-faced woman, who looked to be about twenty-five, sat, tapping furiously on her keyboard.

"Good morning," I said, between gasps of air.

Never looking up, her tone was flat when she asked, "May I help you?"

"I'm here to see Amanda Kelly."

Ms. *Friendly* clicked something on her monitor. "She's already gone back for prep."

"Have they taken her to the operating room yet?"

"Sir, I'm not allowed to give out that information in accordance with HIPPA regulations."

"Sorry. It's just... I really need to see her before she goes in for surgery."

"Even if she were still in the holding area, they only let family go back to see the patient."

"I'm her brother."

Her gaze stayed focused on the monitor as she continued clicking.

"Family members are instructed to leave the holding area twenty minutes prior to scheduled surgery in order for the staff to do final prep of the patient. Final prep is already in progress for 7 am surgeries."

Damn, she was hardcore. I angled my head trying to get a glimpse of her name tag.

"Maryann…"

The sound of her name caused her head to pop up and she finally looked at me.

My eyebrows shot up into my forehead as I jerked back in surprise. "Wow!"

Her flat expression turned to concern. "What?"

"You have the biggest and brightest blue eyes I have ever seen."

Concern melted away, replaced by soft eyes and a huge toothy grin. "They're actually cerulean, overlapping into the azure hue on the color spectrum. People mistake them for blue all the time, though."

"I don't know anything about the color spectrum, but they are off the charts on the gorgeous meter." The side of my mouth cocked up into a smirk while I gave her a wink.

She glanced at the computer and then back at me. "So she's your sister?"

"Yep." I nodded.

Maryann reached for a Post-it note, scribbled on it, and handed it to me with a smile.

I looked down at the paper, noticing two things written on it.

"The first number is your sister's room."

"Thanks, Maryann." I took a step back away from the desk.

"And the second number is mine." She giggled, shrugging her shoulders. "I work 'til five, Monday through Friday."

I tapped my temple with the corner of the note, as I backed farther away. "Good to know. I'll keep that info in mind."

I tossed one more wink in her direction, turned, and went searching for Tweet.

My hand was on the doorknob to room three when a stern voice stopped me. I looked up to see a pocket-sized, gray-haired nurse walking toward me with a determined expression.

"Young man, you can't go in there now. She's about to go back to surgery."

"I'm her brother."

"It doesn't matter."

She didn't seem like a flirter, so I gave her the most pathetic sorrowful look I could muster.

"She's my only sister. I'll only stay a second."

"We're on a strict schedule. You should have been here earlier."

"I got caught in traffic."

The door opened slightly and a guy wearing scrubs appeared. I assumed he was the anesthesiologist since they were usually the last doctors to see the patient before heading into the OR.

"He can come in for a few minutes," he said to Nurse Tweet-blocker.

Blowing out a sigh of relief, I smiled at the doctor in appreciation. Nudging past the nurse, my smile widened at her, before entering the room.

Tweet's face lit up at the sight of me. She looked so small on the stretcher, covered in a pile of white sheets and a blanket.

"I just gave her some medicine, so she's pretty loopy," the doctor explained.

"Thanks."

He left the room, closing the door behind him, as I moved toward the stretcher and sat next to Tweet.

The medicine was in full effect. Her eyes were glassy and unfocused, but still gorgeous. I lifted my hand to the side of her face and let my fingertips trail down her cheek and over her jaw.

"Hey, Tweet. How are you feeling?"

"Gooood." Her head wobbled slightly from side-to-side, causing me to chuckle.

Wasted Tweet was adorable.

"I'm sorry I didn't get here sooner. There was an accident and I was stuck in traffic."

"That's alright, my brother. It's all good. You're here now. Grab my clothes and let's go." She grasped the edge of the sheets and sat up, bringing us face-to-face.

I placed my hand on top of hers. "Tweet, you can't leave right now."

Her eyes narrowed and a crooked grin slowly took over her lips. "You wanna hook up?" She leaned toward me like she was about to tell me a secret. "This gown has easy access and I got nothing on underneath it."

My gaze inadvertently dropped down, getting an eyeful of Tweet's chest through the flimsy hospital gown. I swallowed hard and forced my eyes up to hers.

We stared, not saying a word, exchanging *I love yous* in our own way.

The door abruptly opened, startling both of us. Nurse Tweet-blocker appeared. Her expression a little less harsh than when we first met. I wanted to lean forward and give Tweet a quick kiss, but opted for squeezing her hand instead before I stood up. The nurse walked around to the back of the stretcher, unlocked it, and pushed it toward the door.

It was time.

"Nurse Sarah, has anyone ever told you, you were a buzz kill?" Tweet slurred.

The nurse and I both laughed.

"I've been called worse," she said.

Tweet's head lolled from side-to-side, as she raised her arm, waving it around in an attempt to point at me. "This is my Noah. Isn't he hot?"

"He's very handsome," the nurse responded, smiling at me.

"He's an awesome kisser too. His tongue tastes like thin mints. He kissed my thigh under the dinner table with our parents sitting there. Hey Noah! You remember when you touched my boob-bahs... boobesses... booob-aaayz... that's a really funny word," she slurred.

"Tweet, I don't think the nurse cares about any of that." I interrupted, shoving my hands in my pockets.

"It wasn't his fault Nurse Buzz-kill. He accidentality touched my boob-aaayz."

The nurse took one step toward me. "I thought you were her

brother?" She glanced between Tweet and I, then a flash of recognition appeared in her eyes.

"We're a very close family," I said.

I got a knowing look from the nurse before she stepped back behind Tweet's stretcher and pushed her out the door.

I stood in the hallway, staring as the stretcher moved farther away from me. The sound of the rubber wheels squeaking along the sterile floor bounced off the walls. The urge to run after her and make all this go away was overwhelming. My purpose in life was to love and protect my girl, but I was completely useless to her when she needed me the most.

Men

I thought the MRI scan Tweet had was the longest hour of my life. That didn't compare to the two hours she was in surgery and recovery. I circled the hospital at least ten times trying to shake my nerves.

The first couple of days they had Tweet so doped up on morphine that she didn't know what was going on. Her mom stayed with her during the day while her dad and Emily visited at night after they got off work. I took the overnight shift. There was no way in hell I was letting her spend one night alone in the hospital. Fortunately, I knew a couple of the nurses on the unit. When visiting hours were over, they brought me a blanket, and pillow and conveniently looked the other way. I told my mom I was staying at Carter's and I never mentioned anything to the Kellys. I wasn't in the mood for anyone trying to talk me out of being there for Tweet. Mrs. Kelly arrived each day by 8:30 a.m., so as long as I was up and out by then, my secret was safe.

My body jerked awake at the sound of Tweet crying. I bolted out of the recliner and ran to the side of her bed. Tears streamed out of her closed eyes, her head shaking from side-to-side, as her hands fisted the sheets against her chest. She was clenching to the point that her knuckles were white. I glanced at the clock on the wall: 3:27 am. She was having a nightmare.

"Noah!" she yelled.

I placed my hands on her shoulders and shook slightly. "Tweet, wake up."

"Noah! Catch me. Please don't let me fall," she said through sobs.

I put more pressure on her shoulders and spoke louder. "Tweet, wake up. I'm here."

Her eyes shot open. She blinked rapidly, her gaze darting around, before landing back on me.

"Noah." Her voice was weak.

"I'm here. You were having a nightmare."

She nodded, taking in a shaky deep breath.

Shifting, she made room for me on the bed. I crawled in, wrapped my arms around her body, and held her securely against my chest. Her arm draped across my stomach as her head rested over my heart. My right hand traveled along her forearm while my left stroked her hair.

"You want to talk about it?" My lips grazed her forehead.

"I was in this tunnel. You were standing at one end. I walked toward you. When I got close, I suddenly got sucked backwards into blackness. I reached out for you, but I kept falling until I couldn't see you anymore."

We both squeezed each other tighter.

"I got you, Tweet."

Her body tensed. "Have you looked at it?"

I didn't answer for a few seconds. My gaze drifted down to the end of the bed. You couldn't tell she was missing anything with the blanket covering her.

"My leg, have you looked at it?" she repeated.

"No," I whispered.

"Me neither. It feels like it's still there."

"That's the nerve endings messing with your brain."

We lay there, listening to the quietness for several seconds.

"A therapist came in this morning and told me they were going to get

252

me out of bed tomorrow…" She looked over at the clock. "Well, later today."

"It will be alright." I placed a light kiss on her forehead.

"I'm scared."

Tweet's body trembled as her tears soaked through my T-shirt. I pushed her even harder against my body. I couldn't get close enough.

"There'd be something wrong with you if you weren't scared, but I'm going to be by your side. We'll get through it together."

"Noah, you've been here every night, *not* sleeping in that crappy recliner. I can't ask you to stay during the day."

"You're not asking me. I'm telling you."

Looking up, she placed a kiss on my cheek before nuzzling deeper into my chest. "I don't know what I did to deserve you."

"I don't know either, but it must have been something awesome."

After a few minutes Tweet's breathing evened out and she drifted off to sleep in my arms.

Something heavy pressed down on my shoulder and it shook vigorously. My eyes opened, still blurry and groggy. I lay on my side, arms and legs wrapped around Tweet's body. The entire room was lit up in sunlight except for the large shadowed figure of Tweet's dad hovering over me.

Warm breath washed over the side of my face and down my neck. "I'd appreciate it if you'd get off my daughter."

My heart exploded in my chest. I didn't want to wake Tweet or piss off Mr. Kelly more. I quickly but gently unfolded myself and slid off the bed.

"You've been here the entire night," Mr. Kelly said. There was either a sense of relief in his tone or my wishful thinking, but he didn't sound angry.

"Yes, sir."

Holy shit! He caught me in bed with his daughter.

"You've been here every night?"

"Yes, sir."

Please don't be pissed.

He offered me the Starbucks he had in his hand. I glanced from the cup and to him before reaching for it. Bringing it up to my mouth, I drank, cringing at the strong taste. Mr. Kelly lightly brushed the hair off of Tweet's forehead.

"Did she have a good night?"

"Not really." He glanced over his shoulder, eyebrow cocked in question. "Bad dream."

He turned his attention back to his daughter.

"I thought you and Emily usually came by after work." I took another shot of coffee.

He continued to stare down at Tweet. "We do. I have a dinner meeting tonight, so I figured I'd stop by before work just to check on her."

The back of Mr. Kelly's hand ran down the side of Tweet's face, his slumped shoulders rising and falling with a deep sigh. He wanted more than anything to take her pain away, but like me, felt helpless. I sat in the recliner in the corner of the room, giving Mr. Kelly a little privacy with Tweet.

Not looking at me, he said, "Noah."

"Yes, sir."

"Thank you for being here for Amanda."

"I wouldn't be anywhere else."

Grabbing one of the straight-back chairs in the room, he placed it next to me and sat.

"Your dad was always so proud of you. I miss him. He was a great man and a hell of a good listener. I know it's been hard on you and your mom. Nothing will ever replace him in your lives. But I want you to know I'm here, and have two ears, no waiting, if you ever need them."

A slight chuckle escaped me. "I know. Thank you."

We both aimed our focus on Tweet.

"Her mom was a pain in the ass when we first met," Mr. Kelly blurted out.

My head shot in his direction.

"But from the first moment I laid eyes on her, I knew she was my pain in the ass and always would be." He gave me a big smile.

"I haven't done a very good job of hiding how I feel."

"Neither of you have."

"I'd never do anything disrespectful to Tweet, sir."

"I know you wouldn't, son." His large hand slammed down on my shoulder. "Cause I'd have to break your body if you did." He gave me a wink. "Hang in there. Things will work out like they're meant to."

"I hope so. I can't imagine her not being in my life," I said.

"Then don't."

Six days had passed since the surgery. Tweet was doing as well as could be expected. I saw Brooke a few times briefly during the week. Our argument at the condo had blown over and she was being very understanding about my time with Tweet. Although, she reminded me each time we saw each other that Christmas day was still hers. I felt like I owed her at least that much.

Mr. and Mrs. Kelly went all out, setting up the spare room at Emily's place. It was an exact replica of Tweet's room from home. They felt she would be more comfortable surrounded by her things.

Tweet put on a happy face for the sake of her parents and at times even for Emily. She tried to fake me out with the painted-on smile the first day home, but I saw right through it and called her out. I caught her glancing down more and more at where her leg once was. The look in her eyes was familiar. It was the same look I had when Dad died. I had read every bit of information Dr. Lang had given us and did more research on the internet. Tweet was going through the natural grieving process on top of dealing with the chemo treatments that would start in a few weeks.

I tried to supply as much happy in Tweet's day as possible. She was too self-conscious being in the wheelchair to go out, so I brought *out* in. She wanted a manicure, I hired a lady to give her one. She wanted her hair done, I got her hairdresser to come do it. She wanted ice cream sandwiches at eleven o'clock at night, I got her boxes of them at eleven o'clock at night. The happy was temporary, but it was better than none at all.

Emily, Tweet, and I had ordered pizza for dinner and we were watching *Sixteen Candles*, again. Emily was sitting in the big overstuffed chair, while I was sprawled out on the sofa. Tweet was in her wheelchair. For the past half hour she had been unusually quiet. When I looked over at her, she was rubbing the top of her left thigh.

"I'm going to go to bed." Tweet unlocked the wheelchair and started to roll toward her room.

"You alright?" Emily asked.

"Yeah, I think I'm just tired."

I sat up. "You need any help, Tweet?"

"No, I'll be fine. Goodnight."

Fifteen minutes passed when the worse sound I ever heard sliced through the room. Tweet let out a blood- curdling scream. I bolted off the sofa and burst through Tweet's bedroom door. She lay across her bed, holding her stump, screaming and sobbing uncontrollably. I scanned the room, thinking I might see the reason for her screams. Then it dawned on me. She was having phantom pain. I read that some amputees experience anywhere from a mild discomfort to severe pain, like a vice tightening and twisting around the missing limb. Some medications help, but there wasn't much you could do for it, other than applying pressure around the stump and riding it out.

I sat on the side of the bed, scooped her up, and cradled her in my arms. Tweet clenched my shirt and screamed into my chest as the pain grew more intense. Her body convulsed violently with each surge. Emily stood at the end of the bed looking as helpless as I felt, with tears running down her cheeks.

I rubbed Tweet's back trying to calm her down, as I whispered, "I got you, baby. Squeeze me as hard as you need."

One hour turned into two, turned into three. By the time we headed into the fourth hour, Tweet looked completely exhausted. The pain ebbed and flowed. She got a breather for fifteen or twenty minutes and then the process started again. She'd moan in pain, then scream as it intensified, and then convulse several times before the pain let up.

As the sun came up, the pain seemed to subside. I still cradled Tweet in my arms, rubbing her back. Her head rested on my chest. Both our eyes were closed. I was just about to drift off to sleep when the door opened and Emily stepped in.

"Noah, I think she's asleep now. Why don't you go home and try to do the same."

"I'm fine," I mumbled.

"You look exhausted."

"I'm not leaving her, Emily."

She didn't force the issue. The next sound I heard was the click of the door as it closed. My arms tightened around Tweet as she nuzzled deeper into my side and we fell into a peaceful sleep.

CHAPTER 25

On Christmas day we all gathered at Emily's place to exchange gifts and have dinner. When I agreed to spend Christmas with Brooke, I didn't consider Mom, and the fact that this would be the first Christmas without Dad. My focus was so wrapped up in Tweet that everyone else took second place. I felt like a complete jackass being so inconsiderate. I made the mistake of telling Brooke I had to back out while we were at my house one day. Mom overheard and insisted, in front of Brooke, that I go. She wanted me to live my life and not worry. She said the Kellys would take good care of her.

I'd been glued to Tweet's side almost constantly since her surgery. Even though she let me take care of her, I knew the friend zone rules were still intact. It was harder than ever staying within the boundaries when she'd look at me with vulnerable eyes or clung to my body as if I were her lifeline. I wanted to say how much I loved her, but I was afraid if I did, she'd push me away.

Wine was poured and gifts were exchanged before dinner. Mom, Mrs. Kelly, and Emily retreated to the kitchen to put the final touches on the meal while Mr. Kelly went to open another bottle of wine. I was finally alone with Tweet.

She was in her wheelchair, parked at the other end of the sofa. Leaning to the side, I reached in my pocket and grabbed the small black velvet box.

Scooting down the sofa, I sat next to her and held the box up. "There's one more gift. Merry Christmas, Tweet."

Her gaze bounced from the box to my eyes. "Noah, you and your mom already gave me a gift. The cashmere sweaters were from both of you."

"Yeah, my mom picked those out. Today was the first time I'd seen them."

"I'm sorry I wasn't able to get you anything." Her head tilted down.

Placing my finger under her chin, I raised her beautiful face, and smiled. "Would you shut up and open the box?"

She lifted the hinged lid. Her face lit up in disbelief when she saw the pair of yellow diamond stud earrings. Her mouth literally dropped open, no sound coming from it. She looked up at me, stunned.

"I take it you like them?" I smirked.

"I don't know what to say. These cost too much."

"Do you like them?"

"I love them." Her smile widened.

"Seeing your smile made them totally worth it."

Tears quickly filled Tweet's eyes. She attempted to hold the corners of her mouth up, but the tremble of her bottom lip was overpowering, causing her smile to crash. As we stared, that familiar crackle of electricity passed between us, except there was something different this time. Our connection felt even deeper than before. Some couples crumbled under the pressure of facing any difficulty while others create an unbreakable bond. Tweet and I may not have fit the technical definition of a couple, but we were in this together.

I had no clue what was rattling around in that beautiful head of hers. The look she gave conveyed love and drove me crazy. I couldn't stand it any longer. I needed to touch those lips. If she had a problem with it, I'd blame it on whatever crap I could come up with, the emotions of the holidays or mistletoe tradition. I inched my way forward. She didn't stop me. I leaned in more. Still had the green light. My head tilted. Warm breaths mixed. Eyes fluttered closed and...

"Dinner's ready!" Mrs. Kelly yelled from the kitchen.

Fuck me!

Startled, I jumped back, breaking the spell.

I cleared my throat and said, "I better get going."

"You're not staying to eat?"

"I'm having dinner with... um... Brooke and her parents."

Brooke had texted me five times in the past hour making sure I was still coming.

Disappointment washed over Tweet's face. My eyes fell to the floor. I couldn't look at her. She was hurt and I was the cause. This was the first time since the surgery that I was leaving her and it felt wrong. We had spent pretty much every minute together for the past week and I still craved more time with her. Hollow emptiness spread from my chest to the pit of my stomach. I glanced up and caught her wiping away tears with the back of her hand.

Cupping her face, my thumbs ran over her cheeks, wiping away the tears. "Why are you crying?"

Tweet choked out, "I'm just tired and the holidays make me sentimental."

She forced a smile.

"You want me to push you to the table?"

"No. I'll do it in a minute."

I let my hands fall from her face, but hesitated before standing. "You call me if you need anything." She nodded. "Merry Christmas, Tweet."

I love you so damn much.

"Merry Christmas, Noah."

After tearing myself away from Tweet, I said goodbye to the others. As I walked from the condo I had the strangest feeling that the bubble Tweet and I had created over the past week was about to burst.

The Douglases were pretentious people. They were polite and nice in a fake way, as if they were doing you a huge favor by bestowing some of their valuable time on you. I knew the second I walked through the front door of Brooke's house, I would be having a huge platter of awkward with my Christmas dinner. Actually, awkward would have been better than what was served.

The dress code for the evening—a dark suit and tie for Mr. Douglas, a green sparkly dress for Mrs. Douglas, and a tight red dress with matching red heels for Brooke. I, on the other hand, was not dressed appropriately in my navy sweater and jeans, as indicated by the horror on Mrs. Douglas's face when she first laid eyes on me.

Dinner was catered and involved some unidentifiable food, which was brought out in separate courses by uniformed help. I missed my mom's sweet potato casserole, Mrs. Kelly's dressing, and Tweet. I excused myself several times so I could text her from from the bathroom. They must have been busy having fun because she never responded.

I pushed the mystery food around my plate, hiding as much of it under the slice of ham while pretending to listen to Mr. Douglas drone on about his job as an investment banker. After the boring dinner we moved into the living room where the subject of my future plans and intentions with Brooke were the topic of discussion. The disapproving look on Mrs. Douglas's face at my choice of wardrobe vanished when I told them I was going into medicine. I wanted to tell them, as far as my intentions, the only one I had at the moment was to get the hell out of there. Instead, I skirted around the issue. After an hour-long interrogation, I was able to make my great escape.

Brooke hugged my arm as we walked out to my truck.

"So, do you really like your Christmas gift?" She beamed up at me.

"Yeah."

Brooke's gift to me was a stadium seat dog tag and chain. It was similar to the one Tweet had given me when we graduated high school, except it was made from a Dodger Stadium seat. I didn't even like the Dodgers.

"You wear the other one all the time. I figured you'd like to change it up and try something new."

No.

"I really appreciate it."

Once at my truck, I broke away from Brooke's hold. She stepped forward, positioning herself in front of me.

"I love my scarf," she said, playing with the edge of the material.

The other day when Mom asked me what I had gotten Brooke for Christmas, I was caught off guard. I had thought about it, but never got around to actually getting her a gift. Lucky for me my mom always buys a few spare gifts just in case.

"I'm glad. It looks nice on you."

I needed to break things off with Brooke. I fooled myself into believing I could have something special with her. She wasn't a bad person. She had her bitchy moments, but who doesn't. Before we met, she had already planned out her future, which included being the wife of a doctor, a lawyer, or the CEO of a huge company. Brooke liked status. She was accustomed to a certain type of lifestyle and wanted it to continue. Everything was decided, all she needed was a guy to fill the role of husband. The idea of me was more appealing than me, the person. I'd wait until the holidays were over to end things. I was a crappy boyfriend, but not heartless. I wasn't going to break up with her on Christmas.

I leaned in, placing a light kiss on her forehead before reaching for the handle of the door.

"Noah, I want to apologize for the other day at Carter's place. I didn't mean to fly off the handle like that. It felt like I walked in on something. My imagination ran wild and I acted like a jealous girlfriend."

"Brooke..."

She stepped in closer, placing her hands on my chest. "After I cooled down, I understood why you wanted to spend so much time with her. You're going to be an orthopedic surgeon, so naturally her situation was interesting to you."

With my eyebrows furrowed, I looked down, annoyed at her assumption. "She's my best friend. My interest had nothing to do with career choice."

"Well, of course your friendship was a part of it. But now that the whole amputation thing is over and done with, you can back off. Let the family be her support. I'm sure they want to spend as much time with her as possible."

I curled my fingers around her wrist, removed her hands from my chest, and took a step back. "What are you getting at? Tweet's going to survive this."

"That's what we're all praying for. I just figured the respectful thing to do would be to give them time, just in case…"

"There isn't going to be a *just in case.*"

"Look, I don't want to argue on Christmas."

"Then we need to get off this subject."

"Okay." She moved back into my personal space. "If you're staying at Carter's tonight, I can join you. I'll tell my parents I'm staying over at Sandra's. She'll cover for me."

"I'm going home tonight. I don't want to leave my mom alone for long being that it's the first holiday without Dad."

"Oh yeah. That's right."

Rolling up on her toes, she kissed my lips. I pulled away at her attempt to deepen it.

Stepping back, she said, "Want to have lunch tomorrow?"

"I'll call you."

It wasn't that late when I left Brooke's, so I headed to Tweet's, hoping to catch her awake. I drove up to see the condo in darkness. My heart sank a little. I missed her more than usual in the past few hours and wanted to end my day seeing her beautiful face. Since all the lights were out, I hoped that meant she was resting and not having phantom pain that was always worse at night. She got some relief when we wrapped her stump tightly with an ACE bandage. To distract her mind from focusing on the pain, I rubbed her back while playing *Remember When*. It was a game we made up while she was in the hospital. Each sentence started with the words *remember when*, then you give of couple of clues to see if the other person guessed the event. It was silly, but fun thinking back on all great times we shared, and it made Tweet smile, which was the goal.

While sitting in my truck, staring at Tweet's window, Brooke's words played in my head.

Just in case.

I convinced myself that when those thoughts flashed through my mind it was fear getting the best of me. Only when someone else brought up the possibility of Tweet not surviving did it become real to me.

Please God, I'll do anything you need, just don't take her away from me.

Me: *Mornin' Tweet. I missed you last night. How about I come get you and we go out to breakfast?*

Tweet: *Maybe tomorrow.*

Me: *Hey, are you okay?*

Tweet: *I'm fine. I had my phone off. Will chat later.*

Me: *What do you want to do for New Year's Eve?*

Tweet: *Nothing.*

Me: *Can I come over? It's been a few days since I've seen you.*

Tweet: No. I'm too tired.

Me: I like laying around with you. :)

Tweet: Not today Noah.

Me: How about Chinese and a movie tonight?

Tweet: I have my first chemo tomorrow. Not in a movie mood.

Me: Tweet, what's going on? Why won't you let me see you?

Me: You're scaring me Tweet. I have an early class tomorrow, but then I'm coming over.

I was completely blindsided and confused by Tweet. I hadn't spoken with her since Christmas. Her parents and Emily were clueless as to why she wouldn't talk to me and as the days passed, she rarely replied to my texts. I tried to be patient and understanding. I couldn't imagine being in her shoes, having to deal with everything that was happening to her. If she thought she was doing me a favor by pushing me away, she was wrong. It wasn't a matter of her needing me. I needed her.

I didn't wait for Emily to invite me in, instead I pushed my way through the door. "Where is she?"

"Noah, she's having a bad day."

"I need to see her, Emily."

"Now is not a good time. She's very sick. The chemo hit her harder this week."

I walked farther into the condo. "I want to take care of her."

Emily moved, blocking my progress. "Noah, please go…"

"No! She's pushed me away since Christmas and I don't understand why. I made her a promise that we'd get through this together. Please, Emily," I pleaded.

"I'll go ask her, but if she doesn't want to see you…"

"Then I'll go."

I lied.

I followed Emily down the hallway to the bathroom. She glanced back at me before softly knocking on the door.

"Manda, are you okay? Can I come in?"

Tweet's weak muffled voice answered, "Yes."

As Emily opened the door, I craned my neck, wanting to get a glimpse of Tweet, but it closed before I was able. I stayed on the other side of the hall, not wanting to eavesdrop. That lasted all of five seconds. I crossed to the bathroom, pressing my ear to the door.

"Noah's here and he wants to see you," Emily said.

"Emily…"

"I told him you were sick, but… Manda, if you could see the look on his face. It broke my heart. He looks so sad and lost. He wants to be here for you."

"He doesn't need to spend his life taking care of me."

"But I think he wants to."

"I want to go back to bed now."

I heard some movement and then a loud thud, followed by the sound of Tweet crying. I burst through the door to find her lying on the floor sobbing uncontrollably, Emily wiping her forehead with a wet rag. Tweet's new prosthetic leg laid still attached to her, but off to the side, twisted.

I scooped her up into my arms. She was limp and couldn't stop crying as I carried her to the bedroom.

Pressing my lips to her temple, I whispered, "I've got you, Tweet. I'll take care of you."

Emily followed and stood in the doorway of Tweet's room with tears running down her face. I gently placed Tweet on the bed and sat in front of her. My hands automatically touched her face, wiping the tears away with my thumbs.

Her eyes barely stayed open, due to the tears gushing from them, as she choked out, "I'm so ashamed."

"Why?"

"Because I can't do anything for myself anymore. Every part of my body feels sick. I just want to die." Drawing in a shaky breath, she pleaded, "Noah, tell them to let me go."

Her sobs intensified so much, she had a hard time catching her breath. I heard Emily crying louder.

My heart shattered seeing her this broken. There were no words to make her feel better in that moment. I couldn't protect her from the fucking cancer. And she was pushing me away, not letting me love her.

Please let me love you, Tweet.

Shifting, I positioned myself behind Tweet. My arms snaked around her waist, her back securely pressed against my chest. Burying my face in the crook of her neck, I let my own tears flow.

My lips grazed the shell of her ear as I whispered, "I can't do that. I need you too much. Don't you dare leave me."

We finally lay back and on our side, but never lost contact. When I woke up the next morning, we were still tangled together.

CHAPTER 26

Access to Tweet continued to be limited by her choice. I hated it but understood. Certain weeks of chemo hit her harder than others and she spent most of her time being sick or sleeping. I wanted to be by her side, but she insisted I wait to come over until she felt better. I continued to give her whatever she needed, so I didn't force the issue. It was hard staying away. I texted and called several times a day, checking in on her. I also dropped by a few times a week. Occasionally, I got to see her, but most of my visits consisted of getting updates from Emily.

The rest of my life was spent in class or at the library studying. Brooke and I were slowly disintegrating. Each time I approached the subject of taking a break, she'd interrupt, saying how happy and in love she was with me. By the time she finished her monologue, I felt too guilty to make the break. I never gave Brooke or our relationship a chance. I tried forcing myself, falling short each time. I cared about her and it wasn't her fault that things between us weren't progressing. My head had been telling me for years to move on from Tweet, but my heart never gave up on us.

Brooke and I were meeting after class for lunch at the Hungry Lion diner, across the street from the main campus at College of Charleston. It was a small dive that had the best burgers in the area. The place was packed with wall-to-wall bodies. Once we squeezed our way inside, my gaze found her immediately. I blinked a couple of times in case my eyes were playing tricks. She'd been keeping me at arm's length for the past few weeks, using the excuse of being tired and not feeling well. But the picture in front of me was of a smiling and laughing Tweet, at a table with her old roommate, Lisa, and some guy, having a good old time.

Feeling tired and bad, my ass.

The *some* guy sat next to Tweet, his arm draped across the back of her chair with his hand cupped over her shoulder. Every so often, he'd lean in really close as if he were about to kiss her.

Groping Smurffucker.

"Noah!" Brooke's voice pierced through my pissed-off and confused haze.

"What?!"

"I said I'll go put our name down for a table."

"Fine."

As she walked away, I marched over to the three laughing hyenas.

"Tweet?"

She looked great. Happy.

Nervously, she shifted in the seat, moving away from the guy who was snatching a French fry from her plate.

Looking up, jaw slack, she stammered. "No... ah. Hey."

My gaze bounced from her eyes to the guy's hand that was still touching her shoulder.

My shoulder.

"Noah, you remember Lisa?"

"Yeah. Hey. How are you?"

Leaning forward, with her elbows on the table, chin resting in her hands, a huge smile crossed Lisa's face. "Hello, *The* Noah. I'm good."

I nodded.

"And this is Dalton." Tweet introduced us.

"Hey." I extended my hand, he looked puzzled for a split second before shaking it.

Douchebag.

"You and Lisa are together?" I pried.

"No, actually..." He shifted his arm from the chair to Tweet's upper back, pulling her closer into his side. "...my young Grasshopper and I hook up every Monday."

The corners of his mouth curled up into a lopsided smirk, aimed directly at me.

Grasshopper? He had a nickname for her?

My temperature quickly rose along with the tension in my muscles. If he didn't remove that arm from around Tweet soon, I was going to twist the fucking thing off followed by a punch to that smug smirk plastered across his face.

Tilting his chair back, chest all puffed out, he glanced at Tweet and continued. "Yep, we've been at it for about two months, right?" His gaze swung to meet mine. "Our time together wears me completely out."

"He's talking about chemo. We have chemo together on Mondays. Dalton, tell him it's chemo," Tweet blurted out.

Dalton scrunched up his face. "Is that what the kids are calling it these days?"

A snort of laughter came from where Lisa sat. I continued to stare down at the pair, waiting for some clarification on what the asshole was referring to and for him to stop touching my girl.

"I'm just messing with you, dude. We have chemo together. That's all. Unless you consider the blow jobs in the supply closet a relationship."

My gaze shot to a set of panicked teal eyes. "Tweet, I need to talk to you for a minute. Outside."

The sound of my name being called flew across the room as Brooke walked up.

"Our table is ready," she said.

"I'll be right there."

Brooke didn't acknowledge anyone else at the table except Tweet.

"Hey Amanda, how's the leg?"

"Still missing," Tweet said sarcastically.

Clutching my bicep, Brooke tugged. "Come on before somebody steals our table."

"Go sit down. I'll be there in a minute." My eyes stayed focused on Tweet.

Brooke dug her nails into my arm and huffed, before stomping off.

"Tweet. Outside." I walked away without looking back to see if she was following me.

I barreled through the door of the diner onto the sidewalk, pacing until Tweet came out. My hands raked through my hair several times in frustration, confusion, and pure old-fashion jealousy. For weeks I was only allowed to see her for a few brief moments because she wasn't feeling well. And here she was, out, looking amazing, and having fun with some other guy.

Stewart you are hands down the biggest idiotic pussy around.

The second Tweet walked out of the diner I grabbed her upper arm, leading her to the side of the building away from the crowd.

"Who is that asshole?" I snapped.

She shrugged out of my grip. "He's not an asshole. He was just joking around. He does that."

"He likes joking around about fucking you? Is he?" My voice was harsh and angry.

"Is he what?"

Getting in her face, I snarled, "Fucking you?"

"Where the hell is this coming from? Dalton and I are friends, that's all. He was joking. What's wrong with you?"

I leaned away. "I don't like guys talking about you like that. I don't like him."

"Well, I do like him. He's helping me get through all the shit I'm dealing with right now. I need him."

I stumbled back slightly. Her words were like a punch in the gut.

"You used to need me," I said with a shaky voice.

"Noah, I'll always need you. It's just… Dalton understands exactly what I'm going through."

The look in her eyes when she talked about him caused my heart to stop. She had a connection with him that went deeper than the illness they shared.

Glancing away, she mumbled under her breath, "This is ridiculous."

"I don't like how touchy feely he is with you."

"I've watched Brooke climb all over you for months. Not to mention how much she enjoys pointing out the fact that I have a limb chopped off, making me damaged goods."

"This isn't about Brooke. This is about you and me."

"You're right. This is about you and me. You have Brooke and now I have someone in my life to take…"

"My place?"

"No. No one will ever take your place. How come you can have someone and I can't?"

I leaned in so close our noses were touching. "Let me remind you, sweetheart. I never wanted someone else. That was your call."

I pushed past her and headed back inside. Marching over to where Brooke was sitting, I slid into the booth. As I scanned the menu I caught Tweet heading back to her table. Lisa and Dalton stood, the three exchanged a few words, before the girls left.

Dalton turned to the table beside theirs where four pretty girls sat. He made some comment that caused the table to erupt in laughter, and then swaggered toward the counter to pay.

Cocky bastard.

After a few seconds, the cashier tilted her head to the side, giggling at whatever the little prick said to her. My blood boiled over. It was obvious he and Tweet had a connection and here he was flirting with any pair of boobs that entered into his field of vision. I hated that he was in Tweet's life, but I wasn't going to stand by and let him hurt her.

Before my brain had a chance to think, my body propelled itself up and out of the booth.

"Noah... *blah, blah, blah,*" Brooke called out.

Just as I reached him, Dalton turned, almost slamming into me.

"Whoa! Sorry dude," he said, holding his hands up.

"Can I talk to you outside for a minute?"

"You sure like the outdoors."

I walked out the door.

He sauntered onto the sidewalk with the same smug smirk he had earlier.

"What are you doing with Tweet?"

With one quirked brow, he asked, "Tweet? Who the fuck is that?"

"Tweet... Grasshop... Amanda."

"Oh, is that what you call her? Weird."

"I didn't ask you out here to discuss nicknames. But now that you mention it, what the fuck is Grasshopper all about?"

"A private joke." The side of his mouth cocked up in a grin.

What was it with this guy and the fucking smirks?

"Answer my question. What are you doing with her?"

"Whatever she'll let me do."

I grabbed a fistful of his shirt. "Give me a fucking straight answer."

He winced then dropped his gaze to my fistful of material.

"You're holding on to a lot of hair there, dude."

"I just want an honest, non-smartass answer to my question," I said through gritted teeth.

He looked up at me. "Since getting the shit beat out of me isn't on my bucket list I'll answer, but you gotta unhand the follicles first."

My hand dropped and I took a step back.

Rubbing his chest, Dalton said, "We're hanging out."

"Do you love her?" The words were out of my mouth before I knew it.

"In my own way." There was sincerity mixed with sadness in his eyes. He was giving the best answer he could.

I was aware that Tweet had relationships with other guys—Brad the Smurffucker and Matt the dick. It killed me to think of her with anyone.

With those guys I knew she was passing time, wanting to get over this pull we had to each other, just like I'd been doing with Brooke. But with Dalton it was different. I could tell in the brief time I saw them together that what they had was special.

"Don't worry. Nothing's going to happen." His voice snapped me back to the sidewalk.

"Why should I believe you?"

"Haven't you been paying attention? I met her at chemo… bucket list. I'm dying, dude."

I simply looked at him, unable to respond.

"Stage four brain cancer." He said it like it was an accomplishment.

"I'm sorry. I didn't know."

"Makes me less of an asshole in your eyes now, right?"

"No, you're still pretty much an asshole."

"I like you despite your Captain Caveman mentality."

I shook my head. "I have no idea what you're talking about."

"Captain Caveman, it's a classic cartoon."

Narrowing my eyes, I gave him a puzzled look.

"It was featured on Scooby's All-Star Laff-A-Lympics. Don't tell me you don't know who Scooby Doo is."

"I know who the fuck Scooby Doo is."

"Then you're not a lost cause."

This encounter had taken an odd turn, from me wanting to beat the shit out of him to us discussing some lame-ass old cartoon.

"Are we done with this pissing contest?" He stuck his hand out toward me.

Slapping my palm in his, we shook hands. "I think so."

Dalton turned and took a few steps down the street before spinning back around.

"She's a special girl who deserves to be cherished."

"I know and I do," I told him.

He started back down the street.

"Hey, Dalton."

Glancing over his shoulder, he replied, "Yep?"

"Take care of yourself."

"Too late for that, dude."

He gave me one last smug smirk and then disappeared around the corner.

It had been a week since I'd seen Tweet at the diner. Even though both she and Dalton denied having more than a friendship, a deeper connection existed between them. I wanted to be the one person who knew her the best and understood everything she was experiencing, but I couldn't be, not this time, so I backed off. Tweet's happiness was the most important thing in my life. If that meant stepping aside for now and letting Dalton be there for her, then that's what I had to do. I threw myself into school as much as possible, trudging through my day like a lost zombie.

I was living at home with Mom again. Carter had asked me to stay on at the condo after the New Year, and I did for a few weeks. After deciding to give Tweet some space, being only minutes down the street from her was too tempting. Mom and I were on different schedules, so it still felt like I was on my own. She was doing great, keeping busy with work and friends. My aunts decided to surprise her this weekend with a trip to New York, so I had the whole house to myself for a few days.

I was walking in the back door after a marathon study session at the library when my phone vibrated in my pocket with a text. I had put it on silent while at the library.

Brooke: *Where are you?*

Me: *Just got home.*

Brooke: *There's something special waiting in your room.*

As I dumped my backpack on the table I glanced up at the window over the sink. Memories of Tweet flailing her arms and dancing in her own window flooded my mind and made me smile, causing the ache in my chest to intensify. I missed her so much.

Pulling myself away from the window, I walked down the hall to my bedroom. I opened the door to find the *something special* lying across my bed on her stomach, blonde curls piled high on top of her head, and wearing absolutely nothing.

"Hey baby," Brooke said, cocking her head to one side.

"What are you doing? How did you get in here?"

"I wanted to surprise you. I used the spare key under the mat. Surprise!"

"This isn't a good idea."

I tossed my phone onto the nightstand, grabbed the blanket that was draped over the chair next to it, and threw it on top of Brooke.

She sat up, wrapping the blanket around her body. "Your mom is gone for the entire weekend."

"I gotta be honest, being in my childhood bedroom and you mentioning my mom is not a turn on."

Giggling, she slid off the bed and walked toward me.

"I know things have been a little off between us and you seem to be having a rough week. Give me a chance to make you feel good. Give us a chance, Noah."

Brooke held my gaze as she slowly unbuttoned my shirt, pushing it over my shoulders and letting it fall to the floor. Her fingers slipped into the top of my jeans. Walking backward, she tugged me toward the bed. Before sitting down, she let the blanket untwist from her body. It hit the floor at the exact same time my phone lit up with a text.

Tweet: *Hey, I'm at your back door.*

My gaze flashed from the text to a naked Brooke, back to the text, back to naked Brooke. My heart thudded against my chest as beads of sweat popped everywhere sweat could pop. I didn't know what to do. Then I heard three knocks at the back door.

I picked up the blanket and covered Brooke. "Stay here. I need to see who's at the door."

I rushed out of the room, not waiting for her response.

I ran down the hall to the back door and flung it open. Tweet really was at my back door. I didn't imagine the text or the knocks. We stared at each other. She looked beautiful as always, but nervous. My stomach sank. What if she was here to tell me she and Dalton were now together? I stood silent, letting her make the first move.

She inhaled a deep breath before her words came out in rapid-fire succession. "I love you. I've loved you from the first moment we met. I love you deeper every time I see you. I know the timing is awful, but there's never a perfect time. So, no matter what happens, I needed you to know how I feel."

I had dreamed about the moment when she would finally say those words, my response and how we'd end up celebrating, a million times in the past. The moment was here and nothing came out of my mouth. I was dumbstruck.

It felt like we stood staring at each other for hours before I finally said, "Tweet, I..."

No sooner had the words left my mouth when the sound of an irate Brooke screaming my name and stomping in our direction filled the air. She was wrapped in only the blanket. Then it dawned on me that I was standing in the doorway shirtless.

"Oh my god! I thought you were alone. I only saw your car out front." Tweet turned to leave, but I grabbed her before she could get away.

"Tweet, don't go. Just give me some time. Brooke, let's go in the other room."

"You read her text while you were fucking me!" Brooke screamed.

"My phone was on the bedside table. I just glanced over at it."

"You almost broke your fucking neck jumping off of me to get to the door."

Tweet broke free of my grip, walked as quickly as she could to her car, and sped off down the street.

Closing the door, I leaned back against it, rubbing my hands up my face and into my hair. Brooke stood in front of me, fuming.

"I've put almost an entire year into you," she said, clenching her jaw.

"Why did you lie to her about what we were doing?"

"Because she needs to realize you don't belong to her."

"But I do."

"I was the perfect girlfriend—fun, smart, sexy. I pretended to like the stupid music you listen to and baseball. And you could have done anything you wanted to this." She ran her hand down the length of her body. "We look incredible together. Do you have any idea how good I would be for your career? I look like a fucking surgeon's wife!" she yelled and stomped her foot like a two-year-old brat.

"Let's finally be honest, Brooke. From the second you knew I was headed to medical school you had your hooks firmly planted in me. That's what was important to you, the status, not me."

"Like you didn't have ulterior motives being with me. Don't act so high and mighty, Noah. Why were you with me? Oh, I remember now. You were trying to get over your fucking Tweet who didn't want you."

I stood in silence, letting her get all her emotions out.

She paced back and forth, talking more to herself than me. "No matter what, that fucking girl was always in my way. Even when she wasn't physically around she was in your head. Every time she walked in a room your eyes got all googly for her." Stopping abruptly she faced me. "Why didn't you look at me that way?! After all I've done for you—the goddamn cookies I've made for you and I don't even like to bake, the times I gave you the green light to fuck me, and I even got rid of that manipulative bitch for you so you could move on with me!"

"What?"

Tightening the blanket around her body, she walked toward me. "The little girl chat we had at your dad's funeral… I told her to leave you alone. That you deserved better than her. You deserved me."

Pushing off the door, I stepped in her direction. "Who the hell do you think you are?"

"I was your future."

"You were never my future, Brooke."

"Yes I was! You should have loved me."

"I couldn't."

"Why not?"

"You're not her."

"Well… fuck you, Noah."

Straightening her shoulders, she spun and took a few steps away then turned back to me. "For the record, I'm breaking up with you. And don't come running back to me when your precious Tweet is dead."

My jaw clenched as I took a step toward her. "I'm trying to hold it together and not let my anger show because I know all this has hurt you. But do you really want to go out this way, as a cold heartless bitch? Don't blame Tweet for taking something that was never yours. You have three minutes to get dressed and get the fuck out of my life."

Her bottom lip trembled as tears filled her eyes. I had no interest in wasting any more time and energy on Brooke. I needed to go find my girl and start our life together.

"Goodbye Brooke."

CHAPTER 27

I hovered outside the door of my bedroom, poking my head in every few seconds to see if Brooke was dressed. I wanted her to hurry up and leave. It felt like hours had passed since Tweet showed up on my doorstep. I'd been calling and texting her almost nonstop with no answer. I was nervous, excited, and antsy to get to her. Brooke knew it and was dragging this out, wanting me to suffer. The thought crossed my mind to go after Tweet and deal with the Brooke aftermath later. Since Brooke demonstrated some crazy bitch tendencies earlier and had the potential to trash the place, I decided to tie up things with her first. I just didn't realize the level of spite she'd had toward me.

Finally, Brooke appeared in the doorway, fully dressed, and holding her purse. With my palm facing up, I extended my hand. Her gaze fell and her lips formed into a sly smirk.

Sliding her palm on top of mine, she said, "I knew all you needed was a little time and you'd come to your senses."

Dropping my hand, I looked her directly in the eye. "All I need is the spare key you used to get in here."

Reaching into the front pocket of her jeans, she pulled out the key and threw it at me. Turning on her heels, she stomped down the hall and out of my life.

I quickly changed into a pair of jeans that didn't reek of Brooke's perfume and grabbed my gray T-shirt that was a favorite of Tweet's. Passing through the kitchen, the chocolate cake on the counter caught my eye. Thank god my mom had a sweet tooth and a weakness for cake. I cut a huge piece, dropped it on a plate, and wrapped it to go. My mouth watered with just the thought of Tweet, chocolate cake… chocolate Tweet.

I started the search for my girl at Emily's condo. On the way over every pulse point in my body throbbed. The place was only fifteen minutes away, but I caught every traffic light, making the trip feel like another lifetime. When I pulled into the driveway, all the lights were off inside the condo, but Tweet's car was parked out front. I bolted from my truck, sprinting to the front door. Balling up one hand, I continuously pounded on the door, while alternating between calling and texting Tweet with the other hand.

The windows lit up as I heard noise coming from inside. Propping one shoulder against the door frame, I made my expression neutral and hid the plate of cake behind my back.

When the door opened, the sight of her took my breath away. Damn, she looked hot in a black T-shirt with a pair of long black pajama pants covered with hearts and Smurfs. Her hair was down and messy like she'd just gotten out of bed. We stared at each other as if we were both dreaming.

"Hi." I sighed.

"Hi," she whispered.

"Brooke broke up with me."

Simultaneously, her jaw dropped as her eyebrows shot high into her forehead.

Adorable.

I worked hard to keep the corners of my mouth from curling up.

"Oh god, Noah! I'm sorry. I should've waited until you texted me back before barging over. What did you tell her?"

"Goodbye." I unleashed the huge smile that had been begging for freedom since she opened the door.

I brought my arm around from behind me to reveal the chocolate cake. Tweet's eyes doubled in size and her lips parted as she eyed the big glob of frosting I had piled up on the side of the plate.

Note to self: Replace frosting on cake before Mom gets home.

The tip of Tweet's tongue peeked out at the corner of her mouth, slowly gliding over her pale pink bottom lip.

Note #2 to self: Always have frosting.

I was trying to be smooth, take things slow, and not come off like a horny bastard. But the combination of that outfit, the messy hair, and now the tongue sent my body into sensory overload.

Tweet stepped back as I moved forward into the condo, kicking the door closed behind me. Our gaze stayed glued to each other. With a confident stride, I backed her up against the counter that separated the living room from the kitchen.

"Where's Emily?" My tone low and husky.

"She went to Hilton Head for a girl's weekend."

After sitting the cake on the counter, I positioned my hands on either side of Tweet, caging her in.

I ran my nose along the side of her face, my lips barely skimming her cheek. "Did you mean everything you said to me?"

"Every word of it." Her voice was all breathy and shaky.

My fingers gripped the edge of the counter, holding me steady while waves of vibrations hummed through my body.

"I can't believe you're finally mine."

"I was always yours."

"I know. But now we can do *things* to each other and you won't stop...

You won't stop, right?"

"I'm done stopping. It's full throttle from here on out." A sexy smile broke out across her lips. "Exactly, what type of *things* were you thinking about doing?"

"The first thing involves you naked and that chocolate cake." Smirking, I tilted my chin toward the cake before focusing back on her. "What changed, Tweet?"

"Do you really want to talk right now?"

"I figured I'd better get the talking out of the way because once my lips are on your body, they aren't leaving it for quite a while."

"Wow." She sighed.

My gaze traveled from her lips to her eyes. "Fuck it. I don't care what changed."

All the years of pent-up love, want, and need ignited into an explosion of hands, lips, and tongues. Both of us trying to touch and taste every inch of the other at one time. Cupping the sides of Tweet's face, my tongue plunged deep inside her mouth, whipping around wildly, until it made contact with hers. She fisted the bottom of my shirt, tugging me hard against her body. The kiss changed from frantic to deep and slow. As my hands slid down soft curves to her hips, her hands traveled up, tangling in my hair. We were like well-choreographed dance partners. Each of us knowing how to counter the other's moves. Our music, the heavy breathing, and moans that filled the room.

My hands continued their journey down until they finally arrived at the mother land... Tweet's cute round ass. Squeezing, I pulled her forward, her hips rocked, rubbing against me, craving friction. I couldn't get over how hot she made me and we were still fully clothed. At this rate I was going to explode the second I untied my shoe. I needed to slow things down.

I pulled out of her mouth, gasping for air, but kept my lips pressed to hers. "Wrap your legs around me, baby."

As I lifted Tweet up, she opened her legs, placing them securely around my waist. Burying her face in my neck, a prickling trail of heat ran over my skin with each nibble she placed. Her fingers twisted deeper into my hair as we moved toward her room. Once at her bed, our lips reconnected as Tweet slid down my body until her feet touched the floor.

Leaving my hair, her fingers traveled over my shoulders and down my back. The nails applying the perfect amount of pressure, causing my dick to convulse. I broke from her lips long enough to raise my arms, while she grabbed the bottom of my shirt, sliding it up and off. A shiver ran through my body as her hands glided over my bare chest. Tweet shuddered, causing me to smile at the way our bodies affected each other.

My tongue slipped into her mouth, for a slow deep kiss before my lips started their trek across her jaw. Moving to her neck, I sank my face into her hair and inhaled.

"I love you more than anything else in this world," I whispered.

Traveling south, I kissed my way down the center of her body, coming to rest on her stomach. I slid her shirt up to expose the soft skin. As I nuzzled into her, my tongue circled her navel interspersed with light kisses just above the waistband of her pajamas.

"Oooh god, Noah," Tweet moaned, my lips vibrating across her stomach.

The sound almost made me come. I smiled against her skin. My hands ran up and down her firm ass, lightly squeezing as my tongue continued swirling.

Slipping my fingers under the waistband of her pajamas, I slid them down her legs, my lips following close behind. I sprinkled light kisses along the top of both thighs before burying my face between her legs. Tweet let out another deep guttural moan right before her knees buckled, landing her on the bed. I slid her pants the rest of the way down and off, leaving her in only a T-shirt and panties.

My hands slowly glided over her legs. Looking down, my gaze froze on her prosthesis. All the times I was with Tweet, she hid it by wearing long pants or skirts. This was the first time I'd seen it. Earlier, I was so lost in the feel of her body and the taste of her lips, the leg never crossed my mind, not even when it was wrapped around me. For a split second the sight of it was surprising.

"Are you okay with me taking this off? I won't if you don't want me to."

"It's pretty clunky, so I guess off would be best," she said, the quiver evident in her voice.

Tweet's body stiffened as I pushed the button on the side of the leg to release the pin that held it securely onto the liner. Once the prosthesis was disconnected, I slid it off her stump and placed it to the side. I reached for the top of the liner, getting ready to peel it off, when Tweet pulled back. My gaze shot up to meet watery teal eyes.

"Noah, I should go in the bathroom and take care of the liner." She tugged the hem of her shirt, trying to cover the area.

"I can do it. I want to." A couple of tears escaped, trickling down her cheeks. "What's wrong? You look so scared. Breathe, Tweet. It's just me."

Her voice cracked. "The liner is made of silicone and it gets hot when I wear it. It makes me sweat." She swallowed back a sob. "Please, let me go and take care of it."

"What do you usually do?"

"I wash it with warm water and soap."

Shifting forward, I kissed her, then whispered, "I want to take care of you in every way."

I walked into the bathroom and came back with a warm soapy washcloth and a towel. Kneeling on the floor in front of Tweet, I slowly rolled the liner off, revealing her bare stump. I hadn't thought about what my reaction would be when I saw the amputated leg. It looked the same as Tweet's other leg until you reached three inches below the knee, where it was round, tapered, and just stopped. It didn't shock me or turn me off. That missing section of leg wasn't what made Tweet beautiful nor was it the reason I loved her. The amputated leg was a symbol of her strength and grace in the way she's handled her situation.

Smiling up at her, I took the warm washcloth and wiped off the left leg. Then wrapping the fluffy towel around it, I gently massaged while drying it off. Tweet's gaze stayed glued to my hands. Her fingers twisted together in her lap. It was the most vulnerable I'd ever seen her.

Placing my index finger under her chin, I tilted her gaze up to meet mine. "We don't have to do this if you're not ready."

She blinked back tears. "Once you saw it, I wasn't sure you'd want to…"

"Why?"

"I wanted to be sexy and beautiful for you. A prosthetic limb isn't exactly hot, neither is an amputated leg."

Pinning her with my gaze, I said, "I've been waiting years for this moment with you. It would take more than a missing body part to stop me. You are and always have been the most beautiful and sexiest woman I've ever known. I love everything about you, inside and out. Your legs, arms, eyes, heart, humor, and intellect. I love your smartass mouth and the way you scrunch your face when you don't like something. I love when you listen to music, you close your eyes, sway, and play air guitar, getting so lost in it that nothing else exists. I love that you think drinking Diet Pepsi along with eating donuts or cake is a balanced diet. I even love your loyalty to those little blue Smurffuckers." She giggled. "I love all of it because I love all of you. There hasn't been a day in my life that I haven't and there never will be."

Taking one corner of the towel I wiped Tweet's tears away.

With narrowed eyes, I tossed her a flirty grin. "Besides, I've never been much of a leg man. My interests are split."

"Between?"

"Your tits and your ass. Both are phenomenal."

Laughter mixed with happy tears burst out of her.

"I love you, Noah."

I leaned in closer. "Say it again."

"I love you, Noah."

"One more time," I said, moving toward her until there was no space between us.

"I love you, Noah."

Our lips pressed together, moving in a slow steady rhythm. Tweet snaked her arms around my neck, her thighs gripped my hips, holding me tight. Breaking the kiss, her teeth skimmed over my jaw to the spot just under my ear.

Grabbing my earlobe between her teeth, she bit down lightly, then whispered, "I need you inside of me."

I jumped up and slipped off my shoes. It didn't take any time for our movements to become desperate and frantic. Tweet's hands had a field day with my ass, rubbing and squeezing it before moving to work the front of my jeans. As her tongue flicked over my abs to the top of my V, she unbuttoned my pants and slid the zipper down. My dick fought to break free, pushing against my boxers. Tweet's determined hands were all set to slide inside, when I grabbed both her wrists, pulling them away. I bent down and sucked her bottom lip into my mouth.

Pulling back, I said, "I've wanted to get my lips on you for years. I want to taste every inch of you. Let's take our time."

"Okay. I'll try."

Kneeling on the floor in front of her, I sat back on my heels. Tweet's gaze was glued to me as I focused on her amputated leg first. Taking it in my hands, I raised it to meet my lowering lips. My lips drifted over her smooth skin, placing light kisses along the way. Tweet drew in a sharp breath as I reached the top of her thigh. Looking up, I waited for her to give me permission to continue.

"Noah, that felt incredible."

I then gave her right leg the same attention.

By the time I reached the top of her right thigh, Tweet was breathless, propped up on shaky elbows, with her lips in a perpetual "O" shape, and her eyes halfway closed. My lips continued their slow and steady pace, methodically moving up her body. I didn't know how much longer I could hold out. Mr. Dickerson had been waiting a long time for this. Being so close to the edge, it was extremely difficult not to jump off. But I wanted Tweet to feel the way I saw her, gorgeous, sexy, and perfect. I wanted her to feel worshiped.

My kisses got wetter as I inched her shirt up and over her breasts. A growl rumbled from deep within my chest at the sight of her hard nipples pushing against the pale yellow lace of her bra. Her body shook and then her elbows slipped to the side, causing her to fall flat on her back.

Perfect.

Raising her arms, she wiggled from side-to-side, while I got rid of her shirt.

I snaked my arm around her waist, lifting her to my chest, and scooting us farther up on the bed. I stared down at her for several seconds, wanting to memorize how she looked right now. Dark hair fanned out across the pillow, lips parted, cheeks flushed, and teal eyes filled with an infinite amount of love. I'd cling to the memory for the rest of my life of the moment when Tweet became completely mine. My eyes filled with water, causing Tweet's to do the same.

"Thank you for finally letting me love you," I whispered.

Swallowing hard, she said, "Thank you for not giving up on me... on us."

I nibbled along her shoulders, pushing down the straps of her bra. She lifted up slightly as I slid my hands up her back to unclasp it. The lace running over her hard nipples caused a visible shudder to wash over Tweet's body. By the look in her eye, she finally felt the way I saw her.

Lowering my head, I wrapped my lips around one nipple, sucking hard while my thumb circled the other. I then worked my tongue back down her body. My teeth skimmed over one hip, hooking her panties while on the other side my fingers did the work.

As they slid down, I glanced up at her. "You won't be needing these for a while."

I could feel my body tense up with anticipation. My throbbing dick had become unbearable. Moving my hands up her outer legs, I kissed my way up, positioning myself between them. As I ran my tongue over her opening, Tweet fisted the sheets on either side of her. I doubled my efforts, alternating between sucking for long periods and quick flicks of my tongue. Tweet's back shot off the bed, arching as her loud moans surrounded us. The more her body reacted, the faster my tongue moved until I plunged it deep inside of her.

"Noah!" She screamed, her body convulsing, as waves of sensation flowed through her.

I smiled with satisfaction as I crawled up her body.

Hovering over her, I said, "You're my favorite taste in the world."

She looked up, gasping for air. "You didn't get those moves from Wal-Mart."

"I had to up my game for my number one girl."

I climbed off the bed and quickly stepped out of my jeans and boxers. This was the first time we'd seen each other completely naked. I was very pleased at what I'd seen so far, and by the look sprawled across Tweet's face, she was pleased as well.

"What are you looking at, Tweet?"

"What?" She looked up at my grinning face. A blush ran across her cheeks as her gaze darted away.

"I like looking at you too… and undressing you… and kissing you… and running my tongue all over you."

I had one knee on the bed, ready to crawl back on top of Tweet when it dawned on me that, I didn't have a condom.

Fuuuuuuuuuuuuuk!!

"Noah, are you okay? What's wrong?"

"I didn't bring any condoms." I sunk my hands in my hair and tugged. "I brought a fucking chocolate cake, but no condoms."

Biting her bottom lip, Tweet made a poor attempt at hiding her giggles, which soon turned into full out laughter.

"It's okay. I'm on birth control."

Part of me wanted to jump up and high-five something. The other part of me wanted to know when and for whom did she start birth control. Pushing that thought to the side, I refocused on the task at hand.

I crawled onto the bed, settling between her legs. Our eyes locked as my tip made contact with her. The intensity of the sensation was like nothing I'd ever experienced. Every sensory nerve I had was firing on all cylinders. My body always reacted physically to the other girls, but Tweet was the only one my heart and soul ever reacted to. This is what it felt like to make love.

Our hips rocked in perfect unison. Tweet's eyes closed, her head falling to the side.

"Tweet, look at me." Her eyes opened. "I need to see you, hear you, and feel you. It shows me that this is real and that I don't have to pretend anymore."

Running the back of her hand down my face, she held my gaze, never once looking away. "No more pretending."

I slipped effortlessly inside of Tweet. "You feel incredible," I said against her lips.

"I love you so much, Noah."

My breathing became shallow, coming out in short spurts. Staring into Tweet's eyes as we connected physically, I felt an intense energy pass between us, like I was sharing the core of my soul with her. Her legs tightened around my hips and her nails dug into my biceps, as my thrusts became faster and harder. Sweat beaded up across her forehead and her cheeks flushed, as her body tensed around me.

"Noah!"

The sound of Tweet screaming my name as she came was my undoing. My muscles became rigid, my movements going into overdrive as an explosion of energy sent seismic tremors through my body. It was almost too much to handle. Tears flooded my eyes as my body jolted in spasms on top of her. We stayed connected, our foreheads resting against each other, as our bodies calmed.

All of a sudden a wave of sadness crashed over Tweet's expression and tears ran down the side of her face.

"I'm so sorry."

"There's nothing to be sorry about. Don't cry, Tweet."

"I wasted so much time and hurt you."

"Nothing has ever been a waste when it comes to you. Not my time, my thoughts, or my heart. I don't regret anything about my life with you, even the times we were apart. Those times showed me how much I belonged to you. I knew we would be together one day. I just had to be patient and wait. And you were so worth waiting for."

CHAPTER
28

"I love your hair this way."

"It's a mess."

"I like you all messy," I mumbled, nuzzling Tweet's neck.

The past several hours were spent exploring each other, bit-by-bit and inch-by-inch. Repeatedly. That night Tweet suggested, for old time sake, that we take a bubble bath, but promised me it would be completely different from the ones we shared as little kids. I was all onboard for a wet naked Tweet. It was when she mentioned the bubbles that my dick hung its head and cringed. But I never could say no to my girl. Besides, her powers of persuasion were hot. I held out as long as possible, letting her *persuade* me before caving in.

The tub was large enough, allowing my legs to stretch out comfortably, while Tweet sat on my lap, straddling me. Her hair was piled on top of her head, with a few wet strands running down the back of her neck. The light bouncing off her wet body coupled with our recent activity had her skin flushed and glistening. The slightest movement caused the bubbles to splash against her chest, giving me intermittent peeks at her still hard nipples. She was holding the plate of chocolate cake with the look of pure pleasure across her face as she slid the fork from her mouth.

Bubble baths are awesome.

Tweet fed me a forkful of cake with extra frosting.

She really did love me.

Leaning forward, a sexy smirk played across her face. "You have frosting on your bottom lip."

She licked my lip clean before sucking it into her mouth.

"This is the best way to eat cake," she said.

My chest vibrated with a deep moan as she pulled away. The fork dove back into the cake and then her mouth. Staring, I raised my hand, brushing the hair off her forehead and let my fingertips trail down the side of her face. It still felt like I was dreaming, being with her like this.

Tweet's eyebrows furrowed, her lips pursed in a straight line. "Is everything alright?"

"I'm with the woman I love and adore, who also happens to be hot as hell. There's nakedness and cake involved. What could be better?" Her face brightened. "You never got a chance to answer the question I asked earlier about what changed."

"My perceptions. I've wasted a lot of my present holding on to past perceptions. Trying to second guess the future, so it wouldn't catch me off guard. I'm not sure exactly what triggered the way I looked at myself. Some of it was being compared to Emily, but not all of it. There was just something in my DNA that caused me to interpret the things people said about me differently. I always thought everyone else was better than me. That they had all the right answers, but wouldn't share them. When I got sick, I met a friend who shared and readjusted my view."

"Dalton?"

"Yeah. He taught me a lot in a short amount of time." Her eyes shined with tears as her chin quivered. "He passed away last week."

I cupped the side of her face, letting my thumb glide over her chin. "I'm so sorry."

"The only thing perfect is our present because we're breathing, moving, loving, and feeling. We should never wait to let the people in our lives know how much they mean to us. Dalton showed me that."

"You touch my soul. I didn't think I could love you more, but when I found out you were…" I swallowed hard.

A tear rolled down my face. Tweet swept her thumb over my cheek, wiping away the tear.

"Noah…" Her voice was shaky. "I don't want another day to go by without you knowing how much I love you. I've wasted time up to this point not letting you know that I've loved you my entire life. I don't know what's going to happen in the future, but I do know I will never stop loving you."

"Tweet, put it down."

"Huh?"

"The cake, put it down. Now."

She sat the cake on the side of the tub. I reached behind her neck, bringing her to my lips, our tongues knowing exactly what to do. Snaking one arm around her waist, I held her tight against my chest. Her fingers dug into my shoulders as I kissed a trail across her jaw to the spot under her ear.

"You're my everything," I whispered.

"This is the best bubble bath in the history of bubble baths," she moaned.

"Most definitely."

Stretching my arm out, all I felt was air and a cool sheet. My eyes shot open and I sprang to a sitting position, as if a nightmare had jolted me back to reality. I had no idea what time it was, but the room was dark. While I tried to orient myself, my chest tightened as a sinking feeling took over my stomach.

Please, don't let the past several hours have been a dream.

Once my eyes adjusted, I saw light filtering through the doorway from down the hall. I got out of bed and quickly put on my jeans. The feeling in my chest got heavier. I was afraid it had all been a dream, that I was still in the dream, and it was about to turn into a nightmare. I walked in the direction of the light. Reaching the end of the hall I stopped, and faced the kitchen. A deep sigh released from my lungs. She was real and here. Her back to me, she was completely unaware that I stood only a few feet away. Leaning a shoulder against the wall, I crossed my arms, stayed quiet, and enjoyed the view.

Tweet was wearing my T-shirt and her prosthetic leg. My gaze followed the length of her tousled dark hair falling over her shoulders and down her back. She raised her hand toward her face, which caused the bottom of the shirt to hike up, revealing the lower curve of her ass. A hard swallow hit the back of my throat with a thud. I was surprised Tweet didn't hear it and turn around. My mind drifted back to how we had spent the last several hours—the things we said to each other, the plans we made. Every part of my being loved her. I knew I wouldn't survive if she didn't.

God, please don't take her from me. I just got all of her.

I pushed away thoughts of losing Tweet. Breaking the silence in the room, I cleared my throat. Tweet froze, her arm suspended in midair.

"What'cha up to, Tweet?"

In slow motion, she twisted at the waist, looking over her shoulder at me. The plate with the half-eaten cake was in one hand, a frosting coated fork in the other. Her secret identity had been discovered. Tweet was the baked goods bandit. With guilt written all over her face, and a mouth full of cake, she placed the fork down on the plate.

She swallowed, licking her lips afterward. "I was just finishing up the cake. No sense in wasting a perfectly good piece of cake."

In that moment, Tweet was either the most beautiful, sexiest, or cutest thing I had ever seen. I decided it was all of the above. A confident peace radiated from her, evident in her stance and demeanor. My heart exploded with pride. Tweet was finally beginning to see herself through my eyes and believing that she was everything she needed to be right now. Without another word, I pushed off from the wall and walked toward her. The look in her eyes shifted from a panicked, *oh shit I got caught,* to a smoldering, *oh shit I got caught.*

Holding her gaze, I took the plate and placed it on the counter. Goosebumps popped up all over her skin, keeping time with the rapid motion of her chest as it pumped out short shallow breaths. I grabbed her hips, lifting her up onto the counter. My palms flattened against the marble surface on either side of Tweet. Leaning forward, I brought my body as close to hers as possible without making contact. My nose drifted across her jaw and down her neck. The scent of raspberry, vanilla, and chocolate filled the air around us. I pulled back and glanced down at her nipples straining against the T-shirt. Licking my lips, my gaze lifted to meet hers. Without a word, she shimmied her hips from side-to-side, grabbed the bottom of the shirt, and peeled it off. Tweet and I didn't need any words to communicate what each of us wanted right now.

A mischievous sparkle lit up her eyes accompanied by a hotter than hell smirk across her face. As my hands inched along the countertop toward Tweet, a chocolate-covered index finger crept into my field of vision, heading toward her swollen well-kissed lips. The muscles in my arms went rigid. Drawing in a deep breath, I held it, waiting to see what she was going to do with all that frosting. The tip of her tongue slipped between her lips and moved up the finger, capturing some of the sweet. With closed eyes, her head tilted back, a long deep moan flowed from her as the chocolate disappeared into her mouth.

Exhale. Whoosh!

Buckling knees caused my body to jerk. I kept my palms glued to the countertop in order to hold myself up. My dick was spazzing out, attempting to punch its way through my jeans. Standing was becoming painful, but nothing would get me to budge from that spot.

Opening her eyes, she looked directly at me. "You want some?"

"Yes." The word barely audible through my deep husky tone.

As I leaned forward, Tweet held her other hand up, stopping me.

The frosting finger started at her chin, traveled to her neck, and then over her collarbone. Thinking the trip was over I went in for a taste, but Tweet held me back again. The finger moved farther down… *down… down…* landing on her right tit. She ran her finger across the pointy nipple, smearing it with chocolate. My eyes, my heart, and my dick were all popping out. I didn't know how much longer I would be able to last before I grabbed her and buried myself deep inside her.

Sweat dripped down my back as the temperature in the room climbed higher than molten lava. I was on the verge of hyperventilating. My head swirled while a tremor roared through my body. At some point my hands shifted and gripped the counter so tight my knuckles looked as if I had soaked them in bleach. As she gave the same treatment to the other nipple, I shut my eyes and bowed my head, trying my damnedest to stay in control.

I snapped out of my thoughts, opening my eyes at the sound of her voice. "Noah? I seem to have dropped some frosting. Would you help clean me off and…?"

My lips were on her neck before she could finish the question, taking her by surprise. Her gasps and giggles spurred me on. Grabbing her hips, I slid her to the edge of the counter. Her legs tightened around my waist, pulling me closer to her. After cleaning off her neck, my tongue moved to her chin, and then into her mouth. Our chests rubbed together, mixing frosting and sweat over our bare skin.

Mmm… salty and sweet Tweet.

Moving from her mouth, I headed down, cleaning every drop of frosting off of her body. I swept my tongue across her nipple before sucking it deep into my mouth. The moans coming from Tweet were like music to my ears. Her fingers tangled in my hair, tugging, twisting, and holding me firm against her chest.

I pulled back slightly, gasping for air, and whispered, "Fuck Tweet."

"Yeah, fuck me!"

Tweet frantically grasped at the waistband of my jeans and tugged. I stumbled forward, catching myself on the counter. As our tongues collided I felt my zipper open and her hand slip inside, stroking me. A deep growl caused my chest to vibrate against hers. I released her lips. Placing my hands at the back of her upper thighs, I scooped her into my arms, bringing my mouth directly in line with her tits. Her arms encircled my head, and her legs found their rightful place around my waist. I sucked off what frosting remained as I shoved her against the fridge.

I looked up as she gasped and jerked slightly. Big teal eyes gazed down at me.

"It's cold," she said breathlessly, causing me to chuckle.

I lowered her slowly onto me. Every time I slid inside Tweet was better than the last, and each time had been perfect.

Dropping her forehead to mine, she moaned, "Faster, baby!"

My grip tightened around her hips, as I pressed her harder against the fridge. My thrusts had Tweet bouncing up and down so fast, it looked like she was riding a pogo stick instead of my dick. My muscles stiffened as she clenched around me. Jolts of electricity fired through our bodies.

Resting my sweaty forehead against hers. "We're definitely buying lots more frosting next time."

"Most definitely."

"Do you realize that for the past day and a half we have had little to no clothes on?"

Tweet pointed out this fact while I sat on the sofa in only my boxers, with her in my lap wearing a pair of red short shorts and a flimsy white tank top. She was right. Since Friday night, we had been in various stages of undress, emphasis on the *un*.

"Maybe we should become nudists," I said, running my hands up her thighs.

"I wouldn't be able to function. You're distracting enough fully dressed."

"Yeah?"

"Oh yeah." She leaned in, lightly kissing the corners of my mouth.

"Man, you got it bad for me."

Her kisses trickled down to my jaw. "Very bad."

I inhaled a deep breath, letting it out slowly, as my hands slid under her shorts. "You wanna show me how bad? We could stay here or go back to the counter or…"

Tweet's fingers combed through my hair as her hips slowly grinded into me. I kissed the strap off of her shoulder.

"The sofa's not very conducive to what I had in mind to do to you and I've already disinfected the countertop. We should move this into my room," she whispered, her warm breath floating over my neck.

Tweet shifted, reaching for her prosthetic leg that was propped against the coffee table in front of us. Even though she said the leg was comfortable to wear most of the time, it was a little clunky when we were in the midst of our maneuvers.

"What are you doing?" I asked.

"I need to put my leg on to get to my room."

"You think I'm going to unhand your sweet little ass for one second? Oh hell no. I'll carry you."

With my hands firmly planted on her ass, I held Tweet close. Her arms snaked behind my neck. I had taken only one step toward the room when our lips connected. It was impossible not to kiss her. It was also impossible to walk with my eyes closed while kissing her. So, I came up with a system. Take two steps then kiss Tweet for a few minutes.

Step. Step.

Kiss.

Step. Step.

Kiss.

The system was foolproof. Almost.

We completed one of the step phases, landing us just past the front door. We were going at it hot and heavy when suddenly the door flung open.

"Oh my god!" Emily screamed.

In a flurry, Tweet unhooked her legs and lowered them to the floor. She let go of my neck while I reluctantly let go of her ass. She turned in my arms to face her sister, my hands holding on to her shoulders.

"Emily! Um… this is…," Tweet stammered.

"Exactly what you think it is." I finished her sentence.

Emily's mouth opened and closed several times before any words were formed.

"How long have I been gone?"

"Well, things happened kind of quick. Right, Noah?" Tweet's head tilted back as she glanced up at me.

"I wouldn't call nineteen years in the making quick," I said, sarcastically.

Tweet back elbowed me in the ribs. "He's joking. He's a jokester." Awkward pause. "Emily… say something… please."

Sensing that the sisters needed a few minutes alone, I decided it would be a good idea for me to disappear into Tweet's room. Not to mention the fact that I had just realized I was standing in front of Emily in only my boxers.

In one simultaneous flash, I took a step back, dropped my hands from Tweet's shoulders. Emily opened her mouth to talk, and Tweet started tipping over.

"Noah! My leg!"

Emily lunged forward as I flung my arm around Tweet's waist, catching her before she hit the floor. Turning her to face me, I squatted down, wrapped my arms around her thighs, and lifted Tweet over my shoulder.

"Welcome home, Emily," I said, heading down the hall.

"Yeah, welcome home, sis!" Tweet giggled.

"I think the two of you together is fantastic and about damn time!" Emily yelled.

Once in the bedroom I dropped a laughing Tweet onto the bed and fell on top of her.

"We've been found out. How long do you think it will be before she informs the parental units?"

"Knowing my sister, she probably speed dialed Mom before we even got to my bedroom door."

My hand roamed up the side of her body, slipping under her shirt.

"Noah, what are you doing?" Tweet slapped her hand on top of mine.

"I'm following through on our original plan before we got interrupted."

"We can't do that now."

"Why not?"

"Because Emily is in the next room."

"And your point?"

"She'll think we're having *sex.*" She whispered the last word.

"Then by all means let's not disappoint her."

"What if she hears us?"

"You'll just have to keep your cries of sweet ecstasy to a low murmur."

She hesitated. "I don't know."

"Tweet, I did not wait all these years to be cock-blocked by your sister, who, by the way, already knows and is probably expecting us to engage in sexual activity."

Giggling, she said, "You have been a very patient boy."

"Damn straight."

Lifting her head, she kissed the tip of my chin while rubbing her right lower leg over my ass.

"Patience is a virtue."

"It's a big one." The corners of my mouth curled up as I grinded my hips into her.

She slid my hand farther up under her shirt. "And you should be rewarded for your efforts."

"I'm glad you're starting to see things my way."

CHAPTER
29

My gaze was fixated on the pair. It wasn't as if I'd never seen them before. Maybe it was the positon of my head, but from this angle they appeared larger and more engorged than I remembered. More than likely they were always this size. I was just paying more attention to the details now. Sitting by her side with our hands joined, I rhythmically moved my thumb over her wrist. While she read a book, I stared up at the pair of bags containing her chemo drugs hanging above us, dripping hope into her body.

I had taken the day off from school so I could be with Tweet during her treatment. She tried to talk me out of it without success. I'd been in this room plenty of times, transporting patients across the street from the main hospital. But today, when we entered, a wave of anxiety surged through my body.

I watched intensely as the nurses went through the routine of getting Tweet ready. She handled it like a champ, this being a part of her life for the past two and a half months. She didn't even flinch when they inserted the IV needle into her arm. Tweet had started off using a Port-A-Cath, which had been surgically placed in her upper chest area right before she started treatments. It enabled the nurses to draw blood and administer the chemo without having to stick Tweet with a needle each time. She hated having that thing sticking out of her skin, so when it became infected and had to be removed, she opted to leave it out, requiring the chemo nurses to start an IV each time she was here.

I ripped my gaze away from the IV bags and scanned the room instead. In an attempt to make the experience as comfortable as possible for the patients, calming and distracting elements were interspersed with the medical equipment. A bookcase piled with magazines, books, DVDs, and some board games shared the wall with the chemo cart stocked with supplies and drugs in case a patient had an allergic reaction. A flat screen TV and DVD player were mounted on the wall in one corner next to a bulletin board covered with information on local support groups, hotlines, and charity events as well as instructions on what to do in case of a toxic spill. Hand sanitizers and latex glove dispensers were strategically placed on the walls around the room between paintings of the ocean, a field full of flowers, and a sunset. The only other furniture in the room were the chairs lining the walls, each with its own IV pole and small side table. I had seen this exact setup before, but now it felt different. When the person you love claims one of the pale pink hospital recliners, the room transforms from a medical facility to a place where you beg for prayers to be answered.

"There's still time." Tweet's voice caught my attention.

"Still time for what?"

"To bow out. Walk away. I wouldn't blame you."

"I don't understand what you're talking about."

"Don't do that."

"Do what?"

"Play dumb. You're no good at it." She gave me a weak smile. "This is the time in your life when you should be having fun—traveling, going to parties, meeting new people, hanging out with friends… planning your future." Her eyes shined, as tears formed. "I can't attach any of that to my life at the moment, and I don't know if I'll ever be able to."

She blinked a few times and sniffled in an attempt to keep her emotions in check.

Letting go of Tweet's hand, I reached over to the small table next to her chair, grabbed a tissue from the box, and handed it to her. As she dabbed her eyes, the tears slowly leaked out.

I leaned in close, keeping my voice low, and said, "I hate traveling. I've been to my fair share of parties. They're overrated. I don't give a shit about meeting new friends. And my future is with you."

"You deserve to have a normal life and right now I can't give that to you."

I laced our fingers back together. "Where is this coming from?"

"I love you so much, Noah. I want you to have the best."

"I have the best, with you."

"But with someone healthy, someone like Br…"

"I was never with Brooke."

"What?"

"I was never with her the way I've been with you and I never could be."

"I always assumed from her comments that it happened soon after you met. And then at your house that day."

"She wanted you to think we were having sex. And if I'm being honest, a part of me wanted you to think it too when she and I first started dating. I thought it might make you jealous enough to fight for me… for us."

"But you never went through with it?"

"I tried that night you dumped me after Dad died. I went to her house… I know Brooke isn't your favorite person."

"She's a sneaky bitch."

I chuckled. "Yes she is, but there is some good in her. You have to dig pretty deep, but it's there. You've always been the only one in my heart and in my head. Brooke wanted a future. And no matter what her motivation, she didn't deserve a boyfriend who pretended she was someone else when we were together."

"Why did you stay with her so long?"

I glanced away, ashamed at my reason. "She was convenient. When I first met her, I had every intention of trying to move on from you. I mean, you were determined to keep us in the friend zone. I never pursued Brooke. She just kept coming around. Then I saw your reaction to her and thought… It was fucked-up thinking."

"What about Brittani?"

"All she ever wanted was a warm bodied ballplayer. The specific guy was irrelevant to her."

"Just know that I'll understand if all of this gets to be too much for you."

"Nothing will ever be too much for us to handle. You're stuck with me, Tweet."

She leaned forward, brushing her lips against mine. "You're pretty awesome to be stuck to."

"Okay! I'm going to bed! I'm grabbing some potato chips and a glass of iced tea for a snack before I go to my room! I'm pouring the tea now!" A few seconds of silence ticked by. "Just picked up the bag of chips! I am now walking toward my room!" *Tick, tick, tick.* "I'm standing in front of the door to my room! I'm twisting the doorknob, walking into my room, and closing the door!"

The sound of a purposeful slam reverberated down the hall.

"What the hell is wrong with your sister?"

"I'm not sure, but I think she might be going to bed." Tweet giggled.

"No shit," I said sarcastically.

Tweet was helping me study for an English test I had coming up. She was sitting on her bed, leaning against the headboard, legs stretched out while my head rested in her lap with the textbook propped up on my chest.

"I believe that was her not-so-subtle way of letting us know that she'd be out of earshot for the rest of the evening. She's such a goof."

"We should probably take advantage of her early bedtime with a little bedtime of our own."

I tossed the book to the side, sat up, and shifted, bringing me right in front of Tweet's gorgeous face. My gaze traveled down before I nipped at her bottom lip. With a slight raise of her shoulders, Tweet's body trembled.

"Noah Stewart you never cease to give me the shivers."

I raised my hand, slipping my fingers behind her neck and into her hair, as I pulled her to me. I went in for a slow deep kiss. When the kiss ended, our lips stayed connected.

"I love you," she whispered.

"Marry me."

Tweet's gaze moved toward me as the rest of her pulled away.

"What?"

"Let's get married and get our own place."

A huge smile broke out across her face. "We will someday."

"Not someday. Today. Well, not today, cause its eight o'clock at night. Let's do it. I don't want to wait any longer to make you my wife." I gave her a quick kiss on the lips.

"Noah... I can't marry you."

"Why not?"

Her gaze darted away and then down.

I tilted my head to see her face. "Tweet? What is it?"

A mixture of guilt and embarrassment clouded her expression. "My medical bills have started coming in. Things are so expensive. Dad's insurance is great. I can stay on it until I'm twenty-six as long as I remain a dependent."

"Tweet, my dad left me a lot of money. I haven't touched any of it. I can take care of you."

Her head was shaking before the last word left my mouth.

"No. That money is for you and school."

"Between the academic scholarships and my college fund, tuition is already covered."

"Noah, the cost of my chemo drugs for just one treatment is over nine thousand dollars."

"I want to take care of you."

Trailing her hand down the side of my face, she said, "You do take care of me."

"I want to take care of you completely."

"Noah…"

"It's my money, Tweet."

"And I refuse to let you waste it on me, especially since…" Her lip quivered.

"Since what?"

"Since I'm not a sure thing."

My eyebrows scrunched together, not understanding what she was saying. "Not a sure thing?"

She hesitated for several seconds. I didn't know if it was because she couldn't find the right words to say or simply couldn't bring herself to say them out loud.

Drawing in a deep breath then blowing it out, Tweet admitted, "There's no guarantee that the chemo will work."

"You're right."

I had made a promise to Tweet that she could always talk honestly to me about her illness, even though the subject scared the shit out of me. I'd never dismiss any of her feelings and throw clichéd *everything is going to be alright* answers at her.

"You know what they don't mention when you're diagnosed?"

"What?"

"How much control the disease really has over your life, even after it's gone. You get fooled into believing that you have the control when you're given choices on where to have treatment, if you want a port placed or not, or the type of liner you want to wear. And even though Dad's insurance is great, my parents are having to take money from their savings to pay for this fucking cancer. It won't even let me say yes to you. Cancer can swoop in and do whatever the hell it wants to do, whenever it wants. And all you can do is readjust to its aftermath. I don't think about the future, Noah, because I'm scared if I do, the cancer will take that from me too."

I choked back my emotions. I was at a loss as to how to respond to her. We had made a pact, not to let the cancer be the focus of our lives unless it demanded our attention. The reality was, she couldn't honor the pact because the cancer wouldn't let her. It was present in every minute of her life, whether we talked about it on a daily basis or not. The worse feeling in the world was watching the person you're in love with suffer and being powerless against it.

Lifting the bottom of my shirt to her face, I dried her cheeks.

With a raw throat and scratchy low voice, I said, "You don't have to think about the future. I'll handle that."

"I don't know what I'd do without you." She choked out between sobs.

"You'll never have to find out."

Brushing back the hair that skimmed the side of her face, I tucked it behind her ear and placed a soft kiss on her lips.

Pulling away, I tipped my chin up, and my eyes squinted as an idea occurred to me.

"I'm gonna buy a condo."

"What?" Tweet hiccupped.

"There's a great one over where Carter lives. Two bedroom, ground floor. I'm gonna buy it."

Tweet gave me a sideways head tilt. "Are you serious?"

"Yeah. I have enough money for a nice size down payment, I've been working at the hospital for over a year, my credit is good, and I'm sure Mom will co-sign if needed. The only problem is, I need a roommate and I have very particular specifications."

"And what might those be?"

"Delectable dark brown hair, twinkling teal-colored eyes, and plump pale pink lips surrounding a smartass mouth. Curves, gotta have curves. A great rack. Awesome ass. A sensational sense of humor. Intelligence."

"You've become quite loquacious."

Cocking an eyebrow, I said, "Why, thank you. I have no idea what that means."

Laughter brightened her face.

"Noah, don't do this for me."

"I'm not doing it for you. Now, do you happen to know anyone who fits all the requirements?"

"I don't have a job to help with expenses."

"I'm sure we can work out some form of payment." I placed a light kiss on her lips. My expression turned serious. "I want to start and end each day with you by my side. I want to make a home with you Tweet."

Her chin trembled as tears seeped out the corners of her eyes. "I want to make a home with you too."

Tweet pressed her lips to mine, teasing them with her tongue until they parted. She sighed into my mouth.

God, I love her sounds.

"I'm coming out of my bedroom! I forgot to grab the book I'm currently reading! Picking up the book and heading back to my room now!"

Emily's loud narration sent a tremor through my body. Tweet's shoulders shook. Our eyes shot open. Our feeble attempt to hold in our laughter caused our lips to disconnect.

"I'm gonna get things rolling on that condo first thing in the morning," I said, falling back onto the bed.

Craning my neck, I tried to spot what was causing the gridlock. I gripped the strap of my backpack and impatiently tapped the exam book against the side of my thigh. Of all days for me to be running late, it had to be on Tweet's last day of chemo. I hated that I wasn't able to be with her during the treatment, but it was the end of my second semester, and I was in the middle of exams. The professor taught three classes of Introduction to Cell and Molecular Biology. He decided it was a good idea to combine all three classes for the final and have it in the huge lecture hall. All I needed to do was drop my paper on the desk at the front of the room and I'd be on my way. The hold up was one hundred twenty other students were trying to do the same thing and they were bottlenecking.

I pulled my phone out of my pocket to text Tweet when I felt a hand on my upper arm. Glancing up, I saw Angela standing on the step above me. I didn't know her very well. We chatted a few times in class and during a few study group sessions. She had a small frame, short cropped jet black hair, and an unidentifiable swirly tattoo that poked out from the top of her shirt and crawled onto her neck. She was quirky, but seemed nice enough.

"Hey," she said with a nervous chuckle.

"Hey." I started typing out my text.

Me: *Will be there soon. I lo...*

"So, how do you think you did?"

My gaze darted to hers. "I'm sorry. What did you say?"

She swallowed hard before clearing her throat. "The exam. You think you aced it?"

"I think I did pretty well."

"Me too. I mean... I think... I did well. I'm sure you did well too. I was just referring to... never mind."

Finally, the line started moving at a steady pace. I was a man on a mission.

"Are you done?" Angela followed behind, matching me step for step.

"I have two more, English and History. How about you?

"This was my last one."

"Lucky," I said.

"Yeah. Hey, are you still working at the hospital?"

"I sure am."

"It would be great to be able to work there, especially since that's where I'll be going to medical school."

"I'll ask around and see if anyone is hiring."

"Really? That's so nice of you."

"No problem."

Once I got close to the front of the room, I elbowed my way through the crowd of students standing around the professor kissing his ass for a better grade. Tossing my paper on the desk, I turned to leave, almost running into Angela.

"Hey, Noah, would you like to grab some lunch? You know, to celebrate the end of exams."

"Well, I still have two exams." I smiled.

Her face immediately flushed red. "That's right. Sorry. We could just celebrate having lunch."

"Thanks for the invite, but I'll have to take a rain check. I have somewhere very important to be and I'm already running late."

Waving her hand, she took a step back. "Sure. I understand. We'll do it some other time."

I turned to leave when again I felt a hand on my arm.

"If you give me your phone, I'll put my number in it... in case you hear about a job."

"I'm pretty sure I have it. Everybody in the study group exchanged numbers." I scrolled through my contact list, then held the phone up to Angela. "Yep, I got it."

"Fantastic. Call me. It doesn't have to be about a job. We could just hang out sometime."

"I really gotta go."

"Okay. Well, have a nice day."

"Thanks. You too."

I spun around and rushed out the door before anyone else decided to strike up a conversation with me. Jumping in my truck, I tore out of the parking lot. I had one stop to make before going to get my girl.

I leaned against my truck parked in the front of the chemo clinic, holding a large bouquet of yellow, orange, and purple flowers in one hand and a round chocolate cake for two in the other. When Tweet pushed open the glass door, her eyes immediately locked on mine as a huge smile spread around her face. She was radiant and glowing. As she walked toward me, I could sense the pride she felt in herself. She had made it through another hurdle with her signature strength and grace.

I moved in her direction, holding the flowers out to her. "Congratulations Tweet."

Taking the flowers, she said, "These are beautiful. Oh, and cake."

I leaned in and kissed her.

"I'm so proud of you," I whispered against her lips.

She blew out a deep sigh. "Thank you, Noah... for everything. I'm proud of me too."

"How do you want to celebrate?"

Her gaze swung from me to the cake, back to me, as a sexy mischievous smile crossed her lips.

"Damn woman! Am I nothing more than a sex object to you?" I teased.

"You know you love being my boy toy."

"Well, it is your special day."

Grabbing her by the hand, I led her to my truck, jumped in, and sped back to her place to celebrate in style before her sister got home.

The summer was a crazy busy time for both of us. I was eager to graduate from College of Charleston and get started on medical school. I took summer classes just like I had all throughout high school to achieve my goal, along with working at the hospital, picking up as many hours as I possibly could. I wanted Tweet to be my wife sooner rather than later. Until I was able to provide for her completely, which included insurance to cover any medical bills, I knew this wouldn't happen. She wouldn't let me touch my inheritance for her. When we moved into our condo she insisted on contributing to the monthly expenses. I tried to talk her out of it, but she was stubborn and hardheaded, and I wouldn't have her any other way.

Tweet continued to amaze me with her strength. The effects of her last chemo treatment were mild compared to what she'd been through. As her energy increased and she felt good on a regular basis, she decided to send out a few query letters to local magazines for freelance writing jobs. She got hired for each assignment. And she was making plans to take a couple of core classes at C of C during the fall semester. Little by little, cancer was loosening its grip, letting the future back in.

CHAPTER 30

I was in the bathroom staring in the large mirror, my palms resting on the marble countertop. Tiny beads of sweat popped up on my forehead, and my stomach tossed every time I took a step toward the door.

This was a bad idea.

A loud pounding from the other side of the door ricocheted around the room, causing my body to jolt, leaving behind a prickling sensation across my skin.

"Let's get the show on the road," her muffled voice commanded.

Swallowing hard, I cleared my dry throat and said, "I'll be right out."

I grabbed a washcloth and ran cold water over it. Pressing the wet cloth onto my face, I inhaled several deep breaths, trying to work up the nerve to do what I had come here to do.

This was such a bad idea.

I slid the washcloth down my face to reveal terror-filled eyes reflecting back at me in the mirror. Tossing the washcloth to the side, I rolled my shoulders a few times and tilted my head from side to side, hoping to release some of the tension that had a stronghold on my muscles. I glared one more time in the mirror, trying to locate my courage. I opened the door, my eyes focused on the floor. I stepped through the doorway and almost crashed into her.

"Whoa!" she yelled.

I glanced up. "Sorry."

"Are you okay?"

"Yeah, I'm fine," I stammered, my gaze alternating between her and the floor.

"Are you having issues?" Her voice laced with serious concern.

"Issues? What do you mean?"

Leaning toward me as if she were going to tell me a secret, she whispered loudly, "Bathroom issues?"

I scrunched up my face in disgust. "No!"

"I was just checking. You were in there a long time."

"Look, Lisa, I don't think this is such a good idea."

"Are you kidding me?" Her hand came up and swatted my upper arm. "It's a fucking fantastic idea. Besides, everything has already been scheduled. You can't back out now."

Valentine's Day was in a week. It was the first one Tweet and I were spending as an official couple. I felt the corners of my mouth curl up thinking about her and how great she was doing. My life was perfect with Tweet by my side. I was so nervous and indecisive about what to get her for the special day. I'd been giving her gifts forever, but I was *the boyfriend* now and that added a certain amount of pressure. Plus, I felt guilty. Between both of us taking classes during fall semester, my job at the hospital, and the holidays, things had not slowed down. Our time together was limited and then I found out last week that I had to work on Valentine's Day. Tweet was understanding but I knew she was disappointed. Hell, I was disappointed.

I thought it was a good idea to run my initial plans by Lisa. Even though she and Tweet were roommates in college for only one semester, they formed a close bond. I called Lisa and told her my idea. She didn't even give me a chance to finish telling her before my plans got nixed and replaced with ones that she guaranteed would send me into the awesome boyfriend stratosphere. I liked Lisa a lot. She had been a great friend to Tweet, but she was nuts and I wasn't completely onboard with her sure-fire idea. Lisa was getting her Masters in Communication at USC and since she had made a special trip to Charleston to help, I felt obligated to follow through with whatever she had cooked up.

"It's just that… Tweet has never mentioned to me that she would like anything even remotely like this."

"Let me explain something to you, *The* Noah."

I chuckled a little hearing the nickname she had given me.

"You called me because you wanted my help. My advice. You wanted to surprise Amanda with something unique and special. You didn't want the clichéd flowers and candy crap. Am I right?"

"Yeah, I guess," I said hesitantly.

"You're damn straight I'm right. I'm a woman and thus I know what women really want."

Rubbing the back of my neck nervously, I said, "I know, but this is so…"

"So what? So perfect? So fantastic? So incredibly out-of-the-box that it will blow her mind?"

"So weird."

"So weird, cray-cray awesome," she said with excitement.

"Okay, I'll trust you on this, I guess." She seemed really sure of the idea.

Lisa clapped her hands, rubbing her palms together. "Alrighty, let's get this monkey humpin'."

My eyebrows knitted together, baffled by her choice of words.

"I still don't understand why we had to meet here."

"I told you the studio is being remodeled and can't be used," she explained.

"I know, but…"

"Listen, you're having a boudoir photo made. What better place to shoot it than a boudoir?"

I cringed at the word "boudoir". "Don't call it that. It's a picture. I'm having a picture made for Tweet."

Lisa had set up the entire photo shoot with a friend of hers. The photographer's studio was in the middle of a remodel so the shoot was scheduled to take place in downtown Charleston at the John Rutledge House Bed and Breakfast. The room looked like something Tweet would like with pale yellow walls, hardwood floors, and fireplace with flowers on the mantle. A huge four-poster bed took up most of the space.

Rolling her eyes, she huffed out, "Whatever. Now, is that what you're wearing?"

Lisa's gaze ran up and down my body.

"Um… yeah. What's wrong with what I'm wearing?"

I had on navy Nike sweatpants, white Nike T-shirt, and retro air Jordans.

"You look like Nike threw up on you. Take off your shirt."

"Excuse me?"

"You should take off your shirt for the picture, I mean," she said.

"The photographer isn't even here yet."

"I know. I thought maybe you needed me to oil you up." Lisa's eyes appeared to glaze over while they zeroed in on my chest as I watched a large lump slide down her neck.

I took a step back from her.

"What? No, I'm not getting… no."

There was an awkward pause before she snapped out of her trance, cleared her throat, and said, "Well, if my services are no longer needed I guess I'll head out."

"Um… I appreciate all your help with this, Lisa."

"Anything for Amanda. The photographer should be here soon."

"Thanks."

"And you're sure about the oil?"

"I'm positive about the oil."

"Just double checkin'," she said.

"Thanks." I sent a slight smile in her direction.

She patted my shoulder. "Good luck, *The* Noah."

Giving me one last smile, she walked out the door.

Lisa had taken my mind off of my nerves for a few seconds but now that I was standing in the room alone they started to resurface in full force. I walked over to the large window and focused on the street below full of locals and tourists, hoping the distraction would calm me down. I could do this. This was for Tweet. I could and would endure anything for her. The click of the door startled me. Inhaling two extremely deep breaths I turned around to meet the photographer and get this over with as quick as possible.

Everything happened all at once. I turned, saw a big camera, heard a female voice say, "Hey, Noah," and a flash of bright light blinded me before I saw the person.

"Shit," I yelled, slapping my hands over my eyes as I stumbled backward.

"Oh hell! I'm so sorry," she said.

"Tweet?" I asked, confused.

Her fingers curled around my wrist, pulling my hands from my face. I opened my eyes to bursts of light. As I blinked, the spots disappeared and were replaced with the most beautiful girl in the world.

My girl.

With a sheepish look on her face, she dropped my hands, raised her arms up over her head, and yelled, "Surprise!"

A huge smile appeared across my face. "What are you doing here?"

"Happy Valentine's Day!"

Her sexy hips swayed in my direction as she moved in closer, looking up at me through her long dark lashes. My breathing picked up. She looked incredible in her worn jeans that slid over her curves perfectly and a light blue sweater. Her hair was down and fell right between her shoulder blades.

God she was everything to me.

"So this was all a setup?" I asked.

Tilting up on her toes, she whispered against my lips, "Yes."

Her lips traveled across my jaw, causing me to release a deep sigh.

"So there was never a photographer?" My hands moved to her hips and immediately disappeared under the bottom of her sweater.

"No photographer." Her voice was low and sexy as she continued nibbling down my neck.

"This was all planned to surprise me?" My head dipped down, nuzzling her neck while my hands slid farther up her sweater.

She sucked my earlobe between her lips while her hands moved up my stomach toward my chest. "All for you."

"No pictures?" Breathing into her ear, I placed soft kisses just below it.

"Oh, there will be pictures." We pulled away from each other's necks and rested our foreheads together. "We have twenty-four hours of just the two of us. No family checking in, no friends stopping by, no studying, and no calls from work. Just you, me, that big bed, and room service."

"Gee you're swell." I grinned.

I placed a soft kiss on her lips before standing up straight. Our eyes stayed locked. Tweet raised her arms above her head, allowing me to peel off her sweater. The bra she had on was pink with white hearts on it. My eyes landed on her chest, watching as her breathing picked up. I swallowed hard. My fingertips traced the outline of her bra. Starting at the strap, my hand slowly traveled down to the top of one breast, then across to the other, and then to the second strap. I stopped halfway up the strap and slid it off her shoulder, revealing the small scar she had just below her collarbone. The tips of my fingers ran gently over the scar. It was one of the permanent reminders of a terrifying time in our past. I glanced up into water-filled teal eyes.

"No sadness today, Tweet," I choked out.

"No sadness," she said, blinking back tears.

I lowered my lips to hers and placed soft kisses over her mouth. Tweet whimpered breathlessly, causing me to deepen the kiss. My tongue connected with hers immediately. My hands slid down her body as hers traveled up mine. Her fingers worked their way into my hair. Grabbing her ass, I lifted her up, carried her to the bed, and laid her down. I took off my shoes, pants, and shirt in record time. Without any hesitation Tweet removed her prosthetic left leg and liner. Reaching toward the nightstand, she grabbed a couple of baby wipes from the container and a hand towel.

Wow, Tweet had planned for our Valentine's Day in bed.

I loved how comfortable she was with me, no embarrassment or self-consciousness about her amputation.

After she cleaned her stump, she kicked off her right shoe, and shimmied out of her jeans.

Hot damn! The panties matched the bra.

"Leave the bra and panties for me," I told her, throwing a grin and a cocked eyebrow her way.

Tweet scooted to the middle of the bed. As she settled back, I settled between her legs. Propping myself up on my elbows, I gazed down. Her cheeks were flushed pink, her hair fanned out, and the tip of her tongue kept peeking out between her slightly parted lips.

She brushed the hair away from my forehead, and let her fingertips trail down the side of my face. Her eyebrows knitted together as a deep breath escaped her.

"You okay, Tweet?"

"Yeah… Sometimes I get overwhelmed with how in love I am with you."

"Ditto." I grinned.

I teased her, nipping at her lips, her chin, along her jaw, and down her neck.

Giggling, she said, "That tickles."

Tweet shifted to the side allowing me to move my hand behind her and unclasp her bra. My lips followed the path of the lace as it glided over her nipples. She slipped her arms through the bra straps and tossed it to the floor. Taking one nipple in my mouth, I sucked hard while massaging the other breast. Tweet's fingers dug into my biceps.

Pulling away, I gasped, "I can't get enough of your body."

A low growl escaped her as I placed open-mouth kisses across her chest. I wrapped my lips around her other nipple. Her right leg rubbed up and down my ass, attempting to push down my boxers. I licked down her stomach to her hips. Tweet lifted up enough for me to slide her panties off. I jumped off the bed, causing the mattress and Tweet to bounce. The best laugh in the world came pouring out of her as I frantically stepped out of my boxers.

"This bed is awfully chilly without you." Her hand traveled down her body.

That's my girl.

Pouncing on the bed, I wasted no time devouring her. My mouth moved down her body. I was about to nuzzle between her legs when it suddenly hit me.

"Fuuuuuck," I mumbled against her skin.

"Oh god yes," she moaned.

"I can't."

"What's wrong?"

I looked up to see her propped up on her elbows, glancing down at me. "I didn't bring any condoms."

Even though Tweet was on the pill, we had decided it was better to be safe than sorry and doubled up on protection.

"Front pocket of my jeans," she said, dropping her head back on the bed. I rolled off of her and grabbed her jeans, finding the condom. "There's an entire box in the suitcase."

"Suitcase?" I asked while dropping my boxers.

"I packed a suitcase. It's in the closet. Noah, I'm so not in the mood to talk luggage right now."

I rolled on the condom and got back to business. Positioning myself between her thighs, I rocked into her. Our eyes locked. Sweat coated our skin. Tweet's arms and legs gripped my body as my movements sped up. Moans and a squeaky bed filled the air. A wave of convulsions took over our bodies as the throbbing inside of her intensified and we came together.

The next morning I got up early and left to pick up my original Valentine gift for Tweet. When I returned she was still sound asleep, lying on her side, her hair fanned out over the pillow. To say last night was incredible would be an understatement. We spent the time making love, sleeping, and eating. Repeatedly. She had given me the best Valentine gift I could have asked for. Her. Us.

I placed her gift on the nightstand and crawled into bed beside her. I nuzzled the crook of her neck and whispered, "Wake up, sexy."

Her eyes stayed closed but a huge grin appeared across her beautiful face. "Mmm… mornin'. Let me sleep a little longer. You gave me quite a workout last night."

I chuckled. "I have your gift."

Tweet's eyes shot open and her head popped off of the pillow. She scanned the room before her gaze found me.

"You got me a gift?" Excitement was in her expression and tone.

"Of course I got you a gift. I'm the boyfriend now."

She leaned toward me and kissed the corner of my mouth. "Yes you are and a mighty fine one at that."

"Hmmm… minty fresh." I looked at her, confused.

"I may have gotten up before you got back and brushed my teeth," she confessed.

"And here I thought you didn't even notice I was gone."

"You know I can't sleep when your sexy arms aren't wrapped around me."

We stared at each other for a few seconds, both knowing what the other was thinking. Tweet and I didn't need words to communicate. We never did.

"When is checkout?" I asked, glancing from her eyes to her mouth.

I wanted her so badly right then. Who was I kidding, I always wanted her.

"In an hour," she said.

"If I do to you what I want, then I don't think there'll be time for your gift before we have to leave. I want to go slow and long."

"Yeah, slow and long," she said dreamily.

Clearing my throat, I broke our trance. "Gift time."

Tweet sat up straight in bed, letting the sheet fall to her waist. She was wearing one of my T-shirts she had packed. I grabbed her gift and sat back down facing her.

Her eyes grew to the size of saucers when she saw the huge arrangement of red roses in the crystal vase. "Oh Noah, they're gorgeous. I love them. I love you. Thank you."

Resting the vase on the bed, I held it between us. She buried her nose in the flowers and inhaled deeply.

As she pulled back she had a curious look on her face. "The flowers have tiny scraps of paper pinned to them. What are they?"

"Take one and read it," I instructed.

She plucked the paper from one of the stems. Her face lit up when she read what was written down. "It's our birthday."

Smiling at me over the flowers, she picked up another piece of paper. "This is the date of our first Lifehouse concert."

Her eyes glistened as recognition hit them. "These are all special dates to us."

"Yeah," I said in a low voice.

She grabbed another piece of paper. "This one is the date of our first kiss, freshman year in high school."

"The greatest first kiss in the history of first kisses, baby."

Tears trickled down her cheeks. She reached in for another scrap of paper. She read the date and confusion crossed her face. She sat in silence for several seconds trying to remember the significance of that date.

"I'm sorry. I don't remember what happened on this date. We were twelve years old."

She turned the paper in my direction. I didn't need to read the date. I already knew which one it was.

Never taking my eyes off of her, I said, "It's the date I stopped loving you and fell in love with you."

Tweet placed the vase on the nightstand. She launched herself into my arms, knocking me backward onto the bed, and showered my face with kisses. Wrapping my arms tightly around her, I did a full-blown belly laugh.

"You are the most wonderful, most thoughtful, sweetest man in the entire world."

"Happy Valentine's Day, Tweet." I smiled up at her.

"Happy Valentine's Day, Noah." She smiled down at me.

My hands slid up her naked thighs, up under her T-shirt, landing on her hips. She rocked back and forth. Her hands were planted on either side of my head. Leaning down she sucked on my bottom lip before her tongue slid into my mouth. The kiss was deep and slow.

After several seconds Tweet pulled away slightly. "This is the best first Valentine's Day in the history of Valentine's Days."

"Yeah. You know if we keep going, we're going to be late for checkout."

"Screw checkout. I'll pay for another night."

That's my girl.

CHAPTER 31

Tweet had my hand in a vice grip while I stood next to her sitting on the exam table. We hadn't said much to each other since entering the room, only exchanging nervous glances every few minutes. Each time the sound of a muffled voice on the other side of the closed door passed by, Tweet's back stiffened. We had been coming to these doctor visits for a year, ever since she completed her chemo. At first it was once a month and then transitioned to every three months. By now we were old pros at the routine, but that didn't lessen the fact that each visit sent our nerves into high alert mode.

A loud knock hammered against the door, echoing through the room. Tweet flinched while my gaze shot up in the direction of the noise. As the doorknob twisted, I felt her pulse quicken underneath my hand. We both drew in a deep breath before the door opened. Dr. Lang's gaze was down, reading the folder he carried as he walked in, followed by his nurse. I squeezed Tweet's hand one more time before letting go and then wiped my sweaty palms off on my jeans.

Looking up from the folder, Dr. Lang greeted us. "Amanda... Noah."

Tweet gave only a weak smile in response.

"Hey Dr. Lang. How are you?"

Handing the folder off to his nurse, Dr. Lang walked back toward the door. Giving the Purell dispenser two pumps, he squirted some into his palm.

"I'm doing just fine," he said, turning back toward us as he rubbed the sanitizer into his skin. He then turned his attention to Tweet. "How are you feeling, Amanda?"

"Good." Tweet gave short clipped answers when she was on edge.

"Glad to hear it. Why don't you lie back and straighten your legs for me."

Tweet always stayed sitting up, waiting until the last minute to get into position for the exam. She hated being stretched out on her back on the table. She said it made her feel too exposed and vulnerable. The doctor would only be examining her legs, so Tweet was allowed to keep everything on except her pants. The lower half of her body was covered with a sheet. She scooted to the middle of the table before timidly settling back. Picking up her trembling hand, I laced my fingers through hers, as I turned my back to the doctor and focused only on Tweet.

I didn't need to watch the exam to know the sequence. With each blink and shift in gaze, Tweet told me what the doctor was doing. She blinked, eyes opening wide as her eyebrows crept up into her forehead, with the initial contact of cold hands on her skin. Her brows knitted together and her eyes glazed over as he placed his thumbs on the lower thigh of her amputated leg, his other fingers slipping behind her knee. The glaze washed away, replaced by water filling to the edges of her eyes. Dr. Lang applied pressure, squeezing hard against the bend of her knee, checking for any indication that the cancer had taken up residence in the lymph nodes. Tweet's eyes closed tight as he moved up to her groin and pushed deep against the area.

When her forehead unwrinkled, I knew the exam was over.

"Amanda, your blood work looks great and I don't feel any abnormalities around the lymph nodes."

Tweet's free hand flew up to her mouth, muffling a happy sob. In an instant, the tension left her body. As she sat up, her arms wrapped around my neck at the same time mine curled around her waist.

Tweet and I broke the hug at the sound of Dr. Lang's voice.

"I know these exams are nerve wracking. How about we do away with some of them. Let's say we go to one every six months," he said.

Tweet finally let out the deep breath she had inhaled when the doctor first walked in the room.

She glanced up at my grinning face and then her gaze bounced to Dr. Lang. "Really?"

"Really."

"Yeah, let's do that." Her face collapsed in relief.

"Keep up the good work. If you have any trouble, call me, otherwise, we will see you back in six months."

Smiling, Dr. Lang patted the side of Tweet's leg and shook my hand before walking out of the room with his nurse.

Turning to Tweet, I raised my arms high and said, "Six months, Baby!"

Slapping her palms against mine in a double high-five, Tweet gave me a huge teeth-bearing smile. "Six months!!"

The year that followed was extremely stressful and exhausting for me. Some days, I wanted to give it all up, drop out of school, find a nine-to-five job, and live with my girl. Then I'd look at Tweet and knew why I was busting my ass. I wanted to take care of her to the best of my abilities and give her a great life. I was trying to build our future as quickly as possible. From the time I could remember I always wanted to be either a baseball player or a doctor. I was a good ballplayer, just not good enough to make a viable career out of it.

I'm not sure how I did it, but I earned my undergraduate degree in three years instead of four, heading straight into medical school during the summer session. My days were spent in classes, lab practicums, studying, or working at the hospital, which left me very little time for anything else, including Tweet. I did manage to get the night off in order to celebrate the second anniversary of her being cancer free, surprising her with a candlelight dinner cruise around Charleston Harbor. But most days I left early in the morning before she was awake and got home late at night after she had fallen asleep.

"Hey, what time did you get home?" Tweet said groggily.

I was sitting at the desk in the second bedroom that we converted into our home office. I twisted in the chair, to find Tweet standing in the doorway wearing my gray T-shirt, her hair down and messy. The sight made me smile.

My hands raked down my face as I yawned. "Not too long ago."

"Noah, its 3 am. Why are you still up?"

"I have a chemistry exam tomorrow and wanted to get a little more studying in."

With the help of her crutches, she walked toward me. Tweet kept the crutches handy at night after going to bed. She didn't want to go to the trouble of putting her prosthetic leg on in case she just had to go to the bathroom. I held on to her hips as she propped the crutches against the side of the desk. She placed her hands on my shoulders, steadying herself as I helped her into my lap. I buried my face in the crook of her neck, one arm wrapped around her waist, the other resting across her thighs.

"You feel so good, Tweet."

"I miss you," she whispered in my ear, her fingers combing through my hair.

Tightening my arm around her, I inhaled a deep breath, slowly letting it out. "I miss you too."

"I'm worried about you."

"Don't be." I nuzzled deeper into her neck. The scent of raspberry and vanilla relaxing me.

"I barely see you. You're working too hard. Why don't you cut back on your hours at the hospital? They'd understand."

"Working there is a good networking opportunity. Knowing the staff and the way the place works will give me an advantage in class and in getting picked for my residency when the time comes."

"I know, but…"

I lifted my head, looking her in the eye. "But nothing. I told you I'd handle our future and that's what I'm doing."

She placed a soft kiss on my lips before resting her forehead on mine. "I know, *but* you're missing a lot of our present."

"It's hard right now getting used to the course load. Medical school is more demanding. I'm trying to find a good balance."

"I know you are. I just don't want you to kill yourself in the process."

"Things will slow down soon. I promise."

I lied. As the months went on things didn't slow down, they got even worse. Medical school was like having two more full-time jobs in addition to the actual one I had. I saw Tweet less than before, if that were even possible. With my class and work schedule being the way they were, some nights I ended up sleeping at the hospital. The night nurses and doctors gave me special treatment since I'd been working there for a while, allowing me to crash in the resident's lounge. Tweet continued to take freelance writing jobs while she got more core classes out of the way. None of the local colleges offered a degree in journalism, so she researched universities that offered the degree online. Our lives were full, so I was confused when a hollow emptiness invaded my chest on a daily basis. Something was missing and it scared the shit out of me.

"My brain is fried," Dan said, stretching his arms above his head.

The five members of my study group had just spent the last three hours discussing the structure and composition of DNA. Our brains and the library were shutting down, so we were calling it a night. We worked well together, each of us having different strengths that formed a well-rounded group.

Dan was good at organizing notes. Jennifer thrived at research. I was the best problem solver. Alex was good for a laugh, there's always one in the bunch. Angela, who had been the only member I knew from C of C, basically excelled at all of the above, except being good for a laugh. She was funny, just not on purpose. She and I had become friends, having a lot of the same classes during our undergrad work. Angela also managed to graduate in three years. Our time together had always been spent strictly at school or in the study group. Other than her academics, I didn't know anything about her.

"Yep, I'm done as well," Jennifer chimed in.

As we packed up our textbooks, charts, and notes, Alex asked, "It's still pretty early. How about we head over to Tommy Condon's for a beer and a bite to eat?"

"I'm game." Dan pushed away from the table.

Jennifer grabbed her backpack and slung it over her shoulder. "Count me in. I'm starving."

"Me too," Angela said.

"I gotta take a pass," I told them, shoving my books in my backpack.

"Come on Stewart, just one beer," Alex pushed.

"Maybe next time."

"Your loss. Alex and I are charming as hell once you've had a few beers," Dan joked.

Putting her hair into a ponytail, Jennifer asked, "Angela, are you coming?"

"Y'all go ahead. I'll be there in a little bit."

The three turned and walked away, leaving Angela and I alone at the table. The feel of a warm hand on my forearm brought my gaze down to Angela's thumb, gliding back and forth over my skin. We were friends but not that friendly. She had always been a little awkward around me, so this was a new uncomfortable development. I shifted away, her hand dropping from my arm onto the table.

"I'm going to be heading out. You outta go catch up with the others," I said.

"I'd rather stay here and catch up with you."

"I'm going home. There, you're all caught up."

Chuckling, she leaned in closer. "You seem stressed."

"Busy with work and school is all."

"Noah, we've known each other for quite a while now. Six semesters to be exact." She tilted her head to the side. "I really like you too."

"Too? Um... Angela."

"Would you like to go to dinner or lunch... brunch... a snack? Any meal you want."

"You do realize I have a girlfriend?"

"Is that still going on?"

"Yeah." I couldn't stop my eye roll.

Her face turned beet red the split second before her hands slapped over her cheeks. "Oh my god! Oh my god! Oh my god! I didn't... I thought you... I mean, you're always so nice to me and sit next to me in class. And tonight you kept smiling at me during the study group."

"I was smiling because Alex was being a dumbass."

"I thought you were flirting with me."

"Because I smiled?"

"Well, it's a pretty terrific smile, Noah!" Her voice increased in volume and pitch with each word.

A chorus of *shh's* broke out around us.

"I'm sorry if I've given you the wrong impression."

"Nooo, it's not you. It's me. I should have known someone like you wouldn't be available. All I do is work, go to school, and study. I keep telling myself that once I have my career established then I can focus on my personal life. I have my head so far in the future that I'm lonely in my present." With her arms folded on the table, her face took a nosedive and hid.

"You'll find someone special one day."

Angela and I had more in common than I thought. The only

difference was, I already had that one special person in my life. Being so focused on our future, I was missing her and missing out. I should have realized that was the emptiness I'd been feeling. After walking Angela down the street to join the others at the restaurant, I headed home.

Walking in our room, I found Tweet already in bed, reading.

Her gaze lifted, a smile crossing her lips when she saw me standing in the doorway.

"Hey. You're home earlier than usual."

Without saying a word, I slipped off my shoes and socks, stepped out of my jeans, and striped off my shirt. Tweet placed her Kindle on the nightstand.

"Wow, I didn't realize I was going to get a floor show. Hold on. I'm positive I have a few one-dollar bills somewhere."

Crawling into bed, I wasted no time taking her face in my hands and devouring her lips. Her fingers trailed down my chest to my stomach. Pulling away, I left her gasping for air.

Her eyes filled with all kinds of sexy. "Wow!"

"I love you and I've missed you so much. I'm cutting back on my hours at work, Sundays are now reserved for you to do with me what you want, and I'll do everything in my power to be home at least once a week in time for us to eat dinner together."

"Hey bestie. It's great to have you back where you belong," she said, pulling me back down to her lips.

Tweet struggled, being too scared to think about the future. I was just the opposite, thinking about the future too much. I needed to step back, find balance in the present, and stop sprinting ahead.

"Lucy! I'm home!" I said in my best Cuban accent, walking in the condo.

I asked Tweet how she wanted to mark her third year of being cancer free. Her answer, *together.* She had been feeling tired for the past few days, so we kept the partying low key with takeout and a movie marathon. I had a bag full of Cuban sandwiches, black bean soup, and fried plantain in one hand, and chocolate cake in the other. We were going old school eighties for the marathon with *Sixteen Candles, The Breakfast Club, and Ferris Bueller's Day Off.*

I was taking the food out of the bag and placing it on the counter when Tweet came in the room.

"Noah."

"I got a Cuban feast."

"Noah."

"Sandwiches, fried plantain…"

"Noah."

"And chocolate cake for dessert."

"Noah!"

I turned to look at a blank-faced Tweet staring at me.

Shit! She was pissed.

I hauled my ass over to her, wrapping my arms around her waist.

Pressing my lips to the spot right under her ear, I whispered, "Happy anniversary, Tweet."

She stood like a statue, her arms remaining down by her sides.

I straightened and rubbed my hands over her shoulders. "Don't be mad, Tweet."

She looked up at me, her eyes more glazed over than pissed. "What?"

"I'm sorry I didn't wish you a happy anniversary before rattling off the menu."

Her mouth opened, then closed, and then opened again. "Noah, I'm pregnant."

"Come again," I said, my head turned, bringing my ear closer to her mouth.

"I'm pregnant."

Blinking several times, my mouth opened, then closed, and then opened. "What?"

"We're going to have a baby."

"You need to sit?"

Keeping my hands on her shoulders, I gently guided Tweet to the sofa. As she sunk down, I paced back and forth in front of her.

"Um… how did this… I mean, I know how it… The thing is, we double dipped with the protection," I rambled.

"I don't know. When I missed my period I didn't think much of it at first. Since the chemo I'm not as regular as I used to be. I was feeling queasy in the morning and I've been so tired. I thought maybe I had the flu."

The sound of a sob hit my ears, causing me to stop. I looked over at the sight of a trembling chin and tears streaking her cheeks.

"I didn't really think I was pregnant when I took the test. I just wanted to rule it out."

I knelt in front of her, wiping the tears away. "Don't cry, Tweet. It's going to be okay."

She drew in a shaky breath. "I'm sorry. I know we didn't expect this to happen."

I wanted to have a life with Tweet that included everything. Once the shock wore off that everything would be coming in approximately nine months my heart filled with joy, excitement, fear, doubt, and then back to joy.

I leaned forward and kissed the corners of her mouth. "You're gonna be an awesome mom."

"You're not upset?"

"Shocked but not upset."

"Thank you."

Tweet laced her fingers behind my neck and rested her forehead against mine. We stayed this way for several minutes, letting the news that we were going to be parents sink in.

"Hey, Tweet, we're gonna have a babeee."

Pushing her back against the sofa, I trailed kisses down her body, stopping at her stomach. Her fingers twirled in my hair. I lifted her shirt, brushing my lips over her skin, kissing it softly.

I glanced up into emotional teal eyes. "We have two things to celebrate. It's a good thing I bought a bigger chocolate cake."

Suddenly Tweet bolted upright, her hands flying to cover her mouth.

She shot off the sofa and rushed down the hall to the bathroom, yelling, "That cake makes me sick! Get rid of it!"

The day Tweet refused chocolate cake, the earth shifted on its axis, and life was about to be turned upside down.

Being as quiet as possible, I let myself into the condo. The class and lab I had tonight ran over. Tweet was in her sixteenth week of pregnancy and though her initial fatigue had subsided for the most part, she still had days that wore her out. I assumed Tweet was already sleeping when I texted her on my way home, but never got a response.

One great thing about working at the hospital was I got to come in contact with a lot of different people, staff as well as patients. It always confused me when I'd see a guy looking at his pregnant wife or girlfriend like she was the hottest thing in town. Once women hit a certain stage, it looked like they were smuggling watermelons in the hospital under their clothes, as they waddled down the hall. When Tweet began to show physical signs of the pregnancy, I realized then, when it was your girl, carrying your baby, there was nothing hotter. Tweet glowed with a new level of confidence in herself and her body.

I crept over to the desk that was now in the corner of the dining room, and gently laid down my backpack. We had moved everything out of the second bedroom, formally the home office, with plans of turning it into the nursery. We'd been looking at possible themes for the room. I had no idea there was an entire baby product subculture. The first-time Tweet told me we were going to the baby store, I pictured a warehouse full of babies. I figured it was a place where soon-to-be first time parents could go and practice things like changing diapers on real babies.

Since Tweet couldn't decide whether or not she wanted to know the sex of the baby early, we had a mix of boy, girl, and non-gender-specific theme possibilities for the room. Square patches of painted on blues, pinks, yellows, and even five shades of gray dotted one wall. Progress was slow, but I was sure the baby would still come home with us even if his/her room was subpar.

As I approached my bedroom, flickers of light and the sound of Jason Wade's voice singing "Everything" came from behind the cracked open door. Poking my head in, I spotted candles covering every flat surface, the sheet and comforter turned down, and Tweet sitting at the foot of the bed. I took a few seconds to soak her in. It was exciting to see the changes her body was undergoing. More curves, more slopes, more everything. Tweet had an effortless beauty. With barely any makeup on, her face glowed. Her hair was pulled to the side in a low ponytail. Wearing a long skirt with a brown, orange, and gold swirled pattern and a plain white shirt, she was out of this world breathtaking.

Her gaze swung to mine when I pushed the door open.

"Hey. I thought you were already sleeping when you didn't respond to my text." I smiled, walking toward her.

She stood to meet me. "I was just busy getting your surprise ready."

Slight panic tinged my voice. "Surprise? It's not my birthday, an anniversary, or holiday. It isn't an anniversary or holiday… is it?"

"No, don't worry. Can't a girl do something special for her fella?" Her hands traveled over my stomach, up to my chest.

"Hell yeah, woman."

Leaning down, I nipped at her lips before my tongue slid in. My fingers slipped under the bottom of her shirt. I felt pressure against my chest as Tweet pushed me back. Our lips disconnected, causing my hands to fall away.

"Not yet big guy. I want to give you the surprise first."

"I thought you looking all hot was my surprise."

Tweet narrowed her eyes. "Are you saying that it's so rare I look hot, that it's surprising when I do?"

Shit!

The thing about pregnancy hormones was that you never knew when they were going to swing into action. I hadn't mastered the skill of being able to tell the difference between teasing Tweet and hormonal Tweet.

"No! I just... No!"

A sly sexy smile crawled across her face.

Teasing Tweet. Thank god.

Taking my hands in hers, she led me to the spot on the bed where she'd been sitting.

"Now, you stay here, keep your hands to yourself, and be a good boy."

I did as I was told. She glided over to the stereo and turned up the volume. Our song surrounded the room. Without turning back to face me, she pulled the tie from her hair. Shaking the waves out, she let them fall down her back. Her hips gently swayed, keeping time with the slow part of the song. Glancing over her shoulder, Tweet threw me a wink accompanied by a sexy smirk. Slipping her thumbs into the waistband, she shimmied out of her skirt.

Fuck me! A private striptease.

A cough flew out of my mouth as I choked on the lump I was attempting to swallow.

Whipping her head around, Tweet said, "Are you okay?"

"Yeah... Fine," I stammered through a few more coughs.

She stepped out of the skirt, grabbing it off the floor and balled it up. I tried to get an eyeful of panty, but her shirt was too long, impeding my effort. Tweet spun around, tossing the skirt at me. I let it smack me in the face and then fall in my lap. Drawing in a deep breath, I shifted, needing to readjust my situation.

Tweet's hands teased the bottom edge of her shirt, slowly pushing button after button through its hole mate. Keeping the shirt securely covering her front, she held my gaze while her slow gyrating hips turned her back around. Little by little my grip tightened around the soft material of her skirt. Glancing down, it looked more like a twisted rope than a piece of clothing. Unclenching my fingers, I let it drop to the floor. I figured it had a better chance of survival down there than in my hands.

Raising my gaze, I was met by Tweet's back, again. She extended her arms, opening the shirt up. Teasing me, she let it slip off one shoulder, quickly pulling it back on before I caught a glimpse of anything. As the tempo of the music picked up, Tweet lowered the shirt more, finally letting it slide completely off her shoulders, to reveal a pink lace bra. Hovering at the small of her back, the shirt still covered her cute rounder ass.

The music began to build, prompting Tweet's ass to shake faster. Inch-by-inch the material was lowered until it finally slipped from her arms, falling to the floor. There were many amazing wonders of the world, but none came close to Tweet's ass in a pair of pink lace boy shorts.

As the song reached its frenetic end, Tweet's booty was out of control, bouncing a la Cameron Diaz in *Charlie's Angels*. Her ass shaking propelled her entire body around to face me. At first, my gaze was mesmerized by the bounce of her tits. Those had also gotten rounder. As she danced toward me, my gaze drifted down. My face scrunched up, a combination of squinting eyes squinting in dim light and confusion. When she was a foot away, my jaw went slack, and my eyes bugged out of their sockets. In big pink letters, written over Tweet's baby bump were the words...

It's A Girl!

CHAPTER
32

I startled awake by the sound of my phone going off. My hand slid across the nightstand in search of it, the ringing blaring in my ears. I didn't bother looking at the screen to see who it was before I answered. The bottom dropped out of my stomach the second Gayle, Dr. Lang's receptionist, identified herself. I don't know why that was my immediate reaction. She could have been calling because we were late for Tweet's six-month appointment that was today. My body twisted toward Tweet's side of the bed. Empty. I glanced at the clock and then at the dresser, where she always kept her purse. Gone. She went to her appointment without me. Dammit. Gayle told me I needed to get to the doctor's office as soon as possible.

"There are a couple of suspicious spots on your chest x-ray. The bloodwork indicates that the cancer is back."

The cancer is back.

The cancer is back.

The fucking cancer is back.

Tweet and I sat side-by-side in front of Dr. Lang's desk, staring straight ahead. Our only reaction to the news was the squeezing of each other's hands.

"I recommend the same chemotherapy as before." He paused. "I'm sorry," Dr. Lang said.

Tweet had finally relaxed a little about these appointments. This was the first one in more than three years that she wasn't nervous about.

"Your treatments can be at The Hollings Center like before and…"

"I'm pregnant," Tweet blurted out.

Looking between the two of us, I could tell by his expression that Dr. Lang already knew.

"Yes, I realize that." He exhaled a deep breath. "I know the recurrence is unexpected. You're still early into the pregnancy."

Tweet and I glanced at each other, not understanding what he was suggesting. When the love of your life gets told she has cancer, it's almost impossible to comprehend anything that is said to you right after the news.

"She's in her sixteenth week," I said dazed and numb.

With his eyes downcast, the doctor said, "It's a few weeks shy of being considered late term, but you're both young and still have plenty of time to start a family."

Jesus Christ, he was suggesting termination.

"Halle." The quiver was evident in Tweet's voice.

Dr. Lang looked up, having not heard what she said. "Excuse me?"

"Her name is Halle Elizabeth," I answered.

"So names…," Tweet said, tossing a French fry in her mouth.

We just spent half the day at the store registering for all things baby. When Tweet told me this was how we were spending our day, I figured it'd be a quick trip. Four and a half hours later, we were finally at lunch. My head still spinning from the amount of baby paraphernalia.

"…For her middle name, what do you think about Elizabeth?"

A huge grin spread across my face. "My mom's name. She'll love that. Any ideas on the first name?"

"I want it to be something you don't hear a lot, but not weird."

"Exactly, no fruit or body parts."

"A name that means something special to us. You're good at naming things." She winked and tapped the side of my leg with her foot under the table.

I narrowed my eyes, not understanding what she meant.

"You gave me a fantastic name."

I chuckled. "Tweet is pretty awesome. And I was just a dumb kid when I came up with that brilliance."

"You held my hand the entire night we trick or treated."

"I was a smooth little dude."

"Maybe something related to Halloween?"

"If you're thinking about naming our daughter Candy, then we need to go back to the store and add stripper pole to the list."

Tweet sat back in the booth, looking up as if the name would appear in midair. "Halloween... Halloween... ween... ween. Hallo... Halla... Halle."

Our gaze locked on each other.

"Halle Elizabeth!"

"I'm having our baby." Tweet's tone was determined.

"Amanda, you know the chemo drugs are aggressive. The risks would be extremely high to the baby.

Her name is Halle.

"Then I won't have the chemo until after she's born."

My head whipped around to look at her. "Tweet..."

With watery eyes, she said, "I'm not going to kill our baby with chemo or any other way."

Dr. Lang stood and rounded his desk. "I know this is a difficult decision. I'm going to step out for a bit, so you can have some privacy."

Once the door clicked shut, sobs poured out of Tweet. Rushing over, I knelt in front of her. Wrapping our arms around each other, Tweet melted into me.

"I adore you." My voice cracked.

"I'm sorry for getting sick again."

Grabbing her upper arms, I pushed her back slightly. "Do not feel guilty. This isn't your fault."

Tightening my arms around her, I pulled her into me, trying to get closer. I couldn't get close enough. We stayed in this position while we processed what just happened. I had to be Tweet's rock and stay strong, while inside my soul imploded. How do you choose between the love of your life and a *life* you already love? Halle was a piece of me and Tweet. She had arms, legs, eyes, and a nose. She wasn't just a blip on a screen. But all I could think about was the very real possibility that if Tweet didn't have the chemo now, there was no chance of her surviving.

"Tweet, you know I want our baby but I need you. My life has to be with you."

"Noah, she's a part of me. She's a part of us. If I have the chemo now it will kill her. I'm not a sure thing with or without it. If I wait and have chemo after she's born, and I don't survive, at least you'll still have our daughter. You won't be alone, our families will help you."

"The entire fucking city could be helping me, but without you, I am alone."

Unable to keep my tears in any longer, I let them run down my face.

"Noah, this disease has taken so much, we can't let it take our baby."

I knew at a young age I wanted to be a dad someday, probably because of how awesome my own dad had been. But it wasn't until Tweet told me we were having a baby, that I realized how much I wanted to be a dad. I felt pointless. The two people I'm supposed to protect in this world, and I couldn't help either one of them. When we left Dr. Lang's office Tweet was at peace with the decision we'd made. My feelings fluctuated from second to second, doubting we were doing the right thing and being pissed off that we were put in this position.

On our way home, Tweet texted her parents, Emily, and my mom, asking everyone to meet at our place that afternoon. They all knew Tweet had her doctor's appointment today, so each dropped what they were doing in order to make it over.

Tweet sat on the sofa, flanked by her mom and Emily. Mr. Kelly stood off to the side. He was already nervous, fidgeting with his watch as he shifted from foot to foot. Mom was in the chair directly across from Tweet. I leaned back against the wall close to the entryway.

Tweet amazed me, holding it together, as she made the announcement. "There's no easy way to tell y'all. My cancer is back."

A combination of gasps and sobs filled the room. Mr. Kelly was the exception. My entire life, I had never heard the man use a curse word. But in that moment, under his breath, he murmured, "Fuck."

"What did the doctor say, sweetheart?" Mrs. Kelly choked out, draping her arm around Tweet's shoulders.

"He recommends the same treatment."

"And what about the baby?" Mom asked.

"The baby more than likely would not survive the chemo."

Emily's hand covered Tweet's.

"I won't be going through chemo until after the baby is born."

All eyes were glued on Tweet.

Emily was the first to break the stunned silence. "Manda, that's pretty risky."

"I know, but Noah and I weighed out our options. And that's our decision."

Options were great to have except when they all sucked.

Clearing my throat caused Tweet's gaze to meet mine. "I'll be back in a little while, okay?"

Tweet simply nodded in understanding.

I had changed into sweat pants, a T-shirt, and Nikes before everyone showed up. I walked toward the door, snatching my keys off of the entryway table. Wrapping my fingers around the doorknob, I started to twist it when Mom's voice stopped me.

"Noah, where are you going?"

"I gotta get out of here."

"For what? Amanda needs you and…"

"Mom, please."

I turned on my heels and walked out the door.

I got in my truck and drove to Folly Beach. It was the end of the off season, right before tourists flocked into town. I knew the beach would be deserted, especially late afternoon. Right now I needed deserted. My mind stayed numb the entire drive, focusing only on the road. Parking my truck at the northeast end of the beach, I got out, and made my trek in the direction of the Morris Island Lighthouse.

I concentrated on the waves rolling onto the shore while keeping my steps at a steady normal pace. The last few hours played like snapshots in my head.

"Suspicious spots on x-ray."

"Blood work indicates the cancer is back."

"Baby at extremely high risk."

"Noah, this disease has taken so much, we can't let it take our baby."

Once they started, I couldn't stop the thought invasion. The feel of burning lungs, pounding heart, and dripping sweat broke through the numbness. My steady pace had turned into a full-out run, hurling myself down the beach in an attempt to escape the thoughts.

"The cancer is back."

The end of the shore was in view, causing me to come to an ungraceful stop, arms and legs flailing uncontrollably.

"The cancer is back."

My lungs couldn't stop pumping out shallow breaths. I was getting lightheaded. Bending over, placing my hands on my thighs, I attempted to draw in oxygen.

"The cancer is back."

I laced my fingers behind my head and paced like a caged animal, breaths huffing out of me.

"The cancer is killing my family."

Relentless tremors bulldozed through my body, shattering the last ounce of resolve I was holding on to. My chest ripped open with sobs.

Looking up to the clouds, I screamed, "Fuck you! She doesn't deserve this! Our baby doesn't deserve this! Fuck you for letting this happen! You need to punish someone?!" Balling my fist, I pounded hard against my chest. "Then give me the fucking cancer and leave them alone!"

With my face coated in sweat and tears, I collapsed on the sand, sobbing, as my body convulsed to exhaustion.

Back home, I showered, changed my clothes, and joined the family for dinner. It was like any other family gathering except for the suffocating silence, each of us playing out individual scenarios in our heads. By the time everyone left, Tweet and I were exhausted. We got ready for bed and lay side-by-side staring up at the ceiling. We hadn't said much to each other since leaving Dr. Lang's office. I wondered if she were having doubts about our decision like I was.

My hand skimmed across the sheet in search of hers. Once contact was made, I curled my fingers around her hand. I turned my head toward her. The moonlight streamed in from the window reflecting off the quiet tears spilling from her eyes. Swallowing the basketball in my throat, my grip tightened, triggering a small sob to escape from her.

"What's rattling around in that beautiful head of yours?" I whispered.

"Nothing."

"Talk to me."

"Having to tell everyone today… it was hard." Her eyes clamped shut, more tears seeping from the corners.

"You were amazing."

"I heard him."

"Your dad?"

"After you left, I was walking down the hall and passed by the bathroom. He was crying and getting sick." She choked back a sob. "I wonder if it would have been better had I died the first time."

My chest deflated. I wanted to take her by the shoulders and shake her. Screaming how insane that was to even think that for a second. But I didn't. Instead, I let her get it all out, no matter how painful it was to hear her say those words, because it's what she needed at the moment.

"All the money my parents have spent seems like such a waste now."

"You're what matters to them."

"Halle wouldn't be at risk and have to face growing up without a mom."

"Tweet…"

"And you could have moved on by now and had a normal life, instead of being a nurse to me."

Propping myself up on one elbow, I leaned over her. I took her chin between my fingers, turning her to face me. "When are you going to get it through that beautiful thick skull of yours that there is no moving on from you for me? I couldn't even do it all those years you were being a pain in the ass, pushing me away."

Leaning down, I kissed her lips softly, lingering for several seconds before pulling away.

"I think we need to plan…"

"Let's do it. You want to go shopping tomorrow and fill up that nursery?" I gave her a weak smile.

"I think we should plan for a future that doesn't include me."

"Tweet, I will do anything you ask, but I will not do that. I can't."

"I want to be a part of our daughter's life even if I'm not here."

That night, Tweet and I planned out how we would raise our daughter. I agreed to take daily videos or photos of us, showing how excited and happy we were getting ready for Halle to arrive. I convinced myself that the three of us would watch these as a family once Halle got old enough. Tweet wanted to give Halle a part of who she was, something lasting. That night she started writing a series of notes to our daughter. I didn't read or ask what the notes were about. There were certain things between a mother and daughter that the dad didn't need to be privy to.

To the outside world Tweet and I were just a young couple making plans and getting ready for the birth of their first child. We were also two people playing Russian roulette with our future. The type of cancer Tweet had was aggressive, the potential for it to spread quickly was great. Dr. Lang kept a close eye on things, having us return to the monthly visits during the course of the pregnancy. As the weeks passed no indication of metastasis or noticeable change in the spots on Tweet's lungs occurred. This was great news. If we could maintain this holding pattern until Halle was born, Tweet's chances of survival increased. But knowing that didn't lessen my fears. My body jolted each time she coughed or cleared her throat. And it was a struggle to keep my nerves reasonably steady and stay strong for Tweet with each doctor visit, unsure if that visit would be the one to annihilate my family. We had a month to go before we officially met our daughter. As Tweet focused more and more on the birth of Halle, I couldn't help but focus on the day chemo would start.

I was in the nursery putting the final touches on the manly projects that involved nails, hammering, and electric tools. Standing on the ladder, I hung the last sage green curtain that matched the large rug covering the dark hardwood floors. I never even knew sage was a color until Tweet schooled me the day I referred to it as just green. I was learning an awful lot about girly things I never knew existed. Looking down at the room from the ladder, I admired all of the work it took to pull this off. Tweet had outdone herself.

The theme was little birds. I loved that she took the nickname I'd given her when we were kids and used it as inspiration for our daughter's first room. Tweet asked Emily to use her artistic ability to create a mural on one of the pale yellow walls. My little girl would be staring up at red, orange, and gold leaves blowing from the tree across her wall, as a variety of pink, blue, and red birds, plus one owl, perched on branches and flew overhead. The white staggered shelves I'd hung housed all kinds of children's books as well as just the right amount of stuffed animals.

"Tweet, can you come in here and give me a hand with this?!"

Appearing in the doorway, she said, "What'cha need?"

"I dropped a nail. I think it fell in the baby cabana."

Chuckling, she walked farther into the room. "Noah, it's a bassinet."

"That's what I meant. Would you mind looking for the nail?"

My gaze stuck to Tweet like glue, nervous of her reaction. Placing her hand inside the bassinet, she felt all around, then froze. Slowly straightening, she held up the small black velvet box. I climbed down from the ladder and tentatively walked toward her. Our eyes locked.

"Tweet…"

"Noah, we've already discussed this."

Medical expenses were an ongoing issue. Even before the relapse, there were still follow-up exams and tests Tweet had to go through. We had decided along with her parents that it was best for her to stay on her father's insurance until the cut off age of twenty-six. Any insurance I was able to provide wouldn't have come close to matching his and with a pre-existing clause, it was doubtful her cancer would be covered until after a certain timeframe. I hated the situation. It made me feel less of a man, not to be able to provide everything she needed. Since we found out the cancer had returned, my desire to make Tweet my wife had consumed me. I wanted us to be officially husband and wife in everyone's eyes.

"Please Tweet, will you…"

"Don't ask me that question, Noah. Not now."

"Then when? When can I fucking ask you?"

"When you don't think I'm going to die!"

"I've loved you forever and have wanted you to be my wife for as long as I've known the definition. How can you think otherwise?"

"I want you to propose when we know there's a future, not because you want to give me your name before you bury me."

"You piss me off so much sometimes." I snatched the box from her hand, as I'd done countless times before, and turned toward the ladder.

"Noah, look at me." I spun around. "You don't have to give me an entire lifetime in a few short months."

"I know, but… I want you and Halle to have my last name."

"Halle will have your last name."

"And you?"

"I will someday, just not today."

My frustration and aggravation subsided the longer I stared at her. Tweet and I didn't have time to waste on being angry. And frankly, there was never an issue more important than spending time showing how much we loved each other.

"If you still won't let me ask when that someday comes, just know, I'm gonna kick your ass."

"I'd rather a thorough spanking."

"Is it beyond perverted that I want to take you right here on the floor of our daughter's nursery?"

"It's time."

A sharp jab hit the side of my ribs.

"What?" I yawned, stretching out my arms and legs.

Tweet and I were spending a lazy Sunday lying on the sofa watching every chick flick known to man. She had been having mild contractions since we woke up this morning. Talking with the doctor, she assured us that this could go on for a few days and was perfectly normal. I dozed off during the umpteenth Drew Barrymore movie.

"Time." Tweet squeaked.

Looking at my watch, I yawned again. "It's 4:15."

"Not *the* time. *It's* time!"

Shit!

I bolted upright, twisting toward Tweet. "It's time?"

She nodded, a smile playing across her lips.

My eyes grew three times their original size. "It's really time? But the contractions are so far apart."

"They've been getting closer the last hour while you were sleeping. I called the doctor and she said to come to the hospital," Tweet said.

My gaze dropped to her bump and then shot back up to her eyes.

"Why the hell didn't you wake me up?"

"Noah, can we discuss this later, like after I've given birth?" she snapped.

I jumped up from the sofa and took one step forward before spinning back around, crashing my lips into hers.

"I love you, Tweet."

"I love you, Noah."

I went in for one more kiss before running to our bedroom to grab the overnight bag we had packed. I sprinted back to Tweet. Extending my hand, she placed hers in mine. I helped her off the sofa and into the car. We were using Tweet's Volkswagen Beetle since trying to get her into my truck nine months pregnant was not a pretty sight.

Tweet pulled out her phone and sent texts to her parents, my mom, and Emily letting them know we were on the way to the hospital. Glancing over at her, I smiled with the thought that we were about to share another *first*.

"I've shared all my firsts with you."

"You're the first girl I've ever noticed and the last girl I will ever notice."

"My first kiss was the greatest first kiss in the history of first kisses, because it was with you."

A nurse and wheelchair were waiting for Tweet as we walked through the door of the hospital. Rolling down the hallway, we passed the waiting room where our family had already arrived. Mrs. Kelly, Emily, and Mom all stood, their faces lit up with bright smiles and happy tears. Mr. Kelly was already nervously pacing in front of the window. As the nurse led us down the hall, Tweet held up one hand, waving at the soon-to-be aunt and grandparents.

Once in the room, I was relegated to the corner of *absolutely no use*, while the pit crew of nurses got Tweet settled. As they were hooking her up to various monitors, beautiful watery teal eyes looked over at me.

"I'll always take care of you and make sure you have candy, Tweet."

"Chocolate cake takes the hurt away and makes everything better."

"Mr. Stewart." The sound of the nurse's voice brought me out of my memories.

"Yes?"

"You can go be with your wife now."

"Thank you."

I walked over to Tweet, scooting the chair as close to the bed as it would go.

"How ya feeling, wife?"

Narrowing her eyes, Tweet pursed her lips.

My hand reached over, brushing away the piece of hair that grazed her cheek.

I leaned in, placing a soft kiss on her lips. "You look beautiful."

Her chin had a slight tremble. "You are so incredible to me."

Suddenly, she bolted upright, her jaw dropped and her eyes popped wide open.

Grabbing my hand she squeezed… hard. "Oooh! It hurts!"

"Try to relax, Tweet."

"I can't!"

"Breathe." I demonstrated by blowing out quick short spurts of air like they taught us in class.

Her gaze nailed me to my spot. "I know how to breathe, Noah!"

Damn!

She blew out air until the pain subsided. Her grip loosened around my numb hand as her body relaxed back into the bed.

I shook my hand, trying to get blood and sensation flowing again. "Feel better?"

"I love you so much, Noah."

For the next ten hours our family, the doctor, as well as nurses drifted in and out of the delivery room. I spent the time being a human stress ball, letting Tweet grab and squeeze any part of me while she suffered through stronger contractions. The doctor and nurses kept reassuring us that everything was going great, slow, but that was expected with a first pregnancy. Mom, Mrs. Kelly, and Emily all offered to take my place for a while to give me a break. None of them were surprised when I turned them down. Nothing and no one was going to separate me from my girl.

"You've always been my girl and always will be. No one will ever take me away from you, Tweet. You're my heart and soul and that's never going to change..."

"You do have me. Every part of me. You always have."

When we hit hour twelve and still no Halle, I told the family to go home and that I would call them when things got moving. Of course, none of them left, opting to stay camped out in the waiting room. All the activity outside the delivery room had quieted and the sun had gone down. Tweet was so exhausted that once they gave her the epidural she fell asleep. I was sitting in the same position I had been for the better part of a day. My hand was lying over her forearm, my thumb slowly moving back and forth over her skin. While I enjoyed the view and feel of my girl, a light drifted in the room from the doorway. As our doctor walked in, I gave her a tired smile.

Checking Tweet's monitors, she glanced over at me and said, "How you holding up, Dad?"

"Hanging in there."

"You're doing great." She patted Tweet's shoulder. "Amanda."

Beautiful sleepy teal eyes blinked open.

"How are you feeling?" The doctor smiled.

"Tired."

"I'm going to check to see if you've dilated anymore."

The doctor snapped on the latex gloves and moved to the foot of the bed. Picking up Tweet's hand, I placed a kiss in the palm and held eye contact while she was being examined.

"Well folks, how about we meet this little girl now."

"Really?" Tweet and I said in unison, our gaze shooting toward the doctor.

From that point everything happened in a blurry whirlwind. Before my brain could catch up, I was standing at the head of the bed, coaching Tweet as she continued to bear down and push.

"Okay Amanda, you need to push a little harder."

"I don't think I can."

"You can do this, Tweet," I said against the side of her head.

"Noah, I'm so tired."

"I know, Baby. All we need to do is push hard a couple of more times."

"What's this *we* shit?" Tweet snapped.

"There's the smartass mouth I love." I placed a kiss on her lips and then looked directly into her eyes. "Let's do this."

Tweet drew in a deep breath and held it, as I helped her sit upright.

"Push, Amanda. You're doing great," the doctor said.

The room filled with Tweet's guttural screams, her face turning every shade of red that existed.

"Rest," the doctor ordered.

I lowered Tweet back onto the bed.

"You're doing amazing. You're incredible. I love you."

"Noah, I can't do anymore," she sobbed.

"Yes you can. You're the strongest person I know. We're going to meet our baby today, Tweet."

"Okay, Amanda. One more good hard push."

We repeated the same process as a few minutes earlier. Tweet let out a blood-curdling scream.

"Fantastic, Amanda. Dad, come down here right now so you can watch your daughter come into the world."

Tweet and I held each other's gaze, our hands staying connected until the last possible second as I moved to the foot of the bed.

The feeling of watching my daughter being born was overwhelming and indescribable. I was in awe as the top of her head first came into view. I gasped, trying to keep it together. Then in a flash, she appeared. My knees buckled slightly as a sob shoved the breath right out of me. She was an actual person living in this world. I recognized her nose, cheeks, and lips, they were exactly like her mom's. She had my eyes and her hair was dark like both of us. Our daughter was exquisite and perfect.

"You're my heart and soul and that will never change."

"Congratulations. Dad, you want to do the honors?" The doctor handed me a pair of forceps.

I flexed my fingers a couple of times before taking them. I thought I'd be nervous cutting the umbilical cord, but it felt like the most natural thing in the world. The doctor handed Halle off to the waiting nurse, who wrapped her in a towel and handed her to me. I couldn't stop the tears. Thank God Travis wasn't here. I'd never hear the end of it. My heart swelled with overwhelming love and pride when Halle was placed in my arms.

"Noah, how is she?"

I walked my daughter over to her mom, placing her on Tweet's chest.

"She's incredible."

Tears poured out of Tweet as she held Halle.

"I love you so much, Tweet. Thank you for giving me Halle."

My kiss started on Tweet's forehead, then traveled down her face, to her lips.

"I love you, Noah. Thank you for giving me Halle," she said, sobbing and chuckling.

The nurse tapped my arm.

"I need to take her for a few minutes."

I looked over my shoulder.

"You can't take her," I said, sounding harsher than I meant.

The nurse giggled. "I have to clean her up. I promise, I'll bring her right back."

Tweet looked at me with panicked eyes.

"Okay, but be very careful," I commanded.

Holding Tweet's hand, my eyes stayed glued to the nurse, making sure she was gentle with my little girl. While my daughter got her first bath, the doctor finished up with Tweet. Finally, after what felt like a lifetime, but in reality was only about fifteen minutes, the nurse brought Halle back to us and laid her in Tweet's arms.

Sitting beside Tweet, gazing down at our family, my heart burst with joy and broke at the same time. Fear seeped into the back of my mind. What if I end up raising our beautiful little girl alone? I wanted to stay in the bliss of this moment, but knowing that the love of my life would be fighting for hers again soon was terrifying. As Tweet looked at me, her face lit up with love, joy, and pride. I pushed the fear aside. I couldn't let the unpredictable rob me of this experience. Our past was a memory. Our future a mystery. But in this moment, with Tweet in my arms, holding Halle, our world was presently perfect.

THE END

EPILOGUE
TWEET

"What on earth are you doing?!"

I couldn't believe what was happening in my very own living room without my permission. I had been gone for only five minutes, tops, to get my vest from the bedroom, and chaos broke out.

"I was adding a bit of pizazz, sweetheart," Mom said in her dismissive *mother knows best* voice.

"No, no. No pizazz needed."

Halle tilted her cute little head sideways. "DeeDee, are you gonna shoot me with that glue gun?"

We'd been having our annual Halloween family dinners for the past six years, ever since Halle came into our lives. Noah was in charge of the menu, which always consisted of his specialty, Lead Bellies—chili, sour cream, cheddar cheese, onions, all sitting atop a big pile of Fritos. For the last two years he'd added to his repertoire for his little bird, Halle. She had him so wrapped around her finger. Thus, the culinary masterpiece, whoodles was born—mac and cheese mixed with cut-up hot dog wienies.

Part of the Halloween tradition, the darker part, was Mom's attempt to inflict her craftsmanship on Halle's costume. Some things never change. Mom had a bottle of glitter poised in one hand, and a hot glue gun in the other. She had Halle in the middle of the room standing on one of the kitchen chairs.

"You're a lot like your mother, you know that," Mom teased Halle.

Halle beamed up at Mom. "I wanna be just like my momma."

"Mom, put the gun down and step away from my child."

Stepping to the side, Mom placed her weapons on the narrow table behind the sofa. I walked over to Halle, helping her down off of the chair.

"Sweetie, go get your trick or treat bag. Daddy will be ready to leave in a few minutes."

Without a word, Halle took off down the hallway to her room.

Swinging the vest around to my back, I slid my arms through.

"Amanda, I'm sorry if I overstepped by trying to give some umph to my granddaughter's costume. My heart was in the right place. I will not do it again."

"You do it every year and then give the same speech. Don't stop now, Mom. It's a family tradition."

"She's a red and blue Lego, Amanda." Her voice went down two octaves on the word Lego. "It's hardly a costume for a little girl."

I glanced over at my dad on the sofa, watching TV and laughing at me and Mom. "Dad."

"Leave the children alone, Abigail."

With both eyebrows cocked up, Mom said, "Is it okay for me to go stir the chili?"

"There's a witch stirring the pot joke in there somewhere." I smirked.

A smile broke across Mom's face as loud laughter burst from my dad.

I heard her before I saw her. The sound of small shoes bounding down the hall filled my heart with joy. I loved to watch Halle do anything, especially run. She did it with such purpose and determination.

Crashing into me, she squealed, "I'm ready to go tricking or treating, Momma!"

Grabbing my hat, I completed the rest of my costume.

"I like your red hat, Momma."

"Thanks. It's a really cool cowgirl hat... right?"

"Really cool." Halle agreed.

"I'll go get your daddy and then we can head out to trick or treat."

"Yay! I'm so excited."

I walked into my bedroom and stopped in the doorway. The breath in my lungs froze. Noah was getting dressed. His back was facing me, as he stood in front of the dresser in his royal blue scrub pants, shirtless. Hence, the lungs not working. He constantly took my breath away, not only with his looks, but his tremendous heart. He was an incredible father, as I knew he would be. He was deep into his residency at the hospital, but always made time for me and Halle. Each time I thought I couldn't fall more in love with him, I did.

Noah proposed a year ago, on the fifth anniversary of me being a cancer survivor. We didn't bother to wait to get married. Three months after I finally said yes to him, I said I do. It was a small ceremony, family and a few close friends. Noah and I had been married in our hearts our entire lives, all that was left was the paperwork.

"Oh doctah! I think I gotta fevah," I said, walking up behind him.

I wrapped my arms around his waist, pressing my cheek against his skin. The vibrations from his laughter tickled the side of my face. He turned in my arms, a huge smile plastered across his chiseled face. Piercing light blue eyes took hold of me.

Slowly leaning down, he said, "Perhaps I should give you a thorough exam."

His left arm snaked around my waist, while his right hand cupped the side of my face, burying his fingers deep in my hair. Placing a soft kiss at the corner of my mouth, his lips then nibbled their way over my jaw and to my neck. I tilted my head to the side to help the guy out. I didn't want him to miss a spot.

"You're definitely hot," he said against my skin.

I slid my palms over his rippling abs, up his chest, and gave him a little push. Giggles drifted out of me as his lips played with my earlobe. Only

Noah Stewart could reduce me to a puddle of girly giggles.

"Our little Lego is ready to snag some candy."

Pulling back, he rested his forehead on mine. "Then we should definitely schedule you for a follow-up appointment."

"I'm so glad you became a doctor."

"I know. The double entendres are endless."

Noah walked over to the bed and grabbed the matching scrub shirt, slipping it over his head.

Holding his arms out to the side, he announced, "I'm ready!"

My parents stayed at our house keeping an eye one dinner and waited for Mrs. Stewart and Emily to show up, while Noah and I took Halle trick or treating. When we started planning Halle's Lego costume, she asked me if she could go up to the doors by herself this year. I was so proud of her confidence. She was fearless. I stayed back enough for her to feel her independence. Noah, on the other hand, stayed within close range. His arms crossed over his chest, displaying bulging muscles straining against the short sleeves of his scrubs. A clear warning to all ghosts and goblins not to mess with his little girl.

He was so overprotective and hot.

I sidled up next to Noah and hugged his bicep. "You look like a bouncer at a medical facility."

"Have you noticed the pint-sized Superman?" His chin tipping up toward the front door of the house where Halle stood.

"Um… Noah, there are about ten Supermans within a twenty-foot radius. You'll have to be more specific."

"The one standing next to Halle. This is the third house I've seen him at, I think he's following her."

There was a small group consisting of a fireman, a princess, a butterfly, a Ninja Turtle along with Halle and the stalking Superman, all waiting for sweet deliciousness to be dropped into their bags.

I bit down on my bottom lip in an attempt to contain my laughter. "Babe, he's trick or treating like the rest of the kids in the neighborhood."

Shaking his head, Noah said, "Look at him."

"Yeah, he's waiting for candy."

"Does he need to stand that close to her for candy? He was also standing close to her like that at the last house." He paused for a second, his stare becoming more intense. "I think he's holding her hand."

Hugging his arm tighter, I teased, "Maybe she's holding his hand."

Light blue eyes shot to mine. I kissed Noah's bicep before flashing a bright smile at him. Out the corner of my eye, Halle's small group trickled down the driveway toward the next house. The butterfly let out a high-pitched squeal as she revealed to the princess the full size Hershey bar she got. The fireman ran by us being chased by the Ninja Turtle. And bringing up the rear was our little Lego, whose hand was indeed clutching the hand of the Man of Steel.

Noah's body stiffened. As he stepped forward, I doubled my efforts, increasing my grip to keep him glued to the spot. Our gaze stayed on Halle and her new friend, watching them approach the next house. Their hands disconnected while they held their bags out, waiting for the door to open. When Santa Claus appeared in the doorway, Halle stumbled back in shock at the sight. Noah broke from my clutches, running toward her. Superman dropped his bag, grabbing Halle's arm before she hit the ground.

By the time Noah reached the top of the driveway Halle and her sandy-haired Superman were walking hand-in-hand away from the door, smiling. As Halle approached Noah, he squatted down, making sure she was alright. She nodded in response and then marched her way toward the next house, still holding on to Superman.

"Looks like Superman has a new friend," said the female voice next to me.

"I'd say so." Glancing over to the very pretty brunette, dressed in a charcoal gray coatdress that fit her curves perfectly along with a pair of four-inch plum-colored heels. "He's yours?"

"Oh yeah. Little Miss Lego, yours?" She smiled.

"Mine and her tad overprotective father's." Her gaze followed mine to a slightly stunned Noah as he watched his daughter ignore him and spend time with another fella.

I extended my hand. "Amanda Stewart."

"Mabry Johnson," she said, giving my hand a firm shake. "I love your cowgirl ensemble."

I beamed with pride. "Thank you. Your costume is great too. What are you supposed to be?"

"I'm a lawyer."

"You look exactly like one."

"No, I really am a lawyer. I had a late meeting and wasn't able to get home in time to change and get Superman out on the street."

Chuckling, I said, "Gotcha."

"Tweet, I told you he was standing too close to her." The sound of Noah's voice grabbed my attention as he walked toward me.

I flashed a nervous half smile at Mabry. "It was a good thing he was close enough to catch her."

"Yeah, well… he needs to…"

I grabbed Noah's hand, interrupting his grumbling. "Noah, this is Mabry Johnson, Superman's mom."

With a sheepish smile, Noah extended his hand to Mabry. "Hey, nice to meet you."

"You too and Superman's real identity is Brandon."

The three of us followed the kids as they moved to the next house.

"Are you new to the neighborhood, Mabry?" Noah asked.

"Yeah, my husband and I bought the place on the corner of Briarfield."

"Oh, the two-story with the big maple tree in front?" I asked, glancing over at her.

"That's the one," Mabry responded.

Noah's gaze continued its fascination with our daughter's handholding as he made an effort to be sociable. "What does your husband do for a living?"

"He's also a lawyer. In fact, that's him walking this way."

With his head tilted down, I wasn't able to get a good look at his face. All that was visible at the moment was dirty blonde hair, a well-tailored black suit, white shirt, and a tie that matched his wife's plum heels.

It was as if someone had pushed the slow motion button on the camera. Mabry's hand shot into the air, waving, as her husband's head tilted up revealing his face. The collective thud that reverberated as mine and Noah's jaws dropped could be heard and felt around the world. I tried blinking the vision away, but each time my eyes opened, he was closer and it was him. Tension and heat poured off of Noah. His jaw set firm, complete with audible grinding of teeth.

With no break in his stride, Brad walked up to Mabry, wrapping his arms around her waist, and placed a sweet kiss on her lips.

Pulling away from Mabry's lips, he said, "Hey Sweetness."

"Brad this is Noah and Amanda Stewart. This is my husband, Brad."

Noah and I stood shell-shocked during Mabry's introductions.

The already big smile widened as Brad's gaze swung over to Noah and I. "Well, isn't this a kick in the nuts."

"Brad!"

"Hi guys. How's it going?"

Mabry's head whipped back and forth between her husband and us.

"The three of you already know each other?"

"We all went to high school together," Brad said.

The sound of Halle crying slapped Noah and me out of our shock. She was standing in the yard of the house we were in front of, gazing down at the lollipop on the ground. Tears dripped from her eyes. Before Noah or I took a step, Brandon reached in his bag, pulled out another lollipop, and held it out to Halle. The second she grabbed it, her face lit up with a smile.

"Don't cry, Halle. I'll always share my candy with you."

Brad poked his head between mine and Noah's. "That's my boy. Wouldn't it be something if those two ended up together in the future?"

Looking straight ahead, Noah said, "Tweet, I need to talk to you for a minute. Alone."

"Sure."

"Amanda, since the kids are getting along so well, we should set up a play date. Hand me your phone and I'll put my number in." Mabry held her hand out.

"Sure." I glanced at Noah before handing her my phone.

Noah tugged on my arm, inching me away. "Tweet."

Mabry finished typing her number into my phone and handed it back to me.

I smiled at her. "Thank you…"

"Tweet."

"…and goodbye."

THANK
You!!!
...

Even though I spend my days and nights using words to create stories that a reader will connect with and feel, there are times when words aren't enough. I could write a thousand books expressing over and over my appreciation to those in my life—family, friends, colleagues, and readers. It still wouldn't come close to showing the depth of my gratitude.

Presently Perfect was a difficult book for me to write for a number of reasons. Alternate point of view books are tricky. You're dealing with an already set timeframe as well as characters and events people know and love. With each book I've written there has to be a point to the story, a reason it needs to be told.

In *Present Perfect*, the goal was to show a heroine with self-inflicted pressure and a disability, who grew into a strong young woman. *Past Imperfect* was a story of redemption and forgiveness. It showed the ramifications of depression and suicide on those left behind. It took me a long time to figure out the point of Noah's story. It's a story of finding a deeper strength within yourself. Following what you know to be true in your heart. The story shows the effects of having to surrender control, witnessing the love of your life struggle with devastating circumstances.

The other obstacle was having to say goodbye to characters that I love. Sure, they live in my head but also in my heart. I've lived with them twenty four hours a day for the past two years. They've made me laugh, smile, cry and at times shake my head. They've gotten me through rough times and brought so much good into my life that to say goodbye hit me harder than I thought it would. It might sounds silly. I mean, I could do whatever I wanted to do with these characters—write more books and continue their story. But I won't. For me, the love story of Noah and Tweet, and Brad and Mabry are complete.

My wish is that the readers laugh, smile, cry, and get their proper thank you and goodbye.

Thank you to my family for all their help, support, and understanding when they don't hear from for days.

Betas: Ladies, you mean so much to me. Your feedback and encouragement push me to be a better writer. I'm blessed to have found y'all. Jennifer Mirabelli, I loved starting my day with your notes. Stacia Newbill, the playlist you made me got me through the final chapters of the book. In fact, I'm listening to it right now. Kiki Amit, what can I say? You make me smile and think. Alexis Durbin, thank you for the time you gave to me. Jennifer Juers, thank you for being fresh eyes to the world of Noah and Tweet. Carrie Horton, the supply of Charlie pictures you sent got me through most days. Kim Bias, thank you for being gentle with me. Melanie Smith, thank you for spreading the Noah and Tweet love. Nicki Destasi, I'm so proud to call you my friend and author sistah. Concepcion Copon, your notes were awesome and added so much to refining the story. Author M. Robinson, I enjoy our friendship and chats more than you know. Tracey Murphy, your understanding and friendship mean the world to me. Christine Estevez, you have a special place in my heart. Beth Hyams, you are my strength.

Tabitha Willbanks, you have been the most incredible assistant/friend anyone could have. Thank you for listening to my ramblings, keeping me on track, and being in my corner.

Linda Roberts, editor: Thank you for your talent, guidance, and patience.

Angela McLaurin, Fictional Formats: Thank you for always taking care of me, and making my books look pretty inside. I'm blessed to call you my friend.

Robin Harper, Wicked By Design: What would I do without you? Thank you for your patience with me and for somehow deciphering my nonsense. Your talent is what causes me to stare at my covers.

Lorie Rebecca, Lorie Rebecca Photography: Thank you for the gorgeous photos for my covers. Both *Presently Perfect* and the redo of *Present Perfect* turfinalened out exactly how I imagined.

Mackenzie Marie, cover model for updated *Present Perfect* cover: Mack, you did a fantastic job being Tweet.

Assad Shalhoub, cover model, *Presently Perfect*—Thank you for your dedication to the project. Working with you was an experience I won't soon forget. I wish you many blessings in your life and career, buddy.

Mary Rose Bermundo: Thank you for all the gorgeous graphics you made for the book, taking us back to the beginning of Noah and Tweet.

Tee Mo Teo: Thank you for being so generous to me with all the beautiful graphics you've created.

Bailey's Broads: You ladies are incredible. You brighten my days. Thank you for the constant support and love.

Blogging Community: The amount of work bloggers do is amazing. So many wonderful blogs have supported me over the course of this "Perfect" journey. I am humbled and honored that they've welcomed me and my characters into their world and continue to support us.

Fellow Authors: I will be forever grateful for the friendships I've made with other authors. From the very beginning they have welcomed me into the indie community. Their advice and support has been invaluable.

To my readers: You spend your hard earned money, give up your time to read and review, as well as spread the word about my books. This is the part in which words are not enough to convey my gratitude. I wish I could hug you all. Thank you, plus infinity. ♡

~*Alison*

ABOUT THE
Author

Alison was born and raised in Charleston, SC. She attended Winthrop University and graduated with a major in Theater. While at school Alison began writing one-act plays, which she later produced. Her debut novel, *Present Perfect*, landed on Amazon's Best Seller List and appeared on many "Best Reads of 2013" Book Blogs. The novel won Best Book at the 2014 Indie Romance Convention Awards. Her second novel, *Past Imperfect*, was published in February of 2014 and appeared on several best books of 2014 lists as well. *Presently Perfect* is the third and final book in The "Perfect" series.

Author Links

Website
http://alisongbailey.com/

Facebook
facebook.com/AlisonGBaileyAuthor

Twitter
twitter.com/AlisonGBailey1

Instagram
instagram.com/alisongbailey

Goodreads
goodreads.com/author/show/7032185.Alison_G_Bailey

Playlist
bit.ly/presentlyperfect

Fan made Playlist (Stacia Newbill)
bit.ly/presentlyperfect2

Other Books by Alison G. Bailey
The "Perfect" Series
Present Perfect (Book #1)
Past Imperfect (Book #2)

66219508R00227

Made in the USA
Lexington, KY
07 August 2017